Da Flip Side
(The Side That's Glorified And the Side That's Never Told)

Jamie Lowe

National Library of Canada Cataloguing in Publication

Lowe, Jamie., 1970-
    Da flip side : the side that's glorified and the side that's never told / Jamie Lowe.
ISBN 1-4120-0769-0
    I. Title. II. Title: Flip side.
PS3612.O93D4 2003   813'.6   C2003-903812-2

TRAFFORD

This book was published *on-demand* in cooperation with Trafford Publishing.
On-demand publishing is a unique process and service of making a book available for retail sale to the public taking advantage of on-demand manufacturing and Internet marketing. **On-demand publishing** includes promotions, retail sales, manufacturing, order fulfilment, accounting and collecting royalties on behalf of the author.

Suite 6E, 2333 Government St., Victoria, B.C. V8T 4P4, CANADA
Phone   250-383-6864   Toll-free 1-888-232-4444 (Canada & US)
Fax   250-383-6804   E-mail   sales@trafford.com
Web site www.trafford.com   TRAFFORD PUBLISHING IS A DIVISION OF TRAFFORD HOLDINGS LTD.
Trafford Catalogue #03-1137   www.trafford.com/robots/03-1137.html

10   9   8   7   6   5   4   3   2

DEDICATION

I dedicate this book to my dad, James Edward Lowe, Jr., my step dad, James Vernon, my Aunt Amma Gene Lowe, my grandmother Lillian "MaMa" Lowe and to my brother, Timothy Edward Lowe. I love and miss you all with all that's left of me.

ACKNOWLEDGMENTS

First, I would like to give all praise and thanks to Allah, The Mighty, The Wise. To my dearest mom, my best friend, who has had my back through thick and thin, always. Whether I am right or wrong.

To my sahaba, Stacey Slaw, who spent a million hours "walking the track", listening to my war stories and advising me on all aspects of my writing. Thank you, brother. You have been an inspiration not only in my writing, but in every facet of my life. We share the same vision.

To Kristi Bruce, this book would still be a dream of mine had it not been for you. When everyone else doubted, you believed in me. You have been my biggest blessing.

To Anthony Miller, Tim Bumpass, Akram, Corey Cunningham, Reggie Spears, Lamont Mack, Akbar Pray, Big Freeze, Vinnie Whitley, Nehron (aka "DC Shorty"), "Port City Twin", Leverne "Peachie" Lockley, Carly Jegbadai, Tim Crippen, Big Mel (aka "Big Greasy"), Rome, Gemini, Crisco Davis, Tom Slick, Ray Dines and Spider for the cover illustration, thanks to you all for reading and giving me your honest opinions and advice on the book. I'm going to need you all to help me on the next one too!

To Mr. Dave Oliver in Jesup, Georgia, thanks for encouraging me to write and for allowing me to read my book to your class.

If I forgot anyone, thank you also. You know who you are.

Da Flip Side
(The Side That's Glorified And the Side That's Never Told)

Author's Note

This is a work of fiction. Names of characters, places and incidents are either the product of the author's imagination or are used fictitiously and any resemblance to an actual person, living or dead, events or locals is entirely coincidental.

James E. Lowe, III

FREEDOM

For months, I tossed and I turned
To and from
I knew You would come

When You came
You didn't stay long
For the life of me
I can't remember how long You actually stayed
But, it wasn't long
I do know for years I've watched You
Through peeking eyes
Only in other people's lives
All of which were Grown folks
Well, I take that back.......
At times,
When Moma wasn't home
You would visit
But, she was never gone long
Maybe, when I reach that age
Grown
You'll come back to me......
So for years I've waited

Finally!
I've reached that age,
That I've waited for
All of my life
Grown....

But, what's happening to me
Isn't what I used to see
I have this one and that one over me
Telling me what to do...
I guess I have to work through
It's just that, if You visit me
At the end of the day
I'll be much too tired to entertain You
What's a man to do?
I've waited for You too long
Not to be able to entertain You...
I've got it!
I know a way that I don't have to work
We can be reunited

Like the times when Moma wasn't home
Cause I'm grown…..But,
This way does jeopardize my chance
Of ever having You back in my life
I'm going to take my chance!

Oh, I'm so glad I took a chance
To be with You
You came back!
No more work; Yet I've got
Tons of cash , cars and chics
This is what I used to see
Through peeking eyes
I am Grown

Until I heard violent screams
"Freeze!"
"Do – Not – Move"
Are you so and so?
You'll have to come with us

Wait!
Please don't go
Ah, how I wish I wouldn't have taken a chance
Now, I realize that
You
Were always in my life
But, now it's too late

Today, I peered through rusty bars
I hoped and prayed You'd come back
I long to see Your face
Are You ever coming back?
If not
I'd rather die
Take my chance on the other side
Maybe,
That's where I'll find You again
Maybe,
That's where I'll find out
I had too much of you
Maybe
I'll never see You again ----- Freedom!

"The key to success; to be ambitious, assertive and relentless in your endeavors." J.T. Hough

"The shortest distance between a problem and a solution is the distance between your knees and the floor. For the one who kneels to the Almighty can stand up to anything…." Author Unknown

Da Flip Side
(The Side That's Glorified And the Side That's Never Told)

CHAPTER 1

"Segregation range stand, up for the four p.m. count!" One of the prison officers yelled loudly. I wasn't standing for shit. I was already in solitary confinement. What were they going to do if I didn't stand up, I thought.

"Styles, you need to stand your black ass up," said Officer Adams.

"I'm not standing up." I said.

He stood at the door, peering into the narrow window. After a few seconds of grilling each other, he counted me and continued to walk.

"Just like I thought," I said, "He can't do shit."

This is one of the things I have grown to hate about being incarcerated. The way we're counted. Daily inventory! All warehoused up and accounted for. We are treated like we are supplies on a shelf. I guess we are supplies to this venal government. All of us. Nothing more than supplies.

Those red necks in Estill, South Carolina, wouldn't allow the Sunni Muslims to congregate and pray except on Fridays. Jummah, the Islamic services, are observed on that day. By federal law, those hillbillies had to do that.

Congregational salat (prayer) is more than essential in Islam. It's vital to a sincere Muslim. Allah says in the Noble Quran, "To establish congregational salat." So the Sunni's congregated on the prison yard and prayed. Subsequently, ten of us were given incident reports, and charged with "conduct which disrupts the orderly running of the institution".

An informant on the compound reported to the investigation staff, that I was the leader of the Sunni Muslims. Tagged with that title, myself and the other nine Muslims were transferred immediately to the penitentiary in Atlanta, Georgia. Just for praying!

For a few months I was in a cell with a Muslim named, Jihad. His name meant to fight for the sake and pleasure of Allah. He was a very high spirited and vocal brother who had the right name. He loved Islam.

One day out of the blue, the guards moved me to a cell by myself. The counselors in Atlanta's prison, elected to make me and Jihad "Separatees". We were said to have too much influence on the other inmates when we were together.

The Jail Administrator, Mr. Randal, (Uncle Tom Bastard) said I was such a bad influence on the other inmates, that I wasn't allowed to have a cellmate nor was I allowed to attend recreation with other inmates.

I stayed in that cell alone for five months. I'm naturally light skinned and almost eight months in the hole without any sun would make Wesley Snipes look like a red bone. You can imagine how I looked. For five months I didn't have anyone to talk to, but God and myself and I openly admit to doing a lot of both.

After five months of being in the cell alone, I finally got a cellmate. His name was Hireen, a white guy from Ormond Beach, Florida. Usually, they don't mix races in the penitentiary, especially in segregation. They try to keep it just that "Segregated!" On this occasion one of the guards heard Hireen saying "As Salaamu Alaikum" to another Muslim. Out of ignorance and miseducation, he laughed. He thought it would be funny to put a white boy, who said he was Muslim in the cell with me. After five months of being alone, I had advised the Jail Administrator that I wasn't going to take a cellmate

1

unless he was a Muslim. Indeed, Hireen was Muslim. It was a blessing for our paths to cross.

I had not talked to anyone in so long I talked Hireen to sleep every night until I left. We made all our prayers together and discussed how good Allah had been to us until the "wee hours" of the morning. I learned that Hireen had been down for seven years. He was about a month shy from going home. He had an armed robbery charge and he had completed his bid.

The night before I left to go back to the penitentiary in Leavenworth, Kansas, he and I were discussing my charges and the day I got arrested. We talked all night until the next morning. Actually, I did most of the talking that night. Just sitting on that small, hard bunk reminiscing. Watching Hireen fall asleep while I told my story in complete detail. He was trying to be attentive with an occasional mod or an "uh-huh" signifying he was still following my story.

"How did the Feds find you?", Hireen asked.

I saw him fighting the sleep monster. He was losing the battle. It didn't make a difference to me though. After eight months in the hole, five of which I was alone, I would settle to talk to someone even if they were falling asleep. So, I continued to talk. Telling my story.

CHAPTER 2

Now that I think about it, it wouldn't be that hard to locate my car in Greensboro, North Carolina. An emerald green SC 400 Lexus Coupe, with 20" chrome Anterra wheels. After all, everyone knew that was one of the cars I drove. "Money!" That's what I called that car. It was like money in the bank. Sleek with more shine that the sun at noontime.

I'm sure the feds got some assistance finding me. Hell, more that a dozen so called homies sold me out anyway.

Have you ever watched a movie and when it reaches it's climax, the director decides to show the scene in slow motion? That's how things happened to me. In slow motion.

Sandy woke me up by shaking my arm and calling my name. "Dana! Dana, get up and get ready for your class. You need to check that damn pager. It has been going off every minute for the past two hours."

When it was all said and done, those two hours could have made the difference of me being free or being incarcerated. It's the Decree if that's what you believe, but either way, there isn't any need to cry over spilled milk.

When I checked my pager, it was Nina. I had met Nina three months earlier at the Myrtle Beach Bike Rally. She had accompanied my cousins, Tina and Jerry on a spontaneous trip to the beach. For myself, I had attended the Bike Rally religiously for years. I was a Bike Rally Vet!

It was late Saturday night when Dakim, a friend of mine, and I had decided that we had seen enough of the Bike Rally. We packed our bags and agreed that we would be more productive back in Greensboro. As we were about to leave someone knocked on the hotel door.

"Who is it?" I asked.

"It's me nigga! Open the door."

"Come on in the door is unlocked." Pookie said, exhaling, choking on L.A.'s finest Hydro.

Jerry opened the door and allowed Tina and her friend to enter. I hugged Tina and kissed her on the cheek. She introduced herself to everyone in the crowded room, and she also introduced her friend, Nina. Jerry knew everyone, but he chuckled and introduced himself anyway.

Nina was gorgeous. The first thing I noticed about her was that she didn't have on any make-up. Then I noticed her eyes. Intoxicating green eyes.

They had arrived a couple of hours earlier and had been stuck in traffic the entire time. Nina and Tina both were irritated by that fact.

"Tina, you and Nina enjoy yourselves. Dakim and I are about to be out." I said.

"Y'all are leaving?" Nina asked.

"Yep! We got here this morning and tonight we decided we've seen enough." I said.

Nina looked at Tina and began to laugh.

"What's so funny?" I asked.

Nina explained that she and Tina had already discussed leaving, but they knew Jerry would be disappointed. My youngest brother, Pookie, said through a cloud of smoke, "Jerry can ride back with us. There is enough room for him in my van if you two want to bounce."

"Then it's settled, " I said. "Nina you ride with me and Tina you ride with Dakim."

Nina and I talked the entire four and a half hours from Myrtle Beach to Greensboro. She was very ambitious and intelligent. She had completed an English degree at Salem College in Winston-Salem , North Carolina in three years. And she graduated from Central Law School, in Durham, North Carolina and was preparing to take the bar exam. We discussed everything from God to sex. She feared God tremendously and she was indeed very sexy. Two things I was attracted to.

Since I had met Nina, she had grown accustomed to paging me on Wednesday evening before I went to class. I was attending North Carolina A&T State University. I was about to complete a Bachelor's Degree in Electronics and Computer Technology. On and off, I had attended A&T for a combined three and a half years.

Enrolled in a curriculum course, that combined both class and lab, I dreaded going to this class. It was only once a week, but it was from 4:50pm to 9:50pm. After that class, I d' rush to my car and head to work.

I promoted the Comedy Zone at Club Sensations. Sensations was Greensboro's hot spot. Owned by my best friend, Neon and his partner, Tino.

Nina would page me on Wednesdays and ask me if she should meet me at or after the club. She wasn't a club head and she would rather wait at my crib instead of coming to the club. Something else I liked about her.

Is this why she is paging me? I thought. Usually, she wouldn't page me but once, maybe twice, but today for some reason she had paged me for hours. Ordinarily, she would not use the universal code for emergencies either. "911". She had done so once before when she wanted to go to the movies. I asked her not to do that unless it was really an emergency. I explained to her that going to the movies did not constitute an emergency. She hadn't paged me like that since then. Now, today she was paging me using 911.

Although, I was use to getting 911 pages, once I met a lady and made her feel like she was the only woman on "God's green earth", and I did not immediately return her page, she would automatically assume I was somewhere else making the next woman feel the same way. Shortly after which, she would start blowing my pager up with the infamous 911! At least, that's what I thought. I have never been so wrong in my life.

"It's just my partner." I said to Sandy. I got up smelling like fresh sex and Tommy Girl and headed for the shower. I was wondering why Nina was paging me like she was crazy? Maybe, I had made her crazy. Crazy about me! I smiled at that ego boosting thought. I had to hurry up and take a quick shower and get to class. It was 4:20pm already.

I showered quickly and returned to Sandy's room to get dressed. While getting dressed, I gazed over my shoulder at her. She seemed to be drifting off to sleep now that she had woke me up. I was tempted to try to get a quickie before I left for class. She looked so sexy spread eagle. Face down in a sea of maroon silk. Sandy was about 5'8", 125 pounds, soaking wet. She had paper bag brown skin, shoulder length hair and the cutest baby face. She could have easily been a model. Her legs were the most attractive to me. Not muscular, like a track star, but very firm and long. Like two small hills at the other end of those mile long legs was the tightest little ass I'd ever seen. A perfect connection.

Sandy wasn't liked at all by the hood rats in the Grove. It's ironic why. She was ridiculed because she wasn't promiscuous. Because of this, the hood rats said she thought she was better than everyone else. They hated on her because the hair that touched her shoulders was actually her's and not weave. She was wanted by every thug and wannabe thug in the Grove. They were all shit out of luck. I had her. The "Prize Possession of the Grove" belonged to me.

She caught the way I was lusting over her brown body and said "Don't even think about it, boy. You need to get to class. This ass won't deprive you of your education." She grabbed the sheet and pulled it over her. Causing her celestial body to disappear. With a trace of sarcasm, she added, "You need to call that bitch that keeps paging you. It's probably that bitch right up the sidewalk. She sees your car down here and it's driving her crazy. Tell that hoe the dick is mine now. Your partner my ass. Yeah right." She said.

I pulled up my Mecca jeans and pulled over my matching tee shirt and slipped on my butter colored Timberlands. I eased into the kitchen so Sandy couldn't hear me calling Nina. I dialed her number quickly. As soon as the phone started to ring, Nina picked up.

"Hello," she said.

"What's up, baby girl? Why are you paging me 911?" I asked.

As soon as Nina recognized my voice she started crying. "Dana, the Feds, DEA, and ATF were here not too long ago. They had a search warrant and they searched our house." Her crying became louder with every word she spoke. "They thought you were here. They're looking for you Dana! What's going on? Where are you?" she asked.

I didn't answer her. I couldn't say anything. I was too shocked to respond. I closed the flip on my cell phone, terminating our call. My heart was beating a million miles per hour. I could not believe it.

I must have screamed or yelled because Sandy came rushing down the stairs.

"What's wrong, Styles? I heard you holler, "what and when" like something had happened."

She walked over, still naked to put her arms around me. I walked past her avoiding her embrace and went into the living room. Uncontrollable thoughts raced though my mind. My heart continued to beat loud like tribal drums.

She asked again, "Styles, what's wrong?"

I walked over to the window and peeked out. Good! I thought. They haven't found me yet. I got to get out of this apartment. Get out of Greensboro! Hell, I'd have to leave the country if the Feds are looking for me. "I'll go somewhere they don't even speak English," I said to myself.

I surveyed the outside once more. Still, I saw nothing. I promised Sandy that I would speak with her later. I told her to go back upstairs. She walked past me smelling line stale sex and Tommy Girl, and headed for the bedroom.

"Make sure you call before you leave the club. I am going to page you just to remind you." she added. She turned around and hopped from the second step and gave me a kiss. "Call me," she said again.

"I am. I promise," I said.

"Yeah, right," Sandy said. She had heard that rooster crow before. She knew that I wasn't going to call her once I left her apartment. I never returned her pages after I left the club.

I made one more call before I left. I called my best friend, Neon. He and I met at Gate City Barber Shop a few years earlier. Although, I had heard of him and seen him race his drag car numerous times at Piedmont Drag Strip, I had never been formally introduced to him.

Neon had a reputation as Greensboro's "Number One Ghetto Super Star". I was fresh out of prison and broke as hell when we met. He had heard about my case. He admired me for doing what I did. Him and I automatically clicked. A couple of days later, Neon introduced me to a guy who helped me get back on my feet.

"What's up, Playa?" he asked in his cool laid back voice. When Neon talked on the phone you'd always thing he was in the bed asleep and you'd just disturbed his much needed rest. With my heart kicking the walls of my chest, I began to explain why I paged him 911.

"I just spoke with Nina and she told me that the Feds were looking for me."

"No shit! Oh my god," Neon screamed. His cool, laid back act flew right out the window. He sounded more afraid than I was.

"What should I do?" I asked.

"You need to get out of Greensboro first, and then we will go from there. Call me as soon as you get to a pay phone. Don't use your cell phone anymore, they may have it bugged by now," he said.

I hung up feeling like things might be alright after all. If there was anyone that could help me now, it was definelty Neon.

I yelled to Sandy and told her I would call her later. Now, I was trying to assure myself hat I would be able to all her later. Paranoid, I peeked out the window one last time and saw nothing. There was usually traffic on Spencer Street, but at this moment, Spencer Street looked like a ghost town. Things just looked to damn still.

I walked out the door and disarmed my car alarm. "Chirp-Chirp". The alarm on "Money" sounded like a giant bird with a cold. Quickly, I walked towards my car. Only ten more feet and I can get into my car and be on my way to freedom. Everything was still cool. No Feds, no DEA or ATF. I was walking as fast as I could but it felt like I was walking in slow motion. Five more feet…four…three more feet and I'll open the door to freedom. Then it happened. Out of nowhere, like a nerve racking clap of thunder. I heard accelerated engines, screeching tires and voices yelling. "Freeze, motherfucker!" All happening in slow motion. Like a scene from so many movies I've watched.

For a minute, I went deaf. I could see their lips moving, but I could not hear a thing. So, this is how it's going to end for me? It isn't supposed to end for me like this. "I'm one of the good guys," I thought.

Slowly, I looked around. Spencer Street had come back to life. Unmarked police cars and spectators filled the street. Damn! Were all these people coming out of their apartments just to watch me get arrested, I thought. I was in a daze. I had the odd impression of having wondered into one of those movie sets. Where is the director of this movie? Tell these people to stop moving in slow motion. Who cast me for a part in this movie? Nobody gave me script?

Suddenly, I heard one of the agents scream, "Get up against the fucking car, asshole. You move the wrong way and I'll blow your goddamn head off." He had his Glock 10mm, aimed right between my eyes. The barrel appeared to be the size of a small cannon. This fool looked like an excited child on Christmas Day. His eyes were bright, sparked with the excitement at hand. I was the present he had been longing for all his life.

"Is there a problem, officers? I asked.

Wasn't' it Eddie Murphy who used that line?

"Yeah! You were the problem until just now. We've been looking for you for a couple of days," he said.

Another agent appeared with a photo of me in his hand. Simultaneously, looking at the picture, and without looking at me, he asked, "Are you Dana Styles?" Without giving me a chance to answer, he began reading me my rights.

Again, I looked around. In the midst of the spectators, I saw a small girl I called Precious. Prior to this scene, everytime I saw Precious I'd give her about ten dollars. Just like a "Ghetto Superstar" should do. She would look up at me, as cute as a button, and thank me. Then she'd run straight to the Groove Store.

At this precise moment, I was more concerned about Precious than I was for myself. She had witnessed her father getting gunned down by the Greensboro Police Department, not too long ago. She had been traumatized every since it had happened. She looked frightened. Somehow, I managed to flash a smile, trying to convince her that things were going to be ok for me. She turned and ran away crying. The instant she ran away, I began to think about my son and daughter. Tears formed in the wells of my eyes and started to rise. Slowly, but surely those tears reached the rim of my eyelids. One blink would have caused those tears to spill over the rims like Niagara Falls. "Don't blink! DO NOT BLINK!" I said to myself.

I fought the tears from over flowing. A battle I didn't think I had a chance to win. I didn't want these federal pigs to get it twisted. I can't let them think I'm about to cry because I'm afraid. I'm scared as hell, but they'll never know it.

"The main thang is to maintain your cool, Rock! The main thang is to maintain your cool."

Uncle Roy's voice kept going through my mind. Playing like a scratched record. He must have known before he passed, that at some point in my life those word would be crucial to me. Vital, like my own heartbeat. I didn't blink. I'm maintaining my cool. Uncle Roy would have been proud of me.

"Do you understand your rights, Mr. Styles?" the flunkie agent asked me with a shit eating grin on his face. "Of course you do. You're a smart college boy." He started to laugh loudly in my face.

"Put him in my car," the one who seemed to be in charge said. A black agent. Some fake ass Billy D. Williams looking nigga. Who does this nigga think he is? He came to arrest me and he doesn't even have his weapon out, I thought.

I was patted down and thrown head first into the back of his brand new Ford Crown Vic. The leather smelled like it had just been put in the car before they came to arrest me. I used to love the smell of new leather in cars, not anymore!

I watched from the backseat of the Crown Vic, as the fibbies searched my car. Violating "Money". Ripping her apart.

"Pop the trunk." A white agent with long, greasy hair called out to the rapist inside of "Money". He walked to the rear of the car. He looked back at me and smiled the same shit eating grin.

"Damn!" I said. "Do they teach that stupid grin in the federal academy?"

As soon as he raised the trunk the white agent saw the boxes. I couldn't wait for the contents of those boxes to hit the streets. But the way it seemed, it wasn't going to happen. At least, I wasn't going to be the pusher. He knew he had found what they were looking for. He took his right foot and propped it on the back bumper of my car. I saw his pointed Dingo Boots, and I knew he was scratching the paint on "Money".

I looked out to my right and I saw the "Head Nigga in Charge," (HNIC) talking to Sandy. She seemed to be handling things well. She glanced at me and I could see the hurt in her eyes. Then she turned to lead the fake as Billy D. and his crew into her apartment to be searched.

Wasn't that hurt in her eyes? I thought.

"Sir!" Cowboy, with those fake rattlesnake skin boots on, yelled out. "You might want to see this first."

The HNIC turned around and taking exaggerated steps, quickly made his way to the trunk. Cowboy dug deep into his pocket and pulled out a butterfly knife. Flicking his wrist twice, magically a long silver blade appeared. With all eyes on him and the boxes he commenced to cutting. His cutting was wild. Out of control like some country bumpkin skinning a deer. He almost cut Billy D.

"Sorry, sir," Cowboy said.

"Just get the goddamn box open Williams," Said the HNIC.

When the box split open, little styrofoam pieces, in the shape of macaroni went everywhere. Cowboy put his hand deep inside the box. Billy D. was about to explode from anticipation. For a second Cowboy fished around with his hand. Everyone looked extremely disappointed when he pulled out a handful of my latest rap CD's.

"Keep searching, Williams," Billy D. said.

Along with three other agents, the HNIC turned and escorted Sandy inside her apartment. All of a sudden, I felt my pager vibrating. To my surprise, the agent had failed to take them from me when I was patted down. I had to get to my pager. With my hands cuffed behind my back I was facing a difficult task. I had some numbers locked in my pager that I couldn't allow the Feds to get. I knew I didn't have much time to reach my pagers before one of those hot shots figured out what I was trying to do. For the moment, everyone was occupied with searching my car and Sandy's apartment. I tried over and over, but I could not reach my pagers. Both were located in the front of my pants. Clipped onto my belt. I took a deep breath, so there could be space between my stomach and belt, making my pagers loose. I rolled over on my stomach and got on my knees in the floorboard. My pagers caught the tip of the seat and fell to the floor. I got up as quick as I could and started to stomp both of the pagers. Cowboy heard the stomping and came running to the car. H looked through the window, down on the floor and spotted the pagers.

"What do we have here?" The Boss loves to call numbers back for notorious drug dealers," said Cowboy.

How long can he continue to wear that stupid grin, I thought?

One of my pagers was a local number pager and the other was a nationwide sky pager. The local number was only used for personal pleasures. Sandy for example, that's the number she had. The sky pager was my business pager. When anyone wanted "Work" nothing less that a kilo, the sky pager was their ticket. First class! Beam me up Scottie.

When Cowboy picked up the pager from the floor, the local pager was still in tack. I had stomped the sky pager until the battery had fallen out. When the battery comes out of the sky pager it loses its numbers. It did not have a memory like the local pager. Being the meticulous planner I am, I made sure that was one of the features before I purchased it. My connections and buyers were safe as long as they didn't page me from this point on. The local pager still had its numbers in it and it was still going off. I didn't care though. I had accomplished what I intended to.

My connection had called a lot of people to tell them not to page me. I'm glad he did that. He saved himself and a bunch of other guys. That's what best friends are for!

Billy D. emerged from the apartment still looking disappointed. When he looked over at me, I gave him the same "shit eating grin" his boys had been giving me. Cowboy ran up to Billy D. and thrust the pagers in his face.

"I forgot to give you these earlier. Sir." He was craving accolades from the HNIC, but he received none. He didn't mention that I had stomped the battery out of one of them. That would have exposed his negligence.

With all that was happening, I failed to realize the even larger crowd that had formed. Everyone wanted to see me getting arrested. This way they could have their own rendition of how I got busted. Sandy, the prize possession of the Groove, was seeming to enjoy the extra attention she was receiving from the masses. I think she was excited that she would forever be a part of the story, "When Dana Styles got busted." And where he was when he got knocked. She would at least be the talk of the town for a while. I told myself that she had to be hurting.

Putting his right hand up in the air, and making fast circles, Billy D. motioned to the other agents to get ready to go. Cowboy announced to everyone that the show was over. He instructed them to clear the streets. When the crowd did not immediately break up, he threatened them to move along or there would be others accompanying me. Billy D. didn't approve of his final comment. He gave him a "shut the hell up look, " so Cowboy did just that.

"The show is over." Isn't that what the Cowboy just said? So this is a show? Billy D. must be the director.

Ok guys, you said this is a show. You said that it was over. Why am I still in handcuffs? Cut! Stop the tape! What was the Hollywood term? So much was running through my mind.

Billy D. got in the car and slammed the door. He had the audacity to sigh like he was having a bad day. Another agent, one I saw standing amongst the spectators got in too.

"Which way, sir?" he asked.

"Go back the way we came," said Billy D.

The crowd finally following Cowboys' orders was breaking up. Resuming their everyday activities, in slow motion. I started to think about my son and daughter again. I wondered where Precious had run off to. As we pulled off I nodded my head at Sandy. Searching for a teary confirmation in her brown eyes that would prove she was hurting. For some reason, I felt like if she was hurting, I would feel better.

Placing her hand up against the right side of her face, like her hand was a telephone, she exaggerated the movement of her lips and in slow motions she said, "Call me tonight."

Now, she would be sure I'd call! As she strolled back inside her apartment, she was surrounded by those two and four faced hood rats that hated on her. She was the star of the show now that I was being driven off the set. I watched as they all filled into her apartment. They looked like ducks. All in a row. I counted them. One, two, three, four, five, six seven of them. Sandy being the eight duck. All eager to hear her side of the story. The "Prize Possession of the Grove" was soon to become someone else's prize.

It felt like it took an hour to get off Spencer Street. We turned left on Market Street to go downtown, still appearing to move in slow motion.

"Damn!" I said to myself. Then I began to think. If I would have called Nina two hours ago, I would be two hours ahead of these clowns!

"Well, well Mr. Styles," Billy D. said. "It looks like you're going to miss class for a very long time."

CHAPTER 3

Twenty days after I graduated from Madison-Mayodan High School, I joined the United States Army. A patriot, I arrived in Ft. Benning, Georgia, on June 26, 1988. I was nervous as hell. Although, I had an idea of what to expect because my brothers, Rodney and Tim, were already in the Army. They had pulled my coattail on the shock treatment I would run into head on.

"Get the fuck off of my cattle truck. Don't look at me, private. You are wreckless eyeballing," Drill Sergeant Lacy yelled.

Drill Sergeant Lacy, Toussaint and some huge drill sergeant with a thick Jamaican accent were yelling out obloquies. The huge Jamaican drill, grabbed me and my duffle bag with two giant hands. We were nothing but small bags of potatoes to him. He threw me and my possession out of the cattle truck with ease. My duffle bag hit the ground like an atomic bomb. It came open and my property went everywhere.

"Get at the position of attention you dingle berries," he yelled out.

I began to bend over to pick up my things that were on the ground.

"Don't' you even think about picking up shit," he frowned and said to me. All around me bodies and duffle bags continued to fly, like migrating bird joining the formation. The worse part of all this was it was raining golf balls. My property spread like cake icing on the ground was getting soaked. I couldn't even think about picking up shit.

For twelve weeks, I went through Basic Training and Advanced Infantry training (AIT) excelling in both. I received the Army Achievement Award, along with the M-16 Expert Badge for completion of Basic Training and AIT. Those three Drills I learned to hate but respect at the same time.

Usually, upon completion of Basic Training and AIT, a soldier would take a two week vacation. In my case, after graduation I was shuttled along with a gang of others across post to another school. Airborne School!

The only reason I was attending Airborne School was because if I graduated I was guaranteed a permanent duty station in Ft. Bragg, North Carolina. Less than two hours away from home.

The only thing in the world I was afraid of was heights. But, if getting me close to home meant overcoming that fear, I was willing to take that chance. Just the thought of being less than two hours from home was a motivational factor throughout Airborne School.

Airborne School consisted of three weeks. Each week having it's own significant name. The first week is called "Hell Week". Appropriately named, it is without a doubt, physically the hardest week of Airborne School. Hell Week is designed to weed out the weak links in the strong Airborne chain.

I was in First Battalion in Airborne School. We started the class with approximately six hundred soldiers, eager to become paratroopers. Needless to say, when we reached the end of Hell Week there was a drastic reduction in the number. First Battalion had a total of three hundred and twenty soldiers going into the second week.

The second week is called "Tower Week". This particular week we learned all about the paratrooper's equipment and how it was properly worn. Also, we learned how a paratrooper exits a high performance aircraft while in flight. And of course, how to perform a correct parachute landing fall (PLF). After four days of diligent training we were taken to the towers. Once there, each "wannabe" paratrooper slipped into a parachute harness and waited for his or her turn to be raised two hundred and fifty feet into the air. Once we were hoisted to our high destination, we were dropped. We descended gracefully back down to the precious earth. If you didn't implement what you were taught during tower week and some soldiers didn't, it was evident when the PLF was conducted. Some twisted and broke ankles and legs. Others realized at that point that two hundred and fifty feet was too high and fifteen hundred feet wouldn't be an option. Therefore, reducing our total number of soldiers to about three hundred.

The final week of Airborne School is called "Jump Week". Mentally, this was the most challenging week. I was far beyond being nervous this particular week, I was scared as hell! I continued to think if I really wanted to be close to home, I'd have to graduate from Airborne School.

The night before my first jump, I could barely sleep. I tossed and turned having terrible dreams of my parachute not deploying. When the jump instructors, better known as "Black Hats" came to wake us up, I wasn't asleep. Everyone in the unit was probably doing what I had been doing. Lying there in my small bunk, contemplating whether to jump or not! I wondered how many of the soldiers were from North Carolina? Willing to jump out of a perfectly good airplane to be stationed close to home.

Airborne School was a voluntary school. It wasn't frowned upon if you didn't graduate. You had balls just for trying to make it. Evidently, that was sufficient enough for some of the soldiers that morning. Eleven of them quit instead of attempting their first jump. I'm sure those eleven were up all night tossing and turning. Indomitable thoughts getting the best of them. The remaining two hundred and eighty-nine were loaded onto cattle trucks and shuttled to Houghton Airfield.

"Nervited" is a term I created. It's a mixture of being nervous and excited. That's how I felt when we reached the airfield, "nervited". Butterflies fluttered in my stomach by the thousands, but my adrenaline rushed. I saw some of the largest airplanes I'd ever seen. Then it crossed my mind. Hit me like a ton of bricks. I had never flown in and airplane before. Now, here I was getting ready to jump out of the first airplane I set foot on. I closed my eyes so tight it made my headache. Silently, I started to pray that God would give me the courage to overcome the fear of jumping. He was probably receiving two hundred and eighty-nine of the same prayers.

"OK, listen up soldiers," Black Hat McGrady called out. "Today will be the first day of the rest of your airborne lives. Get in a single file line and pick up your chutes and your reserves. I hope you don't need your reserves." He said as he laughed and walked away.

I got in line and picked up my T-10 Bravo Chute and reserve chute. I walked slowly back to where I'd been sitting. I stared at the T-10 and reserve. They both looked just like the chutes I had seen in my dreams.

"Damn, I hope I don't need this," I said looking at the reserve. I sat the reserve down. More scared than nervous or excited, I began to put on my equipment.

"The bird will be taking off in fifteen minutes." said McGrady.

When I looked around at the other frightened faces, I recognized a friend of mine. Barnett was from Los Angeles, and he and I were field buddies while in Basic Training. Now, here we were in Airborne School together. His face was baptized in fear.

"Hey, what happening Barnett," I said.

"Nothing dawg," he responded. "I'm just ready to put my knees in the breeze."

Barnett tried to sound cool, but the eyes don't lie. He was scared as hell too.

"Yeah, me too dawg. I'm ready to put my knees in the breeze. I've been ready. I couldn't even sleep last night because of anticipation."

The truth was, I could not sleep for fear of jumping. I wandered if Barnett could read my eyes like I could read his? Oh well! I couldn't quit now. My mouth had written a check my ass had to cash.

"Let's go! Let's go!" Some unidentified Black Hat screamed out. "Your prayers belong to Jesus, but your ass is mine." He said.

I looked over at Barnett and gave him two thumbs up.

We all were instructed to form two lines and move outside toward the aircraft. A huge black and green C-130 Hercules.

"Man damn, this is a big ass bird," I said to Barnett. With stretched eyes he just shook his head up and down.

Barnett and I were smart and got at then end of the line. If we refused to jump, we would be the last two on the plane and no one would see us refuse. At least, that's what I was thinking. After twelve weeks of Basic training and AIT, I knew Barnett was thinking along those same lines. I convinced him to get in front of me. That way if I refused to jump, even he wouldn't see it.

When paratroopers load a C-130, the entire rear of the bird opens. It looked like a gigantic tailgate on the world's largest pick up truck. We were loaded on the plane in two lincs. One for each side of the bird. I assumed that the C-130 was like a commercial aircraft with the doors located toward the front of the bird. To my surprise, the door of our exit was located in the rear of the bird. The C-130 started racing down the runway and I realized that my plan had backfired.

Ever since I was a child, I'd sit in the front of any class I was in, race to be the first in any line and tried to be the first in everything I did. Why? I thought. Why did I go against my own grain and try to go last today? I was going to be the first one to jump or the first one to refuse.

"Twenty minutes." Black Hat McGrady yelled out as soon as the bird lifted. That's the first jump command. Everytime that a command is given, it is repeated by every paratrooper to ensure that the command was heard. Twenty minutes until "T.O.T" Time on Target.

"Out board personnel stand up! In board personnel stand up! Hook up!" As I hooked my static line onto the static line cable, my hands were shaking frantically. My adrenaline was turned up to the red zone now.

"Check static line!" McGrady was yelling the jump command to the top of his lungs. His voice fighting a loosing battle with the loud hum of the C-130's engine. He looked at me and flashed a wicked grin. He knew I was scared to death. He'd seen fearful faces a thousand times on new paratroopers. He took pleasure in seeing those faces.

Suddenly, I felt a ghastly gust, like a tornado had been unleashed in the plane. The Air Force safety had opened the doors.

"Mannnnn, damn." I said.

McGrady started laughing loud and deviously. Abruptly, stopping his laugh he screamed, "Check equipment." A few seconds later he yelled, " Sound off for equipment check."

When this command is given, the last paratrooper turns around and allows the next to the last paratrooper to inspect his equipment. Then he turns back around and inspects the next to the last guy's equipment. If everything is correct, he smacks the trooper on the ass and screams, "OK!" This "OK" is like a domino effect. Each paratrooper checks the person's equipment in front of him and screams the same thing if the equipment is correct.

"Ok!" I heard Barnett scream as he smacked me on my ass. Stomping my right foot and pointing my left hand directly in Black Hat McGrady's face, I yelled out as loud as I could, "All OK jump master!"

McGrady gripped the sides of the doors and arching his back he hung out of the bird. He looked like a grown ass man enjoying himself on the playground. The wind was blowing so hard it was disfiguring McGrady's face. This was heaven for him. He checked the outside of the doors. Gliding his hands over the skin of the metal bird, to make sure there wasn't anything that could snag our equipment. When he returned inside, he yelled "Ten minutes!" It was repeated by everyone except for me. I tried to say it. I moved my lips, but nothing came out. I peered out of the door as we passed through the clouds. My knees were shaking but ironically I was really anticipating the jump.

McGrady stomped the platform at the base of the door to ensure it was locked in place. He returned again and yelled, One Minute!"

"That's the fastest nine minutes in the world." I said to McGrady.

"Are you ready, airborne?" He asked.

Eyes wide, mouth open and speechless, I shook my head up and down, very fast.

"Stand in the door." said McGrady.

I inched my way to the door. I assumed a good door position. Knees slightly bent and my back straight just like I was taught in Tower Week.

"When you see the green light come one," he pointed to the red and green bubs beside the door, "Wait for my smack, then go."

In Airborne School they train you not to look down once you're standing in the door, but I had to look. The earth's surface looked like it was a million miles away.

"Damn, is that a house?" I said to no one. It couldn't have been. It was smaller than one of those monopoly houses!

"Thirty seconds," McGrady yelled from behind me. I raised my head and looked straight out into the horizon. Beautiful blue skies and fluffy clouds awaited me. I was about to become one with both.

"Green light, Go!"

McGrady smacked me hard on my ass, almost pushing me out the door. I jumped up six inches, out thirty-six, like I had been trained to do. The propt blast grabbed me, shaking me like dice. I felt like a piece of paper being thrown out the window of a speeding Porsche.

"One thousand, two thousand, three thousand." I counted with my eyes closed. As four thousand pierced my lips, I felt a sudden jerk. I looked up and inspected the sphere of silk. It was the most "Beautifullest" thing in the world. I felt great. I yelled out as loud as I could, "Airborne!"

As I descended, I observed the other silk chutes in the air. I yelled over to Barnett, but he didn't respond. I guess he was still shook. I looked up at the sky and thanked God. The heat from the sun warmed my face. The sun was an incandescent beauty. I was as close to it now than I would ever be. This was freedom. My prayers had been answered.

I hit the ground, keeping my feet and knees together, tucked and rolled. A dynamite PLF is what McGrady would have called it. I had the same experience for the following three days. My last jump was a night jump. A requirement in order to graduate from Airborne School. Hell, all my jumps were really night jumps, because I kept my eyes close when I went out the door!

Proudly, I graduated from Airborne School and returned home for a much deserved vacation. I received my orders in the mail to report to Ft. Bragg, North Carolina at the end of my vacation. Less than two hours away from home.

I was sure that being close to home was going to be great and at the time it was, but now that I sit here and think about it, I probably would not be here in this situation if I had been ordered to serve my tour elsewhere. I have truly learned what looks good or seems good isn't always good for you. It has been a hard lesson learned.

CHAPTER 4

I arrived at Ft. Bragg, North Carolina in mid November 1988 with uncontained zeal. I was so "gun ho" that it I would have been given a Kamikaze Mission, I would have accepted it with honors. I reported to the 82nd Airborne Division (ABN DIV) Hold-Over Center. New paratroopers, commonly referred to as "cherries", had to wait at this center until they were assigned to a unit.

I was assigned to Alpha Company (A.Co) 3rd 505 Parachute Infantry Regiment. Once there I had to under go further assignment. I finally got designated to first platoon, first squad. Sgt First Class Marero was our platoon leader. He ordered an informal formation in the unit's day room, so I could be introduced to everyone.

"Ok, Ok! Listen up everyone. Let me have your attention. We received a new cherry today, so let's give him a first platoon welcome."

When Sgt Marero said that the day room erupted. "Cherry! Cherry! Cherryeeeeeeeeeeeeeeeeeeeeee!"

"What's your name, cherry?" a voice from among first platoon said.

"Styles. Private Styles." I said in a firm voice.

"Styles!" I heard someone say, mimicking the way I said my last name.

"Well, get your ass on the ground and give me fifty pushups in style."

For the next hour, I did pushups, sit-ups and side straddle hop non stop. Everyone was having a ball at the expense of my sweat.

"That's enough! We don't want to kill the cherry before we go to the field next week," said Marero. Breaking up the cluster, he along with the others who had just tried to physically torture me with exercise welcomed me again. This time they shook my hands instead of making me work out.

Drenched in sweat, I proceeded to my room to seek some solace. Sgt. Marero assigned me to a room with a white guy named, Scoot Poosh from Troy, Ohio. He had been in A. Co. for two and a half years already. Poosh entered the room and spoke.

"Hey, Cherry! You put your things on that side of the shelf. That's my bean bag," he said, taking a big bite of a microwaveable cheeseburger. "I don't allow anyone to sit on my bean bag. How did you like your cherry party? It's been some time since I had mine." He held his head back, squeezing his eyes tight as if he were trying to remember something. "Things will get worse before they get better."

I began to unpack and Poosh continued to talk. "Cherries have to do all the shit details. You better hope we get another cherry soon. You got here at a real fucked up time. We go to the field for three weeks in three days. Are you ready?" he asked.

Poosh was talking fast. Asking questions and making statements in the same breath.

"Your cherry blast will be a battalion mass tact," he said.

"What do you mean "cherry blast"? I asked.

"Your first jump with A Company. It will be with the entire battalion. That's a lot of silk in the air." Then he added, "That's scary, cherry!" He smiled like he had really come up with something creative. Then he cut his smile short as if he had been overwhelmed with a serious thought. "A black cherry!" he said smiling again.

When Poosh said that, I jumped in his face. I snapped!

"Lookah here, motherfuckah, I know I go this cherry shit coming, but that black cherry shit, that racist shit, I ain't having it."

Even though Poosh was substantially larger and much taller than I was, he took a few steps back and flopped his beet red face down on his beloved beanbag. He was shocked at my unexpected outburst. I could see it in his blue eyes.

"Damn dude, I didn't mean anything personal by what I said. It was only a joke. I'm not racist. In high school, my best friend was black."

That's the first thing a red neck says, I thought. "Yeah, right!" I said.

I hoisted my duffle bag onto my bunk. I continued to unpack and organize my locker. I was still exhausted from my cherry party.

Alpha Company was comprised of roughly 150 soldiers. Out of the 150, nine were black, six were Spanish and one was Vietnamese. The rest were the hardest charging white boys I'd ever seen. Ready for war! Ready to die!

Airborne Infantry wasn't a popular M.O.S. (Military Occupational Status) for blacks. That was a job that required you to work ten times as hard as any other job. Needless to say, you had to do this after you jumped out of a perfectly good airplane. Black soldiers weren't having that!

Since the number of blacks was so low in the Airborne Infantry Units, they automatically stuck together. Staff Sergeant Scott was a brother from Tampa, Florida. He was the squad leader for the 3rd squad in my platoon. He introduced me to the other seven blacks in Alpha Company and took me to meet the other brothers throughout the battalion.

Eddie Hunt was a brother from Pittsburgh, Pennsylvania. He was a squad leader in Bravo Company. Huntman (pronounced hunt-man) as he was called, had been in Bravo Company for almost four years. He had completed Ranger School and had been promoted to E-5 a month earlier. B Company was our Battalion's Mecca for black soldiers. It had seventeen brothers.

Huntman and I hit it off as soon as Sgt. Scott introduced us to one another. He was listening to some song that was kicking some powerful lyrics.

"What's that you're listening to?" I asked.

"That's that new cat, "Two-Pac", Tupac or something like that. He used to rap with Digital Underground. This is his joint by himself called "Brenda's Got a Baby".

"Word! I like that, " I said.

It was music that we had in common at first. Then I saw what Huntman was pushing. A new Blazer dropped with "100 Spokes" with some serious sounds in the back. To be a sergeant this was a cool guy. Almost too cool to be in the Army. He acted like he was still a civilian. He wore a thick herring bone necklace and a matching bracelet. To top it off, he had a gold nugget watch that was gleaming as well. The Army was being good to this nigga, I thought. His material things made me second guess why I had joined the Army? For the love of my country or to have the money to purchase the things like he had? But, I knew it was for the love of my country that I joined the military.

Two days after meeting Huntman and the other brothers in 3rd Battalion, we all went to the field for three weeks. I was "nervited" when I made my cherry blast, but now I wasn't a cherry anymore. I had six jumps. At least that's what I thought. During those three weeks in the field, I found my niche in first squad. I felt more like a part of our "Ivory Family" despite my soulfulness.

When you return from the field after a long period of time you crave civilization. To take a good shit on a toilet, instead of squatting behind bushes while trying to align your ass over a hole you've dug, is priceless. And a hot shower was worth more than that. After all the equipment is accounted for, the planning for the parties began. Actually, they are planned before we go to the field and just fined tuned when we return.

"Hey Cherry, you want to go and get drunk with us?" Poosh asked. That invitation was a sign that I was officially a part of the A Company Gang. He said they were going down Hay Street, in Fayetteville, to the Dollar Bar.

"Hell naw, I ain't going with all ya'll white boys to get drunk. I know what happens at those types of parties, " I said laughing. "I don't drink anyway. "

"The Cherry is sober." Palagonia, an Italian guy from the Bronx, New York said in his distinctive New York accent.

"First Platoon needs a designated driver, " Poosh said.

"Nah, I'm going to just chill out and rest, " I said. I escorted the rowdy group of white boys out of the barricks, advising them not to get to drunk.

When I came back inside the barricks, the CQ, (the soldier assigned to answer the phone) told me I had a call. I did not know we could even receive phone calls. "Damn, I am still a cherry, " I said to myself.

"Hello, " I said.

"Yo, what's up Styles? This is Huntman. Me, Moe and Wilk are getting ready to ride out. Do you want to go with us?"

"Yeah, I'm down, " I said.

"We'll be ready in about thirty minutes, " he said.

I hung up the phone and rushed back to my room. I grabbed my freshest gear and got dressed. Public Enemy blarred from Poosh's stereo as I got dressed. I sprayed some cologne on, that was sitting on his side of the shelf. It was a dark bottle that didn't have a name on it. It smelled pretty good so I sprayed it once over my shirt. I was ready in five minutes.

I walked out of A Company's rear door and took about thirty steps and walked into B Company's front door. Before I reached Huntman's room I could hear NWA's "Fuck the Police," like Eazy E, Ice Cube, Dr. Dre, Ren and Yella were performing

16

live in his room. I knocked on the door and it was unanswered. Then I kicked the bottom of the door. Still there was no response. I opened the door, slightly. Huntman, Wilk and Moe were all standing around a desk in the corner of the room. They still hadn't noticed me.

"Yo! " I yelled. Their necks snapped like the command eyes right had been given.

"Damn, Moe!" Huntman said. "I thought you locked the fucking door."

"Hold up one second Styles," Wilk said, already closing the door. I backed slowly out of the room. I was straining to see what they were worshipping on the desk. All I could see was what looked like a plate.

"Wait in the day room for us, " Wilk said.

Curiously, I walked back up the hall. Eazy E, and the rest of his crew had faded since my invasion of the room. After a few minutes, I saw the guys emerge from Huntman' s room. They whispered to each other coming up the hall.

"Styles, you want to drive?" Huntman asked.

"Man you know I don't have a car yet, " I said.

He shook his head and smiled. "I know you don't have a Whip yet. I'm talking about my Whip."

He tossed me the keys. We walked out to the parking lot and got into the Blazer.

"I need to stop by the bank teller to get some cash flow first, " I said. When I said that, Huntman turned around and looked at Wilk and Moe. The three started laughing.

"Cash! Nigga, you don't need any cash when you're rolling with us. We are cash." Moe said.

"Pullover there." Moe pointed to the other side of the huge parking lot. "I need to get something from my car. Right here. Stop!" he said.

Moe hopped out and disarmed his car alarm. It was a black 1988 Mustang GT convertible.

"Damn, that's Moe's whip?" I asked.

"Yeah, one of them. He has three Mustangs, " Huntman said.

Moe returned to the Blazer concealing something under his shirt. When he got in the Blazer he handed Huntman an incredibly large pistol.

"We might need some heat in Big P' s tonight, " he said.

Huntman cradled the large pistol like it was a newborn baby. That Ranger School had enhanced his love for weapons.

"Yeah, you're right. Those Fayetteville niggas were grilling us the last time we were in there," Wilk said, with a devious smile. "That's why I already packed my shit." He raised up his silk shirt and unveiled an equally large pistol. This amused us all and we laughed all the way to Big P's.

When we arrived at P's, I parked the Blazer side ways, taking up two parking spaces.

"Yeah, park like this. These niggas will park close to you just to open their doors to hit your ride," Huntman said.

We bailed out and headed for the entrance to the club. It was still relatively early and there wasn't much activity going on in the parking lot. As we approached, all the bouncers spoke to Moe. Moe spoke back to them and walked over to where they were huddled. We stopped our stroll when Moe raised his hands up for us to stop. After a few words, he turned and motioned for us to advance forward. We were escorted in and seated in the VIP section.

"What ya'll want to drink?" A cute waitress asked.

"Give me a Ginger Ale on the rocks, " I said, winking my eye, inspecting her from head to toe. "I'm the designated driver."

"Give the rest of us Hennessey and Coke and put three bottles of Dom on ice for us," Moe said. She smiled at me and before she walked off she said,

"It's good to know that there are still some responsible men left in this world. I was getting worried. "

"I practice safe sex too, " I said. "Is that responsible enough for you?" I asked watching her every move. She smiled, but didn't answer me and floated away. The guys thought that was funny and all of them laughed.

It didn't take long for a crowd to accumulate. Big P's had transformed from a stream of partygoers, to a sea of party animals. As Guy's "Grove Me, " pumped like blood through the large Bose, people moved about with high intensity thru the thick clouds of Mary Jane smoke. Huntman and Wilk were seated in the opposite corners of the VIP section from Moe and myself. They were facing the entrance and we faced the DJ booth. Watching each other's back. I set there listening to the Ghetto Boys now. "Mind of a Lunatic" seemed to have the club rocking. I wondered how many large and small pistols were being concealed by all this flea market attire.

One of the bouncers, a large dark skinned dude with a curly kit, kept directing traffic to Wilk and Huntman. Each time Wilk would dig deep into his coat pocket and pass plastic bags to a culprit. In return for the bags, Huntman was accepting folded and rolls of cash. No wonder I didn't need any money, I thought. These cats got something that everyone seems to want. This routine went on for almost two hours before Wilk looked over at Moe and nodded his head back slowly with his lips poked out. Moe got the big bouncers attention, who had directed traffic so well. He motioned for him to come over to the VIP section. When he did, he handed the big guy a roll of money and shook his large hands. Walking towards the exit sign, I noticed the grilling faces, and the evil eyes that followed us. Now, I realized why Huntman and Wilk were strapped. I felt naked without a gat. The next time I visited Big P's, I would definitely be strapped. We made it safely to the Blazer, despite all the "Go to hell" stares.

"Boy, we rolled tonight." Wilk said.

"Where to now?" I asked.

"Huntman, its 1:15 now, and I told my girl to meet me a 1:30, so we better get over there." Moe said.

"Turn left here and make the next left at the intersection, " Huntman said pointing to the road to our left. We cruised down Bragg Blvd. on our way to meet Moe's girl. Wilk and Moe counted money in the back while Huntman continued to mess with the stereo system.

"Make a right into this parking lot, " Huntman said.

The parking lot was packed. I read a flashing sign that said "Lashockas." It seemed like every ride there was a fly ride. It looked like Five Star rims or Hammers decked every whip on the lot.

"There she is, Styles. Pull up to the Green Mustang." Moe jumped out and ran to the passenger side of the Mustang. He hopped in the car and disappeared behind the illegal limo tent. Just as fast as he hopped in he popped out of the Mustang. Growling like a savage beast, the Mustang pulled off.

"Go ahead and park where she was, " Moe said.

"Hell no! We're not parking right here for some nigga to scratch my paint. We are parking over there. " Huntman pointed way to the other side of the parking lot.

"Damn man, we are driving my car the next time we go somewhere. I cannot be doing all this fucking walking. We didn't walk this much in the field," Moe said shaking his head.

We got out and hiked across the parking lot. The same thing that took place at Big P' s took place here at Lashockas, with one exception. The bouncers greeted Huntman and Wilk this time, instead of Moe. I watched as they explained who I was. I guess they recognized Moe's face. The bouncers didn't inquire about him. Wilk and Huntman looked back and nodded at us both.

We marched into the club with two bouncers leading the way. The crowd parted like the Red Sea as we made our way to the VIP. The VIP section was already occupied with a gang of intoxicated and boisterous hoodlums. Huntman stepped up on the elevated section. "What's happening my nigga?" He said.

Easily identifiable with the most gold chains, and surrounded by three fat booty chickenheads, the gangs leader slapped Huntman's hand. "Y'all niggas make room for Huntman and his crew, " Sammy B yelled.

In unison, the entire gang shifted like synchronized swimmers. After slapping hands with the whole gang, we finally took our seats. Moe took refuge in a seat right outside of the VIP. Shortly after we were seated the traffic began just like at Big P's. We stayed in Lashockas until it was closing time."This is ya last chance to slow dance, " the DJ announced. Couples shuffled to the dance floor. "Piece of My Love" by Guy, serenaded those who remained to grind one last time, before going to purchase a cheap room on Bragg Blvd.

We hiked back across the parking lot to the deserted Blazer. "I sold them all except for one," Moe said.

"We'll get rid of it tomorrow at P's" Huntman responded.

We all went back to the barricks and called it a night. I went back to my room, undressed and got into bed. I thought about all that had happened. I was tired and I fell asleep thinking about how could I really get down with the guys to make some of the money they were making.

7:30 AM, THE FOLLOWING MORNING

"Styles, wake up nigga. You still asleep?" Huntman asked. He stood over me looking like he had been awake for hours, and he probably had. "This is my third time coming over here to see you and you've been asleep."

"Third time! " I said. He had been up for a while, just as I expected.

"How much money you got in your bank account?" Huntman asked.

"Why? "

"I'm trying to do something. I need to borrow some money. Whatever you give me I will double it when I pay you back, " Huntman said.

"Double it?" I asked.

"Yeah! Whatever you give me I'm going to give you twice that amount back. "

"When?" I asked.

"It'll take three or four days, maybe a week, but you will be straight. Trust me, " He said.

Something wasn't adding up. I just saw these cats make a million dollars last night, now he was in my face before the early bird wakes up asking me for money. "I'll have to wait until Monday to go to the bank," I said.

"They have banks on post that open at 8:00 on Saturdays, and I need it ASAP. I'm trying to do something real big, " He said to me.

I got up and took a shower. Then I rode with Huntman to the bank. I had made up my mind to only give Huntman $500. That way it wouldn't hurt me much if he didn't pay me back. But, I had figured out a way I could get my money back if he didn't pay me. The wheels on his Blazer were worth three times the amount he wanted to borrow. I wouldn't have any problems sitting that pretty Blazer on blocks and selling those wheels back in Greensboro.

Three days went by and I hadn't heard anything from Huntman. I accepted the fact I had been beat. I vowed to leave that Blazer on blocks though.

Wednesday, after the 4: 30 p.m. formation, Huntman finally showed his face. He came down to my room and knocked on the door.

"Here you go dawg," he said. He handed me fifty twenty-dollar bills.

"I'll probably do the same thing next week if you want to get down. "

"No doubt, " I said.

'We're going back out to the clubs this weekend, do you want to come with us?" Huntman asked.

"No" I said "I'm going to Greensboro this weekend. You all need to come up there. "

I started to tell him about all the things that were happening in the Gate City. He said it sounded like fun. "Let me ask Wilk and Moe if they want to ride up there. I'll let you know tomorrow. "

I didn't want Huntman to see how excited I was about the $500 profit. I could barely contain my excitement. I had never made so much money so fast without doing anything. Hell yeah, I was with doubling my money next week and any week he wanted to borrow it. Next week I was planning to get out all of my money in my account. Drain that bitch bone dry! He slapped my hand and walked out of the room. "Let me know what y'all are going to do tomorrow. " I yelled.

Thursday afternoon I saw Huntman and Wilk in the chow hall. They all were looking forward to a change of scenery this weekend. We agreed to leave Ft. Bragg at 6:30 p.m. the following day.

Friday at 6: 23 p.m. the CQ called for me. I ran down the hall to the phone. Huntman said they were on their way to the parking lot with their bags. I hung up the phone and dashed back to my room to grab my bags.

"You going home this weekend, Cherry?" Poosh asked. He was sitting on his precious bean bag eating a big bowl of "God only knows what?"

"I'm on my way now," I said.

"Have a good time and get laid for me." He said.

20

I ran back down the hall and out the barracks. When I got to the Blazer I opened the rear door and threw my bag on top of the other bags. Huntman was relaxed in the passenger seat and Wilk and Moe were stretched out in the back.

"Since you like to drive so much," he said smiling, "you can drive to Greensboro."

I jumped in the drivers seat and ejected the NWA tape, and I put in my Keith Sweat tape. It was something I could listen to while I cruised down the highway. When I pulled out of the parking lot Keith started begging. Nobody begs like Keith. It was going to take about an hour and a half to get to Greensboro and Mr. Sweat was going to take us all the way!

Highway 421 North is a boring drive from Ft.Bragg to Greensboro. Keith was pleading, "Make It Last Forever." I wondered if he was singing about a relationship or long ass 421 North. He must have been singing about a relationship, because 421 finally came to an end and turned into Martin Luther King Jr. Drive, in Greensboro.

"Y'all niggas wake up, we're here," I said. I pulled up to the Red Roof Inn on Meadowview Drive. We checked in our rooms and unpacked our bags.

"What are we going to do first?" Moe asked.

"We are going to ride over to North Carolina A&T State University first. You all think there is a lot of women at Fayetteville State, you haven't seen shit. A&T has ten times the women as FSU, and they look better. Then we're going across the street to Bennett College. The all black female college I told you all about. It's a closed campus but being the Airborne Infantry men we are, we shouldn't have a problem infiltrating. " I said. Laughter filled the air as we prepared to go "Ho-Hopping!"

Traffic on High Point Road was horrendous. Some rock and roll concert was taking place at the Greensboro Coliseum. We bobbed and weaved through traffic and finally made it to Greensboro's East Side. A&T was having some type of gym jam, and the campus was packed. My partners were tripping because they couldn't believe all the fine, young sisters they were seeing.

"Damn, look at how fat her ass is, " Wilk said, almost breaking his neck to follow the sister's ass.

"Look over there, " Huntman pointed to a group of girls standing about twenty deep.

"Ain't no way in hell I would have joined the Army if I was from up here." Wilk said.

We continued to cruise through and around A&T's campus. Sweating the tenderonis and being sweated. We made a few pit stops to exchange numbers with some of the young queens. Promising to call and come back later. Promises that would be kept.

"Where are the projects and drug spots at around here?" Huntman asked.

When he asked that I knew immediately that our trip to Greensboro wasn't just about a change of scenery. It was an undercover, set up shop trip. These niggas wanted to scout Greensboro for a spot. A section they could put their product down. One thing was for certain. If they wanted to put down in Greensboro, I was going to eat a piece of the cake. A huge piece.

We rode through most of the hoods in the Gate City. The Blazer was a foreign vehicle in each project. We were attracting suspicious stares in every hood. Were we the

Feds? Were we lost? We had to be if we were cruising thru these hoods. One stop and we would be victims of a robbery, I assured my comrades. So we never stopped.

As we passed through the hoods a series of questions would take place. What's up with this hood? Who runs this spot? Is this spot hot? I answered the questions to the best of my abilities. For almost two hours we checked out spots. The Hill was our final hood for tonight's observation.

The Hill was a notorious spot in the Gate City. I explained to my partners that the police didn't even come up on the Hill. That's how bad it was.

"My type of spot, " Huntman said.

Wilk added, "If the police don't fuck with the cats on the Hill, those niggas are hustling without a care in the world."

"We need to join that party, " Moe said.

"I know a few niggas that get money up here. Tomorrow when the heat tab rises, I'll come up here and find them. I'll have to come alone though, because if I bring an unfamiliar face up here, them niggas will think the person is five "O''. I'll find out what's going on and let you all know," I said.

We took Lee Street to English Street and headed for Side Effects. Things were slow on Fridays but I assured them that on Saturdays it would be packed.

"We're going to scout Side Effects out too," I said.

"Yeah, that sounds good to me," said Huntman. "But right now let's get back to AT&T."

"Its A&T, not AT&T," I said.

"Whatever it's called let's get there. I promised," then he paused and looked at the name on the small piece of paper, because he had forgotten her name. "...Pricilla, that I'd see her later. Right now, would be later," Moe said.

CHAPTER 5

During the daytime, the Hill looked more like a forty ounce land field than the projects. Bottles of "Ole E" stood abandoned on curbs, and some broken. Actually, most of the bottles were broken and the glass sparkled like diamonds in the sun, on the cold pavement. Trash accompanied every broken bottle. Philly Blunt boxes and Burger King bags added to the ghetto decoration.

The Hill Store never closed. It was a safe haven for drug dealers. Shabob, the store owner, was all about the money. He didn't care how he made it. The drug dealers paid him to keep packages behind the counter in his safe. When I pulled up I recognized a face leaving the store. I tooted the horn and called his name.

"Kiwi!" Kiwi was so black he got his nickname from the Kiwi shoe polish. He was half smoker, whole hustler.

"What's up Blacker than me?" I said.

"Styles what's up? Damn, it's been a long time. I heard you went into the Army or some shit. Trying to be all you can be before nine in the morning. "

He stopped and giggled at his own joke. "However ya'll say it. What happened? Uncle Sam kick your ghetto ass out already?"

Kiwi walked to the window and smacked my hand. "Dis your ride?" he asked. "I seen this ride come through here last night. You better be glad you did not come back through here. Them crazy ass niggas had planned to shoot this pretty bitch up. "

Kiwi looked bad and smelled worse. Worse than I had ever seen him. He probably hadn't taken a shower in days.

"You just in time for breakfast, " he said. He turned the big bottle dressed in brown paper, all the way up. "You want a drink?" He asked. He took the back of his hand and dragged it across his chapped lips.

"No, I don't drink," I said. "Check this out Kiwi. I got a hook up and I'm trying to move some work up here. "

"Nigga, you know you can't just set up shop on the Hill. These crazy ass niggas ain't going for that. "

"I'm not trying to set up shop. I'm just trying to give a better price so everyone can make money, " I said.

"What kind of work you got?" Kiwi asked.

"What you mean "what kind"?"

"You got hard or soft?" He asked.

"Nigga, I got both," I said, with a serious grit on my face.

"When can I try some of it out?" If it's any good I'll sell all you got. These niggas been having garbage lately, " he said.

"I'll be back up here in an hour and I will let you know something, " I said.

Kiwi and I slapped hands again and I started to back out of the parking space. "I'll make sure I'm here in an hour," he said.

Before I pulled off Kiwi called me. He asked if I had ten dollars he could borrow. He promised to pay me back later. I guess this was his way of testing me. If I had a hook up, I should have ten dollars to spare. I handed him a twenty and told him not to worry about paying me back.

"Just be up here in an hour, " I said.

I left the Hill and rode over to the Grove. I didn't tell my partners I had people over there too. My cousins Red and Chug hustled in the Grove. It would be easy to hit them off with some work and get a few buyers lined up.

Red was at home when I stopped at his house right outside of the Grove. I gave him the run down of my situation. He said I could count on him moving all the coke I could get. That was all I wanted to hear him say.

I returned to the Red Roof Inn. Everyone was still in the bed asleep. We purchased two more rooms last night because when we went back to A&T we hooked up with some girls we had met earlier. They said they were looking for something to do. They found just what they were looking for!

When I returned to my room, Lakisha, the cutie I met, was still asleep. I picked up the phone and dialed Huntman's room. I informed him that we needed to talk as soon as possible. He called Moe and Wilk and we met in his room. He had woke his friend up and gave her a hundred dollar bill to go get breakfast for everyone. As soon as the doorknob hit her where the good Lord split her, I began giving them the run down.

"It's not going to be that easy to set up shop on the Hill. I talked to one of my partners and they seen us come through last night. Them wild niggas were going to dump on us had we rode back through. He wants to meet with me in about an hour to try out some of the product. He told me everyone has been getting bullshit dope lately. So our timing is perfect."

My comrades sat listening attentively like three CEO's of a Fortune 500 Company. "How much does he want to try?" Moe asked.

"He'll try whatever I take him and he will work as long as he make a little cash," I said.

Before anyone could comment, I decided to let them I had already expanded my business

"I got a first cousin who said he will buy and sell all the coke I could bring to him in the Grove. "

"Two spots are always better than one," Wilk said.

"I'm going to give you a half an ounce to take back to your friend. It's that butter too. Them niggas will go crazy over this shit." Huntman went to the closet and snatched out his gym bag. He sat it on the bed and unzipped it.

"Here you go dawg." He handed me a small bag of what he called "Butter."

"Don't give that nigga all of this if he smokes. Just give him a piece this big." He took another bag and pointed at one of the broken pieces of butter.

"After he hits that he will find you some buyers. Nothing less than a half an ounce though. We're not selling small shit," he said.

"How much do you want for a half ounce?" I asked.

"I want four fifty for each half, but you need to sell them for five fifty, so you can make a hundred bucks on each sell."

That sounded good to me. One hundred dollars on each sell was more than enough.

"When does your cousin want to get hit off?" Moe asked.

"He's ready now." Huntman dug in his bag and began to count half ounce bags of butter. "How many did you bring?" I asked.

"I brought a big eight," Huntman said.

"How many is that?"

"Its four and a half ounces." Wilk said. "How many do you think your cousin wants?"

"Just give me two or three bags and I will see if he wants to buy them," I said.

"If he doesn't have the money to buy them, front them to him. Tell him you'll pick the money up tomorrow before you go back to Ft. Bragg," Huntman said.

"Front them! You mean just give them to him?" I asked.

"Yeah, don't you trust him?" Moe asked.

"Yeah, I trust him."

"Well if you trust him, we all trust him. That's how we operate," Huntman said. He tossed me four bags. I stuffed them deep into my pockets, being extra careful not to rip the bags. I looked at my watch and I needed to hurry. This meeting had lasted for thirty-five minutes. "I'm getting ready to go back over here and meet this dude, " I said. When I reached for the doorknob, we heard a hard kick on the door.
"Boom-boom-boom! "
Wilk grabbed the gym bag and ran to the bathroom. I jumped back and looked at Huntman and Moe. Both of them looked like they had seen a ghost. "Open the door if

you all want to eat," a soft voice said. When I opened the door Huntman's friend came in carrying several Po Folks bags.

"Dag girl, why you kicking the door like you are the police?" I asked.

"I couldn't knock because my hands were full," she said. "Don't you want your food before you go?" She asked.

"No, but take Lakisha something for me. Tell her I'll be back shortly."

I walked slowly out to the parking lot calculating how much money I was about to make on four half ounces. Four hundred bucks. I had just made five hundred last week when Huntman doubled my money. Nine hundred dollars in less than two weeks. The Army wasn't paying me that much and I jumped out of airplanes.

I got into the Blazer and made a right off of Meadowview onto High Point Road. I was hoping Kiwi would be at the store like he promised. I had given him twenty dollars and he was either going to come back for free goodies or he'd be high as a kite off a twenty dollar rock, I thought. He might be beamed up by now.

This time when I pulled up to the Hill Store, I saw another friend of mine. He appeared to be excited to see me. Maybe Kiwi had spread the word already, I thought.

"What's up Wild Styles," Tory said. I met Tory Wright playing high school football. He was the star tailback for Dudley High School. He was the most sought after running back in North Carolina, until he shot his mother's boyfriend for beating her. He only served nine months in prison, but he never returned to school. Instead, he turned to a life of petty crimes and hustling.

"Nothing much, what's up with you? Long time no see, " I said.

"I'm just trying to make ends meet in these unforgiving streets. You know what I'm saying?" He asked.

"Yeah, I know what you're saying," I said. I wanted to ask Tory why he didn't go back to school? Convince him that he could still make his dream of playing in the NFL come true. But, I didn't. "You seen Kiwi's black ass?" I asked instead.

"Yeah, he's in the store. You look like you doing good, nigga. Put me down. If you're up here looking for Kiwi, I know what's up. He is the biggest crack head up here on the Hill."

"Ain't nothing up. Uncle Sam is being pretty good to me. I'll put you down. Call your local Army Recruiter," I said and winked my eye.

"Recruiter my black ass, nigga you're rolling."

"Go get Kiwi for me," I said.

Tory walked in the store and returned with Kiwi. I put my hands deep inside my pocket, fishing for the most expensive butter in the world. I wanted Tory to see me giving Kiwi a bump. "Here, try this. You can't get anymore of this until someone wants to buy at least a half ounce, " I said to Kiwi.

"You selling weight Styles?" Tory asked.

I responded quickly, "Yeah, I'm selling weight nigga." I hoped that was the right answer. I was green to all of this "Dope selling slang" and I didn't have a clue as to what Tory meant by "weight".

"How much for halfs?" Tory asked.

I started to say four fifty, but I caught myself. "Five fifty, " I said.

Tory dug into his pocket and pulled out some money. He licked his right thumb and started counting. Then he reached into his left sock and did the same thing. He finally produced $543.

"Kiwi, go and hit that rock and tell me if it's any good or not," Tory ordered. Kiwi disappeared and was gone for about ten minutes. When he returned he had a look in his eyes that I had never seen before. His mouth was twisted like he'd had a stroke. He could barely speak. My heart started pounding. I had sold him some bad drugs. I heard and seen on the news where people die from bad drugs all the time. He looked like he was going to fall over at any second.

"Damn, it's like that Black?" Tory asked Kiwi. He shook his head up and down, still trying to speak. After a minute of stuttering, he managed to say, "That shit is fire! "

"Look ah here Styles," Tory said. "I want one now and three more in an hour. The guy who sells weight up here sells his halfs for $600, and they're some shit. I got a couple of boys I'm going to get to buy one a piece."

"OK," I said. "I'll see you in an hour." I looked over at Kiwi and his mouth was still twisted. He tried once again to speak, but I couldn't make out what he was trying to say. I gave Tory the bag I had given Kiwi a piece out of. He didn't notice that he was a rock short of a half ounce. He was seven dollars short anyway. Now we were even. Tory promised to be at the store in an hour. He left the store walking fast like he was going to put out a fire. He was getting ready to start a fire with the "Fire" I just sold him.

"Kiwi get me some more customers," I said. I pulled off and looked into my rearview mirror. Kiwi had bent over and was clutching his stomach. He became smaller as I drove away, eventually fading with the Hill. This butter was something serious! How can someone be addicted to a drug that makes them sick? That's a question I never found the answer to.

CHAPTER 6

I rode over to Red's crib and his ole lady said he had gone over to the projects. I found Red standing in front of the barbershop in the Grove's little shopping center. It really wasn't a shopping center, just a convenient store and a couple of other stores all owned by the same Koreans.

"What's up, Cuz?" I said when I pulled up.

"What's that you listening to?" Red asked.

"The Ghetto Boys. This song is called Money and the Power. "

"That shit sounds good. Money and the Power, huh? Shit, those crackers got that game sewed up. The biggest drug dealers are eating crumbs from their tables. What you got for me?" He asked.

"Hop in," I said. We pulled off and got on McConnell Road. I went fishing in my pockets once more. I pulled out the remaining three bags. When Red saw the bags, he said just what Huntman had said in the hotel room earlier.

"That's that butter! They love that shit around here, Cuz. How much for a half?"

"Five fifty, " I said.

"Is this all you have?" Red asked.

"Nah, I got five more bags."

Red pulled out a big wad of money. He began counting like he was a veteran bank teller. "I want those three now, and bring the other five back as soon as you can." He finished counting the money and handed it to me." Take me back to my spot," he said.

I turned around and took Red back. He jumped out and asked how long was it going to take me to return? He explained he had to go and get the rest of his loot.

"It's going to take me about thirty minutes. Just be right here when I return. Have the money ready. Count it out. Twenty seven fifty," I said. Four hundred dollars in two hours. Nine hundred in less than two weeks and there is still money to be made," I said to myself as I pulled off. A piece of the cake wasn't going to do it for me. This was too easy.

Consumed with thoughts of unmade money, I pulled into the Red Roof Inn. Lakisha and her girlfriends were getting into her Honda Accord. I hit the horn before she closed the door.

"You're going to leave before saying goodbye to me?" I asked. "Is that how you do? Love them and leave them!"

Lakisha smiled, revealing a mouth full of pearly whites. She was brownskin with big beautiful eyes. Her pupils were so black, they looked like coal. She was thicker than cold molasses. She had a soft, but squeaky voice. It sounded like she was making love every time she spoke.

"We're going back to campus to freshen up. Your friends said they were going to call us later this evening. Are you planning to call me?" She asked in a voice so sexy that it made my nature rise.

"Of course I am. Here," I said extending my hand. "Take this and get you something to wear for tonight." I handed Lakisha a hundred dollar bill from the roll of money I had just gotten from Red.

"Tonight?" She asked.

'We're going to Side Effects." I said.

"We can't get into Side Effects. None of us are twenty one, yet."

"Don't worry about that," I said, shaking the money in her brown face. "Money talks! I'll make sure you and your girlfriends get in. Your job is to find something sexy for me tonight."

She gave me a soft kiss and like poetry in motion, walked back to her car. Her hips were swaying from Mecca to America, and I watched her until she pulled off.

"Open the door, Sarge." When I walked in the room I didn't say anything. I just started emptying my pockets on the table." I need the other five bags. My cousin is waiting for me right now."

Huntman was counting the money I dumped on the table. "Three bills of that belongs to me," I said.

"Three! Don't you mean four? " Huntman asked.

"Nah, I gave Lakisha a bill to buy her something to wear for tonight."

"This nigga just started hustling and he is already a trick," Wilk said laughing. "He's a natural trick."

"I gave my bitch two hundred dollars, nigga," Huntman said. We were all laughing now, eyeballing Moe.

"Go ahead and confess, my son," Wilk said to Moe, placing the palms of his hands together and bowing his head.

"Confess what? I didn't give that girl nothing but hard dick and bubble gum," Moe said. He was looking very serious and then he cracked a slight smile. Then he added, "And a new hundred dollar bill."

Wilk admitted giving the girl he was with money before he had sex with her. "Ya'll already know that I'm a trick. That's without saying."

Huntman went back into his stash spot and gave me the remaining five bags.

"What did your friend on the Hill say after he tested the little piece of butter," Huntman asked.

"He couldn't say shit after he hit that rock. I did sell another one of my homeboys one of the halfs. He wants three more too."

"He's shit out of luck because this is all we have with us, " Moe said.

"But next weekend you can get him straight. Just make sure you ride back over there and tell him you won't be straight until then. Don't leave him hanging because that's bad business."

"Your cousin must be doing his thing in the Grove, huh?" Wilk asked.

"Yeah, he is. He said they loved that butter over there too."

"The guy who smoked some of that shit, he'll have you a gang of customers next weekend," Moe said. "It's good you sold the other dude one too. He'll want to continue to get coke from you, especially if they've been getting garbage."

I hurried back out to the Blazer. I wanted to go and make that $500!

BACK IN THE HOTEL ROOM

"I can see now, we're going to make plenty of money in Greensboro. I knew I should have brought more than a big eight. We have to school Styles a little more and he will be alright," Huntman said to Moe and Wilk. Both of them sat listening to Huntman sum things up.

"I don't think we should try to put down in this club that we're going to. If Styles is going to be able to move weight we don't have to worry about paying anyone to let us sell coke. I also need to let him know not to branch out anymore for now. The Grove and the Hill should be sufficient," said Huntman.

Wilk interrupted, "Why did Styles invite those bitches to the club tonight? You don't bring liquor to a liquor house! I hope that bitch don't think I'm her nigga tonight. I'm a trick for life!"

Huntman shook his head at Wilk and picked up where he left off before he interrupted him. "I'll have to school Styles on the price of ounces, bags and quarters. I hope he finds some cats who wants to buy the whole bird."

"This is just what we needed," Moe said. "We had just talked about finding another spot in North Carolina, before Styles arrived. This will give us a break from Fayetteville. We can make more money here than we can down there also. We just have to make sure Styles doesn't get out of control. School him on staying low key in the barracks."

"We'll talk to him on our way back to Ft. Bragg tomorrow," Huntman said.

When I pulled up in the Grove, Red had his head in the front window of a blue Buick, Electric 225. Then he stuck his hand inside and returned with a fist full of green.

The big "Duce and a quarter" waited for Red to step back and it pulled off fast. When he saw me he jogged over to the truck, faking like he was bow legged.

"Another satisfied customer. That butter got these niggas going insane. You got that?" He asked.

"Yeah, I got it, " I said.

"Do you have anymore?"

"No, but next weekend I'll be straight as an arrow," I said.

Red reached inside his jacket and pulled out a roll of money wrapped in plastic with a rubberband around it. "It's all there," he said. "Twenty seven fifty. You could have made it an even twenty seven."

"You could have made it an even twenty eight. You round up, not down," I said laughing at Red. I passed him the five bags and told him to meet me at Side Effects tonight.

"The club won't pay the rent, Cuz. I got to go to court in two weeks, so I'm hustling to make this money to pay this cracker."

"What are you going to court for this time?" I asked.

"For the same thing I went for the last time. Selling that poison."

"I'll yell at you later," I said to Red before I pulled off.

I took a different route to the Hill this time. I hated showing up empty handed. Tory stood on the side of the store towering over four prostrated bodies, that had one dollar bills scattered everywhere.

"Bet two that he hits nine," one of the young cats said.

"That's a bet," another one yelled.

"He can't hit Nina Ross, that's my bitch," the young cat said.

Tory heard the stereo system banging and walked over to the truck. "Man, my people ran out. I won't be straight until I come home next weekend," I said.

"Shit! I needed that dope. I already had them sold. As good as that dope is I could have sold a million dollars worth of that shit tonight. Next weekend, huh?" Tory asked. "The Army let's you come home every weekend?"

"Yeah, if I'm not working," I said. I didn't even try to explain to Tory what type of work I actually did. He didn't want to hear that right now anyway. If I wasn't talking dollars, I wasn't making sense to him.

"Make sure this is your first stop next weekend. I'm usually up here by the store. This is my domain. I got this little bit on lock," Tory said.

"You seen Kiwi?" I asked.

"That nigga somewhere still twisted by the blast you gave him. You don't have to worry about fucking with that nigga. Just call me when you get home. Here is my pager number and home number. That nigga ain't nothing like he use to be. This crack shit…" Tory paused and shook his head from side to side.

"This shit broke him all the way down. He is a real shady cat now. Can't trust a nigga smoking."

I took heed to what Tory had said. He was telling the truth. Kiwi couldn't be trusted. He would do anything to get high. I decided to make Tory my main man on the Hill. He could be trusted. At least more than Kiwi!

I pulled the plastic bag of money out of my pocket. I took the rubberband off and started counting. I was going to get my cut in twenties this time instead of all large bills. Five hundred in twenties, looked like a million dollars to me. It would look like two million when I pulled it out in Side Effects, I thought. I couldn't wait.

"Damn, what was I thinking about inviting Lakisha and her friends to Side Effects?" I said to myself.

CHAPTER 7

Everyone had taken a shower and was ready to go joy riding when I returned. I gave Huntman the money and went back to my room to shower. After I got dressed, we went to Four Seasons Mall. Compared to the mall in Fayetteville, Four Seasons was humongous. It was crawling with fine young sisters. Some even promised to come to Side Effects.

During our shopping spree, each one of us bought new outfits to sport to the club. We were making sure that we were going to look like we belonged in the VIP section.

We left the mall and rode over to A&T and hung out for a while. It didn't matter that we had met some girls there already. Our philosophy was, "If we found willing girls that easy the first time, the second time the willing girls would come looking for us. Needless to say that didn't happen but we did meet new prospects. After hours of hanging out and wasting gas, we all agreed to return to our rooms.

I had been home for two days and I hadn't even called my family. I was caught up in making and spending money. I'd decided to see them the following weekend.

We all met in Moe ' s room and laughed and talked about what we were going to do once we got to the club. We planned our every move. That was our infantry training crossing with our personal lives. From our entrance into the club parking lot to our exit was discussed. A limo even came up during our brainstorming, but that idea was shot down because we packed everywhere we went. We couldn't leave weapons in a rented limo.

It was 12: 27 when we pulled into the crowded parking lot of Side Effects. The line to get in looked like it was a mile long. As soon as we were about to approach the front of the club, I pushed the NWA tape into the deck. "Woke up quick, at about noon, just thought that I had to be in Compton soon, Gotta get drunk before my day begins, before my mother starts bitching about my friends… "

Our entrance had gone just as we planned it. As soon as we turned into the parking lot, push in the NWA tape and turn the volume all the way up.
Slowly, with serious looks on our faces, we rolled through the bumper to bumper traffic. "Nigga, it looks like a fucking parade out here, " Wilk yelled over "Eazy E's high voice.

"What's that over there across the street?" Huntman asked.

"That's another club called Moore's. We're not going over there. That club is for the niggas and bitches who can't get in Side Effects. They shoot over there every weekend. More than Matt Dillon busted his gat on Gun Smoke, " I said.

We finally made it out of the parking lot and made a left onto Bessemer Avenue, then a quick right on English Street. As soon as we made the right on English we turned right into the Advance Auto store parking lot. This parking lot served as a second parking lot for the club.

"That line is long as hell, " Huntman said.

"It's mostly women though, " Wilk added.

"Lets hurry up and get in line because they'll stop letting people in shortly," I said.

"Line my ass. Membership has its privileges," Huntman commented. "Styles, do you know the owner of this club?" he asked.

"Yeah, his name is Bobby something, but I don't know him like that." I responded.

When we got out of the Blazer I hit the alarm. There were people who came to Side Effects weekly just to hang in the parking lot. They were hanging extra deep tonight. They stared at the new ride and the unfamiliar faces. We trotted across Bessemer, back into the crazed parking lot. Then we walked to the back of the line and stood, realizing that we were mortal. We had to wait just like everyone else. Somewhere in the medley, Huntman disappeared.

"Where did Huntman go?" I asked Moe.

"He's on some Airborne Ranger, stealth shit tonight," Wilk said, starring at the long line of fat asses.

"Isn't that, " Moe said pointing at a parked Honda Accord. "Our girls from AT&T?"

"It's A&T," I said.

Lakisha and her girlfriends had parked in front of the club. They were going to make sure they saw us before we went inside. They got out of the car all wearing one thing in common... smiles from ear to ear.

"We thought we had missed ya'll," Lakisha said in a voice that would melt fire.

"Darlin girl, you look good, " I said.

"I got this outfit just for you. "

Lakisha had bought a pair of gold and black pants that hugged every curve on her hind parts. Her top, black trimmed in gold was just as tight revealing perfect breast.

"Do I look good enough to eat?" she asked me seductively.

One of her girlfriends covered her mouth, "Gurrrrrrrrl, you so crazy," she said between her skinny fingers.

Wilk and Moe stood looking at me. Waiting to hear the answer to her hot question.

"Don't you mean, eat again?" I responded coolly.

"Oh shit!" Wilk said. "Nigga you da'man."

"Umm girl," her other girlfriends said, smacking Lakisha's arm. She glanced at her friends as if to say, "I told you so, " and smiled.

"Where is Huntman?" Asked the girl who had brought breakfast from Po Folks.

"He's around here somewhere, " I said.

"He disappeared, " Wilk added.

A bouncer wearing a t-shirt that read "Security" on the front approached with a flashlight in his right hand, smacking it against his left palm.

"Your name Styles?" He asked.

"Why? What's up?" I said.

"'The owner instructed me to escort you and your friends inside the club. " Huntman paid the bouncer to bring us in the club. I walked passed everyone looking like I shouldn't have been in line anyway. Money may not talk, but it will prevent you from standing in long, cold ass lines.

Traffic inside the club was worse than the hectic traffic in the parking lot. Side Effects wasn't a very large club, and I'm sure that the occupants exceeded the fire code weekly. When you entered the club the first thing you'd notice was the raised dance floor that had a steel cage around it. It almost looked like a holding cell! Traditionally all the wild, freaky dancers would get their groove on in the cage. There was a large bar in the front of the club and a smaller bar in the rear. When we walked in Huntman was already seated at the front bar talking to a fine red bone. He didn't know we had hooked back up with the college girls. When he noticed our entourage he politely excused himself and walked to where we were standing. He spoke to everyone and gave the breakfast girl a hug.

"What do you all want to drink?" He asked. This was a question that the college girls had prepared for while waiting for us to arrive.

"We'll have three strawberry daiquiris and one sex on the beach, " Lakisha said.

"Who's having the sex on the beach?" I asked devilishly. Lakisha looked at me and smiled. She was having the sex on the beach. I didn't know about sex on the beach, but I did know about sex in the Red Roof Inn.

Big Daddy Kane, "Ain't No Half Step'n" had the entire club either dancing or bobbing their heads. Lakisha and I went inside the cage and started dirty dancing. Riding and grinding each other like mating animals. I looked through the massive crowd searching for my fellow soldiers. Upon location, each one of their faces was elated, filled with verve. These cats were having a ball.

We still managed to mingle and exchange numbers, despite our A&T girls. They didn't mind. They were just excited to be in Side Effects. While mingling, I ran into a couple of my friends from my hometown. Tone and Geno were both from the Madison, Stoneville area. The two towns are only a few miles apart.

It had been some time since I'd seen either of the two. We engaged in small talk, exchanged numbers and promised to keep in touch with each other. Tone said he had heard about Ft.Bragg and Fayetteville. He wanted to came and spend a weekend down there with me. "I heard the clubs are twice as wild as the clubs are around here. I heard those G.I. 's wives go buck wild when they are out in the woods," He said.

"As soon as I get straightened out down there, you can come and hang out with me, " I explained to Tone.

After the club closed, we followed tradition and fell into the long formation of fly rides. A caravan of caroused and voracious drivers were speeding to be the first to order breakfast once inside of I-HOP.

All of us ate breakfast and returned back to the hotel for round two with our school bunnies. It had been a successful weekend as far as we were concerned and there was only one way to cap it off. These gorgeous book smart but naïve college girls were about to find out that we were indeed GI's. Hardcore, freaky GI's. We planned a 'Switch-A-Roo!

As soon as we pulled into the Red Roof Inn's parking lot, we got out and started laughing and talking to each other. The girls sat in the Honda doing the same thing .We motioned for them to get out after a few minutes of joking around. When they did, we handed each of them our room keys, and told them to head on up to the room, we promised to be there in a second. Our plan was that Wilk goes to Huntman's room and Moe goes to my room and vice-versa. From there it was every man for himself. Whoever had the best talk game would score.

I was very confident in my talk game. I could talk a cat off the back of a fish truck, so talking this tenderoni out of some ass wouldn't be a problem for me.

When I knocked on the door, Moe's friend Pricilla opened it. She was standing behind the door peeking, dressed in only her panties and bra.

"Where is Moe?" She asked still holding the door and peeking.

"He told me to come and keep you company for a while, " I said.

"What?" She started to close the door and I stopped her.

"Wait Pricilla, " I said. "When we all met each other last night, my intentions were to get your number not Lakisha's. I wanted your number because, " I paused and began to stutter a little. But, it was all a part of my game. Stuttering proves one or two things. Either you are lying through your teeth or you're being sincere and you're pouring out your heart. "…because… I… I.. I think you're beautiful. I got a thing for dark skin women. Especially, when they are as fine as you are. That's what Moe and I were discussing when we pulled up. It's crazy how it happened, because he wanted to hook up with Lakisha."

The door started slowly opening. I walked in licking my lips, telling her how fine she was again.

"Why didn't' t you say something last night before I slept with Moe? I was telling Lakisha tonight, while we were waiting on ya'll, how sexy you are."

"Moe is over in the room right now talking to Lakisha." I said.

"So she is fine with all of this?"

"I don't know, and I don't give a damn. I know what I want is standing right here in front of me, and I'm use to getting what I want," I said smiling.

"Is that so?" Pricilla asked. She sat down on the edge of the bed, legs slightly open. She was fine as frog hair. I didn't lie about that. Her swarthiness was definitely a turn on to me. So far, I hadn't used much of my razor sharp game. That even surprised me!

The phone started ringing and I knew who was on the other end before I answered it.

"Yeah, " I said.

"Styles! What in the hell is going on?" Lakisha asked, in a tone of voice that sounded so foreign coming from her. "I just made your lame ass friend get out of here. I don't know what kind of games you're playing, but I don't get down like that."
Moe had left Lakisha's room and got in the Blazer. That was a part of our or scheme. If you get kicked out of a room and the other guy was still in your room, go back to the Blazer and wait until further notice was the rule.

"Calm down girl, " I said. "I am not playing games. I'll be over there in a minute."

"Is that Kisha?" Pricilla asked. "I knew she wasn't with this the way she talked about your black ass today. "

33

I hung up the phone and walked over to the bed. The real game was about to be implemented now. I was getting ready to kiss her. If she kissed me knowing that Lakisha wasn't with the "Switch-A-Roo," then I knew that the pussy would be mine in the future. If she denied the big sexy soup coolers that Lakisha had vaunted about all day, the pussy would be a little difficult for me to get.

I bent over Pricilla and grabbed the back of her head. Passionately, our lips clashed like two trains on the same track. I took her hand and placed it on my dick so she could feel how bad I wanted her. My hands started to explore her voluptuous body. Passing slowly down her lower back, stopping at her thick ass. Pricilla was panting heavily. Now, I knew she wanted to fuck me just as bad as I wanted to fuck her. Gently, I pushed her back with my left hand. My right had ventured deep inside of her panties. The "Nappy Dugout" wasn't nappy at all. It felt like new velvet. I took my middle finger and parted her. We continued to kiss.

"Shit! " she said when the phone started to ring again.

"You answer it, " I said. "Tell her I'm gone already." I got up hating the interruption also. I rubbed my dick and it was harder than woodpecker lips! I took my middle finger and stuck it in my mouth, tasting Pricilla's sweet juices. Then I took my finger out of my mouth and let her suck it.

"You are a freak! " she said. "I don't want you to go over there and fuck her. I'm not fucking Moe anymore. I'm going back to campus."

"Hello! He's gone girl. I don't know what kind of games they are playing. I want to drive your car back to campus and I will come back and pick you all up in the morning. No, he didn't say anything out of the way to me, " Pricilla said to Lakisha.

I kissed Pricilla on her forehead while she was still talking to Lakisha and then I turned and opened the door. She held up her finger, signaling me to wait. Turning her thick, black ass up in the air, she crawled to the head of the bed and grabbed her pocketbook. She wrote her number down and handed it to me. Covering up the phone, she said in a sweet whisper, "Please don't let Kisha see this number." I put the number in my pocket and backed out of the door.

Moe was in the driver's seat of the Blazer. He opened the door as soon as he saw me coming.

"What happened? What did Pricilla say?" he asked. "Huntman and Wilk came out and went back to their own rooms. They told the girls they were just tripping," he said all in one breath.

"Pricilla is going back to campus. She is pretty hot right now," I said. I meant that in more ways than one. It would hurt Moe's pride if I told him that, so I didn't.

"Fuck her, let her go. I just want to get some rest anyway, " he said.

"Pride is a bitch, " I said to myself.

Lakisha opened the door and rolled her big pretty eyes at me. "It takes you ten minutes to roll those big, beautiful eyes," I said. She didn't think my comment was funny.

"I don't play those types of games, Styles."

"It was just a little joke, " I said.

"I'd appreciate if you don't ever joke like that again with me."

If Lakisha was upset, it didn't last long. She was completely naked when I got in the bed. She couldn't wait to sit on my face again. She had talked about it all day. I took one last whiff of my middle finger before I started kissing Lakisha's soft body all over.

34

Pricilla's celestial body was mired in my memory. I stuck that same middle finger in Lakisha's mouth. Although Pricilla had gone back to campus, I made love to her in my mind. Lakisha was reaping all of her benefits.

We got up Sunday morning and packed our things. Lakisha and her two friends walked down to the lobby to wait for Pricilla. We started carrying our bags to the Blazer in preparation for our trip back to Ft. Bragg. Hugs and short kisses followed with promises that would probably be broken. Moe stood alone watching like he could care less, but you could tell his ego was bruised. When he saw Pricilla pull up he walked out of the lobby to the truck. Pricilla was staring at me while the girls put their bags in the trunk. They loaded up and pulled off.

For an hour we recapped the weekend events. Then we discussed the business end of the trip to Greensboro. Huntman advised me not to expand anymore. "At least not right now, " he said. I'll just go with the Hill and the Grove. Between those two spots, you'll be straight." Then he explained the weights and prices of the cocaine. "The more they buy, the better deal they're going to get." He assured me that I would still make money. His cardinal rule was never deal with anyone I didn't know. He said, when someone in the Grove wants to get served, let Red serve them and bring the money back to me. The same thing applied to Tory and the Hill.

"If a nigga can't trust them to do business, then that nigga can't be trusted, " he said. That made sense to me. That's how it was going to go down too.

As soon as Huntman stopped talking, Wilk picked up the lecture. "When we get back to Bragg, and if anyone asks you about your weekend, just tell them you kicked it with you fam. When you start getting money, be careful of what you buy. These crackers watch us like hawks."

Wilk continued with the "Do's and Don'ts" of Ft. Bragg, until we reached Spring Lake, which was three miles from post. Everyone was extremely exhausted and we all dreaded the infamous 6:00 a.m., formation that would come to soon. Exchanging soul shakes, we agreed to see each other after work the following day.

I walked back to the barricks with my bag tossed over my shoulder. I had truly enjoyed myself this weekend. I was looking forward to the next weekend. When I walked into Alpha Company, my name was scribbled on the black board above the CQ's desk signifying that I'd had a phone call. I checked the list and it was a call from my mom. Instead of going to the phone, I made a mental note to call her later. I unlocked my room and threw my things on my bunk. Poosh had left his radio on and Huey Lewis was singing something about he wanted a new drug! I didn't bother to listen to the rest of the words before I changed the station, but those few words I did hear triggered a thought. If he wanted a new drug I'd have the butter next weekend! Somebody call Mr. Lewis and tell him to meet in Greensboro!

CHAPTER 8

Our battalion wasn't scheduled to go to the field for another five weeks. That was five weeks of making money the way I figured it. Two days had passed since our "Tour de Greensboro," and I hadn't heard from or seen any of my Crew. They were doing details for the S.E.A.R (Search, Escape and Rescue) School, aiding the Special Forces. It was a three day detail. The detail was assigned to Bravo Company, Monday morning by the Sgt. Major.

Wednesday night 2 1/2t ton trucks flooded Gila Street. Bravo Company was returning from the S.E.A.R. School detail. I walked out to the large, muddy trucks and welcomed my partners back to civilization. They jumped from the rear of the trucks with war painted faces. It was hard to believe that these were the guys who dressed in expensive "GQ" clothes in Side Effects just a few days ago.

"Damn, ya'll niggas are filthy, and ya'll smell just like ass," I said, exaggerating my facial expression.

"But we're off until Monday. You just make sure you have your clean, good smelling ass in the formation in the morning at 6:00a.m." Wilk said.

Huntman looked like a black Rambo. He had a M-60 machine gun, strapped over his shoulder with a belt of blank rounds crossed over his chest. He added, "We're getting ready to go shit, shower and shave right now. We'll call you in about an hour or so." They rushed into the barricks excited to be a part of civilization again.

Instead of calling, the three came over to Alpha Company once they were dressed. They were starving and wanted to go get something to eat. For three days they had eaten M.R.E's (Meals Ready to Eat), and they were eager to dig into same real food. Unanimously, Vic ' s was the restaurant of our choice. Famous for pork chittlings, anybody who thought they were somebody in Fayetteville dined at Vic's.

When we entered Vic ' s I instantly knew that these three guys were regulars. Everyone employed in Vic' s, greeted them with smiles. Happy to see them like they were cousins you only seen once a year at family reunions. Some even spoke addressing my partners by their names. I was introduced to the ones who used names when they spoke. This officially made me the fourth wheel on the car and I was ready to roll.

We ordered from a fat waitress name Antoinette, who acted overly excited about helping us. We began to discuss what was going to take place the coming weekend.

"Styles we're not going to be able to go to Greensboro this weekend, " Huntman started to explain.

Before he could continue, I interrupted. "Man damn! I was planning…"

"Hold your horses, Speedy Gonzales, " he said. Just as quick as I cut in, he cut me off.

"We're going to let you go alone. Can you handle that?" He asked.
Without even thinking I answered him. "Yeah, I can handle that. But how am I going to get there?"

"I'm going to let you drive one of my cars, " Moe said.

"One of your Tangs?" I asked.

"Yeah, but don't speed. I don't need another speeding ticket on my car insurance. "

"Yeah, I can handle that," I said again. I was excited as hell and I didn't care if they could tell. I had been waiting to go out and drive one of Moe's cars. The Mustang GT was my dream car. Now, I was going to get to drive Moe's Mustang home. "Hell yeah I can handle it."

Antoinette returned with our plates. No one had ordered the chittlings and I was thankful for that. The terrible smell that some loved so much was already heavy in the air, almost choking me. A plate at our table would have been too much for my stomach to bear.

Between voracious bites, each one took their turn to drop jewels on points that they thought were vital. I listened to them but in my mind, I was already driving up Highway 421 North.

"You hear me, Styles?" Moe asked.

Snapping out of my daydream I answered him. "Yeah, I heard you. " I was lying my ass off. I hadn't heard shit. "When are you going to give me the coke?" I asked.

"We'll give it to you when you get off of on Friday. I'll have to show you where the stash spot is in my car," Moe said.

We finished our food and conversations. Each one of them left a twenty dollar bill on the table. The total cost of our meals combined was only twenty-six dollars and some odd change. No wonder Antoinette was happy as hell to serve them I thought. The largest tip I had ever left anyone was a dollar, but things like that were going to change as soon as I started getting money.

Cruising down Murchinson Road or "The Dirty Murk" as it's referred to in Fayetteville, we made a right into what appeared to be the only hang out in Fayetteville. F.S.U. (Fayetteville State University) was swamped with niggas and fly rides. And Murphy's Law says, "Where there are niggas and fly rides, you'll always find fly chicken heads." The girls at FSU added a new dimension to the term "Chicken Head". Legend has it in Fayetteville, that if you park at FSU and place a box of Kentucky Fried Chicken on your fly ride, the chicken becomes a chicken head magnet! It was no longer a legend. I witnessed it with my own eyes. At least ten of the fly rides had large boxes of chicken on the roof. Those rides are where all the chicken heads were gathered. As always, our presence caused heads to turn. Except for those heads, whose mouths were filled with KFC's best.

Since I had to have my clean ass in formation early the next morning, we pushed on through the crowd. They planned on returning after I was dropped off at the barricks. I hated I was going to miss out on the fun, but I'd have my fun the weekend coming, I thought. I was dropped off and I watched as they pulled off quickly. Headed for the first KFC they could find.

When I got off of work Thursday, I called Tory .He wasn't home but I left a message with his mom, that I would be home Friday night around 7:30. Then I called my mom and told her I'd be home Saturday afternoon.

Friday morning I was the first one standing in formation. Anticipation wouldn't allow me to sleep. I hadn't felt like that since Airborne School. This time it was excitement not nervousness. I had been thinking about the money I could make. It wouldn't be long before I would have enough money saved to buy my own Mustang GT. I was ready to grind this weekend.

Four thirty p.m. finally came. I stood in formation listening to the First Sgt., complement us on how well the barricks looked. For our hard work, we would not have to work until Tuesday. First Sgt. thought he had all the sense. It was written on the black board that he was having a birthday party on Sunday and all the NCO's were invited. He would be to shit faced to come to work on Monday anyway! It really didn't matter to me why we had off, all that mattered to me was we had a long weekend. After he dismissed the formation I walked over to Bravo Company. None of my partners could be found. I did an about face and went to my room. I packed my things earlier in the week, so all I needed to do was shower, get dressed and locate my Crew.

When I returned to my room from the shower, Huntman was in my room. He was seated comfortably on Poosh's bean bag, waiting for me.

"Sit in that chair over there Huntman, Poosh will have a baby if he saw you sitting on his bean bag." I said. He got up and did not respond about Poosh or his beanbag, and sat in the chair.

"You're not ready yet?" He asked. "We're meeting Wilk and Moe right outside of Spring Lake in twenty minutes. So you gotta hurry up and get dressed."

Huntman and I crossed Ardenes Street and walked across the parking lot. As we approached the Blazer, I started for the passenger side. Huntman continued to walk past his truck.

"Where are you going?" I asked.

"We're not riding in the Blazer, we are riding in that." He pointed to an old, orange Grimlin. There was a guy sitting in the driver's seat of the car smoking a cigar. Clearly, you could tell by his long corn rolls that he was a civilian. I opened the passenger door, speaking to the brother. He looked like he was younger than I was.

"Styles, this is Justice. Justice this is my main man, Styles." Huntman introduced him and I then he added, "We need to hurry up. I don't want them sitting at the store with that shit in the car."

When we arrived at the store, Moe was pumping gas into his car. Wilk was inside of the store, paying for the gas and a couple of forties.

"Styles, I only use 93 octane gas from Exxon. I've hid that for you in a spot underneath the drivers seat. It's nine ounces, broken down in halves. Eighteen bags in all. My cell number is behind the mirror that's on the sun visor," Moe continued. "When you get to Greensboro, get that shit out of the car. Don't ride around with any of it unless you're dropping it off. Make sure you don't speed, and be careful.

I eased into the drivers seat. The H-Pipes and Flow Masters Mufflers on the Mustang made it sound like music to my ears. I turned the stereo off and patted the accelerator, "voom-voom-voom. " Moe and Wilk had squeezed into the back seat of the Grimlin. They made a right heading back towards Spring Lake .I made a left and watched them disappear in the rear view mirror. I changed gears and began to accelerate. Before I realized it I was running 90 mph. I shifted to fifth gear and eased up. I promised Moe I wouldn't speed.

I stopped in Sanford and washed the car. If I was going to be driving my dream car, it was going to be clean. I got back on the highway after I washed it and the Mustang was gleaming. In less than an hour I would be in the Gate City. Just like I told Tory's mom. My T.O.T (Time on Target) would be around 7:30. There wasn't going to be any Red Roof Inn this weekend. I had money and the means to make more of it. I pulled into the Embassy Suites. I had brought a girl there before, knowing I didn't have the money to buy a suite. This had happened earlier in the year, when I was still in high school. I lied and told her they didn't have any vacancies. She was very credulous. She believed me despite the huge parking lot that was almost completely empty. She rewarded me anyway and gave me some pussy in the parking lot. She said I got an "A+" for effort. Now, here I was a few months later with a pocket full of money and able to pay for my first suite. "I've always been amazed at how so much can change in so little time, " I said.

"Me too, " said Hireen. "Things can change at the drop of a hat. What happened next" he asked.

Flirting with the girl at the front desk, I requested a suite on the top floor. Symbolically, representing where I was going to take this dope game.

Cool now, I walked back to the car to get my bags. I searched underneath the driver's seat and finally found the stash spot. I put the dope in my gym bag and pimped back through the entrance. I hopped on the elevator and press number eleven. The top floor!

I opened the door and looked around the spacious room. It was nice. It had a large living room with a bar and a small kitchen. I dropped my bags and walked back into the bedroom. I had never seen a bed that was so big. I executed a swan dive and bounced on the soft mattress. Then I rolled over and picked up the phone. When I called Tory this time he was home. He had been waiting for me to call he said. He went on to say he had enough money for an ounce and a half. I got directions to his crib and told him I would see him shortly. Next, I paged Red. It took about ten minute before he called me back.

"Who dis?" Red asked.

"Dis me fool, " I said.

"Oh, what's up, Cuz? You're back in G'boro huh?"

"Yeah, I'm back. Are you trying to see me?"

"You got the same shit as before?" He asked.

"No doubt, that Parkay!"

"I want 2 1/2 ounces now, " Red said.

"Give me about 30 minutes and I'll be there. I just got in. I got to get things in order first, " I said.

After I called Tory and Red, I called Pricilla. Her answering machine picked up on the fourth ring. I left her the phone number and the room number where I was staying and I emphasized "Embassy Suites". I took eight bags and stuck them in the inside pocket of my jacket. I had a feeling that eighteen bags weren't going to be enough for the entire weekend. If I had to, I'd drive back to Ft. Bragg to pick up some more coke, I said to
myself.

When I pulled up at Tory's house a big black and white pit bull guarded the front door. I tooted my horn, and I saw the curtains being pulled back. The door swung open and Tory came out onto the porch. I guess he was expecting me to be in the Blazer, because he looked surprised to see me in the 5. O Mustang.

"Damn nigga, that's sharp. That's your Boss?" he asked. I've never been the one to front about things that were not mine so I didn't lie. Well, not totally.

"Nah, this is my partner's. He's driving mine," I said. I knew that it wouldn't be long before I had my own Mustang, so I thought it would be safe for me to respond that away.

"What color is yours?" he asked.

I was hit! Caught in a lie, I thought. He had me.

"Ah, mine is a color you'll love. You will see it soon enough."

"Come on in the house, my mom ain't tripping. She knows what time it is with me .She might want to buy a couple of ounces her damn self, " Tory said laughing. I walked in not being able to conceive my mom buy anything illegal. We walked through the living room into a small kitchen. Tory sat at a small, round table that had pieces of folded toilet paper beneath two of the legs to keep it from rocking.

"Don't sit there," he said pointing at the chair I was about to sit in. "That chair is broken." There were only two chairs in the kitchen, so I remained standing while Tory counted his money. He inquired about how much dope I had and how long I would be in Greensboro.

"I don't have much work, but I'll be here until Monday night. I'm sure I'll be finished by then. I got some more cats to hit off later," I said. I wanted Tory to think I had a million cats to serve. Create a sense of urgency and he'll work hard to sell what he had so he could re-up. He already knew that the dope I had wasn't going to last long, and he wanted more than an ounce and half.

He counted out enough money for three ounces, leaving me with one ounce in my pocket. "This should last me a couple of days. If not," Tory paused. "How can I contact you? You got all this dope and no pager."

"Nigga, I'll call you," I said to Tory. I did need a pager though. I hadn't thought about that. Right now I wanted him to think I was on some top secret shit. "You just call me back when I page you, " I said.

Tory's mom walked in the kitchen while he was examining the cocaine. She looked young. Hip almost. She gave birth to Tory when she was only 13 years old. She spoke to me without making eye contact. Even if she would have made eye contact, I wouldn't have noticed. My eyes perused her just like Tory examined those bags of butter. To me she was Butter! Tory noticed how I was looking at his mom.

"Come on Styles, let's bounce, " he said. Frowning his face.

I tried to play if off as we left. "Bye Ms. Wright, " I said. Even though Tory failed to introduce us, I added, "Nice meeting you. " She twisted her heart shaped ass over to the refrigerator and opened it. She turned her head and flashed me a subtle smile. Now I understood why Tory shot the bastard who was beating his mother. I didn't even know her and I wanted to blast his ass again.

When we walked out of the front door, onto the porch, I noticed the big pit bull hadn't budged. "That's a big ass dog, " I said.

"That shit eater won't bite fried steak. Don't ever worry about him. He loves people; he just hates other dogs, " Tory said.

I didn't care how much Tory claimed he loved people, I wasn't going to walk up to that door ever, unless he was standing there. Not with "Petey" guarding the door.

"I'll call you tomorrow to see what's up," I said.

I cranked the car, pressing the gas pedal. "Voom-Voom. " The curtains in the living room were pulled back again. Tory didn't know his mom was looking out of the window. Surprisingly, she waved at me. I waved back at her and he thought I was waving at him. He looked puzzled. I had to look stupid, smiling and waving like I was some homecoming queen in a parade. Damn his mom was fine, I thought.

Red stood there wondering who I was invading his spot. There were about ten youngsters running from car to car making sells when I pulled up. One ran up to the

Mustang, as I was getting ready to get out. I opened the door and before he could make any propositions, I screamed on him, "Do I look like a fucking crack head?"

"Oh shit," Lil Kenny said. "What's up Styles? I didn't know who you was."

Red was walking towards me shaking his head. "Damn Cuz, every time I see you you're in something different." He reached inside his coat and pulled out a roll of money. "This is twenty-seven fifty, " Red said handing me the money.

"I only have two halfs with me right now. I'll bring the other ounce and a half back in thirty minutes. "

"Thirty minutes, " Red said loudly. "I need them now. "

"I'll be right back," I said. "When do you go to court?" I asked Red.

"Next Friday. I'm trying to get the rest of this money for my attorney today, so hurry back." Red wasn't pressed for conversation. He needed that butter to flip his money.

I jumped back in the car and peeled out. I took Lee Street and got on Highway 40 West. It was going to take me about fifteen minutes to get to the Embassy Suites. I rode calculating the money I had made. Eleven hundred dollars and I just got home. Four more weeks like this and I would have my own Mustang.

I ranged walked through Embassy Suite's lobby, to the elevator. I pressed number eleven and ascended to the top floor. I opened the door and went straight to my stash spot. While I was digging down into my pillowcase, I noticed the little red light on my phone was blinking. I read the directions on how to check my messages and followed them.

"Hey Mr. Styles! I'm glad you are in town. I've thought about you all week and I can't wait to see you. Call me as soon as you get this message. I'm not going anywhere. I'm waiting on you, " Pricilla said on the answering machine.

I dialed Pricilla's number as fast as I could. She answered on the first ring. "You must be expecting a call, Chocolate, " I said.

"What's up Mr. Styles? " she said in the same voice I had heard on the answering machine. "Where are you?"

"I'm in the suite. What's up?" I asked.

"I'm trying to see you tonight," she said.

I explained I had some important business to do and that I'd pick her up in an hour or so.

"I'm going to start getting dressed now. What are we going to do?" she asked. "I'm kind of hungry. That cafe' food isn't good at all. "

"We'll go and get something to eat and maybe a movie," I said.

Twenty minutes had elapsed by the time I hung up the phone. I should have been on my way back to meet Red. I rushed out of the room and onto the elevator. When I reached the bottom floor, I ran through the lobby to the car that I had left running. I jumped in the car and did a vicious burn out leaving the hotel parking lot.

When I came off of the ramp to enter the highway I was going 70 mph, and I was still in third gear. I didn't see any State Troopers, so this was a perfect time for me to see what this car was really made of. I pressed the accelerator. The tachometer went from 4O00rpm's to 7000rpm's in a matter of seconds. I shifted into fourth gear and I was going 95 mph. I felt like Muhammad Ali in his prime. I bobbed and weaved through the traffic. During my hasty observation for State Troopers, I hadn't bothered to check behind me .I only checked in front of me. Low and behold, one lurked, camouflaged in the traffic behind me. He was in an unmarked car. A Mustang LX 5.0! The State Trooper came speeding up behind me. I looked in my rear view mirror and by the distinctive headlights, I automatically knew it was another Mustang. "Oh, this bitch wants to race, huh?" I said out loud to myself. I pressed the gas pedal harder, trying to push it through the floor. Now, I was running over 100rnph. The Mustang behind me was sticking to my ass like crazy glue though. Speed is a rush for me. At this moment I was on cloud nine. Until. Suddenly the Mustang behind me was illuminated with flashes of blue lights.

"Oh shit!" I yelled. I took my foot completely off of the gas pedal. I was too shocked to press my breaks .As my speed started waning, I pulled to the right of the highway, being extra careful not to run off the shoulder of the road. I didn't want "my" tires to get dirty. Finally, I came to a complete stop. The State Trooper, who had just tricked me into racing, sat in his car for a few minutes. I needed to get the dope out of my pockets, and put it underneath the driver's seat in the stash spot. I had to do it without looking like I was trying to hide something. It only took me a second to realize that, that wasn't going to happen. It took me ten minutes to find the stash spot before. "Damn, I should have listened to Moe," I said. I took the three bags from my pockets. Then I turned the interior lights on. I wanted the State Trooper to be able to see what I was doing. That would make him less suspicious. I opened the glove compartment and retrieved Moe's registration, simultaneously placing the dope behind a heap of other papers. The whole time I hawked the Trooper in my rearview mirror. His interior light came on when his door opened, allowing his black face to be seen. He placed his round hat on his baldhead before he stepped out of the car. Coolly, he strolled to the car and bent over, peering in the window.

"License and registration sir. Why were you driving so fast?" he asked.

I handed him the registration and open my wallet to get my license. I pulled out my military ID instead. I handed it to him intentionally, but I acted like it was a mistake.

"Pardon me sir, I handed you the wrong ID." I handed him my driver's license in exchange for my military ID, but he continued to study it. "Not that it vindicates my speeding, but I thought you were this guy who I've had some problems with. He drives a Mustang too. When I saw your headlights I thought you were him. He saw me in this car today. "

The Trooper didn't seem to pay any attention to anything I was saying. He probably knew I was telling a lie. "Where are you stationed Private Styles," he asked. Damn, this nigga thinks he's in the Army now with this private shit, I thought. "In Ft. Bragg with the 82nd Airborne Division," I answered proudly and as cordial as possible.

"Oh yeah! I just left there last year. What unit are you in?" he asked.

"I'm in A Company 3-505."

"Get the fuck outta here, " he yelled. "I was in 2-505." He had gotten excited now. "Do you know a guy who has a Mustang like this but his is a hard top? His name is Pouncy?" he asked.

"Hell yeah, " I said. "That's my dawg."

He handed me my license, ID card and registration back and began to tell war stories about Ft. Bragg. I wasn't tripping though. I'd stay there all night kicking the "Willie Bobo" if he wanted to.

"When are you going back to Bragg?" he asked.

42

"Monday night," I said.

"Tell Pouncy, Parker said what's up? Tell him I'll be down there next weekend. I've tried to call him, but they're in the field and they won't be back until Wednesday. I'm not going to write you a ticket but you better slow down." Before he got back to his car he yelled, "Don't forget to tell Pouncy I pulled you over." He was proud of that.

"I will, " I said. "I'll probably see you when you come down next weekend too." I dodged a big bullet. I pulled off very slowly. Fortunately, for me there wasn't too much traffic coming, so I eased back onto the highway. As soon as I saw Officer Parker cut across the grass and speed off in the opposite direction I started laughing. "Who in the hell is "Pouncy"?" I said. Oh well, there won't be a thing Parker can do about it me next weekend. I would be in Greensboro anyway. I decided not to speed anymore though.

Red had dragged an old, dirty Lazy Boy chair from the dumpster to his spot. He had covered it with a sheet from his place. He was laid back like a King on his throne when I pulled up. Quickly, he jumped to his feet.

"Man what took you so long?" he asked.

"This State Trooper pulled me for speeding."

"Did you have that dope on you when he pulled you?"

"Yeah, I had it." I opened the glove compartment and handed Red the dope.

"Boy, your ass is lucky. If that would have been my ass, he would have searched the fucking car. "

"Get some fucking license and that won't happen, " I said. "I got to bounce. I got this fine broad over at A&T waiting on me."

"Page me later, " Red said.

Before I got to A&T, I stopped at John's Curb Market to use the pay phone. I wanted to make sure Lakisha wasn't around to see me pick up Pricilla.

"I'm about two minutes from campus. Come on down to the parking lot. . Lakisha isn't around is she?" I asked Pricilla.

"She's around here somewhere, but I don't care. "
I did though. Lakisha was straight. I didn't want to mess that up if I didn't have to. I wanted my cake and eat it too.

Pricilla stood at the front door of Barbie Hall waiting on me. When I pulled up I had to toot my horn because she was expecting to see the Blazer. She had on a black dress that was tight as a tick on a dog's dick. It revealed more curves than any road I'd ever driven on. She wanted me to notice her curves too, because she held her coat in her hands. The dress was short too. It reached her mid thigh. She began walking towards the car and I leaned over and opened the door for her. Those succulent thighs slid across the seat like black ice. She had on heels that were taller than Kiss boots. When she closed the door I was still looking at her legs. The dress was even shorter now that she had sat own.

"Damn girl, you look like a million bucks."

"Thank you, but I want to look good enough to eat. Do I look that good?" She asked. Pricilla had remembered the question Lakisha asked me at Side Effects, so she asked the sane thing.

"You look so good that if I start eating you, I'm afraid there won't be anything left when I'm done. "

She started to smile showing all her pretty teeth, approving my answer. We started discussing the types of food that we liked. We came to the conclusion that

Darryl's Family restaurant would accommodate both of our differences in taste. I began to rub her seductive thighs. She responded by opening her legs. My hand ventured deeper beneath the darkness of her dress. I pulled her panties to one side and started to finger her. She grabbed me tightly around my wrist and pulled my hands away.

"Wait!" She said.

I thought she meant wait until later but that's not what she meant at all. She pulled her panties off and hung them on the mirror. She placed her right leg on the dashboard and her left leg across my lap. Again, but with a stronger grip she grabbed my wrist and inserted my middle finger deep inside of her. She began to slow roll and moan. Her wetness allowed me to slip another finger inside of her. When it started to feel good to her she started to thrust and it felt like she was going to break my wrist, but I wasn't going to stop. I fingered her until we took the High Point Road exit. The Darryl's sign was visible now.

"We're almost there, baby," I said in the smoothest voice I could muster. Just like before, I removed my fingers and stuck them in my mouth. I sucked them like I was a breast feeding baby.

"Dag, I was about to come," she said in a whiny voice. She grabbed my hand and sucked my fingers.

We sat in the car a few minutes once we arrived at Darryl's. I had to wait for my dick to deflate. Pricilla thought that was cute. I handed her her panties and she hung them back on the mirror. She got out and left her pink and white, Victoria Secret panties on display.

I requested a seat on the upper floor when we entered the restaurant. "A corner table" Pricilla added. Our waiter led us upstairs and to our table. I pulled out Pricilla's chair. She thought I was trying to be a gentleman, but I was just trying to make sure she sat with her back towards the stairs. I had watched to many gangster movies and the guy who sat with his back to the stairs always get whacked! I sat with my back against the wall staring Pricilla in her round, black face and keeping an eye on the stairs. She took her shoes off and put her feet between my legs. I started to massage her small, soft feet. She wiggled her feet from my hands and started to rub them against my pulsing dick.

"What are you going to order?" she asked.

"A chocolate Pricilla Pie," I said.

"You got one of those already," she replied smiling. "When are you going to taste it?"

"What are you guys having tonight, " the waiter asked

"I'll take the lobster platter with baked potato and lemonade, " Pricilla said.

"Give me a chocolate Pricilla Pie," I said.

The waiter looked confused. He hadn't heard that ordered before. Maybe it was something new. He took one of his menus and opened it. As he scanned the menu, Pricilla and I started laughing. He finally figured it was a joke and smiled. He was probably thinking how silly I was or how lucky I was.

"I'll have the grill chicken platter with fries and lemonade, " I said. My dick was harder than a cat's paw now! A midget could do pull ups on it. Just When I thought it couldn't get any harder, Pricilla asked me a question that turned my dick into Kryptonite!

"Have you ever had a blow job in a restaurant?" She whispered.

"Ahhh...Ahh no! But there is a first time for everything," I said. I looked around. I had already noticed there wasn't to many people in the upper section. The closest people to us were on the other side of the restaurant. They looked like they were trying to do their own freaky thing.

"Come sit over here, " I said to Pricilla.

I pulled the chair next to me back from the table. With an ogling look on her face, she eased around to the chair and took a seat. The couple across the restaurant couldn't see her now because a large artificial plant obscured their vision. As soon as she sat down she, unzipped my pants. Helping her, I pulled my fly open to allow her easy access to "Franky" (A name given to my dick by my high school sweetheart). She took Franky tightly in her hands. She observed her surroundings to assure no one could see her before she went down town to pleasure me. "If you see anyone coming up those stairs, you better let me know, " she said.

She bent over, licked the head of Franky and slowly started to insert him in her mouth, inch by inch. She moved her hands up and down and her head followed. Gradually, she began to speed up. I placed my hands on the back of her head and followed her rhythm. This would have been a two-hand double dribble if I were playing basketball!

Although the couple across the restaurant could not see Pricilla, they could still see me .I was paranoid, wondering if they were watching? Pricilla started to moan with every stroke. She was almost humming. She was enjoying giving me head, just as much as I was enjoying receiving it. This really turned me on. Being paranoid flew right out of the window. I slid deeper into my seat and tried to lean back. I dribbled her head faster now. I closed my eyes and my legs became stiff. I didn't care if the President of the United States was watching me. Pricilla was making me feel like I'd never felt before.

"Oh shit, " I said, trying to suppress my voice by clenching my teeth together. They say pressure will burst a pipe! I must have been full of pressure because my pipe exploded!

Pricilla didn't miss a drop of my eruption. She slowed down to her original speed. When I opened my eyes, the waiter was standing in front of our table holding two steaming trays. His mouth was as wide open as his eyes were. He smiled and shook his head up and down. Speechless, he sat the hot trays on the table without disturbing Pricilla and quietly stepped off. I had never been so embarrassed, yet so proud in my life. I tapped Pricilla on her shoulders. She jumped up, napkin already in hand and wiped the corners of her cum filled mouth.

"'What did you stop me for?" she asked. "I don't see anyone coming, but you! " she said, slightly laughing. Then like a turd in a punch bowl, Pricilla noticed the two steaming trays of food that sat on the table.

"Oh my god! Did he…?"

"Yep! He saw us," I said.

"I asked you to watch the stairs, " she said, fixing her hair that I had messed up.

"I did watch them until I came, " I said with a half grin. "Then I closed my eyes. I couldn't help it. I'm sorry. Kill me for feeling good!"

"Did it feel that good that you couldn't keep your eyes open?" she asked proudly.

"Hell yeah! " I zipped my pants up and took a good deep breath. "'Whooooooooooooo, that felt great! " I said again. I put my hand up for Pricilla to slap me high five. She slapped my hand and started laughing.

"Boy you are truly crazy. "

"Crazy about your fine ass. "

"She just polished your knob in a public restaurant and she has the nerve to call you crazy," Hireen said, shaking his head.

She excused herself from the table and went to freshen up. (Rinse her mouth out I suppose) I sighed in disbelief as she walked away. She returned after a few minutes and we began to eat our food that had cooled off some. We tripped about what had happened. The waiter had went down stairs and told everyone about his "x-rated" story. . One by one, everybody found some type of business upstairs. Eager to get a glance at the one who was getting head, and the one who was giving it. Even the dishwasher walked up the stairs and acted like he was looking for something.

We finished eating and I left a twenty dollar tip for our waiter. Then he returned to clean our table and I handed him the twenty dollars.

"Sir, " He said. "You take your ticket and pay it on the way out. "

"Yeah, I know but I give you the tip, don't I?" I asked.

"Thanks! " He said with a huge smile on his face. "This is the second largest tip I've received since I've been working here."

"What's your largest tip?" I asked.

"Forty dollars! " He said excitedly.

"Well you won't beat that record tonight, " I said laughing. Pricilla, who was still embarrassed, smacked me on my arm.

"Be nice Dana. "

"But, I bet you the people who gave you forty dollars didn't put on a show like I did, " I said.

The waiter, who was laughing now, agreed and began to walk away. "Thanks for the tip and the great show," He said.

Pricilla wanted to go to the car while I paid for dinner. I understood why! Everyone was giggling as I paid for our food. I would be remembered forever in Darryl's and I'd always be a hero to that waiter.

When we walked past the large waterfall in the front of the elevator, Pricilla commented on its beauty. She looked around impressed. "This is much nicer than the Red Roof Inn. " She pinched me on the ass and kissed the back of my neck while we waited for the elevator. "You think I made you close your eyes in the restaurant, you wait until we get in the room. I'm going to make you pass out."

"You must have forgotten what Lakisha told you about me, " I said. She didn't think that was funny, but I didn't intend it to be. I was dead serious!

"Ding-Ding" the door sounded like one of those bells beside a boxing ring when it opened. I allowed her to enter first then I stepped in behind her. I pressed number eleven and we began our rise to the top floor. I opened the door and Pricilla walked into the suite.

"You are a gentleman, " she said. She walked straight to the bedroom, hopped on the bed and picked up the remote control. Then she reclined and kicked off her heels.

"What's this in this pillow case?" She asked. She pulled the covers back and before she could pick up the pillow, I snatched it off the bed.

"It's…it's…" I stammered.

I didn't know what to tell her. I walked out of the bedroom and closed the door behind me. I examined the bags to make sure she had not crushed any of the dope. I walked over to the bar and hid the remaining seven bags in the iceless cooler. When I came back in the room, Pricilla had shed her skintight dress and lay face down on the top of the covers. I undressed in record time and started to kiss her down the crevice of her back. My tongue glided across her shinning black body, stopping on her thick ass. I bit her left butt cheek softly, then I spread them apart. I licked her ass and performed oral sex from behind her. It's a good thing I moved the dope from the pillowcase, because Pricilla had put over half of the pillow in her mouth. Her moans were still louder than whatever was on t.v. I rolled her over onto her back and continued to eat her until she came in my mouth. Then I entered deep inside of her, almost melting. We sexed each other for the majority of the night and some of the morning. Finally, we passed out. Both extremely tired and satisfied!

CHAPTER 9

It was only 8: 15 a.m., when the phone started ringing. It was Red, pleading with me to come through early so he could get five more bags of butter. I needed to get up anyway. I had promised my mom that I would be home Saturday afternoon. I told Red that I would see him before 10: 00 a.m.

"Before ten, " Pricilla said, looking at the bright red numbers on the clock that punched the darkness.

"I got to get up anyway. I promised my mom I would be home this morning. I thought you were still asleep, " I said.

"I was until the phone rang." She got up and twisted to the bathroom. My eyes followed her natural choreography until she closed the door, causing a teepee to be built underneath the covers.

The t.v. had been on all night and now, Gargamel ran across the screen chasing little blue Smurfs.   I turned to channel 12 and watched the Gummy Bears bounce through the forest until the bathroom door opened.

"Is that a gun or are you happy to see me?" Pricilla asked, licking her full lips.

"Its a gun. The same one the blasted a cap in your ass last night. "

"Well shoot me again before we go since it appears to be loaded, " she said.

For the next hour we fucked and sucked. We decided it would be best if we took our showers separately, for fear of starting allover again.

Red ordered 2 1/2 ounces, leaving me with one ounce. I called Tory to see if he wanted the last two bags.

"Hello, " his mom said.

"Hey Ms. Wright. I apologize for calling your home so early. Is Tory there?" I asked.

"Its Rena," she said. "My name is Rena, Mr. Styles, and Tory isn't here."

"How did you know who I was?" I asked surprised.

"You're the only one of Tory's friends who calls me Ms. Wright."

"It won't happen again Ms. Rena," I said sarcastically.

"Call back later. He'll be here soon and if not, I will. Maybe you can talk to me. "

Without giving me a chance to say anything, Rena hung up the phone. Did she just flirt with me? I thought. That situation was a time bomb ticking, if that's just what happened.

When I pulled in front of Barbie Hall, at least six girls were being dropped off. I kissed Pricilla and promised to call her later. I wanted to hurry up and get off campus because I was afraid Lakisha would see me.

It was 10: 30 when I pulled up to Red's spot. He had on the same clothes as the night before.

"Damn Cuz, did you spend the night out this bitch?" I asked.

"Nigga, I'm on a serious mission right now, he said. He handed me the money and I passed him the coke.

"I only have one more ounce left, " I said.

" Just one more?" he asked. "I don't have the money for it right now but I want it."

I didn't want to ride around dirty anyway, so I fronted the ounce to Red.

"I'll get the money tonight or tomorrow."

"I'll be right here on the block or at home," he said. "I can't go far I'm on house arrest, but the ban is on my dogs leg now."

I laughed at Red because I knew he was telling the truth. Some people are born just to break the law and he was one of those people.

I got on Battleground Avenue and took 220 North to Madison. When I got home, I hugged and kissed my mom. I updated her on the current events in my life leaving out a few things. Then she inquired about the car I was driving. I explained a friend had let me borrow the car just for the weekend. Mama had cooked my favorite meal too. Fried apples, home made bread and chicken. Just the smell alone made me want to go AWOL. When I finished eating I called Kami to let her know I was home.

Kami and I started dating my 12th grade year in high school. Contrary to the past couple of weekends, I was very much in love with her. Or what I thought was love.

Saturday afternoon was spent with my mom and youngest brother Pookie, visiting family and friends. Answering questions every time I talked to someone.

"How does it feel to jump out of an airplane? Do you get scared? Have you ever seen anyone whose parachute didn't open?"

My mom didn't like that question. Any mom of a paratrooper wouldn't! Saturday night Kami and I stayed together and discussed future plans. She wanted to get married and have a baby. Despite all the dirt I was doing I wanted the same thing, but I wanted to wait a little while just to make sure. I didn't tell my mom or Kami that I didn't have to work on Monday. I did not tell Moe either. I called him Sunday morning before I left my mom's house and told him I wouldn't be back until Monday night. I let him know that things were running smoothly, but I had a few more bags left to sell. He agreed that I should stay and get rid of them before driving back to Ft. Bragg.

When I got back to Greensboro, I went out to Red's spot. To my surprise he wasn't there, so I knew he was at home .I went over to his house and he said he was expecting me .He disappeared into his bedroom and returned with a handful of cash.

"I'll be straight again next weekend, " I said. "I will page you from Ft. Bragg, Friday. I'll put code 22 behind the number so you'll know it's me. That's just to let you, know I'm on my way home."

"That's if I don't get looked up," he said.

"Think positive, Cuz," I said. "You'll be ok."

I left Red's and without calling drove to Tory's crib. Petey laid stretched out in front of the door slightly raising his head up when I blew the horn.

I was really hoping Tory wasn't home. When the door opened it was him, instead of his mom.

"Come on inside. Don't worry about the dog. I told you that before. My mom told me you called. I was hoping you called back because I ran out."

"Me too," I said.

"I thought you said you had a connection?"

"I do," I said. "In Ft. Bragg not Greensboro."

Rena walked out of the back room and my heart skipped a beat. She was so fine.

"Hey Rena! How are you?" I asked.

"Fine, Styles. How are you?"

"I'm fine." I wanted to say now that I've seen you, but I would have had to kill Tory right then and there. Rena had a Ford Escort that she shared with Tory .He was about to make a run right before I came, he explained.

"Hurry up and get back Tory, I need to go to the grocery store, " Rena said.

"I'll be back in a few minutes."

As we walked out the door I offered Rena a ride to the store. Tory didn't look bothered. Now, he wouldn't have to hurry back.

"I'll call you next weekend when I get home Tory," I said.

" Just page me,' he said. He closed the door on the dirty black Escort and drove off.

"Your girlfriend isn't going to get mad is she?" Rena asked.

"She probably would if she knew about me giving you a ride," I said.

"Why didn't you call your boyfriend to give you a ride?"

"I don't have one of those," she said.

"Then we should be safe because my girlfriend doesn't live in G'boro. Lenny Williams poured his heart out on this song, didn't he? I asked.

We rode to Food Lion both singing "I Love You". Rena was surprised that a "Jitter Bug," as she called me listened to that old school music.

She shopped and I pushed the basket. Watching her float up and down the aisle. I was bragging on how well I could cook when she said that I could cook for her tonight. I accepted the offer without even thinking. I just continued to run my mouth about the different types of food I loved to cook.

"My mama raised five boys and she taught us all how to cook, " I said.

"I'll be the judge of that tonight," Rena said.

On our way back to her house I asked Rena what was Tory going to think about me cooking for her?

"I'm Tory's mother, he isn't my father. I run my house." She said.

"I don't think that will be a good idea right now. Maybe I can take you out to eat next weekend."

"Next weekend would be fine, " she said.

Blue Magic was playing on our way back to Rena's house. "Let the Side Show Begin! " That's what was about to happen. A sideshow!

I helped Rena bring in the groceries. Before I left I asked would it be alright to call her from Ft.Bragg this week. She said she expected me to call her. Even though I had only messed with one older woman. (The manager at the McDonald's I worked at while I was in high school.) I learned that an older woman would tell you what she expects. That eliminates all the guessing. I hugged and kissed Rena on the cheek. I felt like I was betraying Tory, but I felt like asking her if I could spend the night!

I drove to a pay phone and called Lakisha. She was excited to hear from me. I told her that I was going to be in town for one night. She said she had an 8:00 a.m. class that she couldn't miss, but she wanted to stay with me. I picked her up and we got a room at the Red Roof Inn. It would crush Lakisha if she knew that the night before I had sexed one of her girlfriends crazy!

Most of that's her fault though. A woman should not brag to her girlfriends about how good her man is in bed. Especially, if he can eat some pussy like myself! The worst type of woman is a curious woman. A curious woman won't stop being curious until her curiosity is satisfied!

CHAPTER 10

The CID (Criminal Investigation Division) had been investigating Huntman, Wilk and Moe since late 1987. They teamed up with the Feds, who were conducting an investigation on a drug ring in Fayetteville. Huntman was said to have ties with the guys in that particular ring. An informant had reported that the drugs that were being dealt in that ring were coming from Miami, Florida.

Chuck and Supreme, (AKA Preme) were the two guys responsible for the drugs coming from Miami, according to the informant. Both had been stationed in Ft. Bragg, during the mid 80's, but got out at the end of their four year obligation. According to the informant, Chuck got out to do "Bigger and Better" things, and Preme just wanted to make some "Serious Cash." Supreme returned to Miami and became deeply involved with the drug game. Later, he ran into his old comrade, who was dealing drugs, but on a much smaller level. He convinced Chuck that they should operate as a team instead of individually.

For years, while stationed in Ft. Bragg, Chuck and Preme had scouted Fayetteville for "could be" spots, if they decided to return. Not knowing that they both had the same thing in mind. Now they had hooked up they discussed going back to North Carolina to do their thing. They were both familiar with the drug prices in Miami and knew they were much lower than the North Carolina prices. In Miami, they could purchase a kilo of Bolivian Flakes, for 12 to 15,000 dollars, and the Bolivian cocaine was the best coke. In Fayetteville, a kilo of any kind of coke sold for twice that amount. Knowing this information, "Operation Hurricane" as it was later called, began.

Preme had been a mediocre soldier in Bravo Company, 3-505. He and Huntman roomed together for two years before he got out of the Army. . He use to constantly talk about what he was going to do once he got out of the Army. He'd say he was going to become a drug dealer and make some serious cash. He would also talk about the cars he would have once he started making some real money. The jewelry he would own would cost as much as the average home, he would brag. Thus, when he returned to Bragg he immediately looked his old roommate up.

Huntman had told Preme that he was living in a fantasy world. He added that he didn't have the street smarts to be a drug dealer. Now, Preme was back with sweet vengeance. Eager to show and prove. Huntman was astonished when he saw Preme .He was driving the biggest Benz he'd ever seen with a diamond infested Rolex wrapped around his wrist. Every pocket on his Gucci Jeans were swollen with cash.

"Fantasy world, huh nigga?" Preme said to Huntman.

Huntman was speechless. It was unequivocal that Preme had reached his goal. All his crazy talk hadn't been in vain. Actually, now that Huntman thought about it, it wasn't that crazy. And just as he promised, Preme returned to shine! Preme propositioned Huntman to join the "Supreme Team." To jump on his band wagon and make some serious money. Briefly, Huntman was in a state of apprehension. Then he sat aside his patriotism to see the conceptual picture. He too, wanted the things Preme had showed up with. His Army check wasn't going to get him a new Rolex and it sure as hell wasn't going to get him a new Benz. After a day of thinking, Huntman called Preme asking him, "How can I be down?"

Preme had a plan for Huntman. He knew that he could be trusted more than anyone of the guys he dealt with in Fayetteville. For two months he escorted Huntman, introducing him to the guys he dealt with in Fayetteville. During those two months, Huntman observed the art of dealing cocaine, which he mastered quickly. He later brought Moe and Wilk on board to assist him locking Fayetteville (DaVille) down. Now, that I became the forth wheel on this rolling car, I too, was a part of the investigation that extended from Miami, Florida, to Madison, North Carolina.

The problem with the investigation was there hadn't been any control buys, pictures of deals or telephone conversations, incriminating anyone involved. The main informant was a female, who occasionally fucked Chuck when he came to DaVille. The investigators, lead by Agent Goodwin, had not figured out a way to infiltrate the "Supreme Team's " airtight family.

When the female did meet with Chuck it was always in a different hotel and he never called her when he arrived in Fayetteville, only whenever he was leaving. This was a big problem for Goodwin. This never allowed him the opportunity to pen point the "when and where abouts" that is essential in an investigation.

Huntman only dealt with the guys who were introduced to him by Preme and Chuck. Agent Goodwin knew they would not sell to an undercover agent. They were too smart to do something that careless. He was moving slow on this investigation. He wanted to make sure things were in order before he made a bust. One wrong move could destroy the entire investigation. He knew he could expect a promotion if he caught these guys. His superiors had started to press him to move things along. Speed things up because he was taking too long to give the investigating department feedback. They wanted some action!

Goodwin harassed some of the guys who were supposed to be connected to the drug ring in Fayetteville. He had not been successful in busting anyone "red handed" though. Those whom he harassed reported immediately to Huntman. Huntman would chill out dealing with that particular person for a couple of weeks until the smoke cleared.

That was a part of the Supreme Team's agreement. If anyone got harassed or busted it was incumbent to advise those higher up. Higher up in DaVille was Huntman. He would in turn advise Preme or Chuck.

Goodwin realized too much time and money had been spent for nothing. His boss wanted some results and fast. The Supreme Team had to be dealt with at all cost or it was his narrow ass.

CHAPTER 11

Huntman called me about 6:00 pm, that evening. I hadn't left my room since I got back from Greensboro.

"PFC Styles," I said.

"Pretty Fucking Crazy, " Huntman said laughing. "What's up? Did you sell all of those t-shirts?" he asked.

"Yeah, I've been waiting for one of you to call me. "

"Meet me in front of our company so I can get that from you. I want to make sure you're straight for next weekend," he said.

I hung up the phone and returned to my room. I got the money out of my locker and stuffed it inside of my coat pocket. I went out the rear door of A-Company, headed for B-Company's front door. Before I reached the steps Huntman and Moe were walking out of the barracks. I followed them out to the Blazer and we all crawled inside.

"You didn't get any tickets in my car this weekend did you?" Moe asked.

For a brief second my heart stopped. It was like Moe knew about my close call with the State Trooper. "Man nah, I didn't get any tickets. I never went over 55 miles per hour, " I said. "Here you go." I pulled out the money and handed it to Huntman.

"But I did get Pricilla, " I said smiling.

"You did for real?" Huntman asked.

"Nigga, I tell a bunch of lies, but I don't lie on my dick!" I said.

Clearly in his feelings, Moe blurted, "I don't care if you fucked her. I don't love that bitch. I don't even know her ass." You could tell by his voice that he was hot!

"Is the pussy any good, Styles? Moe was just talking about how good it was today, " Huntman said. He continued to ask me silly questions about Pricilla. He knew it was bruising Moe's ego.

"This week we're going to give you the same thing, Styles," Moe said, trying to change the subject.

"So you fucked her while driving Moe's car?" Huntman asked.

"But it's going to be powder. If we get more than we usually get, we're going to give you more, " Moe continued, ignoring Huntman.

"Did she suck your dick?"

I tried to hold back the laughter, but I couldn't any longer. I erupted with laughter.

"Man fuck ya'll niggas," Moe said. He got out and slammed the door. Then he opened it again. "Give me my damn keys!" He jerked the keys from my hand and we watched him disappear between the barracks.

"His pride is hurt, " Huntman said. "He was just talking about that girl today."

Huntman met with Preme and Chuck later that night. They hadn't been able to transport what they wanted to transport, so Huntman was given his usual issue of five kilos.

Chuck followed his normal routine after business was conducted. He waited for Preme and his girl to leave Fayetteville. Preme carried the money, safely tucked away in a hidden compartment in a big Chevy Van back to Miami. Chuck would then call his friend Tanoka to let her know he was about to pick her up. She stayed with Chuck once a week when he came to Fayetteville.

Tanoka had been busted for selling cocaine, but turned states evidence, (Snitch) on her boyfriend in 1986. She had been working with the Fayetteville Police Department, FBI and DEA since she got popped. She worked for anyone who could help her support her habit. Shopping!

She had caused three guys to get busted since 1986. None of them ever suspected her of setting them up. She was never called to testify, because everyone she had been involved with had been busted "Red Handed." Subsequently, they all took plea bargains. Now, Tanoka was dealing with someone who was much more discreet and expected everyone to be out to get him. She had been cautious not to ask Chuck too many questions about his business. She knew that would make him suspicious of her. But, those "Folks" were putting pressure on her to get some type of information concerning the drugs coming from Miami.

She started asking Chuck questions about Miami. She also asked him to call her before he left Miami, to let her know he was on his way to Fayetteville. She concealed her questions by adding that she was tired of spending just one night a week with him. She ended by saying she just missed him and wanted to spend more time with him.

Tuesday, after formation, I caught up with Huntman while he was walking out to his truck.

"What's up?" I asked.

"Nothing much, I'm going to Airborne Sewing on Yadkin Road, to pick up my uniforms. I had a couple of them that did not have my Ranger tab on them, so I'm having them sewed on. You want to ride with me?" he asked.

I jumped in and got the run down on how things were going to go the coming weekend. Since they didn't get what they thought they were going to get, I'd be given the same thing as last weekend. I would drive Moe's car again, Huntman explained. The plan was to meet sometime Friday, after the last formation.

Friday morning, while I was eating breakfast, Wilk came in the chow hall. He ordered a cheese omelet and pancakes and joined me. Huntman had given him my "work," as he called it. He said he'd meet me at the same gas station as last week at 5:30. He handed me the keys to Huntman' s Blazer, and continued to explain that I would be driving Moe's Mustang once I met him at the store.

"It's better if everyone sees you leave in the Blazer, " he said. "Then you can drive the Tang to Greensboro."

At 5:30, Wilk was parked by the pay phone along the side of the store. He stood facing the entrance of the store and conversated on the phone. I sat in the Blazer admiring the Green Mustang. This was the same car Moe's girl was driving when she met us at LaShocka's.

Wilk motioned for me to get out of the truck. When I walked towards him, he covered up the bottom of the phone and said, "The keys are in the car. I've already put gas in it and the shit is in the same spot as it was in the black Tang. Moe said don't speed and to be careful."

That was something that didn't need to be said. I was wary of the speed limit after last week's scare. I would be on cruise control all the way to the Gate City. I clapped Wilk, and slid into the Mustang. This one sounded even better than the black one.

When I got to Greensboro, I checked into the Residence Inn. I took the 18 bags of butter, and hid them in the fireplace. That was a safe place because I had no intention of starting a fire.

I called Tory's crib and as the phone started to ring I realized I had not called Rena like I had promised her. I had been so busy being a soldier, I hadn't had time to call.

"Hello,'" a sweet voice from the other end of the phone said.
"What's up Ms. Wright?"

"Hey stranger,'" she said. "I must have scared you because I didn't get my phone call like you promised. I don't like to be stood up. "

I explained that I had this big jump and that I was in the field the entire week. She said she understood, but she refused to be stood up for dinner. I promised her that wasn't going to happen.

"Is Tory there?" I asked.

"Yeah, he's here. He is standing right here as a matter of fact, looking down my throat." Tory had heard Rena's entire conversation with me. It was evident he didn't like it when he took the phone.

"What's up Styles?" he said in a harsh voice.

"You straight?" I asked.

"Hold up nigga! " he said. "What's this shit about you taking my mom out? Don't end up like that last sucka with holes in his clothes, " he said. "And no I ain't straight. "

Tory had made a real slick comment and threatened me .I didn't respond because I would feel the same way if one of my partners was trying to take my mom out to eat.

"Are you trying to get straight or what?" I asked.

"Bring me three ounces, " he said. "I'll be here waiting on you."

I paged Red and began to unpack my things. I dialed my mom's number and no one answered. Then I called Kami and her mom said she and her cousin were gone to the mall. I paged Red again. It wasn't like him not to call me right back. I figured he must be tied up somewhere, handling business.

I took three ounces from behind the fire logs and stuffed them deep into my pockets. I had decided to ride through the Grove to see if I could locate Red after I dropped Tory's package off. I called Lakisha and made plans to see her later on also. Next, I called Pricilla and her answering machine came on. As I was leaving my message Pricilla picked up the phone.

"Hello, hello, " she said.

"What's up Pricilla? I'm in Greensboro. Are you trying to see me later?" I asked.

"I am, but not if you are going to see Lakisha this weekend too, like you did last weekend. I heard her telling someone she saw you also last weekend. No wonder you didn't have a chance to call me back. You were to busy fucking her." She continued to fuss then she abruptly said, "As a matter of fact, I'm going to chill. You probably don't want to see me anyway. I'm on my period. "

After she said that, she hung up the phone. I started to call her back. I dialed six numbers, then I hung up. She needed to cool off.

When I pulled up at Tory's, I got out despite the big pit bull sitting in front of the door. To my surprise, Petey didn't growl, bark or anything. He only raised his large square head up and wagged his hard tail, causing it to smack against the screen door. I knocked on the door and Tory jerked the door opened.

"I thought you were scared of the dog?" He said, stressing the word scared.

"Cautious," I said. "I'm not scared of shit. If it was a scared bone in my body, I'd cut it out myself. " We walked into the kitchen and both of us took a seat. It was a different table with matching chairs.

"Look ah here, Styles, " Tory said. "I don't approve of you trying to date my mother."

"Hold up Tory! " I said.

"No! You hold up. My mom is a grown ass woman, and she is going to do what she wants to do. I've never approved of any guy my mom has dealt with. Including my sorry ass daddy. Just don't ever lay a hand on her. This is her house, but respect me because it's my house too."

When Tory finished talking, I didn't say anything. I shook my head, signifying I understood how he felt. He reached into his pocket and I expected a gun, but he pulled out his money and laid it on the table. I handed him the bags of butter and he slid the money over to me.

"Hold up, " he said. "This is powder."

"You don't want powder?" I asked.

"No, no...I mean yeah! Powder is how I rather have it. These guys just asked me for powder. They are going to be happy as hell. They can cook it themselves and put more cut on it."

Being as green as I was in the game I didn't have a clue what he was talking about when he said cut, but I agreed.

"I got to go," Tory said. "I got some cats waiting on me now. Mama!" he yelled as he walked out the kitchen.

Tory had asked Rena to allow him to speak with me "Man to Man" and she agreed. When I heard the front door close, Rena emerged from the bedroom, wearing a peculiar grin.

"That son of mine is so protective over his mother. Hey!" she said. "We're still going out for dinner aren't we?" she asked.

"Yeah sure, " I said. "I got to make a run and I will be back in about an hour. " This wasn't a good time for a hug or a kiss so I hurriedly walked out of the house to the car.

Tory was pulling off as I walked to the car. "So, that's your Mustang, huh?" he stopped and asked.

"No, this one belongs to a friend too. Mine is parked." He pulled off and I wasn't far behind.

There were only a few youngsters standing at Red's spot. I recognized one of them and called him over to the car.

"What's up Lil' Kenny?" I said. "Where is my cousin?"

"You haven't heard? Red got locked up today. Those crackers crossed him up in the courtroom, " he said.

I hated to hear that for more than one reason. I thought Red was going to beat those charges. I guess he didn't think positive like I told him to do, I thought.

"How much time did he get?" I asked.

"I don't know all the details Styles, I just know he got locked up."

I rode by Red's house to see if his girlfriend was there. She was not, so I left her a message under her door to call me at the hotel.

Rena and I went out to eat at Darryl's. I walked in recognizing faces from last week. The same waiter who witnessed me having an orgasm, rushed to seat me .He was wearing a wide smile as he seated me in the lover's corner, on the upper floor. He gave us menus with promises of returning shortly.

The events were not quite as exciting as last weeks, but Rena and I had better conversation. She wasn't looking for a man she explained. She just wanted a friend! I could handle that. All I was looking for was another piece of pussy.

During the course of our meal the entire staff made their way upstairs, one by one, acting like they were looking for something or someone. Rena thought that was strange. She finally commented after the dishwasher showed up, dripping wet.

"I hope they hurry up and find what they're looking for," she said. She didn't have a clue that she was what they were looking for. She just wasn't doing what she was supposed to be doing!

Rena and I finished our meal and I took her home. I walked her to the door and gave her a small kiss. This time, on her soft red lips. She thanked me for a wonderful dinner and made me promise to call her later. I promised I would call her and I made my way back to the car. I had six ounces of coke left and I was going to call and locate Tory anyway. I wanted to talk to her but I wanted that money more. At this point, if I talked to her that would be a plus, but my primary mission was to sell the coke I had remaining.

When I returned to Red's house Page still wasn't home. I could see the corner of the yellow piece of paper I had slid under the door. As I turned to walk away I heard a voice saying, "No ones at home. Ain't been there since morning. You know that boy you're looking for Red, I think that's what ya'll call him? He had to go to court today for selling them damn drugs. I recon he got locked up cause he ain't been back since dis morning. He usually brings me a Pepsi and some nuts everyday. I didn't 't get em' today."

Red's neighbor was an elderly man who sat on the porch day and night watching everything that moved. Evidently, Red had told him about his case. The old man sounded real disappointed. He missed Red. He missed his Pepsi and his nuts.

I returned back to my room and chilled. I had to figure out a way to get rid of the rest of the coke. Someone had to replace Red. I had made a promise not to branch out, but when a paratrooper is faced with a problem he adapts and over comes. Even though I could bank on Tory purchasing more from me I still needed a contingency plan.

I rode over to the Grove to where Red's spot use to be! Traffic had picked up, but nothing like the traffic when Red was there. Lil 'Kenny saw me pull up and ran to the car.

"'What's up Styles? You straight?" he asked.

"Not right now, but I can be." I said.

"I can't buy ten and twenty kilos Styles, but I can buy ounces at a time. I also know all the cats who use to buy from Red. I use to make most of his sales for him. Now that he is gone, I'm going to hold his spot down until he comes back."

"What do you need now?" I asked.

"I'll take two ounces now and two later, " he said.

That was cool. Red only purchased 2 ½ at a time. There wasn't going to be much difference if any at all. I could deal with that. Between Lil' Kenny and Tory, I was still going to make my money.

After dealing with Lil' Kenny, I picked up Lakisha from campus.   I prayed that I didn't run into Pricilla while I was picking her up. Thankfully, I didn't .She wanted to go and eat but I had already been to dinner. She was satisfied with ordering a pizza once we got to the room. She took a shower while waiting for the pizza man to come. I called Kami while she was in the shower and promised to see her the next day. She thought I was still in Ft.Bragg. (You could do that before *69!)

Saturday morning, I checked out of the Residence Inn and dropped Lakisha off at her dorm. I wanted to stay at the Residence Inn another night but I was afraid that since she knew where I was staying, she might show up unexpectedly. I told her I was going back to Ft.Bragg.

Kami's mom had just finished cooking breakfast when I arrived at her house. As always, we were happy to see each other. She invited me in and fixed me a big plate of her country cooking. Eggs, grits and home made bread. Not to mention the different meats she had cooked.

I told Kami that I had borrowed my friend's car just to drive to Stoneville to see her. I explained that I couldn't stay long because he needed his car later on that evening. Kami and her mom thought that was sweet of me. I promised to come home and take her Christmas shopping the following weekend.

Tory wasn't home and Rena was still asleep when I .got back to Greensboro. She insisted that I come in. She claimed she was about to get up anyway. Rena had on a nightshirt that barely covered her butt cheeks .She pranced backwards and forward past me a few times, always checking to see if I was watching her. And I was! After about five minutes of this prancing the front door opened and Tory walked in. Immediately, I knew he thought I spent the night with his mom.

"What tha…?" he started.

"Hold up, I just got here five minutes ago," I said.

"Dag mama, put on some clothes, " he said frowning up his face. "What's up Styles? Nigga you need a pager. I ran out last night and I needed to get in touch with you but I couldn't.

"I'm going to the mall today and get one. I didn't want to look like a drug dealer, " I said.

"That's what you are, nigga, " he said looking relieved that I didn't stay with his mom last night.

"Whatcha need?" I asked.

"The same thing," he said. "Three ounces."

Since I checked out of the Residence Inn, I had the coke with me. Tory wanted three and I had four ounces left. I went to the car and brought back all four. I told Tory as soon as he sold the first one he could get me straight. I hadn't fronted Tory anything until then. When I did, it hit him like a Mean Joe Green tackle. "Maybc, if he eased up on me with his mom, he could get a lot more fronted to him." I saw it in his eyes. Greed!

I should have stopped selling drugs that day when I realized that greed would cause you to pimp your own mother just to get that mighty dollar. Unconsciously, that's what he was willing to do. Greed is a motherfucker!

"I really appreciate that," Tory said.

I got up and headed for the door. Rena reappeared with some black biker shorts on. Her ass looked like a teardrop!
"Dag Ma, what do you have on now?" Tory asked, shaking his head in disapproval. He stuffed the bags in his pocket and walked out the door.

"I'm cooking dinner today Styles, around two or three. I'll see you then, " Rena said.

"Damn, I love that in a woman," I said under my breath.

"Excuse me," she said smiling. "you love what in a woman?"

"Nothing, I was just thinking out loud. I'll see you when its time to eat."

I got a room at the Howard Johnson's on Meadowview Road. I checked in and took a much needed nap. When I woke up, I took a long, sweltering shower and went to the mall. I had to find a pager so I wouldn't continue to miss money. A nexus for the fast life!

CHAPTER 12

The nerdy looking sales man had paged me twice already to make sure my pager was working. I asked him to page me once more as soon as I left the store. When I exited the Motorola Store, I was busy playing with my new toy when I heard a tranquil voice call my name .It sounded like a thousand angels singing a love song!

"Dana!…Dana!…Hey!" I looked up and fixed Celeste with a sharp, brown eyed gaze. Celeste was from Madison too. She and I attended high school together, but she was two grades behind me. She had on some tight jeans that looked like they were painted on, revealing her "Coke-Cola" bottle shape. Actually, her pants had been airbrushed. Her name sprayed on the left thigh and a small kitten painted on her right thigh.

"Hey, what's happening Celeste? Damn you've grown up, " I said. I complemented Celeste on how well she looked at least three times in our short conversation. I asked her how was her family doing? Her brother Orlando and I had planned on being the next big thing in the rap industry after Run DMC and Jam Master Jay. But, things didn't go as planned. Orlando joined the Army also.

She and her friend Vicky, a tenuous cutie herself, were in the mall Christmas shopping, she explained. As she continued to talk, my mouth watered for her. She gave me her phone number and I promised to call her later. When she walked a way, I seen a big smiling cat painted on her ass. I watched her until she walked into the Women's Foot Locker. I never thought I would see the day when I would trade places with an airbrushed cat! My pager finally went off, breaking my train of thought about Celeste's ass.

I arrived back at Ho Jo ' s, thinking about the cat on Celeste's jeans, still. It was forever airbrushed in my mind. I picked up the phone and dialed Tory's number. He wasn't home, so I gave Rena my pager number to pass on to him. She reminded me that dinner would be served in a couple of hours. I told her to page me when she was finished cooking.

I fell asleep watching the Pittsburgh Steelers, crushing the Dallas Cowboys. I had a dream that I was back in the mall. I met a queen while I was shopping. She was so beautiful. A real queen! She had the crown, gown and the whole nine. Today, I realize that was a dream that came true before I went to sleep!

I woke up hearing a beeping sound. I thought it was the alarm clock going off, but it was my new toy. I hadn't got use to the sound of the pager yet. When I pressed the big gray button on the side, it displayed Rena's phone number. I picked up the phone, and slowly dialed her number.

"Come and get it," she said, when she answered the phone.

"Come and get what? You or the food?" I asked.

"I could mean both, but you're not ready for me."

"Yeah, I'm ready for you and the food."

"Well come and get it like I said. We're both hot!"

Rena had changed into a silk Calvin Klein pajama suit. She had planned to spend the entire day inside where it was nice and warm. She gave me the money for the ounce I fronted Tory after she gave me a wet kiss.

"He brought it back a few minutes after you left the first time. I guess he doubled back to see if you really left," she said grinning.

"What's that trash you were talking on the phone?" I asked.

"Me! You were talking shit too, " she replied.

"Didn't you just tell me over dinner that we were just going to be friends or some bullshit?" I asked Rena.

"That's just what it was, " she said. "Some bullshit I was talking. What do you want first, your desert or your plate I fixed for you?" she asked.

Before I had a chance to answer, Rena pushed me back onto the sofa and started kissing me fervently. Intensely, I returned tongue for tongue. Then I stopped thinking with my dick.

"Look Rena!" I said, pushing her off of me. "I don't want to do this right here. I have a room at the Ho Jo's, and after I eat…," I paused and rubbed my stomach. With a full smile on my face, I added, "After I eat, I suggest that you come over to the room. " I could see the lava boiling in her eyes. She was hotter than a firecracker on the 4th of July. After a brief look of disappointment she agreed to join me after I ate. Rena packed her bags while I ate. If the pussy is anything like the food I would be in love before the sun came up, I thought. Her macaroni melted in my mouth and her greens were seasoned perfectly. I began to hope that Rena didn't give head! At least not good head, because I would really be fucked up!

After I finished eating, I gave her the room key to our tryst. I wanted to check on Red's girl, Page first. I told her I would be there soon. But, before I checked on Page, I rode by Red's old spot to check Lil ' Kenny out.

Lil' Kenny was kicked back on Red's "x" throne. He saw me and he popped to his feet like he had been caught doing something wrong, by reclining on the old chair. I pulled up and he ran over to the car.

"What's up Styles? What happened to you yesterday? I thought you were coming back, " he said.

We walked in the Grove Store and I explained I had run out of coke. I gave him my pager number and told him I would see him next weekend. I bought a huge bag of Platters Peanuts and a 32 oz. Pepsi, and I drove to Red's crib.

Pops was sitting in his normal place on the porch. He had his feet placed on the railing of the porch. I walked over and gave him the bag of peanuts and the cold soda. He smiled at me like I had restored his youth.

"I'm in the Army in Ft.Bragg, so I can't bring this daily like Red, but when I can I will."

Pops thanked me and went on to say that Page had finally came home.

"She just got in an hour ago, " He said. Then he thanked me again.

"Who is it?" Page screamed when I knocked on the door.

"It's Dana."

She opened the door and invited me inside. Before I could ask her about Red, she started giving me the run down on my Cuz.

"He got sentenced to eight years. That will be cut to four years once he is processed in the system. After a fourth of four years he could get paroled, so he'll be straight. He is suppose to call me in an hour."

"Do you need anything?" I asked.

"No, I'm fine right now, but I might need something later on down the road."

I gave her my pager number and told her to call me if she needed anything. I also gave her two hundred dollars to send to Red.

"When he calls tell him I said to keep his big head up. Call me if you need anything."

"I will, " She said.

I walked through the lobby and got on the elevator. The top floor was my destination. I knocked on the door and Rena opened it. She was as naked as a J-Bird! She turned without saying a word, leaving a trail of sparkling water, and walked to the bathroom. Following the trail, I admired Rena as she slid into the tub and turned the jets on full blast. I stood, frozen in disbelief. Rena was sexier than I'd imagined. God had to break the mold after her created her!

I undressed, trying not to show how excited I was. I stuck one foot in the gushing water to test the temperature. Slowly, I eased into the hot tub filled with scented bubbles. Rena took a bath cloth and began to bathe me. I relaxed as much as I could. I laid back, feeling like a king being washed by his slave girl. She took "Franky" into her hand and gently passed the bath cloth over his sensitive head. Passionately, I began to kiss her. My tongue exploring her mouth. She dropped the bath cloth and slowly mounted me, digging her painted nails, red as vintage wine, deep into my chest. I grabbed her ass and pulled her down, thrusting Franky deep inside of her. She rose up and down and I quickly caught her rhythm. As we danced, she started to pause on every down stroke. Tightening muscles of her pussy around my dick. Pleasantly choking Franky! The inside of Rena was as hot as the water in the hot tub. That thing she was doing with her pussy was driving me insane and she knew it. She started moaning that she was about to come.

"Let's come together," I almost cheered.

Rena shook her head, but didn't say a word. Her facial expressions looked like she was in pain, but the pleasurable moans proved otherwise.

"I'm coming! I'm coming!" Rena started saying over and over again. She dug her nails deeper into my chest, almost breaking the skin. I could feel the juices from her pussy making the temperature in the hot tub rise. I came and it felt like the entire world had been lifted off of my shoulders.

She sighed climatically and said she had never had an orgasm like that before. She made that statement at least four more times during our stay at the Ho Jo' s. The first couple of times I believed her. Then I realized that she said that after every orgasm. I quickly came to the conclusion that the pussy was indeed better than her gourmet cooking. Gourmet pussy! And the head was the bomb!

I woke up at 5:30 a.m., and Rena was still asleep. I walked over to the window and observed the pinkness in the morning sky .The sun had started to rise and just as I had predicted, since the pussy and the head was the bomb, I was fucked up!

After we checked out, Rena followed me to the Waffle House on High Point Road. While she ordered I used the pay phone to call Lakisha. After I lied to her about where I was, I called Pricilla. She said the only reason I hadn't seen her during the weekend was because I knew she was on her period. She hit the nail on the head, but I assured her that wasn't the reason. I was busy taking care of important business, I explained.

"Not to busy to fuck Lakisha," she said and hung up on me again.

Rena and I ate and I promised to call her and see her later. I took my time going back to Ft.Bragg. My mind was flooded with thoughts. Thoughts of Red and his jail situation. My "Real " girlfriend, Kami. Rena and Celeste. Lakisha and Pricilla. I knew that situation was going to blow up in my face, but not this quick. I couldn't wait to get back next weekend to see Celeste.

I was definitely was going to call her from Bragg. It seemed like it took me less time to get back to Bragg compared to the times before. I didn't even speed either. I guess it was all the things I had on my mind. Like the muscles in Rena's pussy. Thoughts like that still make time fly by today. Just not fast enough!

CHAPTER 13

Sunday night I called Celeste. She and I laughed and talked for over an hour. I let her know that I was coming home again the coming weekend. I asked if she was going to be busy? Her cousin from Baltimore, Maryland was coming down she said, but they would be out and about in Madison.

"Just call me before you leave Ft.Bragg," she said.

If they were going to be riding around in Madison, it wouldn't be hard for me to find them because the town was so small and everyone knew each other, I thought.

"I'll call you before I leave, " I said to Celeste.

I also promised Rena that I would call and let her know I made it back to Ft.Bragg, safely. We also conversed for a while. She went on and on, talking about her repeated orgasm. How nobody had ever made her have them back to back. She sounded as fucked up as I was. Later that night, despite our early formation, we all went out. Wilk had a few ounces left from the weekend and we decided to go to Lashocka' s to get rid of them. I watched as they worked the joint, moving the coke. These cats were smooth operators. After an hour, we left the club. Sold out!

I broke the bad news that Red had been locked up, but I also gave them the good news too. Red's partner Lil ' Kenny had taken up the slack. I would not miss a beat, I promised.

Instead of going back to the barricks, we went to Moe ' s house. Huntman and Wilk had cribs too, but not in their names, they stressed. The more I hung out with these guys, the more I found out about the things they had going on outside of the Army.

The same broad that met Moe at LaShocka's was setting in the living room watching t.v. When we walked in the house, without saying a word, she got up and went straight into the bedroom. Moe followed her.

"I'll wake ya'll up in a few hours so we can go to formation. " he said before disappearing behind the closing door.

There were two other bedrooms. Wilk went into one and Huntman went into the other. I was left to hold the couch down.

Wednesday night, Moe and I were at the carwash on the "Dirty Murk" when Chuck paged him. He jumped in the car quickly and dialed Chuck's number. Chuck wanted to meet Moe at his house, so we finished shinning the tires and rolled out.

Chuck was parked in front of Moe ' s house when we pulled up. His jet black Caddy sat with the park lights on, under the dog wood trees that covered Moe's drive way. He had a woman in his car and that didn't sit well with Moe.

Chuck agreed not to ever bring anyone to Moe's crib. Now, he had violated. "What's up Moe?" Chuck asked. "This must be your man you all were telling me about. "

"Never mind who he is, who in the hell is she?" Moe asked, pointing his finger at the girl laid back in the Lack.

"Oh, that's my girl, Tanoka. She is a local chick. She's cool. She doesn't know what's up. She thinks I'm just visiting one of my old Army buddies," he said.

Chuck could tell by the look on Moe' s face he was angry, but he didn't really care. He wanted to relay the message from Preme and kick rocks. He had other things he needed to do.

"Preme told me to holla at you all, to let you know we're going to be extra straight this time around. So y'all will probably get ten or fifteen bricks instead of five. "

"Ok" Moe said. "But, make sure you don't ever bring that girl back to my house. I don't care how local she is. Those are the worst kind. "

Chuck jumped in the Lack and pulled off. You could hear the bass from his stereo system pounding, minutes after he left.

"You hear that, Styles?" Moe asked.

I heard everything, but I acted like I didn't hear shit.

"I couldn't hear anything for that loud ass stereo." I said.

Moe explained that I could take more dope to Greensboro this weekend. At least a half kilo. A whole kilo if they got fifteen.

Tanoka had received half of what she asked for. She had convinced Chuck to spend more time with her. She also saw where Moe lived. Agent Goodwin was going to be pleased when he received this information. He needed some information to pass on to his supervisors.

Since Chuck had been in Fayetteville this time, he hadn't mentioned Preme. Tanoka was cautious about asking questions about him. She figured he hadn't come to Fayetteville yet with the coke. Tanoka suggested to Chuck that they go back to the room.

He agreed with her. Quiet is kept, Tanoka had Chuck turned out, opened, sprung! He looked forward to coming to Fayetteville once a week just to see her.

Once they arrived at the room Tanoka said she was hungry and she asked Chuck to go and pick them up something to eat. She added that she had a surprise for him when he returned. He went to China Town to get egg rolls and fried rice, thinking about his surprise along the way.

When she entered the room she immediately called Agent Goodwin. She assured him that nothing had gone down with the Supreme Team this weekend, but it was about to. She confirmed the address, what was perceived to be Moe's.

"As soon as Preme comes to town, I'll let you know," she told Goodwin.

He got off the phone and called his boss to fill him in on what was going on with Operation Hurricane.

Supreme arrived in St.Pauls, about five minutes after Tanoka had gotten off the phone with Goodwin. He paged Chuck from their home in St.Pauls. St.Pauls was thirty minutes from Fayetteville. No one but Preme, his girlfriend and Chuck knew about the house in St.Pauls.

While Chuck waited for his fried rice and egg rolls, he returned Preme's call. He told Chuck that he would get with Huntman and the rest of them in two hours. He needed to set up somewhere first he explained. He said he'd call him back as soon as he did.

Chuck paged Huntman, Wilk and Moe. It didn't matter which one he talked to. Either one could inform the other two about what was going down. Moe was the first one to call Chuck back. Chuck relayed the message and told Moe to be on stand by in two hours. "Its going to be on and popping," he said to Moe.

Moe then called Wilk and Huntman and we all went on FSU's campus. We decided to kick it there until we heard from Preme or Chuck again.

Chuck hurried back to the room, anticipating his surprise. When he opened the door Tanoka had on a red and white Christmas teddy. She turned around twice, displaying her ornaments for him.

"You like, " she asked Chuck.

"No! Me love," he said and pushed her back on the bed.

An hour later, long after he had enjoyed his surprise, Chuck's pager began to go off. Preme put code "777", and Chuck knew that meant that everything was ready. The "777" also represented a location. He was at the Fairfield Inn, next to the mall. After Preme paged him with the location and the "OK" code, he paged him with the room number followed by how many kilos he was going to give Huntman. "214-*15".

"Who is that that keeps paging you?" Tanoka asked Chuck.

"Its Preme, " he said. "Let me call him back to see when he is coming up here."

Tanoka's antennas went up when Chuck said he was calling Preme back. She almost sat straight up in the bed to listen. Then she rolled over instead, acting like she wasn't paying attention.

Chuck paged Moe and hit him with all the codes at once. "777*214*15". "I couldn't get through, " he said to Tanoka. Then he dialed a number he just made up. When an old white lady on the other end said, "Hello, " Chuck began acting like he was talking to Preme.

"What's up my Nigga? Oh yeah! You'll be here Friday morning. That's cool.

I'll see you then."

The old white lady just sat puzzled, and listened. She didn't hang up until Chuck did.

We were in the middle of being signed into the female's dorm when Moe received the page from Chuck.

"Damn! " he said. "I knew it."

We started to shake our heads in unison. We knew it had to be Chuck or Preme.

"Lets ride y'all " Moe said.

"Y'all go ahead. I'll be right here when y'all get back, " I said, hugging one of the girls we'd just met.

"Me too," Wilk said. "I'll be right here with Styles."

Moe and Huntman rolled out to handle the business. Wilk and I stayed in the dorm with all the fine girls.

Thursday night Chuck left Tanoka in the hotel and told her he would be back later. He thought she had acted very strange the entire time he was in DaVille. She was asking questions she normally would not ask. Just like the other three guys she had set up, Chuck had no idea she was working with the "Folks". He was under the impression she was trying to have him set up to be robbed. The girls down in Miami did it to out of town niggas all the time so he was hip to the game.

Friday morning when Tanoka woke up, Chuck still hadn't made it back. She paged him and he never returned her pages. Now, she knew why he had left two hundred dollars on the table. To pay for the room and to catch a taxi home.

I was on the road to Greensboro before six o'clock with a whole "Joint." Thirty-six ounces! I went back to the Embassy Suites and checked in for the weekend. I called Tory and let him know I had something big for him. He was glad to hear that. The coke from last week was so good, he said, the guys on the Hill wouldn't buy anything unless it was from him. He said he had hoped I had more this weekend. I had hoped he'd say that!

When I pulled up Tory and Kiwi were sitting on the porch. I hadn't seen Kiwi since I had seen him at the store a week ago. His appearance was a lot better than the last time I saw him. He was so clean he didn't look like the same person. To be honest, he looked like the Kiwi I use to know.

"What's up fellas?" I asked.

"What's up G.I. Styles?" Kiwi said in return.

"Come on in the house Styles," said Tory.

Tory opened the screen door and I opened the door and walked inside. I sat down in the living room and turned on the t.v.

"Turn it to channel 45," Kiwi said. "Ultra Man is still on."

I threw him the remote control and he started flicking through the channels.

"Come on in here Styles," Tory said, as he led the way to the kitchen and sat down. I followed him carrying the bag of coke. I opened it up, exposing the ten ounces.

"How much money you got?" I asked.

"I got enough for six ounces, " He said.

"If you buy six, I'll front you the other four," I said holding up four bags in my hand. "You just got to get me the money back before Sunday evening."

"Don't worry about that. Consider all of this sold. Do you have anymore?" he asked.

"Yeah, a lot more," I said. "And I need to sell it all before Sunday."

"If it's the same coke as last week, I'll get rid of all of it for you, " Tory said.

I placed the money in my bag and walked back into the living room. I gave Kiwi a soul shake and I bopped out the door.

Lil' Kenny's block was jumping now. He saw me pull up and ran to the car.

"It ain't nothing but garbage coke out here, Styles. If you got some good work I will move it all today."

"How much money you got?" I asked Lil 'Kenny.

"I got enough to buy three or four eggs, " he said.

"If you buy four eggs," I said trying to sound like I already knew that eggs were ounces, "I'll front you four." I held up my fingers.

Lil' Kenny immediately started to count his money. "I need the money for the four I'm fronting you before tomorrow evening," I said.

"I already have these bitches sold."

"I'll be back in a few to get you straight, " I said.

When I returned, Lil' Kenny was resting on his throne, waiting for me. I gave him eight ounces in exchange for four grand. He said he would page me as soon as he sold the first four ounces.

When I got to Madison there wasn't anyone at my mom's house. I decided to call and invite Celeste over, but she wasn't at home either. Then I remembered that she told me she would be out with her cousin, joy riding in Madison.

I cruised around Madison before making a pit stop at the Café' .The Cafe ' was Madison's main attraction for the blacks. Young ones and old ones alike. It was a little hole in the wall joint, ran by Ms. Cathy. She sold chicken plates, bologna sandwiches and cold malt liquor to anyone who had the money to buy it.

I parked under the "Tree" beside the Cafe'. I walked over to the Cafe' and the first person I saw was my friend Tone. I hadn't seen him since the night I saw him at Side Effects.

"What's up Styles?" Tone said. "I won't ever get a chance to come to Fayetteville if you keep coming home on the weekends."

We embraced, patting each other on the back. "When are you going to be ready for me to come down there?" he asked.

"I go to the field in two weeks," I explained. "Then I'm going to have a break when I come from the field, because we're going to Alaska for a month. During that break, you can come down and kick it with me. I still have your number and I'll call you and let you know."

I continued to speak to everyone in the Cafe' I knew them all. I ran my mouth for almost an hour then I decided to walk across the street to the "Block". The "Block" was a huge parking lot that everyone flocked to on the weekends and parked and chilled. It was packed tonight. Everyone knew I was in the Army and they were glad to see me home. I slapped a million high fives and answered just as many airborne questions. While I was talking to one of my homies, I felt a tap on my shoulder. When I turned around I saw the same beautiful, unframed artwork that I had seen at the mall a week ago. I hugged Celeste and told her I had called her a couple of times. She explained that she and her cousin Mechelle had been riding around and visiting other family members. Mechelle walked, (bow legged) over to where I was standing. After speaking to me she told Celeste that she was about to evade the Block. She and Moochie were about to go on their own joy ride.

"What am I suppose to do while you're riding around with Moochie?" Celeste asked.

"You and Dana ride around for a while. You've been talking about him all day anyway." Mechelle started laughing and eased off to Moochie's car. Celeste was in shock from Mechelle' s clever deception.

"So you've been talking about today, huh?" I asked Celeste.

"No, well yeah, sort of. I did kind of talk about you today. " Celeste started to blush.

"Are we going joy riding or are we going to stand up here with all these knuckle heads?" I asked.

Celeste was driving her father's car, a midnight blue, Corvette Stingray. When we pulled off I gave the peace sign to all my homeboys who wished they could have been me at that moment.

We rode and talked for a couple of hours. I was impressed with how mature Celeste was. She was ready to graduate and matriculate into some university. She had not made up her mind what school she wanted to attend.

I knew when Celeste dropped me off at the Tree that she was going to be a part of my life for a long time. Sometimes people meet and they instinctively know that. I knew! Like myself, Celeste was an "esoteric. " A person understood by only a chosen few.

When I got back to Embassy Suites I called Rena. She had paged me twice, she said.

"It must be something wrong with this pager, because I didn't receive any pages." Honestly, I had turned the pager off so Celeste could have my undivided attention.

"When are you going to stop staying at those hotel, and start staying with me?" she asked.

"Are you coming over or are we going to talk on the phone all night?" I said avoiding her question.

When Rena arrived she had on a knee length Shirolen. It was button all the way up.

"It isn't that cold outside, " I said.

She dropped her bags as soon as she was in the room. Then she kicked the door closed and smiled. "It is if you don't have on anything underneath your coat."

Rena unbutton her coat and allowed it to fall to the floor. A mountain of sheepskin formed around her leather Agna boots. I rubbed my head, bewildered, but very excited. I didn't only love a woman who knew exactly what she wanted, but I also loved a spontaneous woman.

She said she practiced the whole week, contracting the muscles in her "Stuff" as she called it. She had noticed the week before in Ho Jo's how that drove me crazy. I had scratched her back, everytime she made her "Stuff" choke Franky. It would have been hard for her not to notice.

When the "Side Show" began, it was evident that she had practiced. Franky got strangled to death! Saturday morning, after a night of super sex, I asked Rena to cook for me. She agreed to fix me some of her macaroni and cheese with the blue berry muffins.

Before I went to check on Lil' Kenny, I took Pops a Pepsi and a big bag of peanuts. He informed me that Page wasn't home and she hadn't been for two days.

"When that boy Red was home she didn't go anywheres. I guess since he's locked up her hot ass can run wild as a pack of stray dogs. I had a dirty bitch to do me like that in 1960."

When I walked away. Pops was still talking cash shit about Page.

"She ain't worth a hill of beans. That boy ain't been gone a good gotdamn week and she's fucking out of both draw-legs….. I tell you what……. "

Lil' Kenny wasn't at his spot when I rode over there. I drove to the barbershop in the Grove to see if he was there, but he wasn't. So I paged him from the barbershop. He was still at home in the bed.

Unlike Red, he didn't come in for a while and then go back out to the block. He would stay out until he ran out of dope, or until money stopped coming. Then and only then would he go home. The money was still coming when Lil' Kenny ran out of dope early this morning. He wanted to make sure he didn't miss me so he got up and came to the barbershop. He asked for the same deal. Four for four. He paid me for the four I fronted him and for four more. I told him I would meet him in an hour at the barbershop.

Tory wasn't home, but he left the money he owed me with Rena .I paged him while I was at his house to see if he wanted anymore work. When he returned the call he said he wanted the same deal also. Six for ten. That left me with nothing but time to do what I wanted to do.

I wasn't worried about Rena popping up unexpectedly, so I paid for an additional night at the Embassy Suites. Before I went back to meet Tory and Lil' Kenny, I called Kami like I had promised. She was waiting on me because I gave her my word that we would go Christmas shopping this weekend. I told her to meet me at the Piccadilly Cafeteria in the Four Seasons Mall.

Back In Miami

Supreme and Chuck were having dinner at the Polo Club off of Biscayne and 162nd Street. Chuck was explaining to Preme how Tanoka was acting strange the entire week.

"She was asking me all kinds of questions, Dawg. She asked when you were coming to DaVille? Where do you stay, when you are there? Shit like that. I think she is trying to have us robbed by some of those Fayetteville niggas." Chuck said.

"Maybe she is "Five-O" Preme said laughing.

"Yeah right! She ain't got sense to be the police, " Chuck said. He continued, "I had her twisted this week. She didn't know if I was coming or going. She wants to come down here too. I'm going to see what she is really up to this coming week. "

"How do you plan to do that?" Preme asked, with a mouthful full of lamb.

"I'm going to put her in a hotel room and tell her I'll be back shortly. I'm going to tell her that I have some things to do for you. I'm going to tell the people at the front desk to keep telephone records for me until I check out. Then after I get the numbers she's calling, I can call them back to see who it is that's going to try to rob us," Chuck said.

67

"Damn nigga! You're on some Inch High-Private Eye shit, huh?" Preme said.
"Better safe than sorry." Chuck replied.

Back In Fayetteville

The Crew had ten more kilos than they normally had. They had already sold seven but the remaining seven was going kind of slow. Moe decided to buy two keys for himself. He had a side hustle going on that nobody else in the Crew knew about. One of the rules of the Supreme Team was never start doing your own thing, outside the rims of the Team. If anyone had potential buyers, you had to bring it before everyone. That allowed everyone a chance to decide if the potential buyer was going to become a part of the Team! Moe had broken this rule. A rule that he created and stressed from day one. He paid Huntman for the two keys and told him he was going to deliver them. He took them directly to his crib and hid them in the ceiling tiles in his bathroom.

Back In Greensboro

I dropped the rest of the coke off and told Tory and Lil 'Kenny that I'd see them Sunday morning. I met Kami at the mall and she and I had dinner. After dinner, she shopped for over an hour.

"Whatever you want for Christmas, you can have, " I said to her.

"I just want you, " she replied.

"You already got me!"

I meant Kami could get whatever she wanted except for a ring. I had "Ring-Ophobia! " I wasn't ready to commit and buy one.

"I thought you said I could have anything I wanted?" Kami said. She stared at the one karat ring on her skinny finger.

"Get the ear rings, " I suggested.

She gave the sparkling ring back to the white girl, who looked like she was afraid we were going to run off with it.

"Give me the ear rings and the necklace," Kami said to the white girl. She was going to make me pay dearly since I didn't want to buy the ring. She had told everyone that I was buying her one for Christmas. It didn't matter to me how much it cost. I was spending money that I didn't lift a finger for.

"Where are we going now?" Kami asked.

"Just follow me, " I replied.

Once we got to the Embassy Suites, I gave Kami the room key and told her I would be back shortly. Rena had promised to cook for me and she had paged me once already. I had played with my food at Piccadillies, but I was going to devour her food.

"What's up for tonight Styles? Are you going to stay here, or are you going to stay at the hotel again?" Rena asked me.

With a mouth full of blue berry muffins, I started to answer her. "I'm going to stay in Madison tonight, I guess. My mom is complaining that she doesn't see me enough when I come home. I will call and see you later, " I said.

I ate until I was about to pop and I still took a plate to go. I wanted Kami to taste some of Rena's good cooking so she'd know what I expected when we got married. I kissed Rena and bounced.

When I got back to the Embassy Suites, I told Kami I stopped by my Aunt Amma Gene's house and she fed me and made me take a plate to go. I let her taste the home made muffins and told her that's what I would be expecting once we got married. She wasn't suspicious about where I had been. She knew she had a good man that loved her enough not to cheat on her.

Sunday morning I got up and paid for extended check out. Between our lovemaking, Kami and I laid around watching t.v. and talking about our future plans together. She said she was ready to leave Stoneville. She wanted to be wherever I was. We even discussed having a child. If it were a boy, it would be named after me, but if it was a girl she wanted to name her Sheneka.

At 1: 30 pm, we said our goodbyes and made promises to see each other the following weekend.

Petey wagged his tail and jumped up as I walked to the door. It startled me because he usually just stayed on the porch. I stopped not sure of what he was going to do. He brushed up beside me demanding to be rubbed. I started walking again and rubbing his huge square head. I looked through the window and Rena was on the sofa asleep. I watched her jump when I knocked on the door, hard like I was the police. She opened the door, and cruised back to her comfortable spot on the sofa.

"Don't knock on that damn door like that," she said, stretching her legs.

"Have you seen your son, Ms. Wright?" I asked.

"Yeah, he said for you to page him when you got here. " She pointed to the phone. I paged Tory and went over and lay on top of Rena.

"Dana, your black ass is heavy," she said.

"I wasn' t heavy the other night, " I said.

She smiled and kissed me .My hands went underneath the small ass Winnie the Pooh t-shirt she had on. Suddenly, the phone rang.

"You just got saved by the bell, " I said to Rena. I got off of her so she could answer the phone.

"You answer it! It's probably Tory calling you back," she said.

"Hello!"

"Damn Styles! You got it like that? You're answering the phones and shit now. I got your cheese. It's going to take me about forty- five minutes to get there though. I'm in Durham."

"Awright, I'll be here waiting on you," I said. I hung up the phone and made a b-line to Rena. Little did Tory know he had just given me the green light to help myself with his mom. I got down on my knees and my head went under the t-shirt this time .The way I ate Rena out drove her wild. She bucked like a wild stallion. This was pay back for exercising those pussy muscles and choking Franky!

Rena was showered and dressed before Tory arrived. He paid me and asked if I had more coke?

"Not until next weekend," I explained.

"I got the whole Hill locked down now,'" Tory said. "I still have most of what I bought from you. I sold what you fronted me first. The rest of it will have to last me until next weekend. "

"You better start sitting on a few ounces, " I said. "In a couple of weeks I go to the field. Then in February, I go to Alaska."

"Alaska!" screamed Rena.

"Yeah, for thirty days. We got to do some winter training. We might have to fight some Russians or something."

"Man, fuck dat, " Tory said. "I ain't fighting shit in the cold. "

"Are you going to call me this week, Styles?" Rena asked.

"Yeah, I'll call and check up on you to make sure you are doing fine."

I slapped hands with Tory and hugged Rena and walked onto the porch. Tory walked me out and said, "That was a good looking out this weekend. I needed the money," he said. "I'm trying to get my own crib."

"Sometimes I will be able to look out for you, but there are going to be times I won't be able to. It all depends on my peeps in Ft.Bragg."

Lil' Kenny was standing against a black Buick Regal when I pulled up. He was talking to his girlfriend who was twice his size. They were and odd couple, if I've ever seen one. He politely excused himself and pimped over to where I was parked. He dug deep into his right pocket, pulling out what appeared to be a million dollars. Just as quick as he pulled it out, he stuffed it back into his pocket.

"Wrong stash, " he said. Then he entered his left pocket and pulled out a stash that was folded with ponytail holders wrapped around it.

"Here you go Styles. Four G's. Now you can go back to Ft. Bragg and play like you're a soldier. You got those crackers fooled," he said.

"I'll be back next weekend and I'll page you to let you know I'm in town."

I pulled off and put Keith Sweat in the tape deck. I turned it all the way up and headed for the highway. I rode back singing along with Keith. I had 36,000 dollars. I had never seen that much money in my life. I took my time, being extra careful not to speed. I stopped in Siler City to get some gas, then in Sanford to grab a bite to eat.

When I got to Bragg, I put the money in my bag and went straight to my room. Poosh was in the room reclining on his beanbag listening to some very heavy metal music, that I couldn't understand. I took my bag and locked it in my wall locker. I needed to be in the room alone so I could count out the money and get what was mine. Poosh was eating some potato chips from the vending machine. He was always eating.

"You have fun at home this weekend, Cherry?" he asked spitting little specks of chips in the air.

"Yeah, I had a great time, " I said.

"Did you get laid?" he asked.

"Does a bear shit in the woods?" I asked. "I got laid by two different women. It could have been more but I didn't have enough time," I said.

Poosh looked at me like he didn't believe me and said, "Yeah right!"

"Are you hungry Poosh?" I asked, already knowing the answer to that question was "yes", but this a way I could get him out of the room.

"Yeah, why? Did you bring some soul food from home?"

"No, but I'm hungry too. If you fly, I'll buy."

Poosh jumped to his feet. That sounded like a winner to him. "What cha want to eat?" he asked.

"Pizza will be fine with me," I said. I gave Poosh a twenty-dollar bill and he was on his way to the Pizza Hut.

I watched through the window as he walked out and got into his car. I locked the door as soon as he started his engine. I pulled the money out and started counting. I counted $37,000, instead of $36,000. I counted it twice, just to make sure. Someone had given me an extra thousand bucks, so I put $4,600, in my locker with the $2,800 that was hid in the back.

Things had picked up for Huntman and the Crew. They ended up selling the remaining five kilos and needing more. Moe was determined to sit on his two keys he had bought. He had plans to break them down to sell in his own little spot.

When I paged them, they were at Huntman's house. They gave me directions but I still got lost. When I called them again, Wilk came to where I was. I followed him back to Huntman's house and joined in on the fun they were having. Some of Huntman's friends from Pittsburgh had flown down for the holidays. They drank in the den, while we counted money in his bedroom. Huntman was surprised that I sold an entire kilo.

"I could sell more than that if I went to a few more spots," I told them. They all insisted that what I was doing was more than enough for now. Huntman handed me a roll of
money after we finished counting.

"I already got my money," I said.

"I know you have, just take this and consider it as jump pay" he said smiling.

It was a thousand dollars! Since there were only three women from Pittsburgh I told them I was heading back to the barricks. Nobody tried to stop me. They all said their "later on's" as I walked out the door.

An empty pizza box sat on the table in my room. Poosh was on the beanbag asleep. I laughed as I eased my clothes off and got into bed. He had gotten drunk and ate all the pizza.

CHAPTER 14

It was business as usual Monday morning. We ran twelve miles and did a muscle failure, push-up, and sit-up routine. Wilk and I had started to meet each other every morning at breakfast. But, this morning, I was too worn out to even think about food after the PT session.

When he finished eating he came to my room to see why I hadn't met him in the chow hall. I was stretched out on the floor when he knocked on my door.

"Yeah, its open, " I said.

"Damn, dawg, they ran y'all like that this morning?" Wilk asked.

"They ran us all the way to the Delta Force Compound, then we ran down Long Street and back to Fire Break Six. After all that running we did muscle failure, push-ups and sit-ups. I'm tired as ten niggas on the back of a pick up truck that just finished priming tobacco, " I said.

Wilk thought that was funny. "Don't let Sgt. Marero hear you say that."

"What's up?" I asked.

"I'll probably go with you to Greensboro this weekend. Chuck called yesterday and said he has something for Moe and Huntman to do this weekend, so I'll hang with you. We can get with our girls at A&T."

"I don't know about that right now," I said. "It seems that they're, upset with me."

"They're mad at you not me," Wilk said. "We are going to drive my car this weekend. You haven't seen my wheels. "

Wilk told me he would get with me later on in the week to make plans for leaving Ft.Bragg, to go to Greensboro. He left the room screaming something about I need to get up and take a shower.

The next three nights I talked to Celeste on the phone. Rena, Lakisha, and Pricilla had all been conquered by Wild Styles! I could tell that Celeste was going to be totally different. Things naturally moved slowly when we talked. We agreed on seeing each other when I came home.

Wednesday night, Chuck met with Huntman and Moe. He explained to them the situation with Tanoka. Moe was pissed off to the highest degree!

"That's why you don't bring people with you when you come to my crib. Especially, a bitch. You know to keep a bitch out of your business." Moe said. He continued to fuss and Chuck couldn't say anything because he knew he was dead wrong.

"Now I have to creep in an out of my own damn house!"

"Just leave the bitch alone, " Huntman suggested.

"I can't do that, " Chuck responded quickly.

"Why?" Huntman and Moe asked in unison.

"Because, if I cut her off now and she is trying to rob me, she going to direct the stick up kids to Moe's crib for sure."

It made sense. The best thing was to go along with Chuck's plan. Get the phone list from the hotel and get the addresses through information. Once the addresses were obtained, then they would watch the house or houses and find out who was who?

"These motherfuckers think they're playing with some rookies, huh?" Huntman asked. That Ranger School shit, twinkling like new chrome in his eyes. "We will watch the niggas who are suppose to be watchin us. Don't them niggas know we do this shit for real?" Huntman started getting hyped.

"I'm the best that ever done this shit! " he screamed.

After Huntman cooled down, Chuck informed them that Preme was already in DaVille. He was waiting for Chuck to page him to let him know all systems were go. Preme was at the Cotton Aide Inn, on Yadkin Road. When they arrived, Huntman and Chuck went into the room while Moe stayed outside to be the lookout. Preme gave Huntman five kilos and assured him he would get more coke the following week.

"Now what's up Chuck?" Huntman asked. "What cha gonna do about that sorry bitch?"

"Drop that coke off and I'll page you back later to let you know what I'm going to do. She knows I don't carry much money, so I don't think nothing is going to go down, unless she thinks Preme is going to be around. I already got a room at the Ramada Inn down town, and I've talked to the front desk clerk to arrange for me to get the phone list when I check out. I'm going to go and pick her up now, " Chuck said.

Chuck pulled up in front of Tanoka' s house. She hadn't heard from him since he'd left Thursday night, and she wondered if she was going to ever hear from him again. She was pleased to see him when he pulled up but, when he knocked on the door she opened it cursing.

"Motherfucker! Where do you get off leaving me in a hotel room alone? Yo ass is crazy! You haven't returned any of my pages then you show up at my door almost a week later like nothing has happened. "

"Something came up, " he said.

"Something came up! Nigga, that's what phones are for, " she yelled.

After a few minutes of masquerading, she gave Chuck a tight hug and kissed him on the lips. If she was really upset she would have fussed more than that, Chuck thought. Now, she was hugging and kissing him like nothing was wrong. He knew something was up with her. She was changing personalities like the seasons change.

"You know I get busy Honey, " he said. "I apologize. " Tanoka kissed him again.

"Are you going with me?" he asked.

"Are you going to leave me again?" Chuck shook his head no and smiled his half smile.

"In that case let me grab my things, " Tanoka said. She packed her bags quickly. Then she went into the kitchen and wrote her mom a note. "I'm gone with Chuck, I'll call you later." She hung the note on the refrigerator and they left.

When they got to the Ramada Inn, Chuck started volunteering information that Tanoka wanted to hear.

"Preme won't be in Fayetteville until Friday night. His van broke down last Thursday night, that's why I had to leave so fast. I didn't want to leave my partner on the side of Highway 95. I got some big business to do this weekend while I'm here. Do you want to go with me back to Miami this weekend?" he asked her.

Jackpot! Tanoka thought. "Yeah, I'll go." She tried not to sound like she really wanted to go. Chuck found that to be strange also, because that's all she had been talking about. Going to Miami! He made mental note of all her funny signs.

She dropped her bags on the floor and stretched out on the bed. Chuck hoped she wasn't trying to have him robbed. He was really starting to dig her and the sex was great! If he had to, he thought, he would leave her alone and advise Moe to move to another spot.

Three hours had passed and there hadn't been any pages from Chuck. Huntman became very concerned and paged Chuck himself. Chuck and Tanoka were sound asleep when his pager went off. It woke Tanoka up. She eased the pager off of his pants and pressed the square button. "555-3033, " was displayed on the screen. Tanoka wanted to copy the number down. She reached across Chuck to get the pen and Ramada Inn pad. Her arm brushed his shoulders and woke him up. Chuck didn't move though. He wanted to see what she was doing. She grabbed the pen and pad. When she pressed the button again to display the number once more, Chuck quickly turned over.

"What da fuck are you doing!" he screamed causing Tanoka to almost jump off the bed. "Why are you getting ready to write that number down?"

Tanoka was a veteran at playing games. She could think on her feet quickly.

"I know you got another bitch in Fayetteville, Chuck! I know that's who's always paging you when we're together. I also know you left me Thursday and went to stay with that bitch! I don't believe you had to pick up Preme. I love you Chuck. If I got to go thru your shit to find out what's going on with you I will."

Tanoka started to cry softly. Chuck embraced her tightly. Now he realized he had become paranoid for nothing. Of course she would ask all kinds of questions if she thought he had another woman in DaVille.

"I'm sorry, Baby Girl," he said. "I shouldn't have yelled at you like that. I don't have another woman in Fayetteville. I don't have another woman period! You're all I need. I'm sorry," he said again.

As he held her close, she wiped her phony tears from her face. She looked into the huge mirror on the dresser and smiled at herself.

Chuck picked up the phone and called Huntman back. In a few words he explained that he had been, totally wrong about the entire Tanoka situation. He was, "Way off" he continued to say. Everything was cool. Back to normal. He told him he would page them next week.

When Chuck woke up, he didn't wake Tanoka up. He showered and put on his clothes. When he quietly reached for his keys, her hand swiftly grabbed his wrist.

"Where are you going? Are you leaving me again?" she asked.

"No, I'm going to get you some breakfast."

She looked over to make sure there wasn't any money left on the table. If he was going to leave, she knew he would at least leave her some money to pay for the room and a ride home. The table didn't have any money on it just an unused ashtray and a Mt.Dew can.

"Trust me, Honey, I ain't going nowhere until Saturday morning and you'll be with me then."

As soon as the door closed, Tanoka was on the phone. "Hey mama, " she said. "How are you? I might not be home for a few days because Chuck is suppose to take me to Florida. I'll call you and let you know."

After she called her mom she dialed Agent Goodwin' s number.

"Goodwin," He said when he answered the phone.

"Hey, dis is Tanoka .I'm in the Ramada Inn with Chuck now. The drugs are going to get here Friday night, but I don't know what time. Also, he is taking me to Miami this weekend. I suggest you hold off your hungry dogs so we can locate the bigger fish down there."

Goodwin was overjoyed. He told her to call him back every time Chuck left the room. He wanted to be kept informed of his every move. She agreed and hung up the phone. She lay back to watch t.v. not believing how she had flipped the script on Chuck when he caught her red handed. She looked in the mirror again, admiring the beautiful reflection, and smiled.

Wilk sat down with his normal breakfast, a couple of pancakes and a cheese omelet.

"What time are you going to be ready tomorrow?" He asked.

"I'll be ready as soon as the formation is over. I am not even changing my clothes. I'm wearing my BDU's (Battle Dress Uniform) home," I said.

"Fuck dat," Wilk said. "I got to change my rags. I am not trying to look like Rambo." We laughed and continued to eat.

Wilk said he had to pick up the coke after formation. He said he would be ready to bounce at 5: 30. "That would give me enough time to shower and change my clothes after all, " I added.

Tanoka didn't even want to leave the room, instead she sent Chuck out for everything. While on an errand for Tanoka, Chuck called Preme and explained how he had been wrong. "I was assuming things, " He said.

"Don't assume things," Preme said. "When you assume, you make an "Ass out of "U" and "Me". That old saying flew right over Chuck's head.

Friday morning when Chuck and Tanoka were checking out of the Ramada Inn, the front desk clerk gave Chuck a copy of the phone list. He did not need it now, he thought. He decided to throw it a way. When he started for the trashcan Tanoka called to him, "Chuck! The police is getting ready to write you a ticket. "

He stuffed the paper in his pocket and ran to his illegally parked car. His pleadings worked because the police allowed him to move his car from the handicapped parking space. He pulled in front of the Ramada Inn and Tanoka rolled his bag out and threw her bag in the back of the car.

"How long does it take to get to Miami, " she asked.

"About 13 or 14 hours. I'm glad you're riding with me, you can help me drive," Chuck said as he put the car in gear and pulled off.

I drove Moe's car back out to the gas station. I knew I was going to be riding with Wilk but I didn't know what type of car he drove. It wasn't hard to figure out as soon as I pulled into the parking lot of the gas station. Wilk had a flip-flop purple Escort GT. It was lowered about five inches from the ground. We never rode in his car because only two people could ride in it. The entire rear was consumed with speakers. Moe and Huntman, still in their fatigues, sat waiting on me.

"Leave it running, " Moe said when I pulled up. He got out of the Blazer and into his car. As soon as he shut the door Huntman tooted his horn and pulled off.

"We got something to do," Moe said. "Ya'll be careful, and don't speed," Moe added.

I thought he only advised that when we were driving his car. He knew how important it was to take precautions.

"Get your yella ass off the phone and let's roll, " I said to Wilk. "Time is money." I lowered myself in the Escort. It felt like I was sitting in a go-cart. The music wasn't turned up, but Wilk's pride and joy vibrated with every bass drop. He got in, closed his door and turned up the music.

"Lets ride," he yelled out.

When we got to Greensboro, my head was about to pop. Eric B and Rakim had blasted my eardrums for an hour and a half. I jumped out of the car and slammed the door. I was happy to see the Embassy Suites. I had become a regular at the expensive hotel.

When I walked in the front desk receptionist, Brianna, spoke to me before I had a chance to sit my things down.

"Hey Mr. Styles! I see you're back with us again this weekend."

"Wilk looked impressed that she knew my name. "Oh you've been staying here instead of the Roof?" he asked. "Boy, you are a true trick "

Brianna started smiling. I hadn't noticed how cute she was until that moment.

"The top floor, please, " I said, with an angelic smile.

We unpacked our things and I picked up the phone. I paged Tory and then Lil' Kenny. Lil' Kenny called me back first.

"Yeah, did somebody page Kenny?" he asked.

"What's up Lil' Kenny?" I said.

"Who is this?"

"This is Styles."

"Yo! What's happening Styles?" Lil' Kenny said. "I'm glad to hear from you. It's bone dry around here. When you coming through?" he asked.

"Yeah, what do you need?" I asked.

"Since it ain't nothing around here, I'll buy eight if you front me eight."

"OK, I'll be through there in about an hour."

"Please hurry up. I'm missing a lot of money right now," he said.

A couple of minutes later Tory called me and said he wanted the same deal as last week. I talked him into buying ten instead of six, and I told him I'd front him ten instead of four. When I hung up with Tory, I told Wilk that I had sold the whole kilo that quick.

"We don't move them that fast in DaVille," he said in disbelief.

"Dope Man, " by NWA, pounded the speakers in the Escort GT when Wilk pulled up on the block, the flip-flop, purple paint and his extremely loud stereo made everyone and their mama, stop doing whatever they were doing. Cool cats pointed and bobbed their heads at his fly ride. He loved this effect. He laughed at people when they paused to admire his purple creation.

"Gotdamn, this bitch is nice as fuck," Lil' Kenny said. "Styles, you just in time. That's that shit playing right there. "Dope Man, Dope Man, Yeah that's me!" Lil' Kenny cried out. He passed me two stacks of paper. "That's four "G's" each."

I handed him the bag and put the money under the front seat. "This is a come up for me," he said. "I'm about to lock this whole Grove down, fucking with you Styles."

He walked off picking up on the lyrics of Dope Man.

"Fuck you bitch, who am I, the Dope Man......." I yelled and reminded Lil' Kenny to page me when he finished selling the first eight. He agreed and disappeared into the Grove Store, still bopping his head to NWA.

"Hey stranger, " Rena said, when she opened the door. She gave me a hug and invited Wilk and I inside. "Tory! " she yelled.

"Damn, " Wilk said in a voice loud enough for Rena to hear. I pushed his arm and told him to chill out.

We sat down and Rena went to get Tory.

"Who the fuck is she?" Wilk whispered.

"That's the older lady I was telling you about."

"The one with the great pussy?" he asked.

"Yep!" I said.

"Dawg, she is fine as hell. Her son is gonna kill you."

Rena came back in the living room and said Tory would be out in a second and then she walked into the kitchen.

"What's up Styles?" Tory said.

"What's up Tee? This is my partner from Philly, Wilk, this is Tory."

They slapped hands and we all sat down. Wilk pulled out the bag of coke and handed it to Tory. He handed me the money and started to explain how dry it was in Greensboro.

"If I had this two days ago, it would have been gone two days ago," Tory said. "Y'all staying for dinner?" he asked.

"Nah, we got to go to Madison tonight, " I answered.

"I'll page you tomorrow and let you know if I finished your ten, " Tory said.

"Tell your mom I said I will talk to her later."

"Nigga, you go and tell her. Don't get shy now!"

I walked in the kitchen and eased up behind Rena. I kissed the back of her neck and she turned around quickly with a big knife in her hand.

"Styles, you're gonna get hurt," she said.

"You gonna hurt me?"

"Not intentionally," she said as she put her arms around me. "Are you staying for dinner?" she asked.

"No, I'm going to Madison."

"Are you staying down there again?"

"I don't know yet. I doubt it."

"Are you going to be home tonight?" I asked.

"I don't know yet. I doubt it," she said trying to be funny.

"Alright, I'll be back here tonight around 12:00."

She gave me a kiss and softly bit my neck. "I'll see you then." -

When I walked out of the door Petey was laying in his usual spot. I hadn't noticed when I got there that he wasn't on the porch. Wilk bugged out when he saw how big the dog was. He wouldn't leave out of the house until Tory walked Petey around the back of the house. When he did, Wilk ran and jumped in his car.

"Dag, I love the paint on this Escort. Who did you get to paint it?" Tory asked Wilk.

"My man in DaVille painted it. His name is JD. His shop is on the Dirty Murk."

Tory didn't have a clue what the Dirty Murk was. He just shook his head like he knew what Wilk was talking about.

I stopped by Celeste's house as soon as I got to Madison. She was at home babysitting her niece. She and I talked for about an hour while Wilk watched t.v. and played with her niece. I intended to stay longer, but I could tell Wilk was getting bored. I hugged and kissed Celeste softly on the cheek before we left. I promised to call her the next day.

Since Wilk wanted to see his friend at A&T, I didn't even visit my family while I was in Madison. I would see them later, I promised myself.

We drove back to the room and I called Lakisha as soon as I got to the phone. She wasn't in her room so I called Pricilla.

"Hello, " she said.

"Hey Chocolate Bunny."

There was a small pause before Pricilla finally spoke. "Hey, " she said.

"Are you busy? 'I I asked.

"No, I'm just watching t.v. and talking to one of my girlfriends."

"Are you trying to see me tonight?" I asked.

Another pause and then came the response, "Yeah, why not?"

"Ask her where is her girlfriend at?" Wilk said in the background.

"Wilk said where is your girlfriend?"

"Tina is in her room, but she has a very bad cold. She won't be coming out, " Pricilla said.

"What's up with your friend in the room with you now?" I asked.

Pricilla whispered to me, "She might be too big for him. " Then she spoke up and said, "Yeah, she's cute."

I began to laugh lightly. I didn't want to let Wilk know that something was funny.

"You two come to the Embassy Suites. We are in room 1112."

"Tina has the flu, but Pricilla has another friend who is coming with her, " I said to Wilk.

"What does she look like?" he asked.

"Pricilla told me she was cute. "

Wilk jumped up and ran to the shower. He was getting ready for Big Mama and he didn't even know it. This was definitely going to be funny to me.

"That's them knocking at the door, " Wilk said. He rushed to open the door and before he did, he blew himself a kiss in the mirror.

When he opened the door, Big Mama, who was very cute, glided her fat ass in smiling from ear to ear. Wilk was speechless.

"Y'all can go in the bedroom. We'll stay in here," I said.

"I'm Deborah." she said to Wilk, leading the way to the bedroom. She sat on the end of the bed and kicked off her shoes.

"I'm Wilk." he said. "Please to meet you." He looked back at Pricilla and me and started shaking his head.

"Hell Naw!" he said, balling up his face. I pushed him into the bedroom and closed the door.

"You still mad at me?" I asked Pricilla while I hugged and kissed her neck.

"I just don't want you to lie to me. I already know you're sleeping with Kisha. Hell, you fucked her first, but don't lie to me. I can handle you seeing her, but just don't lie to me."

Pricilla kissed me and then pushed me back onto the sofa. She unzipped my pants, and I took a look at the clock on the wall, it was 10:45. I had an hour and fifteen minutes to satisfy Pricilla and to come up with a lie that didn't sound like it was a lie. I was not going to stand Rena up because I knew she wasn't going to stand for that.

Pricilla and I laid beside each other, on the pullout sofa bed.

"It's pretty quiet in there, isn't it?" I asked. "I hope your big ass friend hasn't killed my partner."

Pricilla started laughing. "She needed to get her some. That's all she talks about is sucking dick. "

I looked at the clock and it was 11:50. "Oh shit!" I said.

"What is it?" Pricilla asked.

"I forgot I am supposed to be somewhere at 12: 00. "

"You should have thought about that an hour ago. "

"This guy owes me some money and I am suppose to meet him. " I got up and started putting on my clothes. I threw Pricilla her panties and bra.

"Get dressed and I'm going to drop you off at campus. "

"What about Deborah?" she asked.

When I knocked on the door Deborah answered instead of Wilk.

"Yeah, what's up?" she said.

"Wilk, give me the car keys. I'm going to meet... "

Before I finished the sentence, the door cracked open and a big hand with gold bracelets, dropped the keys to the floor. I picked them up and turned toward Pricilla.

"Don't worry about Deborah, " I said. "Worry about Wilk."

Pricilla and I both laughed as we got dressed. That eased some of the tension that was there a minute ago.

I dropped her off and went straight to Rena's. Her car wasn't there and I hoped it was because Tory had it. When I pulled up Petey stood and walked to the edge of the steps. I rolled the window down and began to talk to him so he would know it was me. The porch light came on and Rena opened the door. Petey lay back down in his spot and I got out of the car.

I knew I smelled like fresh pussy. It hadn't been thirty minutes since I ate Pricilla. I bent down and rubbed Petey. He licked me dead in my face.

He probably smelled the pussy on my flavor saver, and wanted to taste it himself. I knew what Rena would say when she saw this take place.

"I hope you don't think you're going to come in here and put your hands on me after you sit out there and rub that dog. Then you let him lick you in the face. I'm going to start the shower for you."

She turned and went into the bathroom. "Thanks Petey, " I said as I patted him on his head, whispering into his clipped ears. "You saved me tonight."

I walked to the bathroom and got undressed and showered. I washed off Chocolate Bunny's scent and got in the bed with Rena and made love to her all night.

The next morning, I eased my way into the suite. The bedroom door was still closed. As crazy as it sounds, I had to make sure Wilk was alright. I cracked the door and peeked inside. Wilk was holding Big Mama like he was afraid she was going to get a way from him. She was awake, but you couldn't pay her a million dollars to move. She smiled and I pulled the door closed.

Back In Miami

Chuck and Tanoka had slept all night. Both of them were exhausted from their 18 hour trip. It took extra hours because of the one thousand pit stops. Tanoka had to use the rest room every hour and she had to stop at every Outlet Mall on Highway 95 South.

Tanoka couldn't believe the size of Chuck's house. The living room was the equivalent of their entire house in Fayetteville. Six bedrooms, five bathrooms and a back yard that could be used to play the Super Bowl Game!

Chuck, Preme and a Cuban guy lived in the fairy tale looking mansion, he explained. She asked if she could get another tour of the house. She was sleepy last night, she told him, so he showed her around the mansion again.

The more he showed her the more she started to have feelings for Chuck. Feelings for the house. Maybe she was making a mistake this time around she thought. After all Chuck wasn't like her other three "X" boyfriends. He could give her a lot more than any of them could. Plus, the agents weren't paying her like he would dish out. She'd have to come up with some type of plan to throw Agent Goodwin for good. She could get use to living in a six bedroom mansion in South Beach. She just hoped she hadn't given Goodwin to much information already.

Chuck had a huge walk in closet in his bedroom. It was equipped with a washer and dryer. He took his pants off and emptied his pockets on the shelf. He threw his jeans in the washer along with some more dirty laundry. He grabbed his keys and his money that was in his pocket but he didn't bother getting the room receipt and the phone list.

"So, do you really like the place?" he asked Tanoka.

"Hell yeah, I love it! No wonder you haven't brought me down here. You probably have to beat bitches away from here with a stick, " she said.

It's not about bitches Tanoka, it's all about you," Chuck said in his most sincere voice. He kissed and undressed her, and they made love.

Back In Greensboro

Big Mama walked out of the room and picked up her keys from the table.

"Why did you take Pricilla back last night?" she asked.

"I had some things to do, " I said.

She slung her large purse over her shoulder and started for the door. She had a very silly smile on her face, as if she knew I couldn't wait for her big "Jennifer Holiday" looking ass to leave. She knew I was going to pick with Wilk.

"Nice meeting you, " she said as she closed the door.

Wilk had got up and went to the shower. I turned the knob, but he locked the door. I started knocking and laughing. I even made threats to Wilk that I would ruin his "Pretty Boy" image. Moe and Huntman would pay for dirt like this on"Mr.Trick!" "Mr.Cool Daddy!" with a big girl. "Mr. He likes them like Lisa Bonet"!

"You can't wash her big ass out of your mind. Come on out. " I screamed.

Wilk came out of the bathroom laughing hard "Please, please don't tell nobody about this. Please! "

I was laughing so hard I was crying now. "I saw you holding her this morning." I put my arms out in a big circle, like I was holding a 55gallon drum. "I hope you didn't eat Big Mama," I said.

"Hell nah! But laugh if you want to, Big Mama can suck a bowling ball through a coffee straw. She had me popping my toes last night."

I looked at Wilk and he hadn't noticed that she had put a dark hickey on his yellow neck. That put the icing on the cake. I thought I was going to die!

We went to the mall and did some Christmas shopping. Christmas was next weekend and I hadn't bought any presents except for Kami's. I had accumulated a lot of people on my list in the last month. I was having sex with the girls, at least I could do was buy them a present. To keep it simple I bought everyone the same sweater. I did get different wrappings on the boxes. I shopped for my mother and Granny too. I spent the entire day delivering presents. Just in case I didn't make it back next weekend. Saturday night, Wilk and I were at Rena's when Lil' Kenny paged me.

When I called him back he was ready for me to come get my money. We rode over to the Grove and picked up the money and Lil ' Kenny asked me if I was going to be straight next weekend since it was going to be Christmas? I told him I would be.

"Just because it's Christmas, doesn't mean we can't get money. Hell yeah, I'll be straight. I'll sell Santa some coke if he wants it," I said making everyone laugh.

When we got back to Rena' s, Tory had made it home .He had locked the Hill down and he had set up shop at another spot in Durham. He had met a guy from Durham, named Clark, while he was in state prison for shooting the bastard who beat his mom. He and Clark had hooked up and were conducting business.

"Styles let me holla at cha, " Tory said.

We went back to his room. He handed me the money and asked me to count it.

"Why?' I asked. "I trust you."

"I want to start doing it like this because I lost a thousand dollars last weekend, handing niggas money and not counting it."

"That was you?" I exclaimed. "I knew someone had given me an extra grand. "

"You got it?" Tory asked.

"Yeah! You gave it to me."

"At least I know you are not petty. A petty nigga would have kept that shit. "

"Just give me seven thousand instead of eight and we'll be straight. "

Tory counted out a thousand dollars and handed me seven thousand.

"It's seven thousand. I have counted it twice. I really appreciate it, Styles, " he said.

From that point on Tory never tripped on or said anything else about his mom again.

Big Mama must have had some great head, because Saturday night, she stayed with Wilk again. He didn't care who found out about it!

Sunday afternoon, we packed our things and were preparing for our short trip back to Ft.Bragg. Pricilla and her friend had packed their things too, to go home for the Christmas holidays. They were going to leave Saturday but Wilk had convinced Big Mama to stay one more night.

Once we got on Highway 421, I went to sleep, despite the Kenwoods that were beating my brains out. Wilk drove all the way back without stopping.

I got my $2,600 from the $36,000, and Wilk held on to the rest of the money. He dropped me off in the parking lot across from the barricks and kept going.

I walked in and noticed my name was on the board. When I checked the message list, Celeste had called me twice. I went straight in the dayroom and got on the telephone. Celeste and I talked for hours, until we both were about to fall asleep on the phone.

CHAPTER 15

Chuck had treated Tanoka like royalty over the weekend. That was evident when she tussled with her Gucci luggage, filled with Fendi and Loui Vitton as she walked into the airport. It contained enough Christmas presents to last a lifetime .She checked in her bags and requested a window seat. Tanoka wasn't fond of flying, but in this case it was much better than driving 18 hours.

Tanoka craned her neck to look out of the window. From the sky, Miami looked like a huge patch of grass, sandwiched between swamp and sea. She looked into the cotton daub skies and thought of how she could wiggle her way out of the web she had weaved. Agent Goodwin wasn't going to be pleased at all. Fuck him! She thought. She would be extremely happy in Florida with Chuck.

After dropping Tanoka off at the airport, Chuck returned home to pack his things. He was taking a flight two hours later, but he told her he would arrive in Fayetteville on Wednesday. Even though he felt like he could trust her, he still didn't want to involve her in his business. Preme had left the night before, on his weekly drive to North Carolina, Chuck knew things would be popping when he arrived.

He walked into his closet and started grabbing clothes off the hangers. He reached inside of the dryer and neatly folded his favorite pair of jeans. He laid them on top of the other folded clothes in his own Gucci bag. When he turned to exit the closet, he noticed the hotel receipt and the phone list. He opened the phone list for the first time and glanced at it. He was familiar with a couple of the numbers. He recognized the pay phone number Preme always paged him from in Miami and Tanoka's home number. He had made a couple of calls himself to some folks in DaVille, but there were a few more numbers he did not recognize. But, one particular number appeared on the list five times.

Chuck checked his pager to see if it was one of the numbers Huntman had paged him from while he was in Fayetteville. Then he stopped checking because he knew he didn't call anyone at the same number five times. He reached for the phone and before he touched the receiver, it began to ring. It startled Chuck a little and he laughed slightly. He threw the paper on his dresser an answered the phone.

"Hello, " he said.

"You still at home?" Preme asked.

"Yeah, my flight doesn't leave until another hour or so."

"I'm glad I caught you. Look in my bedroom and bring me my yellow gators when you come to N.C. " Preme said.

"That's all you called me for?" Chuck asked. He sighed deeply and hung up the phone. He threw his bag over his shoulder and went to Preme's room.

After he packed the gators, Chuck drove to the airport.

Back in Ft. Bragg

First Sgt. stood in front of A-Company with razor sharp creases. He took a deep breath and began to speak. "This week will be spent in preparation for the field exercise next week. Actually, we're only working three days so we got to bust our balls getting things in order. Platoon Sgts., I have the operations order now, so we will have a meeting in the dayroom after this formation. Fallout!," he yelled.

I walked from our formation over to B-Company. They were still standing in formation. I stood against the building and waited for their First Sgt., to dismiss the formation. When he did, Huntman motioned for me to follow him to his room.

"Since we're only working until Wednesday, what are you going to do?" he asked. "Are you going to wait until Friday to go home or do you want to leave on Wednesday?"

"I'm going to leave as soon as you get me straight," I said.

"I already talked to Preme and he said we should be squared away before then. "

"That's cool, " I said. "I'll leave Wednesday."

Tanoka sat in her bedroom staring at the telephone. She knew she had to call Goodwin. She dialed his number, hoping he would be gone for the Christmas holidays. Her wish was smashed by a voice that sounded like he had smoked since childbirth.

"Agent Goodwin," he said when he answered the phone.

"Hey, what's up? This is Tanoka."

"Oh, Tanoka! How are you? What cha got for me?" he asked.

"I don't have much of anything. I think you are in hot pursuit of the wrong guys. "

"Why do you say that?" Goodwin asked.

"Because, if Chuck and Supreme are supposed to be King Pins they sure as hell don't have much to show for it in Miami. They live in an apartment complex that looks worse than Rose Mary Projects. Chuck purchased a lot of clothes from an outlet mall and he said he sells them every week in Fayetteville. He carries them to the US Flea Market. He is hustling clothes not drugs. Now, I realize why he didn't want me to come down there. I don't think he wanted me to see where he was living. He and I fell out too. I don't think I'll be seeing him anymore," she said.

Goodwin tried to convince Tanoka to continue to communicate with Chuck. His boss wasn't going to like the sound of this. He thought he was close to a huge drug bust. If he takes down a major drug ring he was sure to get a promotion. He was obsessed with getting another promotion.

Tanoka hung up the phone and started to put her new clothes on hangers. "Tanoka, you've done it again girl," she said to herself as she smiled in the mirror. She was beautiful, and she knew it. She picked up her remote control and turned on her radio. Karen White's "Super Woman," was playing. "How appropriate, " she said. "That's just what I am, a super woman."

When Chuck checked in he called Preme in St.Pauls. "I'm here, " he said to Preme

"Finally, " Preme responded. "Did you bring my shoes?" he asked.

"Yeah, I got your ugly ass shoes. What's up for this evening?" Chuck asked.

"I'm trying to see everyone I need to see and be out. I got shit I got to do in the Bottom. "

"Lets get Huntman out of the way first," Chuck said.

Preme looked at his diamond infested Rolex. He could barely tell the time on it because it had so many diamonds covering the face. "They should be off work by now, huh?" he asked Chuck.

"Yeah, give me a few minutes to get straighten out and I'll call you back. "

"I'm going to be at your favorite spot, room 20, in an hour. Bring me my shoes when you come, " Preme said, before hanging up.

For the past few days Goodwin had kept surveillance on Moe' s crib. He hadn't showed up at the house once since they were there. He ordered his men to pack it up and come in if Moe didn't show up after two more days.

Moe and Wilk met Preme and Chuck at Fairfield Inn. "Where's Huntman?" Preme asked.

"He is still in a squad leader's meeting. He told me to remind you that he has to go to the field next week. Then he won't be here in February .We will be in Alaska, " Moe said.

"Ya'11 are going to NWTC. (Northern Welfare Training Center) It's colder than a witch's titty out that bitch my nigga, " Preme shouted.

"Better ya'll niggas than me." said Chuck.

"I'll be in sunny Miami on the beaches thinking about y'all. Just tell Huntman to hit me up when you all come back. I'm going to miss…," Preme paused. "I'm going to miss the money I get from y'all, " he said laughing.

Huntman told Moe to come back on post after he met Preme. Usually they would not ride on post dirty, but Huntman was planning something different.

The squad leader meeting had ended when the two returned. Huntman told Wilk to put the coke in a duffle bag and bring it inside of the barracks.

"The best place to hide something is right under someone's nose. Nobody would ever look in here for kilos of coke. They know we are smarter than that. We need to start spending more time around here looking like soldiers too. That may kill some of the suspicion about us," Huntman said.

Wednesday the First Sgt. dismissed the formation, threatening if there are any DWI's in Alpha Company over the holidays, that the entire Company would pay.

I rushed in the barricks and changed my clothes. Poosh was going home to Troy, Ohio, and he had found a cheaper flight leaving Greensboro. I agreed to give him a ride to and from the airport, when he returned, Sunday morning.

He carried his bags out to Moe's car and I walked over to B-Company. I knocked on the door and it swung open.

"What's up, playboy?" Huntman said. "Wilk told us about your older lady. He said she is fine as hell."

"Oh yeah," I said. "Did he tell you about who put that hickey on his neck?"

Wilk jumped to his feet and ran towards me.

"Yeah he told us," Huntman said. "It was his fine ass college girl, Tina. "

Wilk was standing an inch from my face now. Begging me not to say anything about Big Mama.

"Man, don't tell these niggas about that," he said.

"It wasn't Tina?" Moe asked. "Who was it then? Wilk didn't tell us bought a new girl."

I tried to look serious, but I couldn't. I spread my arms out as wide as I could and said, "The Michelin Man."

"Oh my god, not Pretty Boy Floyd! " Huntman said.

"A fat bitch put a hickey on your neck?" Moe asked.

We were all rolling in laughter. In the mist of our amusement Huntman handed me a gym bag. I put it over my shoulder. "I don't have the time to give you all the details now, I got to bounce. Poosh has a plane to catch. But, I promise to tell you all later on when I get back."

Wilk had kicked back on Huntman's bed and covered his face with his coat.

Laughter filled the hallway when I opened the door. I could still hear Huntman and Moe after I left the barracks, laughing loud.

I dropped Poosh off at the airport just in time for him to make his flight. He was excited to be going home. He only went home twice a year. He reminded me to pick him up Sunday morning. I assured him, I would be there.

Lil ' Kenny and Tory were surprised to hear from me when I paged them. I told Tory I would be over his house in an hour and told Lil' Kenny I would see him in an hour also.

Chuck called Tanoka to let her know he was in town, even though he had been for three days. He was no longer suspicious of her. He knew that she loved him now and he was falling in love with her also. Tanoka was playing the role to a "T" She was laying it on thick as cold molasses.

"I've missed you, Boo. Where are you?" she asked.

"I'm at Fairfield Inn in room 20. "

"I'll be there shortly. I love you,'" she added before hanging up.
Chuck's smile started on one side of his mouth, but never seemed to reach the other side. Nevertheless, it felt good to be loved, he thought.

I reminded Tory that this was going to be my last weekend for a few weeks. I advised him to buy as much as he could afford. He bought ten so I fronted him ten. Rena was out Christmas shopping, he said, and she would be back soon. I hadn't asked where she was, he volunteered the information. I assumed we were really cool now.

Lil' Kenny was complaining how Christmas was breaking him. He had four kids. Four "Babies Mama's " He intended on buying eight and get fronted eight, but his funds were low. He only had enough to buy six. I played Santa and fronted him the other ten.

Wednesday and Thursday, Rena and I stayed at the Embassy Suites. We only left our room to venture to the pool and the continental breakfast. She loved the sweater I bought for her. I also gave her a few hundred bucks in a friendship card. She really surprised me with a leather coat and matching hat.

Christmas wasn't until Sunday, but she knew I was going to spend that particular day in Madison with my family.

Both Lil ' Kenny and Tory had paged me Thursday night. I was to busy making love to Rena to answer either page. Friday morning, before I checked out of the hotel, I called both of them back. Lil' Kenny was still asleep, but his healthy girlfriend woke him up. He had finished selling eight of the ten, he said. He wanted to know if I wanted to come and get the money or wait until later on that day. I told him I would pick it up later on when he sold the other two.

When I called Tory, he sounded half asleep also. "Styles," he started to yawn. "I sold your ten last night. I paged you because I got a cat that wants to buy a half key. "

"I'm on my way over there now. We'll talk more about it when I get there."

I suggested to Rena that she should go ahead and leave. She was already packed. She picked up her things and said "I'll see you in a few." She kissed me, grabbed my ass and twisted out of the room.

The surveillance team had called it quits after two more days. Moe hadn't shown his face yet! Upon investigation, Goodwin found out that the lease was not in Moe's name. It was contracted to a Ms.Jamika Gray. A background check was conducted and declared Ms.Gray deceased. She was killed when a stray round struck her in the head at a local club less than a year ago. The investigation further stated the eyewitnesses reported the bullet was intended for her boyfriend at the time, Mike Mack.

Mike Mack was a well known drug dealer in Fayetteville. He had beat some youngsters for two kilos of coke and they vowed to kill him on sight. When they saw him at Big P's, they tried to kill him but killed Jamika Gray instead. He escaped their ambush unharmed. Then he disappeared after her death for a couple of weeks. .He didn't even attend her wake or funeral. When he did surface, it was in Grove View Terrace Projects. He murdered both of the guys who thought they had gotten a way with murdering Jamika. Mike Mack was currently doing two life sentences in a maximum security prison in Brunswick County.

Tory was up and about when I got there. He had stacked the 10 "G's" in a pyramid on the coffee table. He got a big kick out of looking at all the money like I did.

"To be honest, I can't do anything for that dude right now. We are leaving next week to go to the field and I doubt if I will be home that weekend. The next weekend I might can help him but in February, I'll be gone to Alaska. He will have to find someone else to hit him off again. "

We both came to the conclusion not to deal with his friend who wanted the half kilo.

"He'll probably try to sell on the Hill anyway, " Tory said.

"Too bad you're going to miss my Christmas meal, " said Rena ."My dressing and turkey will make you swallow your tongue. "

"Oh yeah! Well, my folks are country folks and there will be some tongue swallowing going on in Madison too. "

My brother Tim had come home from Germany for Christmas. He had all the latest fashions. He brought presents from Germany for the whole family. He was wearing what I wanted. A leather coat like Michael Jackson wore in the "Beat It" video.

"Since you're my big, little brother, " he said, "You can have it. " It was just like Tim to give me the coat off of his back because I wanted it. That's why we were so close. Tim called me his big, little brother because I was bigger than he was, but he was two years older than I was.

My mom loved the necklace I got for her. A gold chain and gold cross. Although Christmas wasn't until the next day, we were all grateful to be together as a family.

Jimmy, my mom's boyfriend for "eons" who later became her husband, was there too. He had dated my mom every since I could remember. He had been more than a father to me than my own dad. He was taking pictures and keeping the party alive with his jokes that were not so funny.

I had ordered my real father some cologne and soap from Avon. He loved the Black Suede. He hadn't been around too much when I was a shorty, but I loved him just the same. Since I was named after him, we had established a special bond over the years. One that would never be broken. I drove over to Hayes Chapel, (The out-skirts of Madison), and delivered his gift. He wasn't home so I left it with Mama, his mother. I gave her fifty dollars for Christmas and a big kiss.

Friday night, Mom stayed with Jimmy, like she did the majority of the time now. All four of my brothers and myself, stayed in the Bricks that night, just like the times when we were kids. The good ole days!

Tanoka had spent the past three days with Chuck and was getting ready to fly back to Miami with him. Chuck had made a great impression on her family. He wooed her mother with lavish gifts. Her brother, who really didn't like Chuck before, he loved him now. Chuck bought him a fat gold chain! Chuck even surprised Tanoka after all the gifts he had already showered her with. He presented her with a ring in front of her mother and the rest of her family. Tanoka cried!

While they were preparing to leave the phone rang.

"Tanoka, it's for you," Her mom said.

"Hand me the phone Chuck, " Tanoka said, pointing at the phone.

Chuck placed his big, dark hands around the receiver on the wall and handed it to her. "Hello, " She said.

"I thought you weren't seeing Chuck anymore, " A scratchy voice said. "He sure did look like a black Santa carrying all those presents he bought for you and your family. He must have sold a lot of t-shirts! "

"Who is it, Baby Girl?" Chuck asked. He could see something was wrong by the expression that covered Tanoka's face. She looked like she'd seen the angel of death.

"You're in too deep, Doll Baby," Goodwin said to Tanoka.

Chuck snatched the phone from Tanoka. "Hello, who is this?" He asked.

Click! "Bomb-bomb-bomb! " All he heard was a dial tone. "Who was it? What they say?" He asked her.

Tanoka tried to straighten the wrinkles in her forehead, but Chuck could still see the fear in her eyes. "It was, uhhhh nobody. They had the wrong number, " She said.

"Bullshit! Who was it?" Chuck asked. He grabbed Tanoka by both of her shoulders. "What are you hiding from me?"

This wasn't like Tanoka. Usually, she could think faster than a speeding bullet. She had a brain cramp at the moment. All she could think about was telling Chuck the truth. She started to cry. Big heavy tears filled her Chinese eyes and streamed down her face. She began to talk. "That was my ex-boyfriend. He called me all kinds of names and said he wished I was dead."

"Fuck that nigga," Chuck said. "Fucking coward. That explains why he hung up the phone instead of talking to me. I thought you told me he was locked up?" He asked.

"He said he got out two days ago, " she said.

"He's a fucking coward, " Chuck said again. He picked up the bags and threw them over his shoulders. With full arms, he still somehow managed to have a hand free to hold Tanoka's hand. They walked out of the house and Chuck began to load the rented car. A green Ford Taurus. While he loaded their things Tanoka looked around for one of the undercover cars. She had dealt with Goodwin and his crew for so long she knew them all. She recognized the sky blue, Chevy Citation, as one of Goodwin's own undercover cars. He flicked the lights. When she looked in his direction. She jumped in the Taurus and asked Chuck to please hurry.

Moe ' s girlfriend had gone home to Georgia for Christmas. Huntman and his friends from Pittsburgh were at his crib chilling. They had planned to stay through the holidays. Since they were staying, Moe didn't go home. He didn't need to. He had just as many clothes at Huntman' s house as he did his own.

Wilk had decided to stay there for the holidays too. Between a few deliveries here and there, in which they all took turns, they pretty much stayed cuddled up with the girls from the Steel City.

My youngest brother, Pookie, Tim and myself, hung out all day. We were visiting family and friends. I was driving while Tim and Pookie got drunk. We left Madison and decided to go to Greensboro. I needed to see Lil' Kenny anyway to get my money. When I stopped by his house, I left Tim and Pookie in the car and I ran inside. He had my money in a small brown bag.

"It's ten "G's". I counted it three times to make sure I wasn't giving you too much dough, " Lil' Kenny said.

I didn't want my brothers to see the money so I opened the trunk and placed the bag underneath some rags. We rode around for a while and did a little shopping, then we headed back to Madison. Tim and Pookie were both drunk as skunks! They fell asleep during the twenty minute ride. Once we reached the Bricks, their motors started running again. It has always been something about the Bricks with us three. We loved growing up down there. "The Bricks For Life," was our motto. It just felt good to be home with my brothers.

Sunday morning, I hugged and kissed my mom and all my brothers good bye. When we were kids we would fuss and fight each other all the time. If my mom caught us she would make us hug and kiss each other. Then we would have to say, "I love you, " to each other until my mom got tired! Sometimes that went on for hours. Only to be interrupted with direct orders to kiss each other. On the lips! We hated that more than anything. For fear of this punishment, we stopped a lot of fights before they got started. I heard my Ole Man say to my mom once, "Let them fight each other now, and when they are older they won't fight each other, instead they'll fight with each other. " I was happy when my mom adopted that theory .We still got our backsides toasted for fighting but not as often. "All you got in this world is each other, " my mom used to always say. We've always remembered and believed that. So it wasn't a big deal when I hugged and kissed my brothers bye. On the lips!

I arrived at the airport fifteen minutes later than what I told Poosh. I checked his flight and they hadn't arrived yet. One of the ladies from Delta said that they were at the terminal when I asked her about the flight.

Poosh walked out of the terminal looking around not expecting me to be there. He flashed a big smile when he saw me and he said, "I'm glad you're here. I figured you'd be out getting laid one more time before you went back to Bragg." He smiled and added, "I got laid," he almost yelled.

"We'll talk about that in the car," I said looking around to see who had heard had him.

For almost two hours I heard the story of how Poosh got laid. He only stopped telling me about it when we got back to the barricks. He only did that to start telling Palagonia, the Italian kid from the Bronx.

Tanoka was glad to be out of North Carolina. She felt safe with Chuck. She thought Goodwin was going to do something while they were at the airport waiting for their flight. She knew they were there watching her every move. Everyone in the airport seemed to be watching them. She had been extremely paranoid. But, now she relaxed. She was miles and miles away from Goodwin and her crooked past. She just wanted to forget about her past and start over. She truly loved Chuck now!

CHAPTER 1 6

Tuesday morning we parachuted onto Silicy Drop Zone at 1 : 30. We performed a 15 kilometer movement through the damp brush. My body was there, fully participating in the operation but, my mind was elsewhere. I could still see the smiling cat painted on Celeste's jeans. Lakisha's pearly whites and Pricilla's gorgeous black body, both made cameos in my thoughts while I was beating the wet brush. I had saved over ten thousand dollars since I arrived at Ft.Bragg. All of which was stashed in my wall locker. I could see myself cruising through F. S .U, in my own Mustang G .T. I pictured Rena riding me in the hot tub until. "Whack!" I was brought back to reality when a branch from a pine tree smacked me in the face.

A-Company's mission was to secure MOUT City. MOUT is an acronym for

Military Operation in Urban Terrain. An assimilated city had been constructed to facilitate our training. Despite the rain, sleet and snow we spent 2 1/2 weeks in the field playing war games with other infantry units from Bragg. I only saw my "Partnas in Crime" twice while we were in the field. Both times were when hot chow was being served to the troops. A luxury we only had two times in 2 1/2 weeks.

We returned to civilization Friday, and I called Tory and Lil' Kenny as soon as I got some free time. Both of then were looking forward to my return. Things had been sort of rough for them since I'd been in the field. Neither had a connection that would front them coke like I would. Also, I got in contact with all of my female friends and wished each one of them a Happy "belated" New Year. As promised, I called Tone and invited him down to Bragg to kick it with me.

"What's up Tone?" I asked when he answered the phone.

"Styles! What's happening? he asked. "Are you coming home again this weekend?"

"No, I just came from the field today and I have to work this weekend. I'm calling you to see if you want to come down here next weekend?"

"Yeah, I'm ready to come down there. I thought you'd forgotten about me. Give me directions and I will be down there Friday," Tone said.

I gave him directions and planned to meet him then.

Huntman called Preme to let him know he would be ready to roll again next weekend. He explained he had too much Army stuff to do for this weekend and the coming week. He also called his Fayetteville connects to inform them that it would be "On and popping" next weekend.

Tanoka had been in Miami since Christmas. She really started to have serious feelings for Chuck. In the past few weeks, she had seen a side of him she hadn't known before. A sweet, sensitive side. She truly fell in love with that side of him. Chuck had treated her like a baby the entire time she had been in Miami. To his own surprise, he was happy she was there. Living in the same house as he was. He had been back to DaVille a couple times, but Tanoka stayed in Miami, waiting for her prince charming to return. Her mom and brother were coming down to Miami the coming weekend to see how she was doing. Her mom knew something was going on with Tanoka, but she couldn't put her finger on it to save her life. Some agent had been calling her house, looking for Tanoka. She was coming to Miami to conduct her own investigation.

We worked the entire weekend cleaning rusty weapons and other field equipment. Huntman visited me and asked if I was going to go home the coming weekend. I told him my homeboy Tone, was coming down to kick it with us. He said he was going to plan something for us to do.

Chuck and Tanoka picked her mom and brother up from the airport. He treated them all to dinner and a short tour of Miami before taking them to the mansion in South Beach. Tanoka's mom thought that his house was a part of the Miami tour.

"No ma'am," Chuck said. "This is where I live."

"Damn this is nice," her little brother said.

Her mother smacked him on the back of his head. "Boy watch your damn mouth," she said. She was just as impressed as her son but she contained her outburst. It was all adding up. The agent had to be calling in regards to Chuck, her mom thought. Whatever it was, it had to be serious. Tanoka's mom wasn't going to allow her precious daughter to get caught in the middle of it.

When Tanoka and her mother were alone, her mother began to tell her about the phone calls from the agent.

"Tanoka there has been some agent calling my house. I hope you're not involved in anything illegal. Who is it, and why does he want to speak with you?" she asked.

Before she gave Tanoka a chance to answer, she added, "I'm not going through this bullshit with you anymore. You've been caught up three times dealing with drug dealers. You're not going to be satisfied until your laying somewhere dead!"

Tanoka didn't really have an answer for her mother .She had not expected Goodwin to call her house when he knew she was in Miami with Chuck.

"I don't know who it is mama," she said, shrugging her shoulders, trying to convince her mom. "Maybe it's something dealing with the case I caught in 1986."

"Why would they want to talk to you about something that happened three years ago?" asked her mom.

Tanoka's mom was not a fool. She knew it was more to the agents calling than what Tanoka was admitting.

"Whatever it is, if you get into some trouble this time, " then she abruptly stopped in the middle of her acrimonious statement. She shook her head with disapproval. "Just don't get into anymore trouble TaTa, " her mom said, calling her by the name she use to call her when she wore diapers.

"I won't mama. I promise," Tanoka said.

Her mom forgot all about the trouble talk When Chuck took them all out shopping before they left to go back to North Carolina. She was too busy having a ball, trying to get whatever she could.

Early Monday morning, in formation, First Sgt. , informed us that 3rd Battalion successfully completed more missions than any other battalion on Ft.Bragg. A-Company successfully completed more missions than any infantry unit on Ft.Bragg. He was extremely proud of us, he said. Our reward would be a five day weekend. He just wanted us to take a couple more days to finish cleaning everything and prepare for our exercise in Alaska. The Battalion Commander granted a five day weekend for everyone.

Huntman called Preme to let him know he'd be ready to roll again Wednesday instead of Friday. Preme said that would be better for him, because he had plans for Saturday. If he did not have to leave Friday, things would run smoother for him Saturday, he explained to Huntman.

"Hello," Tory said, sounding half asleep.

"What's up Tee?" I asked.

"Yo! What's happening Styles? Man, pleasssse tell me you are coming home this weekend."

"No, I'm not because I have some more business to handle, but I can meet you somewhere on Highway 421, Wednesday night to hit you off. You'll just have to hold on to the money for me until the next weekend. "

"That's cool, " he said. Tory sounded relieved.

"But I need you to do one favor for me, " I said.

"What's that?" he asked wide awake now.

"You know that other cat Lil' Kenny from the Grove I fuck with?"

90

"Yeah, I know him, "

"I need you to bring him with you because I got something for him too. "

Tory paused for a second. I thought we had been disconnected. "Hello! " I said.

"Yeah, I'm still here," he confirmed. "I'd rather bring back whatever you have for him and give it to him for you. I don't want anyone riding with me when I'm dealing with you, " Tory said.

That was alright with me. "Fine!" I said. "I'll call Lil' Kenny and let him know you're going to get in touch with him Wednesday night, or Thursday morning."

I hung up the phone and called Lil Kenny. I told him how things were going to go down. He didn't care how he got the coke, just as long as he got it.

Agent Goodwin had taken some serious heat rounds from his boss for a few weeks now. His promotion was slowly but surely going down the drain. His star witness, Tanoka, "The Queen of the Double Cross," had triple crossed him. She had given him enough information to continue his investigation though. But, all of his leads were coming to dead ends.

Goodwin was becoming obsessed with making some type of bust. He was in the process of obtaining a search warrant for Moe' s home. He also was trying to find out where Huntman and Wilk lived when they didn't stay in the barricks. Somehow, those two always managed to elude the car that Goodwin assigned to trail them.

Tuesday night, Chuck left Miami in a U-Haul, carrying 50 kilos of Bolivian flakes. They were hidden in the pillows of some old couches. Once again, Tanoka choose to stay at the mansion and wait for her Lover Boy to return.

Preme had taken a flight earlier that day and he was already in St.Pauls, waiting for Chuck to arrive. Wednesday afternoon, When Chuck did arrive, he called Preme to see if he had everything in order. He wanted to conduct business as fast as he could and get back to Tanoka.

Preme had made contact with Huntman and a few other dudes he dealt with. The plan was to do all the moving early Wednesday night. Chuck checked into Fairfield Inn, with two large duffle bags and took a hot shower and a long nap in preparation for the planned activities.

"As soon as you get straight tonight, I need for you to hit me off. I'm supposed to meet my partner tonight on Highway 421. Just because I ain't going home this weekend, doesn't mean I can't still make some loot," I said to Huntman.

"That's cool with me. I'm supposed to meet Preme around seven or eight. As soon as I get with him, I'll come by here to pick you up," he said. Huntman walked out of the barricks and assured me he would see me later.

In the meantime, I called Tory .He said he had been sitting by the phone waiting on my call. I told him to plan to meet about eight or nine in Siler City, a town between Greensboro and Ft.Bragg.

When Tory and I met, I gave him an entire kilo. Eighteen ounces a piece for him and Lil 'Kenny.

"I'll be home next weekend and you can pay me then," I said to Tory.
"Relay the same message to Lil ' Kenny for me."

After Chuck and Preme finished their business in DaVille, both of them took the first flight back to Miami. Usually, Chuck would spend at least a day or two in North

Carolina, but his reason for staying in North Click was in Miami now. Waiting on him to return.

Tanoka picked Chuck and Preme up from the airport when they arrived. They suggested stopping at the Polo Club to eat, but Tanoka explained she had cooked dinner for them. Chuck said he didn't even know that she could cook. He was in for a surprise she bragged.

Every bite of the breaded, boneless chicken breast, made his mouth water for the next bite. Preme was impressed too. He hadn't been to enthused that Tanoka was staying with them. He felt that something about her was strange, but, her cooking was the bomb, he thought. He could get use to her cooking. That's just what he needed, some home cooked meals.

Friday night, I met Tone in Spring Lake .He followed me back to the barricks and we got ready to go out to the club. Huntman had planned for us to go to Big P's.

At 11: 45, we met in the parking lot and I introduced Tone to my Crew. Like myself, Tone did not smoke or drink. So, while my partners smoked la, we caught up on what was going on back home. After twenty minutes of watching my comrades smoke and drink we strapped up and walked to the entrance of the club. Just like before, Moe spoke with the bouncers and we were all escorted inside. Straight to the V.I.P. Tone was impressed at this.

"Damn Styles, ya boys got it like that down here?" he asked.

"'No, we got it like that down here," I said.

Tone was about six feet tall and dark brown in complexion. He had jet black, curly hair and the gift to gab. The women loved him to death. He could dance a hole in a dance floor and put Michael Jackson to shame.

Once inside the club the coke selling began for the Crew, but for Tone and I, the party didn't start until we walked in the door! Tone and I had girls waiting in line to dance with us. (Well, maybe not in line, but we did have them waiting.) We exchanged numbers with a dozen young ladies and continued to dance. Those same "Go to Hell," looks we received the last time we left Big P's, Tone and I were receiving them while we were on the dance floor, doing our thing.

Tone was having the time of his life. He was dancing and didn't even notice the crooked looks. He was too busy trying to get every phone number he could. The DJ slowed the tempo down with a slow song by Al B. Sure and Tone handpicked the finest lady in the club to slow dance with.

As the crooning sounds of Al B. blasted, Tone hugged his handpicked beauty tightly. Sweat glistened from both of their shinny foreheads as the disco lights flashed rhythmically. Tone started to rub the shapely girl like he was giving her a massage. Her hands gripped the small of his back tightly. They felt good to Tone. She raised her head from his shoulder and looked him in his eyes. Tone had just met her three songs ago, but the slow dance made him feel like he had known her for a lifetime. He licked his lips in preparation for a kiss. As he eased his head towards her glossy lips, he felt a third hand grip his shoulder. When he turned around, one of the guys who he had not noticed staring at him, cocked his right hand back. He swung at Tone, trying to knock his head off his shoulders. But, Tone ducked, and the finest woman in the club got knocked the fuck out!

I pushed Tone out of the way and hit the mad "x" boyfriend with a "two piece to the chew piece." Moe, Huntman and Wilk jumped over the rails of the VIP booth and rushed to the dance floor to aid us. When the ex-boyfriend got up, he was backed by an army that was larger than Pharaoh's! Tone looked around, still confused about what was happening. He looked down at the girl with the bloody broken nose. Then to the guys who stood behind the jealous knucklehead, who got the mess started.

"Gotdamn, baby! I know that had to hurt, " Tone said, quickly jumping behind Huntman.

Security turned the house lights on as soon as the confrontation began. It wasn't a secret now that underneath half of the flea market attire was all types of gats. From 22's to 44's!

"Move back!" one bouncer yelled at the Fayetteville mob. He pointed towards the exit sign and instructed a couple of the other bouncers to escort us out of the club before World War III, broke out.

Automatically, we formed a diamond formation, with Tone being the center since he wasn't strapped. Slowly, we walked to the exit. When we reached the exit we started to jog to our rides. Before we got to our cars, the army of jealous cats, rushed the door, pushing the large bouncers to the ground, in hot pursuit!

I heard the first shot ring out when I opened the door to the Mustang. Instinctively, I dropped to the ground behind the door to take cover. I looked over at the Blazer and Huntman started yelling like we were on a field exercise. That Ranger School shit coming to life.

"'Return fire! Return fire!" he yelled.

I pitched my Glock 9mn over to Tone and I pulled out a Mini 14 from under a blanket in the back seat.

"Doom! Dooooom! Doooooo! I started dumping rounds in the center of the pursuing crowd. Tone started to squeeze the trigger on the 9mn. Bodies started to fall and take cover behind parked cars. Most turned and ran in the opposite direction. Once we had their heads down, Huntman yelled, "Get in your car and move out! I'll cover you while you move!"

I jumped in and started the engine. Tone grabbed the Mini 14 and reloaded. He let the window down and said, "Drive over there!" He pointed in the direction of a crowd forming around one of the casualties.

I jammed the car in first gear and did a semi doughnut, turning the steering wheel in the direction of the sobbing casualty. Tone started busting shots and more bodies began to fall. He sprayed a few guys in the back who were trying to run a way from the scene.

"You coward bastards! Take that!," he yelled.

Huntman pulled up behind us and Wilk was in the back of the Blazer with the tailgate down lying in the prone position. With fire jumping from the barrel of his SKS like a dragon spitting flames, Wilk laid down suppressive fire so we could exit the parking lot.

When we pulled into the parking lot back at the barricks, we bailed out slapping high fives. "Nigga, you were busting them bitches, " Moe said to Tone. "you shoot better than half of the niggas in the Army."

"I saw at least a dozen fools burry their dicks in the pavement," Wilk said.

Huntman made no comment. He was busy accessing the damages to his Blazer.

Two windows had been shot out and six holes, almost in a perfect line, were on the passenger side, as a result of the melee.

We need to go and hide my truck until I can get it fixed and painted, " Huntman finally said. "Moe, you need to hide your ride too, for a while. We all need to chill until all this shit blows over. We can't go back to Big P's for a long, long time!" Huntman said, shaking his head.

It was quiet for a minute. Everyone seemed to be in deep thought, as if they had lost a dear friend. Tone broke the silence and said, "I hate that fine ass bitch got knocked out. I was trying to leave with her tonight." Laughter erupted

Moe then said. "Let's go and get something to eat. All this ghetto combat has made me hungry."

Saturday night, we avoided the clubs in DaVille. We went to the movies instead, with some of the same girls Tone and I had met the night before at Big P's .We stayed at the Holiday Inn off of Highway 95 until Sunday morning.

Sunday morning, Tone woke up, got dressed and prepared to head back to Stoneville. He had one of the most exciting weekends in his life, he said. He gave everyone short hugs and promised to come back to visit soon.

Monday morning, Agent Goodwin secured a search warrant for Moe's house. He decided to put another surveillance team on the house before he invaded it. Tuesday they were staked out observing the house, recording all movement.

Huntman had suggested that the Crew should hang around the barricks more and that was what we all were doing. They were making their moves, but instead of going back to one of the houses, they came back to the barricks and chilled.

When Wednesday came, they had sold out and Preme wasn't due back until Friday morning. DaVille was dry. This was a prime time for Moe to retrieve his two kilos from his house. He could sell them for a little more since there was a dry spell.

Goodwin's boys had been staked out for two days and hadn't seen any signs of Moe. They had his girlfriend on tape, arriving and leaving the house, but she had been followed and checked out. She wasn't involved with Moe' s business, or the Supreme Team's operations. The agents doubted she knew what he was into. She was just a naive college girl who thought she was dealing with a career, oriented military man.

Patiently, they sat and waited for him to arrive, in hopes of catching him with coke.

When I paged Tory, he returned my call and told me he had sold his half of the kilo. I told him I would see him Friday night.

Lil' Kenny said he had one ounce left. "By Friday night I'll have all your dough, and I will be waiting on you to come home."

Preme had arrived in Fayetteville, Wednesday morning by plane. Chuck had left Miami Tuesday night for his weekly drive and arrived Wednesday afternoon. No one expected them to arrive until Friday. After Chuck rested, he woke up and paged Moe, Wilk and Huntman.

Wilk and Huntman were at the barricks, but Moe had left. He said he was going to grab a bite to eat. He was really on his way home to pick up the two kilos he had stashed away in his house. He knew when there was a drought and the small dope pushers could raise the price a little and they would sellout faster. The time was perfect for him to hit his little crew off with the coke.

As he was cruising down Yadkin Road, he received Chuck's page and was surprised. He was the first one to hit Chuck back.

"What's up my Nigga?" Moe said, trying to sound like the Florida boys. "We wasn't expecting to hear from you until Friday. "

"Yeah, well we can't allow anyone to pin point us .You know that. Not even our number one customers. Are you all ready?" Chuck asked.

"Yeah, we're always ready," said Moe. He checked his rearview mirror and did a u-turn, terminating his trip home. He pulled into Burger King and ordered a Whopper with cheese and called Huntman.

Friday morning came and there had not been any sign of Moe, just like the last time they staked out his house. Goodwin started to wonder if that was where he really lived. He called his surveillance team in again and started to work on another plan to catch Moe red handed. He had wasted more money for nothing, trying to catch Moe at his house.

He knew it was useless to raid the house. The guys in the Supreme Team were far too smart to do anything as stupid as keep coke in their houses. He still knew that one wrong move would destroy the entire Operation Hurricane. But, he continued to be pressed by higher up to make some type of bust.

When I arrived in Greensboro, Friday night, I drove to Rena's house. Weeks had elapsed since I'd seen her. We were both excited to see each other. She was elated that I was staying with her instead of staying in a hotel.

I paged Tory and he came home and paid me for the fronted coke .I gave him another half key and he was on his way back to the Hill.

Lil' Kenny met me at his house and paid me also. I fronted him another half brick, and hurried back to Rena' s.

Tanoka walked out of the terminal, hiding behind dark Giorgio Armani's. She was greeted by Agent Goodwin and a few of his flunkies. She was floored that he knew she was coming back to North Carolina.

"Everyday I run a check on your name at this airport. With every airline," he stressed. "Just to see if you've made reservations to come back home, Doll Baby."

"What do you want from me?" Tanoka asked through clenched teeth. "I told you Chuck isn't the man you want. He isn't doing anything. Just leave us alone. " Her voice became louder.

"Oh! It's "US" now, is it?" Goodwin asked. He looked around and everyone seemed to be staring at him. An airport security guard had heard Tanoka and started toward Goodwin. Goodwin pulled out his badge and held it up high, not just for the fake cop's benefit, but for everyone.

"I want you to tell me what's really going on? What are you really trying to do?" he almost whispered.

Goodwin knew "good-n-damn well" what Tanoka was trying to do. She wanted to be with Chuck. Her habit of shopping had been overwhelmed, replaced by love. But, he still acted like he didn't know her plans.

"I don't know what you are planning on doing, Doll Baby…, "

Tanoka cut Goodwin off in the middle of his sentence. "Don' t call me that! I'm not your fucking doll baby!"

"You can't win Tanoka. I'll put the word out that you are the biggest rat in Fayetteville. How long do you think you will last then? How long do you think you'll last when everyone finds out you had you last three boyfriends set up? What will Chuck think. about that?" he asked.

Tanoka started walking fast. Goodwin's long legs wouldn't allow her to get a way. Silently, she began to cry. When she reached baggage claim, Goodwin continued to walk past her.

"I'll be watching you Doll Baby, " he said as he walked out of the revolving doors, lighting a Marlboro.

Saturday morning when I woke up Rena was standing over me with beautiful breast and breakfast. She sure as hell did know how to treat her man. She kept my nuts empty and my stomach full!

After breakfast in bed, I got up and drove to Madison. I spent the day with Kami and my mom. They understood, that since I had borrowed Moe's car that I had to return the same day. On my way out of Madison, I stopped by Celeste's house and she and I talked for an hour or more. Before I left, I kissed Celeste. I tried to tie her tongue in a knot. A chill seized my body like never before when we kissed. I promised to call her from Bragg and to take her out on a date the following weekend.

Saturday night, I took Lakisha to Side Effects. After the club I dropped her off at the dorm and crept back to Rena's house. As soon as I walked in Rena undressed me and we made love in front of the door.

Tanoka returned to Fayetteville to pack her things. Chuck said he wanted her to move to Miami with him. For the past two days she worked diligently to pack her things. She continued to think about her unexpected meeting with Agent Goodwin at the airport. She was still shocked that he knew she was coming home. Afraid that he was going to expose her true identity as a snitch, she was becoming a nervous wreck.

Sunday afternoon, I collected my money from Tory and Lil' Kenny and rode to Bob Dunn Ford. I was getting ready to car shop. I'd saved enough money to purchase a Mustang GT. Almost, enough to pay for it in cash, but I knew that wouldn't be wise.

After looking at the fly Mustangs, I decided which one was for me. It was a 1989, maroon Mustang GT. As soon as I returned from Alaska, I would make that car mine.

Huntman received a few reports from some of the Fayetteville workers that they had been harassed by Goodwin. One of the workers added that Goodwin bragged on having an informant inside the Supreme Team. Goodwin also bragged that he would be successful in bringing the Supreme Team down soon with the information he had. Huntman immediately put the entire Team on alert. He suggested to Preme that the coming weekend, which was his last weekend before he went to Alaska, that they chill. Allow the smoke to clear, he said. It should be clear as a glass when we return from Alaska, he told Preme.

I called Huntman when I got back to Ft.Bragg. I met him at Vic's and he gave me the 411 on what was going on. I hated to hear that I wasn't going to have any coke for the coming weekend. I had already promised Tory and Lil' Kenny that I would make sure they were straight one last time before I left. Oh well, I thought. That's how the ball bounces in this game. I may not get to make my $3,600, this weekend, but on the flip side, I'll get to spend more time with Celeste, Rena and Kami!

CHAPTER 17

Monday morning, Captain Blu, with the CID, informed Goodwin that Moe along with the rest of us would be going to Alaska for a month, the next week. Blu suggested to Goodwin that he should try to search Moe's house Sunday night. Since Moe was going to be gone for a month, Blu was certain that he would go home and stay with his lady before he left. Goodwin agreed with Blu and planned the first serious raid on the Supreme Team for Sunday night. This raid would make or break Operation Hurricane.

Tanoka arrived in Miami and she felt better when Chuck embraced her at the terminal. As long as she was miles a way from Goodwin she felt safe. As mush as she hated to drive, she had decided not to fly back to North Carolina. She already knew Goodwin or one of his pesky agents would always give her an unwanted welcome.

"How was your trip home?" Chuck asked.

"It was fine. I didn't do anything but pack and spend time with my mom and brother," answered Tanoka.

"Did that coward call you?" he asked, referring to her ex boyfriend.

"No, " she said. Tanoka grabbed Chuck in a bear hug and buried her round face deep into his thick chest.

"What's wrong?" he asked.

"I just missed you so much while I was gone, " she replied.

"I missed you to Baby Girl. You don't have to worry about missing me anymore. You're here with me now."

I called Celeste Wednesday, like I had promised. She was looking forward to our date, but not half as much as I was. I told her that I couldn't wait until I saw her again.

Tory and Lil' Kenny were hurt that I wasn't going to be straight the weekend. They had just experienced a slump while I was a way in the field. Now they were about to endure another one.

Kami said she had a special surprise for me over the weekend since she knew I was leaving for a month. Everyone knew I was leaving and everyone said they had surprises for me.

Friday afternoon, we got off of work early. Moe had given me the keys to his black Mustang to drive home. I rode, listening to New Edition, anticipating my evening with Celeste, and looking forward to whatever Kami had planned for me. I also planned to see Rena and Lakisha or Pricilla, whichever one I talk to first, before I bounced Sunday night. I had a lot to do in a small amount of time.

The Big P's situation was still keeping my partners from attending any clubs in DaVille. They decided to hang out together for a while and then the plan was to go home and chill out with their old ladies.

When Moe arrived home Friday night, the surveillance team sat two blocks from his house in a utility van. They contacted Goodwin as soon as he arrived. They were instructed to keep close watch on him until Sunday night.

"Don't let him out of your fucking sight, "' Goodwin said to the undercover agent who had called.

Like Moe, Huntman had purchased two kilos himself. Unlike his partner, he didn't have another drug ring he was conspiring with. Instead, he planned to give Justice, the young kid with the cornrows, and the orange Gremlin, the two keys while he was a way for a month.

Justice was the first guy Preme and Chuck introduced to Huntman. He could be trusted as far as Huntman was concerned. After all, he was apart of the Supreme Team.

Rena was coming out of the door when I pulled up. She was on her way to the hair saloon, she said. She added that she was already late for her appointment. After I explained to her that I wouldn't be able to see her anymore during the weekend, because I had to get back to prepare for my field exercise in Alaska, she quickly unlocked her door and rescheduled her hair appointment. For two hours we did what we did best. We had buck wild sex! Both of us were happy that she rescheduled her hair appointment.

I stopped at East Side Grocery Store and called Pricilla. She and Big Mama met me at the Summit Shopping Center and we ate New York style pizza at Elizabeth's Pizza.

"I just wanted to see you before I left for Alaska,". I said.

"I'm glad you choose to see me instead of Lakisha. I've been thinking about you a lot lately, " she said.

"Where is that pretty boy, Wilk?" Big Mama asked.

"He's back in DaVille getting ready for our trip to Alaska, " I said. I knew I couldn't try to see Lakisha now that I had seen Pricilla. Lakisha would talk about seeing me and that would make Pricilla jealous. I didn't have to worry about Pricilla talking about she saw me, because she and Lakisha were friends, and she didn't want to mess that up!

After we ate, I asked Pricilla if I could see her before I left on Sunday night? She agreed to meet me Sunday night at 8: 00, at the Burger King across the street from A&T .

I called Kami from a pay phone in Madison and told her it would still be a few hours before I arrived. She said she had a room at the Margree Hotel, in Eden.

"Please hurry up. I'll be waiting on you. I'm in room 108," she said before hanging up the phone.

Celeste was dressed and ready when I arrived. She had on all black and she looked sexy .I spoke to her mom arid promised to have her precious daughter back home shortly. We caught the 8:00, movie and grabbed a bite to eat afterwards. There was something about her that made me want to take my time with her. So I did.

I took Celeste straight home and walked her to the door. "I had a great time tonight, " she said squeezing my hands.

"'So did I. If I don't leave tomorrow, I'll be back to see you before I go to Alaska. I'll at least call you before I go."

I kissed Celeste like I was one of those cool, soap opera guys. Our heads turned from right to left as we osculated.

"Let me tell you now to be careful, just in case I don't get to see you or talk to you, " she said.

We kissed again and Celeste unlocked the door and went inside.

I checked my watch and it was 11: 34. I drove to the Margree hotel and I saw Kami's car, a little white Chevy Chevette, parked in front of room 108. I tapped on the door.

"Open the door Baby, it's cold out here."

Kami opened the door and the lights were turned off in the room. Candles, which were new hours ago, flickered as the fire continued to eat a way at the wax.

"This is what one of those candles look like when they are new, " Kami said holding up one of the bright red, long candles. "That's how long I've waited on you," she continued, pointing at one of the half candles, burning on the dresser.

"I'm sorry, Baby. It's just hard to do things when you don't have a car. But, when I get back from Alaska I'm going to fix that problem. I'm here now and I want my special surprise! "

In the background, Luther sang something about a house not being a home. I didn't know all the words, so I hummed the tune and grabbed Kami. She smiled and placed her arms around my neck. I untied the belt that was keeping her robe together and put my arms around her thin waist. She had on a lace bra and panty set that appeared and disappeared with the flickering of the candle 1ights .We made love until the flames died all the way out. We didn't come up for air until Sunday morning!

Justice drove over to Huntman's house and picked up the two kilos. He assured Huntman that when he returned from Alaska, he would have all of his money. Huntman warned him about dealing with people he didn't know. Also, he warned him that it was rumored that the Supreme Team had a leak in the once air tight circle.

"That didn't concern Justice. He had everything in order. He knew none of his peeps were the police. "Don't worry about me, dawg. I'll be ok," Justice said. But, Huntman wasn't worried about Justice, he was worried about his money.

Agent Goodwin, and the rest of the Narc Team, was going over the raid plan. Moe had left the house only once since Friday night. He went to the KFC and the liquor store Saturday afternoon, but nowhere else since then. Goodwin actually prayed that they found at least some residue from coke in Moe's crib. If he didn't find that at least, his entire operation, promotion and maybe even his career would go down the drain. But, on da flip side of that, if he found drugs, his career would sky rocket!

I kissed Kami and she began to cry. "Why are you crying?" I asked.

"Because I'm gonna miss you, ' she said.

"I'll only be gone for a month. I'll be home in your arms before you know it."
She wiped her eyes with her sleeve and I opened her car door. Slowly, she got in and I kissed her and closed her door. She waved and pulled off.

I called Celeste from a pay phone and told her that she would be the first person I would see when I came back from Alaska. She said she wanted to be the first and only one I saw when I got back. "Be careful, " she said again.

When I knocked on Rena' s door, she opened it looking surprised. "I thought I wasn't going to be able to see you before you left, " she said. She had her hair wrapped in a blue silk scarf. She finally made it to her hair appointment.

"I had to come back for some more good loving before I left," I said.

"You mean to tell me, you drove all the way from Ft.Bragg just to get some of this loving?" she asked, already knowing the answer to the question.

"I do that every weekend, " I said.

She closed the door and undressed me.   Once again it was on!

When I woke up it was 7: 40 .I jumped in the shower and got dressed. I hugged Rena and told her she would be the first person that I would see when I returned. She made me promise!

Big Mama was in Burger King ordering enough for everyone in Greensboro when I pulled up. Pricilla sat in her car waiting for me. She got out of the car and got in the car with me.

"Where are we going?" she asked. "I know you want some of this chocolate pudding before you go and freeze your balls off in Alaska, " she said with a huge smile on her face.

Big Mama came out carrying a large bag smiling too. She walked to my side of the car and tapped on the window.

"You got to pay for my food since I brought Pricilla over here," she said before I let the window all the way down.

I'd rather clothed her than feed her, I thought! "I don't have a problem with that," I said. I pulled out a crisp twenty and handed it to Big Mama.

"Don't spend it all on one meal" I said and pulled off.

Before we were out of the parking lot Pricilla unzipped my pants and started giving me head. Carefully, I drove over to Bengim Park by the Grove. Pricilla and I got out and walked to the sliding board. I sat down on the bottom of the slide and she pulled off her panties and raised up her dress.

"I want you to think about how warm this pussy is when you get cold in Alaska," she said. She sat on me and pushed me back. She began to roll in a circular motion and I felt the warmth of her pussy and tried to store it in my minds memory bank!

The Task Force had assembled eight blocks a way from Moe's house. Goodwin was more nervous than excited. He continued to pray that he found anything illegal. His boss had decided to work over time to see how the raid was going to turn out. He rode in the Citation with Goodwin.

Moe stepped out of the shower and Treva started to dry him off. She was happy that he had spent the past two days with her.

"I'm going to miss you pumpkin," she said. "I wish you'd stay here with me more often like this." She took his hand and lead him to the bed. The bed was messed up from two days of hot sex. He crawled from the foot of the bed to the top and got under the sheets.

"Turn up the radio up and come on and let's get some sleep." Moe said.

Treva turned the radio up and Ready For The World, singing "Deep" created another sex mood. "Slide over here," he said to Treva.

"I thought you were getting ready to go to sleep," she asked Moe smiling.

"Are you in place Newman?" Goodwin whispered into his walkie-talkie.

"Yes sir, I am, " he responded.

"Then initiate the raid, " Goodwin ordered slowly, looking over at his tired boss. Four agents ran toward Moe's front door with a battering ram. The door gave way after the second hit. Moe pushed Treva off of him and reached under his pillow for his pistol. It wasn't there! He had left it in the living room two days ago.

More than a dozen agents flooded the house identifying themselves.

"FBI! " they all yelled, although most of them were city cops!

Treva jumped back onto the bed and buried herself beneath the covers, hoping she wouldn't be found. The police dog ran in Moe's bedroom and jumped on him biting his arm hard like those police dogs do in the demonstrations.

Moe screamed with half fear, half pain in his voice. He tried to fight the big dog off of him. With mag lights and infared beams cutting through the darkness, the agents secured the house. The plugs were pulled on Ready For The World, and the house lights finally got turned on.

"Get this fucking dog off of me!" Moe screamed to no one in particular.

Treva sobbed uncontrollably from underneath the silk sheets. After what seemed like forever to Moe, Newman called off his attack dog." "Release Lobo, release." The German shepherd released Moe's arm and ran to Newman's side. Blood trickled from Moe's arm and dripped onto the white angel hair carpet. He stood butt naked, holding his injured arm.

After all the commotion, Goodwin entered the house. He introduced himself to Moe, flashing a pink piece of paper.

"I'm Agent Goodwin with the Narc Unit here in Fayetteville. We have reasons to believe you're connected with the Notorious Supreme Team. We have a search warrant to search your house." He looked at Moe's arm and smiled.

"I'm awfully sorry about Lobo. He hasn't been fed in a couple of days." Goodwin ordered the agents to search the house from top to bottom.

"Cover ever inch!" he yelled.

Moe picked up a pair of shorts that were folded up on the clothes hamper at the foot of the bed. Moving like he was still in shock, he slipped both legs through the holes and pulled the shorts up with one hand. He grabbed a t-shirt and a pair of Treva's shorts and put them under the cover for her. She dressed underneath the cover before revealing her red puffy eyes.

Lobo sat beside Newman growling. Drool dripped to the angel hair carpet like the blood from Moe's arm.

"Baby what's going on?" Treva cried.

"Don't worry Sweetheart, it's nothing," Moe said, clearly in pain.

"What are they looking for? Who in the hell is the Supreme Team?" she asked.

Moe could hear the agents going through his house. He heard glass breaking and things being thrown around. He had wrapped a towel around his throbbing arm, and silently began to pray that the agents didn't check the ceiling tile in the bathroom. He knew he should have never brought coke into his house. He heard himself telling everyone else in the Supreme Team, "Don't try to establish side deals. If anyone has any potential buyers, let everyone know." He had done what he told everyone else not to do. He looked out of the bedroom and saw another dog being lead to the bathroom.

Back In Greensboro

"Take this and don't spend it all in one place," I said to Pricilla. I handed her two hundred dollars. I kissed her, sucking her bottom lip.

"You'll be the first person I'll see when I get back from Alaska," I said to her. She opened the dorm door with her panties stilled balled up in her hand. "Be careful and think of me when you get cold, " she said. She shut the door and I watched her until she was out of sight.

Back In DaVille

Moe whispered to Treva to stop asking him so many questions. She was shaking and still crying, but nodded her head, understanding her man's order. One of the agents walked in the room holding the pistol Moe had reached for.

"Do you have a permit for this?" he asked Moe, holding the pistol up in the air.

"Yeah, its in my wallet on my dresser."

Two more agents entered the room. "Nothing sir," they both said in unison.

There were three agents searching Moe's room. "Stand up slowly," Newman said to Treva. "And move over against the wall beside that scum bag, while the bed is being checked.'"

Moe helped Treva up and she gently rubbed his arm, "Are you alright, baby?" she asked. Moe didn't respond to her, instead he asked if she was alright. She just shook her head without saying anything either.

"Nothing sir, it's clean in here too," the agents said after flipping the mattress.

"Gotdamnit," Goodwin said.

Moe started feeling better about the situation. All the agents so far had not found a thing. He began to smile despite the pain he was feeling.

Suddenly, Moe heard loud barking from down the hall. "Sir! Sirrrrrrrr!" one of the agents called out. "In here! In here!"

Goodwin turned and ran out of the bedroom. He was out of breath when he reached the bathroom. The agent stood on the toilet with an excited looked locked on his face. He had moved the ceiling tile and put his arm in the opening and pulled out a kilo of coke. Goodwin jumped up in the air, filled with rapture.

"Hot damn! I knew it. Sum'ah bitch," he said, sounding as country as Roscoe Picoe Train. "Is there more up there?" he asked excitedly.

The agent put his hand in the ceiling once more and fished around .He pulled out another kilo and handed it to Goodwin.

"I knew it. I just had to wait and be patient," Goodwin said. He had went from shit to sugar in a matter of seconds. "Now the money and the time have not been a waste," he said. He was swollen with pride.

Moe dropped his head when Goodwin entered the room embracing the two kilos of Bolivian Flakes. "You don't know what I'm talking about, huh?" Goodwin asked Moe, thrusting the cocaine in his face.

"Arrest him and his girlfriend," Goodwin said to the other agents. Treva went into hysterics. "No, noooooooo!, nooooo!," she screamed.

"Why are you arresting her?" Moe screamed. "Let her go. She don't know anything about this."

It took two agents to hold Treva down to cuff her. Moe felt bad, but he was glad he had kept her totally out of his business. She didn't know shit.

"Put them in different cars," Newman said.

Once at the police station, they began to question Moe. He wouldn't answer any of their questions. He continued to repeat his name and social security number, like he was a POW (Prisoner of War).

Agent Goodwin had decided to hold Treva for questioning to give him leverage on Moe, but it didn't seem to be working. Moe wasn't bending at all! For hours he continued to repeat the same thing. Even after Newman and Goodwin threatened to charge Treva with the drugs, Moe kept saying his name and social security number. Moe knew that the drug charged wouldn't stick to Treva. He knew that this was a game they were playing. Goodwin thought they would use Treva to break Moe down, but it wasn't going to work. Moe was determined not to incriminate himself.

Finally, I made it back to Ft.Bragg. Fortunately, for my tired legs, I found a parking space right in front of our barricks. I threw my gym bag over my shoulder and slowly walked to my room. I was drained Dry! I took a quick shower and drifted off into a deep sleep.

CHAPTER 18

The word had already spread like a contagious disease through 3rd Battalion, that Moe had been arrested for drugs. I stood in formation waiting for someone to come and tell me I was under arrest in connection with Moe. Everyone knew that I hung out with him.

"Birds of a feather, flock together," Sgt. Marero said staring at me. "I hope you're not in on this drug ring Styles. Because if you are, I'll have your ass court martial before you can blink your eyes."

Like a smart ass, I blinked my eyes and opened them wide. "I don't know anything about any drugs." I said to Sgt. Marero.

Moe had not slept at all. He was concerned about Treva and couldn't sleep. He sat wondering how the agents found out where he lived? How did they know he was connected to the Supreme Team? One thing went in his favor. The house wasn't in his name, nor was it in Treva's name. All he had to do is continue to deny that he knew anything about the drugs that were found in the house.

Treva had taken over the lease on the house after her best friend Jamika Gray got killed in the parking lot of Big P's. Two guys from Grove View Terrace shot her trying to kill her boyfriend, Mike Mack. Moe knew that Mike Mack was a known drug dealer. Suddenly he got an idea.

Wilk and Huntman were walking on eggshells the entire morning. Huntman did manage to page Preme and Chuck. He hit them with code "666*82". Both of them would know that meant trouble in Ft.Bragg. Like myself, Wilk and Huntman anticipated someone tapping them on the shoulder, telling them they were under arrest. But, that hadn't happen. Yet!

Our Battalion loaded the C-141, in route for Ft.Greedly, Alaska. All of us were concerned about Moe. We had no idea what they were going to do to him.

When Chuck woke up, he noticed that Huntman had paged him five times, with "666*82". That meant that someone on the "First string" team had got knocked red handed, in Ft.Bragg. He knew he could not call back because that's what the agents expected him to do. Without waking up Tanoka, he rushed to wake up Preme.

"Yo! Wake up nigga," Chuck said shaking Preme.

"What's wrong?" Preme asked.

"It's Huntman. He paged me with 666*82, so something bad has happened in Ft.Bragg."

Preme picked up his pants and pulled his pager off the corner pocket. His screen on his pager read, "10 pages" He pressed the display button and he saw the same pages. 666*82! "Damn, what do you think happened?" Preme asked Chuck.

"I don't know but it can't be good, " Chuck responded. "We'll just have to wait until he hits us back. "

Moe's attorney arrived and sat in the small room, waiting for his client. Moe was escorted in wearing an orange jumpsuit, flip flops, and cuffs, with shackles secured tightly around his ankles.

"Take the cuffs off of my client. I have some papers for him to sign, " his attorney said to the jailer.

"The cuffs can come off, but the shackles are staying on," the jailer said.

"He doesn't write with his feet, so that should work out just fine," the energetic attorney said.

The jailer removed the cuffs and Moe took a seat. As soon as the jailer left the room, Moe asked, "Where is Treva?"

"She's fine. They are going to release her as soon as they finish the paper work. They know she doesn't have anything to do with this mess. They are convinced she doesn't know shit. You on the other hand," he stopped and pulled a tube from his inside pocket. He opened the tube and pulled out a large Cuban cigar. Then he dug deeper into his pocket and pulled out what appeared to Moe as small scissors. The young attorney cut the tip from the cigar and thumped the tip in the corner of the small room. He lit his expensive cigar and continued to speak. "You on the other hand, they think you know everything there is to know. They want to make a deal with you. They want you to bring down the Supreme Team. "

Moe closed his eyes and shook his head. He leaned back in the gray plastic chair.

"I'm not helping them bring down shit. I don't know anything about the Supreme Team."

The attorney kicked his feet on top of the small square table and started to blow thick rings of smoke in the air. He made it obvious that he wasn't paying attention to Moe.   Moe got pissed off and smacked the table hard with both hands and the attorney jumped.

"Look ah here! Are you going to represent me or do I need to spend my hard earned money elsewhere?" Moe asked.

"No, no," said the attorney. "I'm listening. What's your story?"

Moe told the attorney the story about Mike Mack and Jamika Gray. The word on the streets was that the guys tried to kill Mike Mack for two kilos that he took from the youngsters. Jamika use to live in the house him and Treva got busted in. It was obvious that the two kilos that Goodwin and his boys found were the same two kilos that Mike Mack had taken from the youngsters.

"He took the two keys and hid them in Jamika' s bathroom. But after she was killed, he never returned to get them because everyone was blaming him for her death," Moe said raising his eyebrows.

"It's a long shot, but I like the story," the attorney said. He blew smoke from his nose like a raging bull. "This case will generate a lot of publicity once those murders are brought back up." He began to smile. There was nothing more rewarding to him than being in the spotlight of a major case. Not even the money! It was the media that fed his ego. That gave him a hard on. 'The attorney pushed the chair from the table and stood up. His thin frame towered over Moe .He poked the cigar in the ashtray four times, killing the fire. "By god, I think it will work after all!" he said.

He retrieved the tube from his jacket and dropped what was left of the Cuban cigar inside and screwed on the top. "I'll get to working on it right away. Don't you worry about a thing. Don't say a word about anything to anyone. Even Treva! They are going to try to treat you rough, but just be strong. 'They may even try to send you to Ft.Leavenworth, until your court date. It's all a part of their scare tactics. I will be in touch soon," he said.

The jailer opened the door for Moe ' s attorney. Trying to be cool he placed his Oakley's on his tan face and strolled out.

The military had jurisdiction over Moe, so he was moved from Cumberland County Jail, to the 82nd ABN Division Jail, the following day. Goodwin had scared Treva to death. He had her convinced that she was getting ready to spend the rest of her life behind bars. He realized she did not know anything, and that he couldn't use her as leverage to make Moe bend, but he did know she was scared as hell. Even as her release papers were being prepared, he painted a vivid picture of prison life in her head.

"We will release you today if you wear this wire and visit Moe. Ask him a few questions regarding the Supreme Team and you're in the clear. Regardless, of how he answers the questions," Goodwin explained to Treva.

Treva was shaking like a leaf in a windstorm. She couldn't picture herself framing Moe for Goodwin. But, she really couldn't see spending the rest of her life in prison.

"You're too damn smart and much too beautiful to spend the rest of your life in prison. Don't allow this skuz bucket to destroy your life, like he has destroyed his. "

The next day, Treva went to the small stockade on Ft.Bragg, to visit Moe. She sat in a small booth, behind thick plexy glass. The thick glass had a circular hole with wire in the center. That's what I got to speak through, she thought. It looked like years and years of bad breath had traveled through the mesh wire. She positioned herself in the chair and waited for Moe to be brought in.

"Hey Baby! Are you alright?" Moe asked as soon as he sat down.

Treva shook her head yes. "Yes, I'm fine pumpkin. How are you?" she asked.

"I'm ok, " Moe said trying to smile. "I just miss you."

Treva took her hands and put them up against the plexy glass. Moe began to put his hands up against the glass where hers were placed but he paused. He read the writing on the palms of Treva's hands.

"THEY MADE ME WEAR A WIRE," her right hand read.

"MUST ASK YOU SOME " and a question mark (?) was on the inside of her left palm. The word, "DENY" was underneath the question mark.

Moe put his hands against the glass and winked his eye at Treva.

"I love you, " she said.

"I love you too," he replied.

"What's going on Pumpkin?" Treva asked. "Who is the Supreme Team, and how are you affiliated with them?"

"I don't know who they are Baby! I've heard of them, because I know a lot of guys in Fayetteville, and I have heard them mentioned. But, other than that I don't know anything else. You know if I did I would tell you right now. "

"We're you selling drugs Moe? Please tell me the truth! You've never lied to me before, " Treva said.

"Sweetheart, I promise. I swear to God I have never sold any drugs."
Treva continued to asked Moe certain questions she was instructed to ask. He continued to strongly deny any dealings with the Supreme Team. He sounded as sincere as he could with every answer. He was truly grateful for the loyalty Treva had displayed. He made up in his mind, sitting in that small booth, that if he wiggled out of this trouble, he would leave the game forever and marry Treva.

Two days had gone by and Chuck and Preme were pulling out their hair. They had contacted some of their partners in Fayetteville but no one had heard anything about anyone getting busted.

"We have to do something," Preme said to Chuck. "If the folks are on our asses, I don't want to be sitting ducks. We got to find out what the fuck is going on."

Chuck paced the large marble floor with his hands behind his back. He knew what had to be done, but he didn't want to get her involved. He had no other choice right now though.

"I can send Tanoka back to DaVille to see if she can find out anything. I don't want her involved, but I agree with you. We can't be sitting ducks if "Five 0" is on our ass."

Back In Alaska

It was cold as hell!! We had been in Alaska for two days and I continued to worry about Moe. I hoped he was doing fine. I hoped he hadn't told anything on us!

Before we went to the field we had a five day survival course to go through. Everyday after class we had down time to do whatever we wanted to do. The only problem was there wasn't anything to do in Alaska. There was a military store located about a quarter of a mile from the barricks in which we stayed. These barricks were only used for the soldiers coming from other post to participate in NWTC. For that reason, no telephones were ever installed in the barricks.

The PX, (Military Store) was the only place you could go to use the phone. Despite the record breaking temperatures, I hiked to the PX our third day there. Huntman and Wilk had decided to walk to the PX also. This was our first chance to get together since Moe had been arrested.

"What's happening?" I said to Huntman and Wilk.

"Nothing much." Wilk said. "We came up here to call Chuck and Preme to let them know what's going on with Moe. I know they are scared as hell."

"Have they asked you anything concerning Moe", Huntman asked me.

"No," I said. "Sgt. Marero just said if I was in a drug ring he'd have my ass court martialed. "

Huntman pulled out his calling card from his wallet. "Just say you didn't know anything if they question you about Moe," Huntman said. He started to dial Supreme's home number.

Goodwin listened to the tape for the fourth time. He shook his head from side to side in outrage. "Gotdamnit," he said. "He ain't admitting to shit. This tape is useless to me. Did you tell him you had on a wire?" Goodwin asked Treva.

"No, I didn't!" she exclaimed, birthing a serious attitude. "The damn recorder was on before I went inside the stockade. .Did you hear the tape cut off? Did you hear me saying I had on a damn wire? Hell no you didn't! " she said clearly in her feelings. "They have me recorded on videotape too. Go look at the fucking tape if you want to. I've done what I promised to do. If you have anything else for me contact my attorney, " Treva said. She got up, pulling her long hair back in a ponytail and walked out of his office.

Chuck had explained to Tanoka that she had to go back to Fayetteville for him to see what had happened to his partners. She was the only one he could trust, he told her.

"Just fly to DaVille and go to this address. This is our partner Justice. I've called his house number but it's disconnected. I can't find his pager number anywhere. He'll know what has happened. He's very close with our partners in Ft.Bragg. All you have to do is tell him to contact me and Preme immediately."

Tanoka could see Goodwin waiting for her at the airport. She heard what Chuck had said, but she continued to see Goodwin's face.

"I'm not flying Chuck! " she said.

"What? You're not flying? I thought you hated that long ass drive." He said.

"I do, but I hate to fly more," she said.

Chuck did not want Tanoka to drive back alone but she had to.

"Well, get some rest and you can leave first thing in the morning. "

Tanoka knew she was the cause of all of what was happening. If Chuck only knew how involved she was, what would he do? she thought. She went into the bathroom and took a hot shower and did some reflecting. After Chuck knocked on the door and told her to hurry up so she could get some rest, she got out and went to bed, but she couldn't sleep.

Chuck and Preme got with their third roommate, who was ultimately responsible for the drugs, and discussed plans for them to leave the country.

Jesus, said he could arrange for them to live like two kings for the rest of their lives in Cuba. The catch was they could never return to the states. It sounded good to both of them, but they hoped it wouldn't come down to them having to leave.

The phone rang and Tanoka picked it up. "Hello, " she said.

"Hey, is Chuck or Preme in?" Huntman asked.

"No, they're out right now. Who's calling?" Tanoka asked.

"Just let them know that Huntman called. Tell them I'll call back the same time tomorrow." Huntman hung up the phone. "They're not at home," he said to me and Wilk. "I'll have to walk back up here tomorrow after the classes and call him again, " he said. We all purchased chips and drinks and went our separate ways in the frozen tundra.

Tanoka put her things in the car. She dreaded the long ride back to North Carolina. She planned not to even check out the address Chuck had given her once she got back to North Click. Her plans were to get a hotel room and continue to call Chuck and report to him that she could not find anyone at the address. Then she would return safely to her new home in Miami.

Back In Alaska

I walked back to the PX, the next day at the same time, Huntman and Wilk were inside playing Ms. Pacman, waiting for a telephone to become available.

"What's up fellas?" I said.

Wilk. turned around and slapped my hand. Huntman continued to concentrate on Ms. Pacman."

"We're waiting for a phone, so we can call Preme or Chuck," Wilk said. "What's up with you?" he asked.

"Nothing, just cold as hell," I said. "Look! A phones open." I pointed at an empty phone booth.

Huntman turned his head to see the empty phone booth and Ms. Pacman ran into the pink ghost. "Shit," he said. "I got ate. Your turn Wilk, I'm going to the phone. "

"Hello, " Chuck said.

"What's up my Nigga?" Huntman asked.

"You tell me what's up?" Chuck said. "What in the hell happened?"

"To make a long story short, Moe got knocked with two birds in his crib, " Huntman said.

"What! " Chuck yelled. "Where is he now?" he asked Huntman.

"He was in Cumberland County Jail, when we left Ft.Bragg. As soon as I find out something else I'll let you know. We'll be here for three and a half more weeks and I'll hit you as soon as we get back to Bragg. I wouldn't advise you to go to DaVille," Huntman said to Chuck. "I don't trust any of them niggas. Someone is an informant in our circle. "

Chuck's heart pounded while Huntman talked. He wasn't going to go to Fayetteville. He wasn't even going to leave Miami.

When Chuck hung up the phone he began to search for Justice's pager number. He trusted Justice to no end. They had a long history as being good friends. While he was looking for the number, he wondered why Justice's home number was disconnected. He looked in the closet and found nothing. He checked his little black book and still he found nothing. Chuck walked over to his dresser and looked over some phone numbers he had in a Philly Blunt box. He had failed to check there before now. Chuck unfolded a napkin from Lashocka' s and found Justice's pager and cell phone number. He dialed his cell number and continued to browse over the other numbers and papers in the box. He received no answer!

He dialed the pager number and picked up the phone list that had been lying there for weeks. The phone list made him curious again, since he ran across it. He punched in his cell number after the pager beeped and hung up the phone. Then he studied the one number that he had noticed before. The one that had been called five times from his hotel room. He picked the phone up again and dialed the number.

Tanoka was about two hours from Fayetteville. She was tired but determined to continue her drive. For hours she thought of ways to keep Goodwin off balance. She already knew that it was Moe who had been busted. Goodwin didn't know where Huntman or Wilk lived, but she knew he knew where Moe lived. She confirmed his address when Chuck took her to his house. Now, if Moe told on Chuck, she was going to loose out all the way around. She hadn't thought of that until now. She had already crossed Goodwin, so he wouldn't have any use for her. If anything he would throw her to the wolves.

Moe had sat in jail for four days ironing out the wrinkles of his story. He was convinced that the charges could be beat. He had failed to follow his own instructions regarding side deals, and as a result he had got busted. But, he had followed his own advice and as he always said," Kept all bitches out of his business." Since he did that, Treva didn't know shit. He kicked his flip-flops off and laid back on the small bunk. Things could be worse he thought. He could be freezing his balls of in Alaska!

Back In Miami

"This is Agent Goodwin. Hello! Hello! "

"Ahh, I'm sorry .I must have the wrong number," Chuck said as he eased the phone down.

His heart fell to the floor. His stomach started to churn, and he smacked the phone to the floor.

"Oh my god! No! Please god no!" he said. Chuck jumped when his cellular phone began to ring. He was afraid to pick it up. It continued to ring and Chuck remembered he had paged Justice.

He wiped the tears from his eyes, and tried to calm down. "Hello, " he said.

"Yo! Did someone page Justice?"

"Yeah my nigga. This is Chuck. What's up Jay?"

"Nothing Chuck! What's up with you?" Justice asked.

"Why is your phone disconnected?" Chuck asked.

"Too many ho's had my home number and it was causing problems with me and the ole lady. I had to get it changed," he said.

"Have you heard about anyone of my partners getting busted?" Chuck asked.

"No! They gone to Alaska. I saw Huntman Sunday and he said they were leaving the next day. What's going on?" Justice asked.

"I can't explain it right now, but I need for you to go hone. Make sure you are not dirty. I sent a female to look for you, to see if you heard anything about my partners from Ft.Bragg. I couldn't find your pager or cell number. She should be there in a few hours. I need you to keep her there when she arrives make sure she doesn't leave, even if you have to hog tie the bitch up."

Justice started to laugh. He didn't ask anymore questions. He told Chuck that he would call him as soon as he hog tied her.

Chuck fell back on the bed, still feeling sick. He had been betrayed in the worst way. He closed his eyes and began to have flashbacks.

He heard Moe telling him, "Don't ever bring that bitch back to my house." Now Chuck knew why she kept running him on small errands when they were in the hotel room.

"Maybe she is "Five 0, " Preme had said to him while they were having lunch at the Polo Club.

"No, she doesn't have sense enough to be Five 0, " he said to Preme. He was the one who didn't have sense, he thought. He began to think about when Tanoka tried to write his phone numbers down from his pager. She was trying to get the numbers to pass on to the agents. He couldn't understand it! He loved Tanoka so much. He had stopped running the streets because he thought he'd found his soul mate. She really loved him, he thought.

The phone call at her house on Christmas had to be the police. She acted afraid when she was on the phone. He remembered that she was in such a hurry to leave Fayetteville. Now, it was all adding up to Chuck. She wasn't trying to have him robbed, she was trying to have him set up by the agents.

As much as he hated to, Chuck knew he had to tell Preme and Jesus about everything. An informant had infiltrated the heart of the Supreme Team.

When Chuck told Preme what he had found out, Preme hit the roof.

"I knew it was something about that pretty bitch. I had negative vibes about her since day one. I told you at the Polo Club that that bitch could be five 0. " Preme continued to fuss. "You had the fucking police staying here in our crib."

Chuck dropped his head. He couldn't say anything. Preme picked up the phone and paged Jesus. He had to be informed also, since Tanoka had met him.

When Jesus called back, Preme told him about Tanoka. He said that he wasn't worried about her, but he advised Preme and Chuck to prepare to leave the country forever, or deal with her. In his silent rage, Jesus hung up the phone on Preme.

"I've called Justice and told him to hold her when she shows up. Once he has her, he is going to call me back, " Chuck said to Preme.

"I want you to call that psycho Keeby, " Preme said. "Let him handle Tanoka. "

Keeby was the hit man in Danville for the Supreme Team. He was only contacted when serious jobs had to be conducted. He was a cold blooded murderer. If the money was right, he would kidnap the president and murder him! He was a real psycho. But, if you didn't know it you couldn't tell he was a nut case. Keeby was the type of person once you met him, you'd feel like you'd known him for years. People automatically trusted him with their lives, and often he'd take them. Preme liked him because he didn't care who he killed if it was business. Man, woman or child! Just make sure you had his money or you'd become a victim.

Hours passed and Justice had not heard from anyone. He sat at home waiting for some female to come looking for him. He secretly anticipated tying whoever she was up.

Tanoka had gotten a room in Fayetteville, and laid down and went to sleep. When she did wake up she called Chuck to inform him that there wasn't anyone at the house he sent her to. She told him where she was, and told him she'd try to locate his friend later after she rested.

Chuck paged Justice, and Justice assured him that he was still at home. "She didn't come by here dawg. She is telling you a fucking lie. I've been here since you told me she was coming over. I got rope and everything waiting on that bitch. "

Chuck hung up the phone and paged Keeby. Keeby called Chuck back within minutes.

"What's up killer?" Chuck said to Keeby.

Don't call me that, " Keeby said. "I wouldn't hurt a fly. "

"What you doing?" Chuck asked.

"I'm standing in the mirror brushing my hair. I got to put in at least a thousand strokes a day if I want to keep my perfect waves."

Chuck took the phone away from his face and looked at it. He knew that Keeby was a serious fool. A thousand strokes, he thought. It's a wonder his arm doesn't fall off! He did ask him what he was doing?

"Why? What's up?" Keeby asked Chuck.

Chuck looked over at Preme who was staring him down his throat. He thought about how much he loved Tanoka. Maybe he could be wrong about her.

"We have a job for you, " Chuck said. "There is a lady in the Holiday Inn, off of Highway 95. She's in room 806. Her name is Tanoka. I'm going to call her now to tell her you are on your way over there. Ride with her back to Miami. Be extremely polite to her. I don't want her to sense that there is something wrong. We'll see you when you get here.

Chuck called Tanoka and told her he had found out what had happened in Ft. Bragg. He tried to down play the seriousness of the situation by apologizing for making her drive all the way back to North Carolina for nothing. He told her that he finally found Justice's number and he had talked to him.

"Justice moved to another house, that's probably why there wasn't anyone there," he said to her. "Some guys in Ft.Bragg, got busted, but it don't have anything to do with us. I know you just got there not to long ago but I'm ready for you to come home. To make sure that you get back safely, I'm sending one of my friends over to ride with you back, so you won't have to drive all the way back. "

Tanoka was relieved. Things had worked out great, she thought. She hung up the phone and packed the things she had unpacked.

Keeby knocked on the door and identified himself only as Chuck's friend. She opened the door and let him inside. She introduced herself and Keeby told her his name. It didn't really make a difference he figured. He was going to kill her anyway. "Dead people can't tell shit!" was Keeby's philosophy.

Keeby looked at Tanoka as she picked up her bags. He thought she was beautiful, but that didn't matter to him. He walked over and took the bags from Tanoka. She thought he was cute. She couldn't believe that Chuck trusted her enough to ride from Fayetteville to Miami with another guy. Especially one that was as fine as Keeby. The trust that he displayed made her love him more.

For hours Tanoka and Keeby laughed and talked about people they both knew in DaVille. Tanoka felt like she had known Keeby forever. She just thought it was strange that he knew so many people she knew, yet she didn't know him.

"Why do you keep brushing your hair?" Tanoka asked Keeby. "You already got waves going all around your head. You're going to brush them all out," she said jokingly.

Keeby smiled, but he hated it when people made jokes about him brushing his hair. He had to brush his hair. It was the only thing that kept him from killing all the time!

Goodwin was still on cloud nine about his bust. He had caught Moe in possession of two kilos of cocaine. He didn't care that he continued to deny knowing anything about the Supreme Team. Any jury would convict him, he thought. He sat twiddling his thumbs, wondering how he could get Moe to cooperate. If Moe cooperated, he knew that a promotion would be inevitable.

15 Hours Later In Miami

When Tanoka pulled up to the mansion, Keeby looked impressed.

"Damn, I didn't know those niggas were doing it like this, " he said.

"You've never been down here?" she asked.

"Nah, I haven't," he said.

Tanoka knew how secretive Chuck was. It was strange that he would allow someone that hadn't ever been to the mansion to accompany her. Maybe she was just too paranoid, she thought.

They got out of the car and Keeby grabbed her bags again. It was early and Tanoka was sure Chuck and Preme was still asleep, but to her surprise Preme greeted them at the door.

"Good morning early bird, " she said to Preme.

He didn't respond to her. Instead he shook Keeby's hand and welcomed him to Miami. Tanoka felt the coldness in Preme's action. Automatically, she sensed that something was wrong. She picked up her bags that Keeby had dropped, and started for Chuck's bedroom. Her mind began to race. When she reached the bedroom, suddenly the door opened. Chuck stood in the doorway, like he was guarding Ft. Knox.

"Well, well, " he said. "Look who's made it safely back to M. I .A. "

"Good morning, Baby, " said Tanoka. She dropped her Gucci bags and extended her arms, expecting a warm embrace from Chuck. He stared at her coldly, not reacting. He looked angry, yet hurt, Tanoka thought.

"Do you know what M. I .A. mean in the military?" he asked her.

Before she opened her mouth, he whispered, "It means missing in action! " He grabbed her elbow and spent her around and walked her to the living room.

There, Preme. , Jesus and Keeby stood waiting for them. She was smart enough to know that her cover had been blown. She started to beg and plea with Chuck to let her explain. More than anything he wanted her to be able to explain, but he knew no explanation would satisfy his partners thirst for her blood. The past few weeks he had really started to love her. At first, it was her sex. Now, it was the person that he loved. But, he knew that was over.

"Chuck please! I love you, " she screamed. "I didn't know what I was doing. I truly love you. Please don't hurt me, Chuck," she cried.

Chuck knew that Tanoka had to die. That wasn't even a question. The only reason she was brought back to Miami was to see how much information she had given Agent Goodwin. Chuck and Preme began to question her, and Keeby and Jesus looked on.

"How long have you been working for the police? How much do they know about us?" Preme asked spitting in her face as he screamed. He shot questions at her like M-60 rounds. "Do they know where we live?

Have you told them that?" Chuck asked.

"I haven't told them shit! That's why I wanted to move down here. I wanted to get away from them. I wanted to tell you the whole story Chuck, but I was afraid." Tanoka tried to explain herself. Chuck wouldn't look her in the face. He couldn't look at her at all. His chin stuck to his chest. He stared at her feet and squeezed her arm tightly. He was hurting her, but she said nothing.

"They don't know anything about you two. They know your names because everyone in Fayetteville knows y'alls name, " Tanoka said.

112

"They knew where Moe lived, " Chuck cut in. He was furious at himself for trusting her. "How did they know that?!" he screamed. "It was you, wasn't it? You told them where he lived, didn't you? The day you rode with me over to Moe's house. You told them!"

"I told them that you and Preme sold clothes in Fayetteville, not drugs. That's what I told them. " Tanoka's body was becoming limp. Chuck pushed her down on the floor in disgust.

"You tried to write my pager numbers down to give them to the police. You were calling them when I left the hotel room. You were asking me all types of questions because you were trying to set me up to be busted, not robbed! You were trying to have us popped by the pigs. "

Tanoka begged Chuck with her China eyes that were filled with tears. He didn't fall victim to her pleas this time. He bent over and slapped Tanoka as hard as he could.

"Bitch, you ain't shit but a lying tramp," he yelled.

Tanoka dropped her head and wiped the blood from her mouth. She started to cry uncontrollably, but still she manage to speak. "After I realized that I loved you Chuck, I tried to get away from Agent Goodwin, but he continued to harass me. That's why I didn't want to fly to North Carolina. When I went back to get my things, he was at the airport waiting on me .He was still trying to get me to cooperate, but I refused. Christmas Day, it was him that called me. It wasn't my ex-boyfriend. It was him! He was telling me I was in to deep. He said I wasn't going to get away with crossing him. I wanted to tell you Chuck, but I was to afraid to."

Everyone stood around Tanoka, listening to her plea for her life. No one seemed to be moved by what she had said. Taken what she had just told them, they figured that she hadn't caused too much damage to the Supreme Team. They would just have to "steer clear, " of Fayetteville. Preme, Jesus and Chuck stepped a way from Tanoka and Keeby and huddled up.

"So, What do you think?" Chuck asked.

"What do you mean "what do we think"?" Jesus asked Chuck. "I think we need to send a message to the rest of those rats in Fayetteville."

Preme added, "She knows to much Chuck. We got to get rid of her."

Tanoka had managed to stand back up. She looked around like she wanted to run, but figured it would be useless. Then she gazed sadly to where Chuck and his two partners were huddled up. She turned and stared Keeby in his face. His face looked so friendly an hour ago, now it looked stone cold. When she looked back in Chuck's direction, she noticed him drop his head and a large tear cruised down the side of his face. Without saying a word to anyone, he turned and walked out of the room.

"Go ahead and take her, " Supreme said to Keeby.

"Chuck! Chuck! Chuck, please help me! I love you Chuck!" Tanoka screamed. Her cries cut through Chuck like a sharp, hot blade in butter, but he continued to walk away and quietly sob.

Keeby hit Tanoka in the back of her head with the large wooden brush he had stuck in his pocket. She fell unconscious to the marble floor. He picked her up and laid her over his shoulders like she was a huge towel. Preme handed Keeby an envelope filled with cash.

"How do you want it done, Boss?" Keeby asked Preme, like he was some hit man from the mafia.

" Just send a serious message to the rats in DaVille. Make sure she is found real soon, " Preme said.

Keeby carried Tanoka to the car and tied her up. Then he injected her with a tranquilizer to ensure she would sleep the entire trip back to North Carolina.

13 Hours Later

The drug wore off about an hour a way from Fayetteville. Keeby was about to fall asleep himself, when he heard the banging in the trunk. He popped another no-doze, his tenth one, and pulled over on the side of the highway. He opened the trunk and injected another dose of the tranquilizer into Tanoka' s neck.

"That should hold her long enough for me to get some rest once I get home, " Keeby said to himself, while emptying the rest of the syringe.

He pulled the needle from her neck and tossed it in the dark woods. Then he jumped back into the car, still not feeling the effects of the no-doze and pulled off.

Keeby's nearest neighbor was a quarter of a mile a way. He elected to move to Hope Mills just to convenience his murderous business. He decided to go in his house and take a nap before he killed Tanoka. Even if she did wake up before he did, no one would hear her useless cries for help. He was drained and he needed some rest so he could think about a good way to send a message to the rats in Fayetteville. Those stupid pills didn't work for him, he thought. He kicked off his black leather Timberlands and lay on the bed and fell asleep.

Moe' s attorney had hired private investigators who obtained written statements from guys who had witnessed Mike Mack stash coke in Jamika's house. This was great news to Moe. One of the guys even went as far as to say he stashed the coke in the ceiling for Mike Mack at times. Statements like that just about guaranteed Moe his freedom, his attorney said.

"Just be patient, " He told Moe. "God isn't the only one who can work miracles! "

Keeby jumped up and ran to the mirror. He had been sleep for a few hours and he couldn't believe he laid down and didn't put on his "Doo Rag." He grabbed a brush from his medicine cabinet and started to aggressively brush his hair.

"This is all her fault, " he said, looking at himself in the mirror. "She is the cause of me being so tired. The reason I fell asleep without covering my waves. "

He pulled out a Doo Rag from the cabinet and tied it tight around his round head. After he checked the mirror again he ran to the car. He opened the trunk and Tanoka lay lifeless. He poked her in the side with his brush but she didn't move. Keeby grabbed her and pulled her out of the trunk. He heard her moan when he picked her up, so he knew she wasn't dead already. Like before, he threw her over his shoulder and carried her into the house. Tanoka was placed in what looked like an electric chair. Her hands and feet were tied tightly.

"Send a message to the rats, " he kept saying to himself. He paced in front of his soon to be victim. She was starting to wake up.

"Where am I?" Tanoka asked Keeby. "Why do you have me tied up? Where is Chuck? What are you going to do to me?"

Keeby didn't pay any attention to the questions Tanoka was asking him. He continued to pace the floor in front of her. "Send a message to the rats." he said louder. "I got it!"

Keeby took off his Doo Rag and started brushing his hair again. Something he did every time he had a brilliant way of killing someone. He ran to the back porch to where he had a dozen or so rat traps set up. Sure enough, he had trapped two rats while he was away in Miami. He took the two dead rats out of the traps and carried them by their tails into where Tanoka was tied up.

"Please Keeby, don't hurt me. I swear to God if you let me go I won't say a word to anyone about anything. I'll stay out of Chuck's life forever," Tanoka cried.

"The damn thing about it is, I know you will tell something," Keeby said laughing wickedly.

He dropped the dead rats in Tanoka's lap. She began to scream as loud as she could, but it was no use. No one could hear her. But, the cries of someone begging for their life, thrilled Keeby. It made him feel like God. He had the power to take life. He casually walked to the kitchen and picked up a large butcher's knife. He walked back in explaining to Tanoka how he hated to kill someone who was so beautiful. When she heard that and saw the knife, she started making propositions to Keeby.

"If you think I'm so beautiful, maybe we can be together!" She said, trying to calm herself down, but the sight of the two rats were too much for her nerves.

He walked behind her, "We will be together," He said. Tanoka tried to follow him with her teary eyes but she couldn't. Keeby grabbed her by her long, silky hair and pulled her head up, exposing her thin, smooth neck. He pressed the razor, sharp knife against her neck and in one motion, sliced her beautiful smooth neck from ear to ear. Then he forced his hand in the hole he had cut in her neck and pulled her tongue through the hole. "A Columbian Neck Tie!" Just like he had seen in the gangster movies.

"Send a message to the rats, " the Godfather had ordered in the flick, just like he had been ordered to do.

Keeby and Tanoka were together after she died. He was more psycho than Chuck and Preme could ever imagine. After sexing her dead corpse he stuffed her in a body bag, and drove her to the address Chuck had given him. After circling the block three times to make sure there wasn't anyone watching, he cut off his lights and parked the car. He went to the trunk and unzipped the body bag. He pulled Tanoka's dead body out and laid it on her mother's front lawn. He pulled the two rats from his front pocket and dropped them on her chest. Then he bent over and kissed her on the face. Out of respect, he pulled off his Doo Rag and pulled out his brush and began to brush his hair. He turned and walked slowly back to the car.

"What a fucking waste," he said.

CHAPTER 19

Goodwin threatened Moe with a conspiracy to commit murder charge. Moe acted very calm and cool and he had reason to. Unlike the drugs, he really didn't know anything about Tanoka's murder. But, if she was the reason his house got raided, he considered it to be good riddance.

Moe sat in the small stockade and respected Supreme's and Chuck's work. He couldn't believe that Tanoka had been so viciously murdered. He also took heed to the sign of what happens to rats.

Goodwin somehow found out the strategy of Moe's attorney and got permission to go to Brunswick Correctional Institution, to speak with Mike Mack. Mack was serving two life sentences for the murders of the youngsters in DaVille. When Goodwin told him he could get some of the time off of him, if he agreed to testify he never kept cocaine in Jamika's house, Mike spat in Goodwin's face. The guards wrestled Mike to the ground and cuffed him.

"I have two life sentences for murder, motherfucker! You can't help me! You can have me killed like that rat bitch Tanoka!" he yelled at Goodwin. "Don't you ever come here and ask me to help this crooked ass system again. "

The guards pulled him by his legs out of the small visiting room and took him to the lock up unit to calm down.

Moe was scheduled to go to trial in three weeks .His attorney choose to exercise his rights to a speedy trial. That would keep Goodwin from gathering anymore information on Moe. By that time we would be returning from Alaska. Just in time to witness one of the best trials in Fayetteville's history.

Justice told Chuck how Tanoka's body had been found not leaving out a single detail. He said she was laying in the yard as if she was sun tanning on the beach. The autopsy report said she had been raped…after she was murdered. Chuck was more than shocked when Justice told him. He couldn't believe that Keeby was that sick! He was hurt that she had to be dealt with in that manner. He missed her tremendously, but he knew having her knocked off was the best thing for the Supreme Team.

We returned a day before Moe's trial. I called my mother to let her know that I had made it back to Ft.Bragg safely. She told me to make sure I called Kami. She sounded excited. "Kami has something very important to tell you." my mom said.

When I called Kami she told me that she was pregnant. I was floored. But, somehow I knew that was what she was going to tell me. I wasn't ready to have a child. I talked the talk, but I wasn't ready to walk the walk. Not at all!

I knew that Kami was pregnant by me, but I told her we had to have a blood test to make sure that the baby was mine when it was born. I made up a story that I heard she had been messing around on me. We fell out, just like I planned, and I broke up with her.

Huntman tried to get in touch with Justice, but he never returned Huntman's calls. Since Moe had been busted, Huntman figured that Justice was just laying low until the smoke cleared. Then he realized that Justice didn't even know about the bust. Maybe Justice couldn't be trusted like he thought he could be. He hoped Justice would call him back later.

The trial lasted for a week and a half. Goodwin and the prosecution presented a weak case against Moe. On da flip side, Moe's attorney put on an Oscar winning performance. He had witnesses that testified Mike Mack hid drugs in Jamika's bathroom. He was a drug dealer, and Jamika's house was the spot he use to meet his workers. The jurors looked thoroughly convinced that Moe was not guilty. And if they were not, they were when the last witness emerged.

Mike Mack testified that he did hide the two kilos of Bolivian flakes in the ceiling tiles of Jamika's bathroom.

"I took the two kilos from the boys from Grove View. I knew they were going to come after me, so I laid low for a second. I hid the coke in Jamika's house. In the ceiling of her bathroom.

Mike Mack even described how the kilos were wrapped in the brown paper with the yellow tape. After his testimony, the jury deliberated for thirty minutes and returned with a verdict…"NOT GUILTY!"

Moe walked smoothly out of the courtroom a free man, a hero to the Supreme Team and with a multi million dollar lawsuit against the city of Fayetteville for defamation of character.

Mike Mack rode all the way back to Brunswick Correctional, knowing that he would never have to worry about his kids being taken care of, commissary or anything else again. Moe would make sure of that.

Hours after the trial, Moe embraced Huntman and whispered in his ear.

"I'm finished with this hustling bullshit. I can't stand another close call like this one."

Huntman patted Moe's back and said, "Me too, dawg. Me too. I'm finished! No more fucking around for me either. It was fun while it lasted, but it's over now."

"We're just going to have to be regular GI's again from here on out." Moe concluded as they embraced each other again.

The following week, Justice finally surfaced. He had found out about Moe's situation and had been waiting for things to cool off, just as Huntman had expected. Justice paid Huntman and Huntman explained to Justice that he wasn't going to be doing anything else for a while.

"Probably, not ever again," Huntman said to Justice.

I met with Lil' Kenny and Tory to break the bad news to them. Both of them looked like they were going to break down and cry when I told them that I wasn't going to be dealing anymore. I briefly explained the situation and told them how serious it was, and they understood my decision. They were crushed but they respected the highs and lows of the game.

I went to Bob Dunn Ford and put a down payment on the maroon Mustang GT, I had looked at before I left for Alaska. I had saved money in the bank too so it would not look suspicious when I did purchase my dream car.

It was time for me to get back on track. I had to remind myself why I joined the Army. A "Patriot" is what I use to call myself. I made up in my mind that I joined the Army for the love of my country so, I was going to stop using the Army as my camouflage.

After I stopped dealing cocaine, I stopped going back and forward to Greensboro so often. As a result, I lost contact with Lakisha and Pricilla. I talked to Rena on occasions, but eventually I lost contact with her. Of course, I had to keep in touch with Kami, she was pregnant with my first child. Shortly after my return from Alaska, I made Celeste my number one lady.

We all stopped hanging out together like we did prior to Moe being arrested. I mean, we still kicked it, every now and then, but not like we did before. I missed hanging out with my Crew also. I missed the girls at the club jocking us. I missed the money that I use to make most of all!

Moe got married to Treva a few months after his trial and stopped hanging with us all together. He said it wasn't anything personal, but he wanted to change his life. He was a husband now. He won a very large sum of money from his lawsuit against Fayetteville and was transferred by his request to Ft.Gordon in Georgia. After he transferred, I never heard from him again.

Wilk got out of the Army when his time expired later on that year. He moved back to the city of "Brotherly Love." The last time I heard from him, he was working at the Post Office and attending a community college.

Despite his efforts Goodwin didn't get his promotion. Instead, he got demoted for costing the city so much money and embarrassment. He retired after his demotion.

Supreme and Chuck stopped coming to North Carolina. Huntman did speak with Preme at times and Preme said that Chuck was still fucked up by Tanoka's death. I guess he was still in love with her.

On December 11th, 1989, Kami gave birth to my daughter. Just like she had planned it if the baby was a girl, she named her Sheneka. She was as cute as can be. She had my eyes and nose and my mothers complexion. I was a proud father, but just to keep the tension between Kami and I, I told her that we still needed to have a blood test.

Eleven days after Sheneka was born, I made a combat parachute assault into Panama. "Operation Just Cause," really got me back on the right track. I was a "Gun-Ho," patriotic soldier again!

The following year, I was sent to Operation Desert Storm. For eight months, I laid in the desert hoping and praying that Sadaam Hussein didn't drop chemicals on us. Thank God that he didn't.

When I returned from Desert Storm, I was approaching the end of my four year tour. I decided not to reenlist. I was ready to leave Fayetteville anyway. Ready to try my hand at a real "Nine to Five." I wanted to enroll into college also. Exercise my brain. Four years of Airborne Infantry had given me a bad case of tunnel vision. I only knew how to kill! Four years and two wars was enough for me.

I knew how Chuck felt when he said, "He had bigger and better things to do, " I felt the exact same way. I had other aspects of life to explore.

CHAPTER 20

Huntman helped me carry my things out to my car. He wore a sad face and he didn't have much to say as we loaded my Mustang down with heavy, green duffel bags, filled with years of junk. Besides himself, I was the last Wheel from our once rolling car!

"I got one more year left, " he said. "I'm going to get out also." Huntman had been in the Army for almost eight years. He had been through Ranger School and before I left he was promoted to Staff Sgt. When he told me he was getting out of the Army, it went in one ear and out of the other one. I figured he would definitely be a lifer. I felt like I was leaving my best friend in a war zone to defend for himself. We had been through a lot together in the past four years. We embraced each other and hugged tightly. Both of us were too manly to cry .We promised to stay in touch with each other.

It felt great going home a free man. I didn't have to ever worry about waking up at 5:30 am, again to conduct a ten mile run. Didn't have to worry about jumping out of helicopters or perfectly good airplanes anymore. And I sure as hell didn't have to worry about going to another country to fight in a war that wasn't my war!

What I did have to worry about was how I was going to make a living. I had saved up a nice sum of money in the four years I was in the Army. I knew that the money wouldn't last forever. Not even close to forever. There weren't many jobs that sought after guys who were in the airborne infantry. I talked to a few law agencies before I got out of the military that were very interested in sponsoring me because of my experiences in the Army. I'd received an expert badge with every weapon I fired. "They needed guys that could shoot", one Captain of the North Carolina State Troopers said to me. But, I quickly shot down the idea of becoming a police officer. I came to the conclusion that being a cop would be too much like being in the Army. I was tired of uniforms and the whole "Team" thing. I wanted to do something alone. The fact still remained that I had a daughter I had to support, so I needed a job.

A few days after I got out of the Army, I left Donnica's house on my way to Stoneville to pick up my daughter. Even though I was still going with Celeste, I moved in with Donnica. I met her seven months before I got out of the Army at a party in Greensboro. She was a gorgeous woman. Fine as hell! Donnica had long, brownish hair, and hazel eyes. Her skin was the color of creamy peanut butter. Donnica was built like a brick shit house! Her ass was so juicy, that every time we went out, I would always get into a confrontation with at least one knucklehead who would make some type of slick statement about how her ass looked. The first few times it happened I thought that guys were just being totally disrespectful. But, it happened so much, I realized that Donnica's ass just cast guy's brains into a trans. One look made them completely stupid. That's how I met her at the party. I took one look at her ass and I was stupid!

I called Tone to let him know that I was home for good. Since I was coming to Stoneville, he suggested that I stop by the "Back Street," to check him out. He said he had something he wanted to show me. When I turned onto the Back Street, cars were lined from one end of the street to the other. It only took me a second to realize that the Back Street was Tone's dope spot.

I watched as his young workers ran from car to car serving the crack heads. He had to be making thousands a day, I thought. The way I use to make thousands!

Finally, I made it to where Tone was standing and I pulled over.

"What's up Wild Styles?" he yelled, happy to see me. He walked over to the car and hugged me like I was the prodigal son that finally came home.

"I know you're glad to be out of that Army shit, huh?" he asked.

"Yeah, now I don't have to worry about getting up before the sun rises, " I said.

We both began to laugh and catch up on things. After about an hour of discussing old Ft.Bragg stories, Tone said, "I'm going to miss coming down there to see you and your boys. What are you going to do now?" he asked. Before I got a chance to answer, Tone yelled at one of his young workers, "Give her an extra twenty piece." He sounded like a manager at KFC, instead of a drug dealer.

"She has spent more than two hundred dollars, " he said. He turned back to me, "If they spend more than two hundred dollars, I give them a twenty dollar rock as a bonus. Now, what are you going to do now that you are not a slave for Uncle Sam?"

"I m going to get a job somewhere, then I'm going to eventually enroll in college," I said.

Shaking his head in disapproval, Tone began to count some money a worker ran up and handed him.

Tone knew that I was deeply involved in the drug game before in DaVille. He couldn't understand why I was trying to go straight after all the money I made selling drugs.

"You're still worried about that shit that happened last year in Fayetteville, aren't you?" he asked.

I didn't answer Tone. He knew that's what it was. We came to close to getting a case and it had scared the heebie-jeebies out of me.

"Work hard if you want to, I'm not working hard. And as long as crack sells, I won't work at all," Tone said, still counting his money.

We embraced again and I told him I would call him again soon.

Don't wait too long, " he said. "I know a good connection in Winston Salem. It may not be as good as you use to have it, but for around here you will make a killing. I promise you that."

After two weeks of sleeping late and blowing money, I finally got a job at an industrial plant called Kobe Copper. It didn't take me long to realize that I wasn't going to be working there for any length of time. Actually, it took me four weeks and two piss poor pay checks before I quit. After I quit Kobe Copper, I got a job at yet, another industrial plant. Unifi, made anything that could be made with cotton. The pay wasn't as good as Kobe, but the work was not as hard or dangerous. Unifi also had one other plus, it had a lot of women working in the plant. I decided to work there for a while. That would be the smart thing for me to do because I did need the money.

Two months later, I had slept with most of the women in Unifi and I was getting bored with the work. I could not picture myself working in a factory too much longer, even if I was sleeping with half of the women. It was fun while it lasted, but I was ready for another change in my life. So I quit!

My older, but smaller brother Tim, got out of the Army four months before I got out. Just like myself, Tim started working at Kobe Copper when he came home, but he didn't last long either. Now, he was hustling in Madison. He had the Bricks, the projects where we grew up, on lock down. Nobody sold anything in the Bricks that Tim didn't get a percentage of. It was either his coke you were selling, or you paid him for allowing you to sell in the Bricks. Either way, Tim was going to get paid. With a nickname like "12 Guage," nobody in the Bricks ever tried to contest him.

Tim and I decided to go into business together. Once again, I found myself becoming a part of a team. But, the other half of this team was my own flesh and blood. My "Better Half," as we use to say about each other. He was someone that I loved more than I loved myself. So, I didn't mind being a part of a team again.

"How much are you going to invest, Styles?" Tim asked. He always called me Styles, like that wasn't his last name.

"I'm going to put up whatever you put up," I said to my little, big brother.

"I'm going to start out with ten "G's'," he said. "If you match that we can buy enough coke and start selling to them boys in Stoneville. I know they get their coke from Winston. They spend a lot of money with them shady niggas," he said.

120

That sounded like a good idea to me. Tone was going to be surprised when I showed up on the Back Street prepared to serve him and his crew.

Months Later

It had been more than three months since I'd seen Tone last. When we pulled onto the Back Street, he saw my Mustang and jogged over to where Tim and I parked.

"What's up, Styles? What's up, Tim?" Tone said, as we got out of the car.

We exchanged soul shakes and the three of us began to walk in the direction of the old abandoned school that sat off of the Back Street.

"What's happening? What brings you two up in this neck of the woods?" Tone asked.

Tim was a straight up person. He never bit his tongue, or beat around the bush, so he got straight to the point. "I got some great coke from Up Top that I'm trying to get rid of. I'm sure it's better than that shit you all are getting from them shady Winston niggas."

When Tim said that Tone looked stunned that he knew where he was getting his coke from. Tim continued, "I'll beat the price that you are paying now, and you'll save time driving to Madison, instead of going all the way to Winston. And you know as well as I know, that time is money, " he added. "Not to mention you don't have to worry about me and Styles ever trying to rob ya'll." Tim pointed his trigger finger at Tone's head.

"Boo, " he said. "you know those Winston niggas are crazy. You know how they can get."

Tone looked like Tim had scared him with his trigger finger. "Let me talk to Geno and Quayle and I'll get back to you later, he said to Tim. "I see your working career didn't last long Styles,'" Tone said smiling.

"I am working. I'm trying to get your business ain't I?"

We all turned around and headed back towards my car. Tone promised to call me and Tim again. "I'll call ya'll as soon as I talk to my partners, " he said.

A few hours later, Tone paged me .He said they wanted to try nine ounces. Being the businessman I am, I offered to deliver the coke to them. He gladly accepted. "What time do you want me to bring it up there?" I asked Tone.

"Bring it now, we're waiting," he said.

When I pulled up, Tone, Geno, and Quayle stood by their cars talking to some girls. Fine ones I should add. Tone had a van so they excused themselves from the ladies and we all climbed inside to do our business. I pulled out the bag of coke and handed it to Geno. He inspected it and passed it to Quayle. Quayle shook his head, approving the way the coke looked and smelt, and passed it to Tone.

"Take a piece and let someone try it," I suggested.

Tone dipped his fingers into the bag and broke a small piece of the coke. He slid his door opened and called out to his tester. "Yo Tank! " Tank ran over to the van like a slave being summoned by his master. His yellow eyes, the size of lemons, lit up when Tone showed him the rock. "Go and try this out," he said to the short, big head man. "Hurry up and let us know if it's any good or not." Tank snatched the rock from Tone's hand and disappeared. Meanwhile, I got reacquainted with the guys whom I'd known since I was a kid.

"It looks like ya'll are getting money on the Back Street," I said.

121

"We get our share. We're trying to get a lot more if we can get the right connect, " Geno said.

We continued to laugh and talk about things that happened when we were kids. From our little league football days up until our high school days the guys from Madison and Stoneville had beef with each other. To tell the truth they never won!!

In little league football, I played for the Jets and Geno played for the Rams .The Jets came in first place every year I was eligible to play. I was the quarterback for our high school football team, and Quayle was the quarterback for Stoneville. We beat them four years straight. I also beat up Tone and Quayle in high school in two different fights! I had been kicking their asses for years!

Now here I was fresh out of the military with a connect good enough to serve them. Although, I felt like Tone and I were really friends, I felt some tension between Geno, Quayle and myself. But, we were all adults now, with one thing in common. Those green paper backs!

"Man, go and see where Tank's crazy ass is," Geno said to Tone. He opened the door and jumped out in search of Tank. A few minutes later, Tone slid the door open and said, "I found Tank behind the school throwing up." If Tank was bent over throwing up, I knew exactly what that meant. We had some serious coke. "Tank said we should buy everything Styles has to sell. "

Geno pulled out a roll of money and paid me for the nine ounce. "Tomorrow bring nine more up here around the same time, " He said. I shook all of their hands, sealing a deal that promised to make Tim and I a lot of cash. A deal that crushed our past differences, or I thought it did. I got out of the van and jumped back into my Mustang and cruised back to the Bricks.

The following day I delivered another nine ounces to my homies in Stoneville. Tim had made arrangements with our connection Zag, a guy living in Greensboro, by way of New Jersey, that when he bought a kilo, he got fronted a kilo. That a way we could keep the Stoneville Boys satisfied and continue to run the Bricks too.

For three months, things were picture perfect. We didn't only have the Bricks on lock down, but we had Madison, Mayodan and Stoneville on lock. Tim and Pookie moved in together in a new complex in Mayodan, a town that is connected to Madison, called Oakwood Mannor. Tim bought a new Saab and you couldn't tell him shit! He thought the sun rose and set because of him.

Celeste and I were doing good and Donnica never complained, just as long as I came home before the sun came up!

Tim and I were the suppliers for the small time hoods. Well, we were until an ignorant outsider tried "12 Gauge." A few days before Christmas 92', my cousin Hubb was about to race some nigga name Willie. Hubb had just bought a brand new Suzuki GSXR 1100, and was eager to try it out. Willie wanted to race for two thousand dollars. When Hubb pulled out his two G's, Will had raised the stakes to five thousand dollars. He knew Hubb didn't have that amount of cash because his first proposition to Hubb was for three thousand. Willie knew that Hubb' s motorcycle was faster and he didn't really want to race.

Tim and I walked up as the disappointed crowd was breaking up. "What' s up, Hubb?" Tim asked. "I thought you were going to race tonight."

"I was, but I don't have the loot to cover the bet. He wants to race for five thousand, and I only have two and some change, " Hubb said.

"Don't even trip, " Tim said. He pulled out a big role of money from his sheepskin Sherolen. Willie's eyes got bigger than candy fifty-cent pieces. He wasn't expecting anyone to put up the money for Hubb. "Ya'll come back! They are going to race after all," Tim yelled out to the disbursing crowd.

The crowd started to gather again, anticipating a race after all. "Count that for me," Willie asked Tim.

"Nigga, I ain't counting shit. If that isn't enough, then this is." Tim pulled out an even larger roll of money and held it in Willie's face.

"You don't even have anything to do with this race," Willie said to Tim.

"Hubb is my cousin fool! If you're scared, say you're scared," Tim said laughing in Willie's face.

A few heated words was past between the two of them and out of nowhere, Willie pulled out a small handgun and aimed it at Tim. I patted the small of my back, hoping I had my gun, but I had left it in my car.

"Motherfucker, you better use that gun now that you've pulled it out," Tim said to Willie.

"Man, shut up," I said to Tim. "Chill out Willie! Put that gun a way."

"You should mind your fucking business and shit like this won't happen," Willie said to Tim. He began to back up, moving in the direction of his small Toyota truck. Everyone except for me and Hubb had ran to take cover. Willie's pistol bounced from Tim to me to Hubb, until his truck door was opened. He jumped in and cranked his truck and quickly pulled off. As he pulled off, another cousin of mine named Howard pulled up. Tim ran to my car and pulled his sawed off Mossberg out and jumped in the car with Howard. They were in hot pursuit of Willie. I ran, jumped in my car and gave chase to them.

I caught up to them quickly and they were gaining on Willie. I watched as Tim climbed out of the window and sat on the door as Howard's Honda reeled in the slow Toyota truck. He pulled out the shotgun and aimed it at the truck. He shot until he emptied the shotgun, reloaded and shot some more. Willie ran stop signs, and stoplight, trying to get a way, but he wasn't able to escape. A continuous blaze of fire leaped from the short barrel of the 12 gauge Mossberg. After seven or eight double odd buckshots, Tim had shot the tailgate off of Willie's truck. But, he wasn't satisfied. Howard stuck to Willie like white on rice and Tim continued to dump. Finally, Howard got close enough to allow Tim to get a head shot on Willie. Tim aimed the 12 gauge and pulled the trigger. Willie's back window exploded and he lost control of his truck. Howard and Tim continued pass Willie, as his truck plummeted down a steep hill. I slowed down to check things out. I was sure Willie was dead. If the gunshots didn't kill him, I was absolutely positive the wreck did.

"Motherfucker shouldn't have pulled a gun out on my brother, " I said to myself as I looked at the upside-down truck.

If Willie would have known Tim's history, he would have thought twice before he pulled his pea shooter out on my brother. Tim had shot guys for less than that before. He once shot a guy at a stop light for yelling out that his girl friend looked good enough to lick like a lolly pop. This happened in broad daylight on Battleground Avenue. One of the busiest streets in Greensboro. He also shot a guy in the mall that he had beef with. Both times he had gotten a way because he couldn't be identified. Both times he used the "Bitch! " That's what he called his sawed off Mossberg. But, this time there were too many witnesses. Too many people who knew who he was. .

While I continued to follow Howard and Tim, I knew that Tim was getting ready to go to prison for murdering Willie.

The Next Day

Surprisingly, Willie didn't die. Some of the buckshots hit him in the side of the face, and he broke his arm in the wreck. After his surgery on his face, when he wasn't to doped up to write, he wrote a statement informing the police that Tim Styles was the culprit.

Four days later, Tim was arrested and charged with attempted murder, firing a fire arm in the city limits, and firing a fire arm into an occupied vehicle. My daddy was friends with the biggest bail bonding guy in Rockingham County, and he got Tim bailed out. Then we hired an attorney who said he could beat all the charges for ten thousand dollars. He promised Tim and I that Tim wouldn't do one day in prison. " Just don't get into anymore trouble before you go to court, " the attorney advised Tim.

I think that attorney jinxed Tim because less than a week after he made bond he was in Winston Salem buying a half kilo of coke. Zag, his number one connection, had gone back to New Jersey to re-up so he contacted one of his old connects. He wanted to buy just enough coke to hold him until Zag returned. His old connect sold Tim five hundred grams of wax!

"What's up?" I said to Tim, when I answered the phone.

"I need a ride to Winston to pick up some work for us. I was supposed to be there an hour ago, " Tim said.

"Come to Donnica's house and I'll take you," I said.

When Tim showed up he acted like he was in a hurry. This wasn't strange because he had already said that he was late meeting his connect. He grabbed the Bitch, like he always did, and we rushed out the door, enroute to Winston.

The first spot we went to, Tim couldn't find who he was looking for. The second spot we went to, a guy told Tim he had just missed who he was looking for. "He's probably in Cleveland Projects," the guy said.

We rode over to Cleveland Projects and Tim still didn't see his connect. I was getting frustrated riding around looking for this guy. He wasn't the only guy who had coke in Winston.

"Rico and Poncho, are the Florida Boys. They got the best coke in Winston," I said to Tim. I met Rico and Poncho while I was dealing with Chuck and Preme. "I have Rico's number. We should call him and buy some work from him. I'm tired of riding around looking for your partner. He must be a fucking ghost."

"Just take me one more place and we can bounce, " Tim said. We rode over to Boston Projects, (AKA "BDP") one of the roughest projects in Winston.

As soon as I turned into BDP, Tim spotted his connect's car. "Stop right here!"

There is his car," Tim said, suddenly hype. He grabbed his hat and pulled it down, the brim covering his brown face, that had became frowned. He picked up the Bitch and kissed it. "Lets go to work baby, " he said.

"What da fuck are you getting ready to do?" I yelled.

Without answering, he opened the door and began to walk towards the small crowd of weed smoking niggas. The Bitch disappeared! Before the guys realized that someone was easing up on them a shot rang out. Then I heard a second and third shot. One guy fell, and the other four or five ran for their lives. I peeled out, heading for Tim and the guy laying face down. Tim was bent over searching the guy he'd just shot.

"Nigga, bring your crazy ass on, " I shouted at him.

He stuffed his pockets with the guy's belongings and calmly trotted back to my car. I turned around and got out of the BDP as fast as I could. We didn't go back to Greensboro. It was too dangerous to take Highway 40. I knew the police would be looking for us, so we took back roads to Madison instead. Tim tried to explain to me why he shot the guy. He said he didn't tell me he was going to shoot the guy because that wasn't his intentions. I knew that was a lie. I could tell by his eyes when we pulled up that he didn't come to talk to anyone. He came to put in work! I didn't even try to argue with him about it. It was no use. I just wanted to get to a safe place.

Tim got his twelve thousand dollars and then some, when he shot the guy. On the news it said that the guy didn't die, but he'd be paralyzed for the rest of his life. I suggested that we chill out until he went to court. He knew he was skating on thin ice, so he agreed.

The Bricks, and the other spots we had on lock was experiencing a major dry spell, and the Stoneville Boys, took their business back to Winston, when we told them we were going to chill for a while. They had to find a new connect though. Tone told me that their old connect had gotten shot in the back a few times.

"It didn't kill him, but he'll be in a wheel chair for the rest of his life, " he said.

I was convinced that Tone's old connect and the guy Tim blasted was one and the same. I put two and two together, and I figured out that's how Tim knew who Tone's connect was. Anyway, Tim was right about one thing, those niggas in Winston were shady as hell, and they will plot to rob you!

CHAPTER 21

Willie testified that Tim shot him in the side of the face with a shotgun. "When I was struck in the face with the buck shots, I lost control of my truck, " he said, turning his face to the side allowing the judge to examine him. Hubb and I testified that Willie pulled his weapon on Tim first. The judge took that in consideration, but said Tim shouldn't have taken the law into his own hands. "For taking such drastic measures like you did young man, you'll have to be punished," the old gray haired man said, peeking over the round frames of his Ghandi glasses.

Tim was sentenced to four years in state prison. I was shocked! With the money he paid the attorney, he wasn't supposed to get any time. The attorney had promised us both that. Tim's attorney looked back at me like he was surprised at the judge's verdict too. I guess the District Attorney wasn't able to strike a deal with the judge, I thought.

It's sad to say, but I would learn that ten thousand dollars is just a drop in the bucket to most attorneys. Even after you pay them thousands more their word still doesn't mean shit. Their loyalty is to the system not their clients!

The over-paid attorney began to explain to Tim that he'd be home in a year or less. "Four years is automatically cut to two years in the Department of Corrections. You would max that out in a year and four months. The prison system is too crowded for you to max out such a small sentence, " he said.

When Tim called me later that night, he said that he was doing fine. I hoped and prayed that he was doing fine. I hoped and prayed that he was telling me the truth. He left a lot of loose ends that needed to be tied, he said. He gave me specific instructions on what needed to be done and I promised to handle all of his request. "Don't worry Bro," I said. "I'll hold the fort down until you come home. I'll be down there to see you tomorrow," I said.

For more than three months, Tim and I had been together everyday. Hustling, running women and doing whatever we wanted to do. Now suddenly, he had been taken away, thrown to the wolves.

After I hung up the phone with him, I laid across my bed and began to cry. It hadn't been twenty four hours yet and I missed my "Better Half," like crazy.

The following day I contacted Zag and informed him on what happened to Tim in court. We made arrangements to meet each other and discuss picking up where him and Tim left off, prior to him going back to New Jersey.

Ironically, a few days after Tim got locked up, Huntman, who was like a brother to me, gave me a call out of the blue. "What's up soldier?" I asked primly.

"Nothing much, just chilling. I haven't heard from you in a while, so I thought I'd give you a call," he said.

We made small talk, then I inquired about his military situation. "It's about time for you to make a decision isn't it?" I asked. I didn't have to elaborate on what I was talking about, because Huntman knew exactly what I was referring to.

"I talked to the reenlistment officer the other day, " he said.

"I knew it," I blurted. "I knew your brain washed ass was going to stay in the damn Army. "

"I talked to Sgt.Graves," Huntman said, continuing his statement, ignoring my out burst. "He said that since I had been in the infantry for so long, and since I'd graduated from Ranger School, that I couldn't change my M.O.S. (Military Occupational Status) so you know what that means, don't you?" he asked.

"No! What does that mean?" I asked.

"It means that I only have about six months to go before I'm a free man! I'll be in Greensboro, chilling with you. I'm not going back to Pittsburgh," he said.

"Are you serious?" I asked. I was shocked to hear him say he was getting out of the Army. Then again because of our close call, I wasn't that surprised. We all had come very close to catching a serious case.

"Yeah, I'm serious as a fucking heart attack! I'm giving this gun-ho shit up, " he said.

I invited Huntman to come to Greensboro for the weekend. It had been six months since I'd seen my comrade last. He accepted my invitation and said he would roll in Friday evening. "I need you to hook me up with a cutie. Things have been kind of slow for me around here. Those Fayetteville niggas are still pissed off about that shooting shit that occurred at Big P's. I don't get to go out much and meet the ladies like we use to," he said.

I was excited that he was coming to G'boro. Since I was back in the "Business", that he introduced me to, I knew he was going to be an asset to me. Especially since Tim was locked up. I needed another road dog. I could really use him.

"Donnica has a girlfriend that lives above us. I'll introduce you to her. I was going to keep her for myself, but since you're my nigga, I'll let you have her, " I said to my partner laughing.

I decided that I would tell Huntman about what I had going on when he came to Greensboro. From past experience, I knew it wasn't smart to discuss "business" over the phone. I wondered what his reaction would be after all we had been through in Ft.Bragg. "Time will tell," I said to myself after I hung up the phone.

I met Zag at a pizza joint and he agreed to continue to front me a kilo for every kilo I bought. After our meeting, I contacted Tone to let him know that I was back in business.

"I doubt if Geno and Quayle will want to let go of the connection we have right now. Not unless you are willing to make us some deals we can't refuse," he said.

"Check with them and see what they want to do. I'll make you all some great deals, " I said to him. "Call me back later on tonight and let me know what they said. By the way, what are you doing this weekend?" I asked Tone.

"Besides selling coke, I don't have any plans," he said. "Why?"

"Do you remember my partner Huntman from the Army?'1 I asked.

"Yeah, I remember him. The crazy G.I. Joe nigga."

He did remember him, I thought. "Well, he's coming to G'boro, this weekend. You should come and kick it with us," I suggested.

"Just call me when he gets into town, " Tone concluded.

Later that night Tone called me and said that Geno and Quayle were going to keep buying coke from their current connection. "But, I am interested in buying some coke from you if you're going to give me a good deal." We planned to discuss the matter in further detail during the coming weekend.

A Few Days Later

When Huntman arrived, he and I sat down and caught up on things. He explained it was business as usual in Ft.Bragg. Six o'clock formations, long ass runs, foot blistering road marches, and week after week was spent living in the field. Nothing had changed in Ft.Bragg, according to him. As for myself, a lot had changed, but in a sense things had remained the same. I was hustling again, but making more money than before. Now, I was my own boss. I was the Don! No longer the low man on the totem pole. Huntman seemed impressed. His smile radiated his approval. Like an ancient Chinese Sin-Say. His grasshopper had done well!

I began to explain my plans to him. Plans for him and I when he got out of the Army. Even though he seemed pleased with my accomplishments, judging by his facial expressions, and his lack of comments he didn't seem to enthused to join my team. I figured he was still shook by our close call in Bragg. For this reason, I didn't press the issue. When he moved to G'boro and his pockets were on "E" I would confront him again, I thought. Then he wouldn't have much of a choice.

Friday night, Tone joined me and Huntman and we painted the town. After a long night of "Strip club hopping, " we laughed and talked about the good old days in Ft.Bragg, over hot stacks of buttered pancakes at I-HOP. After an hour of reminiscing, Tone and I began to discuss the future business him and I would conduct. Ostentatiously, I made Tone deals that were sure to impress Huntman. I wanted him to see how well I handled my business, hoping he would be ready to jump on the ban wagon.

The following day, I introduced Huntman to Donnica's neighbor, Tammy. She was a slim broad, with a cute short haircut, that made here look like a teenager. She had soft brown skin, with a "Fat-little" butt. She and Huntman clicked as soon as they were introduced. Instead of hanging out with me on Saturday, Huntman accompanied Tammy to the movies. I gave him my house key and told him to let his self in, when he returned. When I woke up Sunday morning, Huntman wasn't in my spare bedroom. I looked outside and saw that his car was parked beside of mine. Before I got back to my bedroom, the telephone rang and Huntman was on the other end.

"What's up Styles?" he whispered.

"Why are you whispering?" I asked.

"I don't want to wake Tammy up," he said. Then in an even lower voice he said, "Boy, I'm glad you didn't keep her for yourself. She is a real live freak. " He said he was going to take her to breakfast when she woke up and that he'd see me later. I was sure when Huntman's six months were up in Ft.Bragg, he'd be in Greensboro. If not hustling with me, then he would be seeing Tammy for sure.

It was bout two or three in the morning. It had to be! I had talked for hours. While yawning, I glanced over at Hireen. He had passed out when I first began telling my story or at least I thought he was passed out. Just as I stopped talking and started to lie down, his red face popped up. "So what happened next?" he asked.

"What?" I said. I looked at him in disbelief. He was just sounding like a chain saw a few seconds ago. "Man, you've been asleep for hours," I said in false disgust.

"I've nodded off, but I'm still with you," Hireen said. "What happened to Tanoka?" he asked.

When he asked that question, I knew he had been sleep for a while. "I told you she got killed an hour ago, " I said. "I'm getting ready to lie down. They'll probably be coming to get me in a few more hours. I'm tired of talking to myself anyway," I said to Hireen. I eased back on the small, hard bunk, and tried to get comfortable. Hireen propped himself up, cupping his face in the palm of his left hand. "I thought you said she went to jail for shooting someone in the face with a shotgun " When Hireen said that, it was evident that he had been drifting in an out, while I was telling my story.

"No!" I almost screamed. "That was my brother Tim. He went to jail for that. Tanoka got whacked. Keeby gave her a Columbian Neck Tie." I took my right pointer finger and slowly dragged it from the left side of my neck, all the way to the right side. Gesturing that she had her neck sliced. Now that I had Hireen's attention again, I suddenly wasn't sleepy anymore. I sat up and crossed my ashy legs Indian style, and began to sort out the story for him. After straightening out the details, Hireen said he was back on track with the story. "So, when you got your connect, and got back on, what happened next?" he asked. Before I could continue the story, Hireen opened his mouth wide and closed his eyes tightly. He yawned for what seemed like five minutes.

"If you're going to sleep let me know now, " I said to Hireen. He assured me that he wasn't.

"I'm listening. If my eyes are closed....................," he paused "Ohooooo" yawning again. 'Sometimes I rest my eyes. "

I knew he was going to go back to sleep, but I had told over half the story, so I decided to continue to talk, even if he did pass out again.

CHAPTER 22

I began to flood the Bricks with coke. It didn't take long before everyone knew I was back on top. Since I didn't have to split my profits, I was making enough dough to give better deals than anyone else selling coke around the Madison area. So, I did just that. In turn, I attracted more customers. More customers meant more dough! The coke I was getting from Zag was so good that the word spread like a wild fire that I had the best coke around. All the crack heads and small timers began to come to the Bricks to cop dope from me. Soon afterwards, Geno and Quayle sent a message to me by Tone. They wanted to reconsider dealing with me. "If you're still willing to give them a good deal, they're ready to do business with you, " Tone said.

At this point, I didn't need their business. I was making a lot of money and I wasn't pressed to deal with them. But, I did like the fact that I would be locking Stoneville down also, if I dealt with them. That would boost my reputation. In the dope game, reputation alone can sell your coke. With this idea in mind, I decided to deal with the two. I even made them better deals than Tim had made them in the past. Everyone was happy. Especially me!

I enrolled into North Carolina A&T State University, in January 1993. I had qualified for the G.I. Bill, while I was in the military, and I was determined to receive all the benefits that I had coming from Uncle Sam. After all, I had fought courageously in two wars for this country, I loved so much, at least they could do was pay for my college education.

Since I love children so much, I decided to major in Elementary Education. I had been through, and seen so much I vowed to become a teacher. I never remembered any of my early teachers stressing the importance of education. Then again, that could be because I never paid attention! But, I wanted to make that impression on children early. Warn them about the snake holes I stepped into. Experience isn't the best teacher. The best teacher is when you can learn from someone else's experience. Although, I was having a ball not working, having loads of cash and fast women, I knew it was all wrong. I didn't want my child or any child, to end up doing what I was doing. So, I made my mind up to become a teacher.

Subsequently, at the end of January 1993, the Federal Government launched an investigation against me, Geno, Quayle and Tone. The beginning of my end! For the next three months I excelled in school and on the block. Tone and I became such good friends, I allowed him to move in with Donnica and me. He was ready to leave Stoneville. He'd out grown the town, he told me. Huntman fell head over hills in love with Tammy. He was coming to G'boro, every chance he got. I made sure he saw how good the dope game was being to me. I flashed Ben Franks in his face that made his mouth water. On the "DL", down low, he observed how I was putting my game down and he became more interested with each trip to Greensboro.

Celeste was also attending A&T. She was constantly upset, because I was constantly in the face of same "fresh woman" despite her being in her feelings, I could always win her over. She knew without a doubt that I loved her. All she wanted was to hear those magic words come straight from the horses mouth. And when I told her, "I love you, " I meant it from the bottom of my heart. Contrary to the other women I loved. With an occasionally shopping spree and some public affection, she would be straight.

A Few Months Later

The parole board turned Tim down on his first hearing. A second hearing was scheduled in four months. His parole officer said he would be paroled if he maintained clear conduct for those four months.

Zag and I began to establish a good friendship outside of the business, also. He wasn't the flashy type and I respected that. He never wanted to be in the limelight, unlike myself. After running plenty of women together, he and I decided to get an apartment to eliminate hotel fees. It would be cheaper for us to pay $620, a month than to continue to pay for rooms at expensive hotels. Now we had a place we could always take our girls.

I never took a blood test to see if Sheneka was my daughter. I knew she was from day one. She looked just like me when I was a baby. I just wanted to keep some tension between Kami and I. I figured I was too young to be tied down, so creating confusion in our relationship was an easy way out for me. Sheneka was three years old now, and the cutest baby I'd ever seen. She was the center of my world. I made sure that I always made time for her. My father wasn't there for me when I was a shorty, and I always vowed when I fathered a child, I would be there to be a part of his or her life. After three years, the tension between Kami and I had long subsided. We became good friends. Occasionally, I could talk her into getting a hotel room with me. I didn't want to take her to the apartment me and Zag had. Out of respect. I knew deep down that she still loved me, and to keep it real, I still loved her too. But, she had grown wiser and stronger over the years from putting up with my bullshit. But, on the other hand, she never built up enough tolerance to completely tell me "No!"

I started spending more time in Greensboro and less time in Madison. I had a few workers in the Bricks that I delegated my authority to handle things for me. Tone served Geno and Quayle for me in Stoneville, so I saw less of them. Dealing with me, Tone came up! He moved into an apartment with his girlfriend. Business wise I met with Tone three times a week to collect my money and to front him more coke. Personally, whenever he or I met new girls who had cute friends, we'd get together and see who could impress the girls more. Since I had the nicer car, and the most money, usually I did.

About A Month Later

I drove to Ft.Bragg, and helped Huntman pack his things. He had accumulated a lot junk over the years and it took us over two hours to pack his shit in the U-Haul truck.

He was more excited to be getting out of the Army than I had been when I got out. I suppose after eight years of doing time for Uncle Sam, it really gave him a sense of freedom. I only served for four years and I remembered how I felt when I got out of the Army. He must have felt twice as good as I had felt, since he did twice the time.

Tammy arranged her things in her apartment to accommodate Huntman and his junk. She worked just as hard as he and I did unloading the truck. She was overjoyed that her man was home for good. "She could get it all the time now, " she had told Donnica. And of course Donnica told me.

I was glad to have someone that I had been through so much with, close by. If I could talk Huntman into helping me hustle, things would run much smoother. He knew all the ends and outs of the game .All the tricks of the trade. I learned a lot from him, and I was willing to learn a lot more. I've never been the type to allow my ego to hinder me from making more money. But, even if Huntman decided to remain "Clean" it was still going to be good having him as a neighbor, I thought.

For the first two weeks after Huntman arrived in G'boro, Tammy held him hostage in her apartment. She was sexing him crazy. If I knew she liked it like that, I would have kept her for myself! He didn't have any complaints about it either. After those first few weeks, she let him come up for some air. We started to hang out like we did back in our Bragg Days. I showed him all of my coke spots, and introduced him to all of my workers. I was trying to entice him to join my team.

When Huntman told me he was coming to Greensboro, I told Zag about him. Zag said he was interested in meeting Huntman. He was impressed with all the Army and dope stories I narrated to him. Zag hadn't mentioned anything about meeting anyone of the other cats I dealt with, so this surprised me. Once I introduced him to Tone, and he didn't like Tone at all. "Something about that dude ain't right," Zag had said about my childhood friend. "Don't bring him around me anymore," he said. I assured Zag that Tone was a good guy. I had known him all my life, I told him.

I didn't know if Zag was more impressed with the Army, "Airborne Ranger, " stories, or the stories of all the coke we use to get in Ft.Bragg. But, as soon as they met, I found out it was a little of both. Zag started by asking Huntman all types of Ranger School questions. He had watched some show on the Rangers on the History Channel and he was impressed with their mental and physical toughness. At first, Huntman seemed to be bothered with all the questions, that seemed like a test, but after he heard Zag was impressed with his all around toughness, he didn't mind entertaining Zag's questions.

Somehow the conversation jumped from parachutes and M-60' s to triple beams and cocaine. The more Huntman discussed types, weights and methods of cooking coke with Zag, the more I was convinced he would soon join my team. But, I knew he still had a lot of money saved up. A lot of money to spend before his pockets would be on "E". He'd saved his money for eight years while in the Army and he had the cake he made from hustling stashed somewhere.

A Few Months Later

Tim got paroled and I had a major coming home party for him. A huge banner that read, "Welcome Home My Better Half' I hung over the entrance of the V.F.W., building. I paid a couple of thousand dollars to have the party catered. Any kind of liquor you could think of I had it at the party. I also paid strippers to work the party, which turned out to be a waste of money. Before the party was over, it seemed like every girl there was half naked anyway. It became so crowded that we had to stop allowing people to come inside. Even then, a party began to take place out in the large parking lot. The spring breeze carrying the loud rap music and smell of Mary Jane, simultaneously, continued until sunrise. I honestly think it would still be going on right now, if the Greensboro, Police Department, didn't come and break it up.

Tim had a hangover and didn't wake up until later that evening. As I was paying the late checkout fee, I felt a tap on my shoulder.

"I haven't seen you in a long while, Mr. Styles." I turned and stared into a smile that was like the sunrise. "I wondered what happened to you?" she asked, in a way that didn't require an answer. Her face looked familiar but I didn't remember her name .I glanced at her name tag trying not to make it obvious."You forgot my name?" she asked, still smiling. She took her left hand and placed it over her name tag, cupping her small, round breast, revealing a diamond ring that hadn't been there the last time I stayed at the Embassy Suites. She was too late though. I had already peeped her name.

"No, Brianna, " I said, undressing her with my eyeballs. I wanted to make that look obvious."How could any man forget your name?" I asked.

She exaggerated her twist, until she was on the other side of the desk. "I'll take care of, Mr. Styles," she said. "You go ahead and take your break." The gay looking white guy handed her the money I had handed him and walked away, twisting as hard as Brianna had twisted.

"Did I hear you say you'd take care of me?" I asked Brianna.

"Yes, you did sir, " she responded in a very professional manner. "And I am taking care of you right now."

"Usually when a woman takes care of me, she does a little more for me. Especially when she has a hand full of my money, " I said laughing. But, she could tell I meant every word I said.

"As many different women as I've seen you with in here, I'm sure they do take care of you. You don't need me for that. " She looked up from the cash register and smiled, still counting. "I'm not going to charge you late fees but the next time wake those lazy chicken heads up and check out! "

I liked the way Brianna flirted with me, with her eyes and body language. She finished ringing me up, and handed me my change.

"You keep that and take your husband out to eat," I said. "Tell him he is a lucky man to have a beautiful wife like you. "

She laid the money on the counter. "He doesn't appreciate a good woman," she said. Her smile vanished into thin air. She slid the money on the counter towards me .I added more money on top of the money that was already on the counter. "'You take this and spend it on yourself, because I appreciate a good woman." I winked at her and walked out of the door thinking if Celeste would have heard me saying that bullshit, she would have killed me!

When Tim sobered up, he and I discussed what I had done since he'd been away. He was pleased with my progress. I broke bread with him and gave him half of the money I had made since his prison stint. Not shorting him out of one cent.

I explained the changes I made and why. "I gave Geno and Quayle a better deal because I wanted to have the Back Street locked down as well as the Bricks. If we lock Stoneville down, we will sell twice the amount of coke, opposed to just having Madison locked down. Also, I put a few of our cousins on the team in Madison, to run the Bricks. That a way, we stay out of the picture but we still make the majority of the money, " I said. I was taking heed of the advice Zag had given me. "Always try to be low key," he had said to me. Letting someone else do my dirt was as low key as I could get. But I still like to be known as "The Man".

Since he was out parting with Tammy, Huntman didn't make it to Tim's coming home party. I told Tim a lot about Huntman, and vice versa. Once before, I even told Tim that he and Huntman acted so much alike, they could be brothers. Tim was eager to meet the guy who I said acted like him. Even he couldn't believe that.

Donnica cooked one of my favorite meals. Cubed steak, mac-n-cheese, fried potatoes and green beans. To top it all off, she fixed Jiffy corn bread that melted in my mouth.

"What you know about that Jiffy?" I asked Hireen. I didn't give him a chance to answer. I kept talking.

I invited Huntman down to dinner and introduced him to Tim. Tim and Huntman began to wet their whistles with 40 ounces of Old English and smoked like they were Navajo chiefs. Tim was digging Huntman, but he couldn't understand why Huntman wasn't a part of our team. "You've sold all that dope in the past and you let one close call make you go straight," Tim said to Huntman.

Huntman explained that that wasn't his first close call. "I've had a few close calls. I've dodged some serious heat rounds. I'm not trying to go where you just came from. "

When he finished telling Tim that he was tired of the fast life, Tim said to him just what I'd thought earlier. "Nigga, you're saying that honest Abe shit now, but wait until that money you've saved runs out. Wait until those pockets are on "E" I bet you'll get down for yours then. "

It was amazing how Tim and I thought alike. All of our lives we have been like "Frick and Frack, " and our ways of thinking proved that to be true. He finished the conversation by saying to Huntman, "You've got to have money to run them ho's. Styles told me that's what you love to do."

Huntman agreed, but maintained his position. Tim respected him for that and they both continued to smoke and drink until they were stoned.

My second semester at A&T, I let Tim run the business, while I buckled down in my schoolwork. I studied the women as well as my work! For the next couple of months the only thing that changed was the women I picked up and the money I made. Both of which, increased.

Jegbadia was one of the women I met at A&T. She was from Liberia, Africa. She was just how I loved my women, bow legged and black as twelve midnight. On a scale from 1 to 10, looks, body and intelligence, she was a twenty. Not one, but two dimes. What ultimately got my attention with her was her Liberian accent. The first time she broke silence with me, I melted. I was in love with another woman! I had my own African Queen.

My world was almost perfect. My pockets were fat as Thanksgiving turkeys, and I had more women than I knew what to do with. Well, I knew what to do with them. I'll say I had more than most men have in a lifetime! Yeah, that's more like it.

My only worries were that more people were going to find out how easy it was to hustle. Then, after they found out it was easy, I was afraid that they were going to start hustling and enroll at A&T before I had a chance to sleep with all the cuties there. Life was great!

CHAPTER 23

"A Greensboro man was shot in both of his knees at a night club called Moore's, last night, by a black male, five feet, nine inches and weighing about 145 pounds, " the newsman reported.

I sat in Celeste's' mom' s house watching the news and drinking grape Kool-Aid. Tim hadn't been home but two months and I knew what the newsman was reporting was his work. The shotgun, the height and weight, the place of the crime, all equaled one thing. "12 Gauge, " or his new nick name "Tim Dawg. " I sat watching the news in disgust.

Tim must have been watching the news also, because as the newsman concluded the story, my pager began to vibrate. I looked at the number and zeroed on the code behind the number. 555-4228*26. Tim's code was " 26 " when I saw that it was him, I called the number directly back.

"Where your crazy, black ass at?" I asked.

"I'm getting ready to bounce. The heat is on me, " he said. "A buster tried me last night at Moore's so I had to put the Bitch on him. "

I knew not to ask where he was going over the phone. I told him to call me as soon as he reached his destination. I wanted to ask more questions, but there wasn't any use. It didn't matter to me what happened, as long as Tim wasn't hurt. He couldn't be wrong in my eyes anyway. The good thing about that is, I knew he felt the same way about me.

A week went by and nobody had heard anything from Tim. My mom was worrying herself sick. She heard a few people say that Tim had shot someone else. I assured her that he didn't and that he was safe. "All those stories are lies. You can't believe everything you hear," I said to her. Although I tried to remain cool for my mother, I was getting concerned myself. Tim and I constantly kept in touch with each other. This wasn't like him not to call me or return my pages.

When the second week went by, I was walking on eggshells. All types of bad thoughts flooded my mind. I was expecting a call at anytime from my mom or someone telling me that Tim was found dead. Instead, I got a page from the 619 area code with code 26 behind it. I sighed deeply with relief when I saw the code 26 in my pager. Before I called the number back I went through a phone book and searched for the 619 area code. It was in San Diego, California.

When Tim answered the phone, he answered it like he hadn't been missing in action for two weeks. "What's up Lil'Bro?" he asked nonchalantly.

"What's up? Nigga, what's up with you? Mama has been worried sick about your crazy, black ass. Where in the hell are you?!" I asked, screaming. I knew he was in California. I just wasn't going to believe it until he said so himself.

"I'm in Southern California. San Diego!" He cleared his throat and began to sing. "It never rains in Southern California," mocking Tony, Toni Tone.

"What the hell are you doing in San Diego?"

"I made my mind up in prison that when I got out and got my shit together I was going to move to Cali. My shit wasn't together, but since the police were looking for me it helped to speed my moving process."

I was glad to hear from Tim. Glad he was safe. I expected him to go to Raleigh, Charlotte, or somewhere like that when he said he was getting ready to bounce. I wasn't expecting him to call and say he was in California.

"What are you going to do out there?" I asked Tim. He gave me a spiel how he had typed a resume and fabricated most of the information. "Lenders Bagel's, was hiring and they needed a supervisor who spoke Spanish," he said. Tim knew "Poquito Espanol," because one of his roommates in the military was from Mexico, and he taught Tim to speak some Spanish. Tim said he typed on the resume that he spoke Spanish fluently and some German.

I sat with the phone pressed against my ear, half listening and half thinking about how much I was going to miss my brother again. At least he wasn't in prison, I thought and I always wanted to go to California anyway.

I called my mother about an hour after I spoke with Tim. She said he had already called her. She was relieved greatly, but also pissed when she heard his voice. But, she was grateful that he was safe. "If he wasn't running from the law, why did he move all the way cross country?" she asked me.

My only answer was that Tim was so unpredictable. "You never know what that boy is going to do, " I said to my mom. She ended our conversation telling me to call my daddy. "He has called here a few times asking have we heard from Tim? Call him and fill him in on your wild brother. I think he has been troubled since Tim has been missing. "

My father and I had grown very close over the past few years. Besides my brothers, he was my best friend. Since I was named after him, I think that created a stronger bond between him and I than any of my other brothers. Also, he had done so much dirt coming up he almost condoned the dirt I was doing now. I could talk to him and confide in him. I loved that. I called and told him Tim was ok. He didn't seem to surprised when I told him that Tim was in California. I filled him in on what Tim had been doing over the past two weeks.

"That's good for him. Maybe he will stay out of trouble out there, " he said.

For the past two months, Tim had been running things while I went to school. A lot of the young guys, who I delegated authority to, had lost their positions when he came home from jail. They hated that, but dared to dispute it. I got things back the way they were prior to Tim coming home. He had terrorized the Bricks for two months, and al-though they would never admit it, all the youngsters were glad he was gone.

Zag laughed when I told him Tim was in Cali. "I wondered why I hadn't heard from Tim Dawg in the past two weeks?" he said curiously. "That dude is wild as hell, " he said. Once again he and I arranged how we would conduct business, minus Tim.

Tone seemed relieved that he would be dealing with me again instead of Tim. I invited him, Geno and Quayle out to discuss getting things back the way I had them. They gladly accepted and we kicked it for the entire weekend. My treat! That was good business.

CHAPTER 24

I had met Mac in Saudi Arabia, during Operation Desert Storm. He was in 319th Field Artillery Unit. His unit was attached to my unit. They followed us wherever we went, but they remained about a half a mile behind us. The artillery units supported the infantry units, just incase we needed mortar rounds to be dropped on the enemy.

Mac and I had two things in common when we first net. Both of us were from the same area, and we both loved to rap. Whenever we had down tine in the desert, we'd get together and mix it up. We spent hours entertaining crowds of home sick soldiers who forgot all about being home sick when we performed.

After the war, and after we returned to Ft.Bragg, we had planned to do big things with our rapping talents. But, unfortunately we both got side tracked doing other things when we returned, and I hadn't seen Mac since then. Until....

When I left one of my girl friends houses, (I can't remember which one) I drove to the Times Turn Around, convenient store to purchase some Gatorade and gas. When I pulled up to the gas pumps, I noticed a guy sitting in the cold, by the phone booth. He had a clothes basket and a trash bag filled with what I assumed were clothes too. He looked too clean and much too young to be homeless, I thought I opened the door and allowed the Indian Head Fragrance to escape freshening the morning air. I eased out of my brand new Honda Accord, I had just bought. It was black with the gold package, lowered, but not slammed, with chrome and gold Enkei wheels. The seats were leather and the rest of the interior was infested with wood grain. The two huge herringbones that were draped around my neck gleamed in the sun. The guy sitting by the pay phone watched as I dapped into the store. We made eye to eye contact and without speaking a word, we spoke the same language. He tilted his head back and I did the same.

He looked familiar, I thought. I may forget a name, but I don't forget a face. But, I struggled to remember where I knew his face from. I walked to the back of the store and pulled out an ice cold Gatorade from the refrigerator. Then I walked to the counter, making small talk with the cutie at the cash register. I was still trying to figure out where I knew the guy from. I paid for the drink and my gas and bopped extra hard when I walked out of the store. I glanced over at the guy squatting by the phones. Again, he and I spoke to each other, this time verbally. It was eating me up, that I couldn't put a name with his face. Nor could I place where I knew him from. I tried not to but I started to stare at him while I was pumping my gas.

I could tell by the way he looked back that he knew me also. I got in my car and drove over to the pay phones, to get a better look at the brother. I got out and walked to the phone booth, opposite where he was sitting. I put a quarter in the phone and began dialing a bogus number. Before I finished dialing the number, I concluded that the dude looked like a guy I was in the Army with named Neil McStevison. But Mac had shorter hair and he wore those "Birth control, " glasses. This guy's hair was longer and he didn't have on any glasses, but he did look like Mac. I peered around the side of the phone and acted like I was talking to someone on the phone. "What's up Mac?" I said. He looked at me and yelled,

"Styles! Damn, I thought that was you. I just couldn't get a good look at you because I don't have my glasses. " I hung up the phone, grabbed my twenty five cents and we embraced each other. "I knew I recognized your face," I said. "You look like a totally different person without your glasses and longer hair. "

"You look different also, but you look like you're doing good," he said. "Where is your Mustang? Did you trade it to get that Honda?" he asked.

"No, I still have the Mustang. I just bought this car." I turned and pointed at the car as if he couldn't see it. "How are you doing?" I asked. I could see that he wasn't doing too good.

"Maaaannnnnnnn, I got serious bitch problems .My ole lady just kicked me out. I'm waiting on a taxi right now to take me to my mom's house," He said.

"Do you want me to take you?" I asked. He explained that he personally knew the taxi cab driver he called, and he didn't want to leave from where he said he would be .I agreed to wait for the cab to come, then I told him I'd drop him off at his mother's house.

When the cab finally pulled up, I gave Mac ten dollars to give to the taxi driver for his troubles. He was pleased and drove off without any complaints. Mac and I began to ride and talk. We laughed as we talked about the long, hot days in Saudi. He said he was still rapping, but he hadn't done anything serious with his music. Like myself, he continued to write and he dreamt of becoming a rap star one day. I suggested that he and I should get together and start working on some music. Enthusiastically he agreed.

When we reached his mom's house, I helped him carry his things to the front door. His mom opened the door and greeted us with a fake smile. She was a lovely looking woman. She didn't look old enough to be his mother!

"Come on in, " She said. Mac hugged and kissed his mother. He introduced me as one of his old buddies from the Army. "You got out of the Army too?" She asked me sharply.

"Yes ma'am. " I said.

She turned and looked at Mac "Neil, if you would have stayed in the Army, like I told you, you wouldn't be having these problems now, " She said bitterly.

I looked around and Mac's mother had a very nice place. Everything seemed to be in perfect order. Although she loved her son, her body language and facial expressions revealed that he was invading her precious space.

"I hope you don't live with your mother too, " She looked over and said to me.

"No ma'am, I don't," I said.

She picked Mac's clothes basket up and disappeared into the laundry room, still mumbling something about we should have stayed in the Army.

Mac was very uneasy with how his mother was acting. I felt bad for him and suddenly I had an idea that would make us both feel better. "Look ah here Mac, " I said quietly. "I have a place you can stay at for a while." I tried to speak quickly before his mom returned. He looked at me and sighed with relief.

"Bring that other bag back here, Neil!" his mother yelled from the laundry room. He got up and walked back to where she was. He found her stuffing his clothes that were already clean, into the washing machine.

"Ma," he said. "I'm straight. I'm going to stay with Styles for a while. I'll be back later to get my clothes." She looked up puzzled. He hugged her and left her in the laundry room stuffing his clothes in the washer.

"I'm ready," Mac said when he came back into the living room. He picked up the trash bag of clothes and carried them to the car.

We rode to the "Ho-Haven," Zag and I had together. Before we entered the apartment, I asked Mac to remove his shoes. I opened the door and Mac was flabbergasted. He had gone from shit to sugar in less than an hour. The apartment was laid out! The living room was decorated with white leather furniture and thick white carpet that drowned your feet with every step. African art hung in fancy black frames, bringing the walls to life. Instantly, Mac knew why I'd asked him to remove his shoes. He looked around like he was afraid to touch anything. His eyes sparkled with approval. "This place is nice," he said.

I showed him which bedroom to place his things. "Don't go in there, " I said, pointing to the other bedroom. "That's my partners room." I went back into the living room and called Zag. I explained the situation to him about Mac and the apartment. He was fine with it.

Zag had met some new honey that was from New Jersey also. She had him wide open like Seven-Eleven. Twenty, four, seven! He hadn't and wouldn't be staying at the apartment for a while, he said.

Mac had a job driving trucks for a company called Old Dominion. I gave him the keys to the Honda so he could have a way to and from work. Since he didn't have a lot of up to date clothes, I gave him the green light to wear anything of mine. Except my underwear! I gave him money to buy his own and a pair of Air Jordan's.

Huntman had a job supervising at a furniture company. With the money he was making, he was still keeping his headway above water. From time to time I would mention that he should be rolling with me, but he continued to blow me off.

I called and spoke with Tim almost daily. I missed him, but I was happy he was safe. That's all that mattered to me.

"It's a small world," Tim said. "I ran into one of my old girls I met while I was stationed in Germany, in the mall," he said rousingly. "We've been kicking it every since." Although, I missed him, if he was happy so was I.

Since Zag had met his new girlfriend, he spent most of his time trying to amuse her. Therefore, instead of fronting me one kilo, he began to front me two and three at a time. "'That way you'll be straight if I'm not around. Robin and I are always on the go," Zag said.

I began to front Tone, Geno and Quayle coke because I had so much of it. They began to sell coke to guys coming from Eden, NC and Danville VA.

My name was ringing as loud as a hundred phones now. In two states! You couldn't tell Dana Styles shit! My "Rep" was growing faster than the speed of light. Everyone was making tons of money. When the moolah started rolling in like tides on a beach, it made our good relationship even better. The four of us became like family.

CHAPTER 25

ac and I started to get serious about our music. We made a couple of demos to see what type of feedback we'd get in G'boro. Everyone who heard our music encouraged us to continue rapping. I persuaded Mac to quit his job and work on the music full time. I was making enough money to support us both. "You don't have to worry about shit, " I said. " Just go to the studio and make music and I'll hold you down. If I didn't think we had the talent to be super stars, I wouldn't waste your time or my cash, " I said.

A Few Months Later

"Malaika is going to have my first child!" Tim said excitedly. "It's going to be a boy! I want you to come out here and meet her."

"Let me make sure everyone here is going to be straight and I'll be out there in a few days," I said to Tim, just as excited as he was. When Tim told me, him and Malaika were expecting a child, I was really ready for him to come home. I didn't want my nephew to be living thousands of miles a way from me. Ok. Let me keep it real! That sounded good but the real reason was, I wanted my Better Half home.

I figured if I went to Cali, I could talk Tim into coming home. I hooked up with Zag to let him know that I was going to San Diego. "I don't know how long I'm going to be gone, but I'm going to let Tone run things for me while I'm a way," I said to Zag.

I don't know what it was about Tone, but Zag didn't like the idea of dealing with him. It took me over an hour to convince him that Tone was a good guy to deal with. "Just hit him off if he needs it," I said.

It took another hour for me to explain to all the women I was messing with that I was going to visit Tim in Cali. It was clear to my women friends how close Tim and I was, so none of them tripped out about me going to the West Coast, but all of them wanted to come with me.

Friday afternoon, I called and made reservations from G'boro to San Diego for the coming Wednesday morning. I had five days to spread myself around. That Friday and Saturday night, I spent with Celeste at the Embassy Suites. And of course I saw and flirted with Brianna while I was there. I told Celeste that my flight was scheduled to leave Sunday morning at 9:45 am. At 9:30 am, Sunday morning, we pulled up in front of the airport.

"You go ahead. I'll be ok from here. My flight leaves in a few minutes." I said, looking at my watch. I kissed her and quickly opened the door. "I'll call you when I get there, " I said. I picked up my bags and walked as fast as I could into the airport. I watched Celeste pull off as I dialed Jegbadia's phone number.

"What's up, Blacky?" I asked.

"Hey Baby! Where have you been this weekend?" Jegbadia asked me in her beautiful Liberian accent.

"I've been trying to make enough money to take with me to California. I don't know how long I'll be there, so I want to take a lot of money with me. I want to be able to buy you something while I'm there," I said.

She understood and asked when was I leaving. I told her that I made reservations to leave Greensboro, early Tuesday morning, and I promised to spend Sunday and Monday with her. She was pleased!

Tuesday morning Jegbadia dropped me off at the airport at 9: 30 am. I kissed her and promised to call her as soon as I got to Cali. I caught a taxi from the airport and rode to Donnica's. I gave her the same, "I've been trying to make money, " spiel. "At least you could have done was answer my pages, " she said. She was upset that I wasn't going to be able to spend more time with her before I left Wednesday morning .I handed her some of the money I said I made, and it killed some of her attitude.

Later that evening, Mac pulled up driving my Honda like it was his. I gave him some money to pay the studio fees and some extra money for his empty pockets. "If there is an emergency, there is money stashed in the back of the freezer in the apartment, you're staying in. Don't mess with it unless it's really an emergency, " I stressed. "I'll be back in a day or so, " I said. I didn't want him to get to wild or to comfortable in my Honda while I was away.

I fronted Tone a few kilos and specific instructions with each one. Also, I gave him Zag's number, just incase he ran out of coke before I returned.

I enjoyed my flight to San Diego. It was the first time I'd been on an airplane since I'd left Ft.Bragg. I didn't have to worry about jumping out for a change. But, I did think about "What if?" the plane started to go down? I quickly came to the conclusion that I would have felt better flying with a T-10 Bravo, parachute!

Tim picked me up at the airport in a new Jeep he'd bought. We embraced and kissed, like our mom used to make us do when we were kids. We had hated having to kiss one another when we were kids, but that was just a form of expressing our brotherly love for each other now. Like the Italians!

We rode and talked until we arrived at his condo in Point Loma. Malaika along with her cousin Maria greeted me when I walked in. Tim had talked to them so much about me, they had to meet me, they said.

Both of them were from Guam. They were short, thick girls. Both had pretty almond skin with long silky, black hair. They almost looked like twins. I know what white people mean now when then say, "They all look alike!"

Tim took a few days off of work to show me beautiful Southern Cal. We did everything from going to Sea World to crashing Mexican house parties. Tim introduced me to a few chicks he had on the side too. I was proud of my "Lil-Big Brother". He had it going on, legally.

I called and checked in with everyone after I'd been there for a few days. I gave the same story across the board. "I'd be home in a few more days."

After my third day there I was staying with Maria. I only intended to stay in California for a week. But, a week went by so fast, I decided to stay a little while longer. Besides, Maria begged me to stay!

Maria's mother was a heart specialist and her father was a plastic surgeon. She was the only child and she was spoiled rotten. She lived in a huge condo in Lahoya, California. The Beverly Hills of San Diego. All she had to do was go to school and make good grades to please her parents. They took care of everything else. What they couldn't take care of I did!

Before two weeks went by Maria was in love. She didn't want me to go back to North Carolina, and I wasn't in a hurry to get back. I pulled out every sex trick in the book and used them on her. She thought she had hit the jackpot with me, and I felt the same way about her, but I didn't let her know that. The things that I did to her, the guys in San Diego weren't doing. Dana Styles had arrived in Cali, and turned her out!

"I have never in my life met a guy who makes me feel like that nigga does. " I heard her brag to Malaika, over the phone. I guess she thought I was asleep, or she wanted to blow my head up. "Girl, once he starts, you have to make him stop, " she said.

When I called to check on Tone, he told me he was about to run out of coke. Mac had had two emergencies, to hear him tell it. So he'd dipped into my stash twice. Celeste, Jegbadia, Donnica and everyone else anticipated my return to North Carolina. They all wanted to know what was taking me so long to come home. Each one of them accused me of having another woman in Cali. I denied it each time and promised to come hone soon.

I tried to convince Tim that he should come back to North Click. I assured him that the police wasn't looking for him anymore. "That shit at Moore's has been long forgotten, " I said in my plea to try to get him to come home. I honestly wanted him home because I missed him. It was like part of me was gone when he wasn't where ever I was. I missed having someone I could trust whole heartedly.

A Few Weeks Later

I had spent the majority of my money partying. I was living large in Lahoya, but I was becoming home sick. I missed my daughter! By now everyone knew that it had to be another girl that was keeping me in Cali. They all knew I loved my brother, but they knew I wasn't about to go a month without some pussy.

Mac had dipped into the stash so much until there wasn't a stash. He claimed he had to pay studio fees, and some speeding tickets that the police were going to lock him up for. Zag was ready for me to return also. He wasn't thrilled at all, dealing with Tone.

I promised Maria that I would be back to San Diego soon. Since my funds were low, she paid for my flight back to NC, and offered to pay for my flight anytime I wanted to visit her.

Tim and Malaika drove me back to the airport. I'd been in San Diego just a little over a month and it hadn't rained until the day I was leaving. "I thought you said, it never rains in Southern California?" I asked Tim.

"That's the city's way of crying. It's sorry to see you go like I am." He said. A tear ran down Tim's face. We embraced each other. My eyes filled and spilt tears also.

"Man, hurry up and come back home, " I said. "I miss you. This place is nice, but it isn't your home."

Right before I got on the plane Maria popped up. "I just wanted to tell you bye again, " she said. Once again I promised Maria that I'd see her soon. She cried like she had known me for years and made me swear to god that I'd come back soon. I did, but I never saw Maria again.

I listened to the Walkman Maria bought for me while I was in route to G'boro. Big Bub's, "Telling Me Stories," seemed to smooth the rough edges in my life. Every time that song would end, I would press rewind and listen to it again. I did this same thing for hours, until we touch down in the Gate City.

Mac picked me up from the airport and carried me to Donnica's house. Luckily, she was at work, because when I unzipped my bag the first thing I saw was an eight by ten, photo of Maria in a bathing suit. Underneath the photo was a pair of her skimpy panties, sprayed heavily with a candy smelling perfume. She had placed the items there while I was in the shower at her place.

I made contact with Tone to make sure things were running smoothly.

"Everything is cool," he said. "I thought you were going to be gone for a few days. That pussy must have been good to you. You said fuck dope, money, school and your local ho's, huh?"

I didn't need to explain myself to him, so I didn't .I had enough women that I was going to have to explain myself to, and the next couple of hours were spent doing just that.

I explained myself and made promises that I knew I wasn't going to keep. I also went to A&T and spoke with all of my instructors. I gave them a sob story about a close relative being shot and killed in California. "Gang related, " I explained. "I've been out West trying to get my family back on track, " I said.

All of my instructors agreed to allow me to make up what work I missed. A couple of them even asked if I needed more time to assist my family. They were aware of the seriousness of the gang problems in California.

It was business as usual after about a week at home. I hustled, went to school and tried to sleep with every woman in Greensboro. And for pleasure, I kept my daughter on the weekends.

Mac and I finally finished our first tape entitled, "On Point. " We decided to call ourselves, The Fugitives, but some group in New York, already had that name copy written. I came up with Natural Life, as a name for our rap group. A name I got off of some prison show I was watching one night. I had copies of the tape made and we began to sell them ourselves in and around Greensboro. After a week of selling the tapes, we had tripled our money. Well, my money! But, I wasn't tripping over any money. I suggested to my partners in Stoneville that we combine our money and start our own record label. "This can be our way out of the dope game, " I said to Geno. "People are getting filthy rich off of this music industry."

Those clowns laughed and made jokes about my idea. They were not visionaries at all. A couple years later Percy Miller (AKA Master P) had the same idea and implemented it. That could have been us................. But anyway!

A Few Months Later

When Tim called and said he was coming home, I didn't bother to ask why? I was just excited he was coming home. That news was music to my ears. For some time, I had been doing things on my own, but nothing was like having Tim by my side. Although, me and the fellas from Stoneville were like family, the fact was we were not family. I trusted Zag, but not like I trusted Tim!

Malaika was due to have Tim's son in two months. Her pregnancy had a positive effect on him. He wasn't about a lot of foolishness anymore. He'd calmed down tremendously. Now, whenever he went somewhere he didn't feel the need to bring the Bitch with him, he would only carry one of his handguns. I know you may think that isn't much different, but before, the Bitch was like Master Card, he didn't leave home without it!

Tim got a job when he returned to Greensboro. This really surprised me. His trip to Cali rehabilitated him more than his prison stint. He had really changed. Well, not totally! He still was a "Super Ho!" He had more women than I did and he stilled loved to drink like a fish. The more things change, the more things remain the same.

CHAPTER 26

Two Months Later

Tim paraded around the hospital as arrogant as a peacock, when Marquise was born. He passed out cigars, masked in blue plastic to everyone who visited his son. A chosen few, including one of the doctors, were issued a dime bag of cannabis with their cigar.

When I arrived at the hospital I showered my nephew with baby clothes from Oshkosh, and Tonka Toys, he wouldn't be able to play with for years. I joked with Tim about his son and told him, I hope that Marquise doesn't end up crazy like he was. Tim laughed at that. Malaika looked at me shaking her head up and down, agreeing with me.

"I hope he ends up just like me, " Tim blurted. "That a way nobody will ever fuck with him. "

A couple of weeks after Marquise was born, Tim mentioned to me that he wanted to get back into the game. He was overwhelmed with hospital bills, milk, diapers and other indispensable items that his son needed. "My job ain't kicking out enough dough. All these bills piling up will make a nigga start hustling again, " he said.

I encouraged Tim to endure, and I vowed to give him anything he needed. Even though one of the reasons I wanted him home was to help me make money. But, I was kind of glad that he wasn't hustling. I knew how anything could, and would happen to him in the streets. He was a trouble magnet! I came to the conclusion that just having Tim home was good enough for me, but I also knew he was going to do what he wanted to do.

When Tim called and said he was ready to get busy, I knew exactly what he was talking about. He'd sat out of "Da Game " long enough. He was checking back into the starting line up.

The guys from Stoneville, like myself loved fast cars, and faster motorcycles. Quayle and I raced motorcycles and Geno and Tone raced a forest green 72 Nova SS, that the three of them had built. Most of their loot from hustling went into building that car and Quayle's bike. We all spent a lot of time together at Piedmont Drag Strip, racing and betting on other races with hustlers from around the area. It wasn't a secret that you had to have piles of money to continuously operate a race car or a drag bike. Very few people at Piedmont had official sponsors to aid them to foot their bills. Hell, it was only three regulars that had sponsors. Melvin Paige was sponsored by Hooters. Anthony Berlin was sponsored by Miller Brew and Chuck Randal was sponsored by Motor Craft. I remember those three because all of them were white guys and they had the three slowest cars at the track. Everyone else that came week after week was sponsored by coke. And I don't mean Coca-Cola!

The faster your race car or bike, the more coke you had. That was my method of determining who had what? If you had a lot of coke, you could afford to spend "Whatever!" on your motor. If you didn't have much coke, your slow ass car or bike would reveal such.

Week after week, a metal flake, royal blue, 69 Camero, owned and operated by Neon Hall, was the fastest car at the track. Neon didn't need a sponsor. He had more cash flow than all the hustlers at the track combined. Or at least that was the word at the track. Geno, Tone and the rest of the "Coke Sponsored, " racers, spent tons of cash on their cars trying to compete with Neon. They never won a race against, "Blue Funk " (The name painted an the side of Neon's car).   Nobody ever came close to winning. From past experience I learned where there are men with money, you'll also find women galore. The track stayed packed with young hotties seeking out, "Bad Boys," with fat pockets. I saw Lakisha one day while I was there racing my bike .I was shocked at how she had developed. She'd gained about ten pounds in all the right places. She looked good enough to eat…again!

I eased up behind her and delicately placed my hands over her eyes. She kindly took both of her hands and started to feel my hands as if she was going to be able to figure out who I was by doing that. After a few seconds of her hand to hand investigation, she impassively asked, "Ok, Who is it?"

"It's your long, lost lover," I said, trying to disguise my voice. Her hands tightened on my wrist and she pulled my hands a way from her soft face. Instantaneously, she turned to see the face that went with the camouflaged voice, that hadn't fooled her.

"Dana Styles! " she yelled. "You sorry dog. Nigga, Where in the hell have you been?"

I tried to explain to Lakisha that a lot was happening with me while I was in the Army. Which wasn't a lie. Then I began to give excuses for not calling or coming to see her. I was getting so tongue tied in my lies that finally she did us both a favor. "Just stop. I've heard enough. Give me your number and I'm going to call you," she said.

She opened her purse and handed me a pen and small pad. After I wrote my number down she turned me around, using my back, and wrote her number down.

"Keep in touch this time, " she said. That was something that didn't have to be said the way she was looking. That same night I called Lakisha three times

Less Than Two Months Later

Because I missed Tim so much, I practically begged him to come back home. Now, I wished I hadn't .He was doing just fine in San Diego and my selfish ass should have left it just like that. Less than two months had gone by and things had gone haywire for Tim.

First, two of his side chicks were pregnant by him. He tried to deny that he had them pregnant, but neither one of them were trying to hear that. Needless to say, this caused major drama between him and Malaika. Oh, I almost forgot. The two side chicks were best friends before Tim came home. Now they hated each other.

As bad as that may sound, that was the least of Tim's problems. He had been busted with two ounces of coke and was out on bond. Then a few days after he made bond, he got arrested again at the drag strip.

A white guy, who was sitting beside us at the track, observed the handle of a pistol that was protruding from Tim's baggy jeans. It just so happen that the white guy was an off duty police officer. He went to the police officers that were working and pointed Tim out. The officers circled and stormed Tim, forcing him to the ground.

A 9 ½ inch barrel, 357, Smith and Wesson, was taken from Tim. The police also took his car keys and searched his car high and low. They discovered "The Bitch, " an AK-47, and a Tech 9mm, cached in the trunk of his car. He was placed under arrest and carried a way to the Guildford County Jail. There he was booked on felony charges of a convicted felon in possession of firearms.

I called my daddy to inform him that Tim was locked up again. "He has a $100, 000, dollar bond,'" I said to him before I even told him why Tim was locked up.

"That boy is a gotdamn fool. What in the hell is he doing with all those damn guns at the racetrack? Was he expecting to fight a war by himself!" he yelled.

Daddy had put up most of his land on Tim's drug bond. He didn't have enough land to cover the entire second bond. He called a couple of his brothers who owned land to see if they would put their land up for Tim's bond. After an hour of calling brothers, sisters, cousins and friends, Daddy hadn't found anyone who would go Tim's bond. His good friend the bail bondsman, was out of town, and wouldn't be back until the next week, his secretary said. Daddy called my mom and told her what had happened. We explained the situation with the bond and mom suggested that we call Tommy and Judy. Old friends of our family, who were like family. "They own a bunch of land, " my mom said. "Call them and I'm sure they'll help us get Tim out."

Daddy called and spoke with Tommy, who agreed to help bond Tim out of jail. I knew that since Tim was already a convicted felon with two felony charges pending, he was facing some serious time in prison. The attorney we consulted with said he was facing up to fifteen years with the charges combined. Twenty years if they box car them. He wanted ten thousand dollars to take the case. The last attorney we hired for Tim, when he shot Willie, asked for ten thousand dollars also. I wondered if ten "G's" was the standard fee for a thug?

This attorney made promises too, just like the last attorney. Promises that would be broken if the DA, and the judge didn't want to play along. We hired him anyway, hoping that he would keep his word. Tim's first court date was a month and two weeks away.

Donnica's tolerance for my bullshit wasn't as high as I thought it was. She started tripping because I wasn't coming home every night. We fell out and I moved all my things over to the apartment where I let Mac stay. It was all gravy though, because in a week's time, that apartment became known as the "Best Little Ho House In Greensboro". I sold my Honda. I needed the money to re-up. Plus Tim's attorney said he was going to need seven thousand more dollars to prepare his defense. I interpreted that as he needed seven thousand more dollars for the big payoff. But, "When the funds are low, the jewels must go!" So, I didn't care about selling the car. Tim's freedom was much more important to me. They made Honda's everyday, but they didn't make Tims!

For the next month or so Tim and I were cemented. I knew his days in the streets were numbered. We did not speak about his court dates at all though. Both of us were too afraid of what the outcome was going to be. Without saying it, we treasured the time we were spending together. Despite all the felonies that were jumping off, we continued to hustle. Loot was going to be a major factor if Tim expected good things to happen inside the courtroom. "You get what you pay for, " is something my daddy taught me. I'd come to the conclusion that I'd go broke if it meant keeping Tim out of prison. I didn't want a shortage of money being the reason he got time.

Tim only had a week left before he was scheduled to go to court. His attorney was very optimistic when we were paying him tons of cash, but now he told Tim that his situation didn't look so good. "The DA wants you off the streets. He says you're a menace to society." He suggested we pay him more money. "For about five more "G's" he said, using street slang to accommodate me and Tim. "I probably can strike a for sure deal. " Disgusted, Tim pulled out a wad of cash and paid the attorney. He turned without saying a word and walked out of the office. "I'd like a receipt for that," I said to the greedy attorney. He began writing the receipt and explaining why more money was needed. He was still talking after he handed me the colorful piece of paper with his John Hancock, scribbled on it. I snatched it from his hand and walked out to the car.

"I don't mind paying that cracker money, it's just the game he thinks he is running," Tim said to me when I got in the car. "He better hope I go to jail, because if I don't I swear to God, I'm coming back here and lay his whole office down. He thinks we're just some ignorant niggas, doesn't he?" Tim asked.

"Yeah, I suppose he does," I said. I didn't want to say much more than that. I didn't want to add fuel to a fire that was already burning out of control.

In the week prior to Tim going to court, he spent as much time as he could with Marquise and Malaika. The other two girls he had pregnant did what ever they could do to rock his boat! They showed up at his apartment asking questions like, "What am I suppose to do if you go to jail? What am I going to tell my baby about his daddy?" Malaika would fly through the roof each time one of the girls would show up at the apartment. Finally, Tim packed up some of their things and went to spend his last two days at a hotel. He was stressed out over all the bullshit!

CHAPTER 27

The Night Before Tim's Court Date

The temptation of painting the town, one last time before court, wouldn't allow Tim to stay in the hotel with Malaika and Marquise. He lied to her to escape the boredom of the small room. "Me and Styles got some serious business to take care of tonight. It has to be done before I go to court tomorrow. " he said to Malaika.

When he left the hotel room, he drove to Claremont Projects and picked up Carista, one of his many girls. He met Carista when he came home from prison at "Twiggy's" a strip club located in the heart of down town Greensboro. "Cash," Carista's stage name, was a dancer that fell in love with Tim's money at first, then later on she truly fell in love with him. On a scale from one to ten, she was a six, in the face, but she was a dime body wise. Tim was very fond of her. He always bragged on how "Down" she was.

After he picked her up, he called me on my cell phone. "Hey Lil Bro! What's happening with you? What are you doing?" he asked.

"I'm laying here naked as a jay bird trying to catch my breath at this moment," I said laughing. Aiesha heard me and smacked me on my arm.

"I should have asked you who you were doing, instead of how you are doing?" he said laughing louder than I was laughing. "I'm going down to Peter Rabbits tonight. Do you want to go?" he asked.

Peter Rabbits was a hole in the wall in Pine Hall. A town about thirty minutes west of G'boro. The joint had a bum reputation. Peter Rabbits was synonymous with stabbing, shooting and murder.

"Hell nah, I'm not going down there to that death trap. I don't even know why you're going down there either," I said to him. "'Are you trying to get into some more trouble before you go to court tomorrow?" I asked. I knew Tim well enough that he didn't have to answer why he was going to Peter Rabbits. He was going there for the same reason he'd go over to Moore's when I went to Side Effects. Moore's was the club across the street from Side Effects. He loved the ghetto thugs, hood rats and all the drama that occurred when the two combined.

"I'm just going to hang out and have a few drinks and some fun. The way that stupid attorney talks, it might be a long time before I get to go out again after tomorrow. You need to catch your breath, wash your ass and come down to Peter Rabbits and chill with your "Big-Lil Bro, " he said.

When Tim made the statement, "It might be a long time before I go out again," it hurt me to the bottom of my heart. The thought of my brother being locked up again saddened me deeply. Briefly, I thought about getting up and hanging out with him, but I declined his offer. My contemplation was overpowered with the thought of what Aiesha had just finished doing to me. I wasn't about to go anywhere.

"'No, I'm going to chill out and get some rest like your ass needs to do. Where are you going to be in the morning?" I asked. "We can't be late for court. "

"I'm going back to the hotel room," he said. "We have to take Malaika and Marquise to the airport before I go to court. She is going back to Cali to stay with her parents. I'll page you early, because the flight leaves at 7:45 a.m. I love you Lil'Bro,"he said, before he hung up the phone.

I hung up the phone and Tim's voice echoed in my mind. "I love you, Lil'Bro," translated into the "Fat Lady" humming. About to sing! It was not over for him yet, but that big bitch was warming up back stage!

I rolled over and gave Aiesha a big kiss on her thick lips. I had met Aiesha a few months earlier in the Four Seasons Mall. Since I'd left Donnica, I started to spend a lot of time with her. She was like Donnica use to be, she didn't trip as long as I came home before the sun started to rise. As long as she stayed like that, the longer I would stay with her!

1:37 am At Peter Rabbit's

Tim ordered his seventh drink and one for his new friend Terrance. They had just met each other while playing a friendly game of pool. Tim was too oiled to notice the odd looks he was getting from some of the guys from Pine Hall. They didn't like it when guys from out of town came through and spent money like it was going out of style. Tim had done just that since he'd stepped foot inside of Peter Rabbits. Even though Cash was with him, he still bought drinks for all the fine ladies in the joint. Something none of the Pine Hall guys would ever do without expecting some pussy in return.

Tim's claim to fame, had reached Pine Hall also. Willie, the guy Tim shot in the face and made wreck was from Pine Hall. Tim had balls of Kevlar showing his face in Peter Rabbits. It was a serious mistake. The odd stares soon became whispers and gestures.

"Fuck you nigga," Terrance yelled to his brother Gerald. Gerald was kind of juiced too. He had been drinking all night.

"Nigga fuck you, " he screamed back at Terrance. Gerald had walked over to Terrance and whispered something in his ear. Whatever it was it pissed Terrance off. In turn, it caused an even stronger, negative response from Gerald. He pushed Terrance back onto the pool table, causing rainbow colored balls to scatter in all directions. A couple of the balls even dropped in the mesh pockets. Terrance jumped up and raised his pool stick to smite Gerald. Tim slid between the two, restraining Terrance.

"Get the hell on partna," Tim said to Gerald.

"Nigga that's my fucking brother. Don't get into family affairs, " Gerald said to Tim.

"If you two are brothers, you shouldn't be trying to fight each other, " Tim said.

Cash stood at the bar talking to our cousin Andre. When she noticed the commotion she ran to Tim's side. "What's up daddy?" she asked Tim, digging deep down inside her painted on jeans.

"It ain't anything, Ma I'm just trying to keep these brothers from fighting each other, " he said.

Gerald seized his bottle of Bull from the corner of the pool table and staggered out of the narrow door, still drinking. A couple of his partners followed him, looking back, grilling Tim and Terrence.

"Let's start our pool game over, " Tim said to Terrance.

"Nah, I think I'll get out of all of this smoke and get some fresh air. Let's walk outside," Terrance said.

After Tim told Cash everything was cool, she walked back to the bar. Now, he motioned for her. She twisted back to where he was standing.

"We're going out to get some fresh air. I'll be right back," he said to her.

"Hurry up, " she said. "I'm about ready to go. You better watch them jealous niggas when you go outside," she added.

Tim and Terrance headed for the narrow door. Before they could exit, a guy stepped to Terrance. "Man, I can't believe you're hanging out with this busta. You think you hot shit, huh?" he asked Tim.

Rage invaded Tim's red eyes. "Nigga you don't fucking know me!" he said.

The guy pushed the door open and held it for Terrance. When Tim approached he let the door go. "Yeah, I know you," the guy said. "You're Tim Styles. A.K.A Tim Dawg! 12 Guage!" he said cynically.

The fresh air breezed across Tim's face and he inhaled deeply, filling his lungs. "12 Guage," he heard the guy yell out. Abruptly, the guy pushed Terrance who was standing in front of Tim, down to the ground. An ear splitting shot rang out. **"BOOOM!!!"** Piercing the silence of the cool night. Then a second and third blast broke the silence. **"BOOOM......BOOOOM...!"**

Slugs, at point blank range, ripped through Tim's brown flesh. Tearing chunks out of his stomach. His favorite Polo shirt absorbed the blood that cascaded from the wounds. He lay on his back, the moon, illuminating his youthful face. The pain was so excruciating that he didn't make a sound. Until**....."BANG...BANG....BANG...!**

Two other guys, one shooting a 38 Special, the other shooting a Byrco 22, filled Tim's small frame with more lead than a thousand pencils. Tim screamed in pain. The bullets ricocheted through his back, arms and legs.

Cash heard the gunshots and bolted out of the club almost knocking the old wooden door off the hinges. The fresh air, along with what she saw, took her breath. "Tiiiiiiiiiiiiiiiiiimmmmmmmmm!," she screamed.

Tim was shrouded with blood. But, somehow his feeble body managed to be walking slowly in the direction of his car. She shoveled deep into her jeans and whipped out a chrome 380. Gerald stood, reloading his 12 gauge and Cash pointed the weapon and began to fire shots at him. He ran and she chased him firing at his head. Before she could close the gap between her and Gerald the guy that was shooting the 22, shot her once in her thigh and once in her hip. She toppled to the ground, screaming for Tim, still. Tim opened the door to his car and pulled out his new 12 gauge shotgun. By now, he was delirious, due to the amount of blood he'd lost. He screamed something out and began to bust shots. But, the guys who had riddled his small body with molten lead, was long gone. After he fired four shots towards Peter Rabbits, Tim dropped to the ground and passed out.

When Andre ran out of the club behind Cash, he was grazed in the arm by one of the 38 rounds. He buried himself under one of the parked cars until the shots ceased. Checking himself out, he jumped up and ran to where Cash laid in a small puddle of blood, sobbing. He picked her up and started to run towards Tim's car. "Don't worry Cash, I'll get you to the hospital," he said frantically.

"Where is Tim!?" she screamed. "Where the fuck is Tim? He's been shot too." She hit Andre in his arm, where he'd been nicked, and tugged on his clothes.

As they got closer to Tim's car, Andre could see what appeared to be a body, laying face down. He could still smell gun power and the stench of burnt flesh in the air. He stopped running when he got closer to the body. He could see that it was Tim. He heard all the shots while he was under the car, and he knew most of them were aimed at Tim. Terrance had tricked Tim to walk into an ambush, he thought.

"Tim.....! Tim.......! Oh my God, " Cash cried. "Put me down, " she demanded. Tim's body lay lifeless in the night. She placed her ear against his bloody chest to listen for his heart beat. "He's still alive!" she screamed. "We got to get him to the hospital. "

Andre carefully scooped Tim's flimsy body from the ground and carried him back to his car. The back door was still opened and Andre laid him in the back seat. Cash hopped around the passenger side, urgently screaming for Andre to hurry.

"The keys? Where are the damn keys?" Andre asked.

"Check his pockets, " Cash said.

He reached over the seats and gently patted Tim's pockets. He felt a roll of money in one pocket and what felt like a bag of weed in the other, but there were no keys. "He doesn't have the keys, " Andre said.

"We got to hurry up damnit! Tim needs some help," she cried ignoring her own pain.

Andre jumped out of the car and ran back towards the club. A few spectators had surfaced since the shots had stopped. He saw Joey, a guy that was from Madison too, getting into his new car. "Joey, Tim needs a ride to the hospital. He got shot up, and he's loosing crazy blood. We can't find his car keys, and I rode with someone up here. They left me when the shooting began. "

Andre was talking so fast he was out of breath. "Please give him a ride."

"I'm getting ready to go home, " Joey said. Then he started to utter something about not wanting to get blood in his new car. When he said that Andre snatched his keys from his hand and got into his car. He pulled over to where Tim's car was parked. Being more careful than before, he pulled Tim's unconscious body out and placed him in the back of Joey's car. Blood was everywhere!

Cash hopped around to Joey's car and managed to get in the back seat with Tim, still sucking up her pain. She held Tim's head in her lap, stroking his face. "You're going to be fine, Daddy. You're going to be fine," she said to Tim.

Joey ran and got in on the passenger side of his car. He looked back at Tim and saw the blood that covered his seats, but he didn't say a word. He knew that Tim needed medical attention as soon as possible. He snapped on his seat belt and silently began to pray that Tim would be alright. He even asked God to forgive him for being so selfish. Andre drove the car like a bat out of hell until he made it to Baptist Hospital in Winston Salem.

CHAPTER 28

7:00 am, Aeisha's House

Aiesha knew I had to get up early so she set her alarm clock for 7: 00 am. I hated the sound that her clock made. It was irritating as hell. It sounded like fire engines, cats fighting, and ten babies crying all at once. When it went off you were going to wake up!

I reached over, stretching my bedroom body, and smacked the round button to silence the nerve racking noise. I hit it so hard that it hurt the palm of my hand.

"You're going to break the poor little clock," Aiesha said.

"Somebody needs to break it," I responded.

"No somebody needs to break that pager of yours. It vibrated all night. So much that it vibrated off the dresser and fell on the floor. Somebody really wanted to get in touch with Dana Styles," she said sarcastically.

I laid back on the bed, and without looking, fished for my pager. When I picked it up, it read, "Over Flow." I pressed the display button and instantly recognized the first number. It was my mother's number, followed by code "911." The second number was my youngest brother's number followed by the same code. I knew something had to be seriously wrong if both of them paged me 911. I continued to check my pager and all the numbers were from family members. All ending with 911.

My heart skipped a beat as I dialed my mom's number. It hammered against my chest. The phone rang and rang, but there was no answer. I dialed the other numbers and the same thing occurred each time .No answer! I hopped out of the bed and began to dial my aunt's phone number as fast as I could. Sweat formed on my fore head and my nose as my heart's pace increased.

"Dana, what's wrong?" Aiesha asked. She could sense something was wrong from the way I jumped up and started pressing the numbers. I didn't answer her, instead, I continued to dial numbers. Finally, while I was calling everyone and getting no answer, my pager began to vibrate again. It was my brother's number. I had just tried to call him, but no one picked up the phone. I started dialing his number again, so fast that I messed up the first time I tried to return the page. I tried to calm myself down by silently counting to ten, and I dialed the number slower, being meticulous with the numbers I pressed.

"Hello?" my youngest brother's girlfriend said.

"Hey, this is Dana. Where is Pookie?" I asked in the same breath.

"Oh my God! Dana, you still don't know?" she asked.

"Know what?" I yelled into the phone. Aiesha crawled over and softly rubbed my arm like I was a puppy. Somehow she knew I was about to hear the news that would hurt me forever.

"It's Tim, " she cried. "Gerald Gibbs from Pine Hall, and some more guys shot him last night. He is in Baptist Hospital and the doctors are not expecting him to live. He was shot about ten or fifteen times " She was still talking, explaining Tim's condition, but I slowly moved the phone from my face.

At a snails pace, I hung up without saying anything.

My eyes filled with tears that streamed down my face. "What's wrong baby?" Aiesha asked.

I laid back in her open arms, my head gyrating on her bare chest. I tried to conceal the monstrous, inner pain, that instantly devoured my soul, but instead, I erupted. "Tim's has been shot! They are not expecting him to live! "

Aiesha held me against her warm body, for what seemed like forever. I felt so much pain, that I didn't feel anything at all. My Better Half had been gunned down.

A few minutes later Aiesha alluded that I should get up and dress and get to the hospital. She handed me my clothes and shoes and I got dressed as quick as I could. By the time I tied my boots, Aiesha was already standing at the door waiting for me.

I hadn't noticed that I was shaking profusely. My nerves were ripped apart, but Aiesha noticed. "I'm going to drive you to the hospital. You better leave your car here," she said. I didn't say anything because I knew she was right in her judgment. I grabbed my hat and trudged out the door.

I noticed things I'd never noticed before in route to the hospital. The small pond that sat behind the condos off the highway. The palm trees that lined the side walk of the

Holiday Inn. I had never seen palm trees in North Carolina before now. I watched a bird flying in the distance and I appreciated it's beauty and grace while in flight. I had been moving too fast to appreciate anything. I said a silent prayer and counted my blessings.

Baptist Hospital was only twenty-five minutes from Aiesha's house, but it took us almost forty minutes to get there. Her Chevy Spectrum, wouldn't go but so fast. The entire ride we didn't say anything to each other. A couple of times I caught her looking at me, trying to figure out what was going on inside my head. Each time I caught her looking, she would snap her eyes back to the road and I would resume admiring God's Creation.

"You go back home, " I said to Aiesha when we arrived at the hospital. "I'll be straight from here."

She reached over and clenched my hands. "I love you Dana. Be careful and please don't do anything crazy. Please!" she begged.

I pulled my hands a way and got out of the car. I wondered what her definition of crazy was?

"May I help you, sir?" The old, blue haired lady asked, peering over her large, square glasses.

I looked over the desk and I could see my own reflection in the windows she had on her face. I noticed the white lines that dried tears had left on the sides of my face.

"Yes ma'am. Do you have a Timothy Edward Styles?" I asked.

She pressed a few buttons on her computer and calmly said, "He is on the 12th floor, in I.C.U., (Intensive Care Unit) 12 D."

I began to walk down the long vestibule in route to the elevators, praying to God that Tim was fine with each step I took. As I approached I observed a crowd of people with concerned looks on their faces. All of them waiting for the elevator doors to open. I looked at a young black guy who had white lines on the side of his face from dried tears also. An older white lady, who must have been in a hurry to get to the hospital because she still had on her bedroom shoes. An even older black lady, with rollers in her hair. She was still crying. I watched the red light above the door drop from the 5th, 4th, 3rd, 2nd, to the 1st floor. The bell sounded and the shiny silver doors opened. I watched the sad faces, which had already been up early this morning or perhaps spent the night with sick or injured love ones, exit the elevator. Then slowly, myself and the other long faces loaded the elevator. I eased to the back, right corner.

"What floor?" the young black guy asked. "7th. ..8th. ...9th," the different elevator occupants called out. "What about you, my man," he asked me.

"The 12th floor, thank you, " I said.

The elevator made periodical stops between floors and finally made it to the 12th floor. Again, the "Ding" sounded and the shiny, metal doors, reflecting blurred faces, opened. As soon as I stepped out of the elevator, I saw my mom crying her eyes out. My older brothers, Ronnie and Rodney, were trying their best to hold her up and calm her down. The doctor she had just finished talking to, stood by, as if he was going to be needed to assist her. I rushed over to assist my brothers with my mom. She hugged me tightly, and said, "They are not expecting Tim to make it through the day! Lord have mercy on my son, " she cried.

152

I walked her into the waiting room. I greeted other family members and friends who sat quietly, silently seeking God's help for Tim. When mama took a seat, I handed her a box of Kleenex that was sitting on a near by table.

"Don't worry, mama, Tim is strong. He is going to be Ok, " I said. I talked to my mom trying to console her. Trying to convince her that things were going to be fine. "That faith you use to always tell us about, you got to have it now," I said to her, squeezing her hand.

After twenty-five, maybe thirty minutes, I realized that I hadn't seen Pookie .I inquired about where he was, and mama said he was in the I. C .U., with Tim. Teary eyed, I walked down the hall looking for the sign that read "12 D." I found the sign and pressed the large square button on the wall. The double doors open sluggishly. Shhhhhhhhhh! It sounded like air escaping from a punctured tire. A few nurses and visitors turned their heads in my direction when the doors peeled. Realizing I wasn't another I.C.U. patient, or someone from their family, they all resumed their working or their grieving.

Pookie' s head didn't turn. He stood with his back to the electric doors, eyes fastened on Tim. I stepped inside and the doors clicked behind me. In a second I observed the entire unit before I took another step in the direction of where Tim's severed body lay.

The smell of germicide and medicine blitzed my stomach causing it to turn. I felt sick. Even though everyone probably had dissimilar complications, they all had one thing in common. The way their lifeless bodies were hooked up to the beeping life support systems. Some patients had family members at their bedside, while the others suffered alone. All of which were too spaced out to realize if anyone was there or not.

As I approached Tim, I could see the tubes that ran from his mouth, nose and throat into three different machines. His arms and legs were wrapped up in blood stained bandages. And worst of all, I could see where the slugs from Gerald's 12 gauge, had ripped chunks of flesh from his stomach and chest.

I stopped a few feet from his bed and silently began to break down. Pookie had yet to turn around. I could hear him sniveling from where I was standing. After a couple of minutes of staring into Tim's expressionless face, I walked up and tapped Pookie on his shoulder. He turned around slowly, his head still lowered, and looked up at me. Huge tears dropped from his tired, swollen eyes. Peacefully, he stroked Tim's left hand. "He doesn't even know I'm here, Dana, " he cried.

I bent over and kissed Tim on his face. "I love you, Bro, " I whispered in his ear. Remembering those were the last words he said to me .I stood back up and eased to the other side of Tim's bed, my hand scaling the rails along the foot and side of the bed. I reached over the rails and gently began to rub Tim's right hand. "You're going to be alright Tim. Just be strong," I said, my voice cracking.

Pookie's moans became louder. He softly placed Tim's hand by his side and walked out of the I.C.U.

There were only two family members allowed in I.C.U., at once. When Pookie left out, he didn't go directly back to the waiting room, so all of the family still thought he was back in I.C.U., with me. For almost an hour I sat alone with Tim. I hoped and made myself believe that he could hear and understand me. For almost an hour, I prayed and cried.

Finally, Pookie returned to the waiting room and my mom came back to the

I.C.U. She told me my Aunt Puddin wanted to come and sit with Tim. I got up and I walked toward the electric doors. The germicide and medicine was still causing my stomach to turn, but not as much. Death, loomed over the I.C.U., separated only by thin white curtains and different pains. I pressed the square button on the wall again and I listened as the heavy doors opened. "Shhhhhhhhhh!"

Less than an hour ago the doors sounded like air seeping from a punctured tire, when I opened it, but now they sounded like someone taking their last breath.

CHAPTER 2 9

"Who is she?" I asked Pookie

"She's some lady that's been in here talking to mama. Her brother is in 12-D, too. He got shot a couple of times, three days ago," he said.

"How are you guys doing?" The woman asked. She must have seen me asking Pookie who she was. " Just put everything in the Lord's hands. Your brother will be fine." She smiled and took her seat behind me and Pookie.

"Listen! " I whispered to Pookie. Or at least I thought I was whispering. "I'm not going to let this shit ride. I'm not putting shit in the Lord's hands. I'm not about to let these motherfuckers get away with this shit. I'm going to Pine Hall right now and air that motherfucker out! " I said angrily.

Pookie didn't say anything. He gave me a blank stare and just nodded his head. I looked over my shoulder and I noticed the friendly lady who spoke to us had been ear hustling. She over heard what I said I was going to do. I didn't care though. She didn't know me from Adam, so I wasn't tripping.

Jimmy, my mom's husband, walked her into the waiting room and they took seats beside me and Pookie.

"Mama, me and Pookie will be back in a few minutes. We are going to go down the street to Wendy's, and get something to eat," I said. "Do you want anything?" I asked.

If didn't nobody in the world know how close Tim and I was, my mother did. Something my father told her a long time ago was true. "If you let them fight each other while they're young, they will fight with each other when they're grown, " he had told her.

That one statement saved me and my brother from a gang of ass whippings. My mom could see in my eyes that I was up to something else. The time had arrived for me to fight for my brother and she knew it. It was her mother's intuition. "Scooter, please don't go out and do anything crazy, " she said to me.

"Hold up! Hold up! Did you say Scooter?" Hireen asked.

"Yeah, I said Scooter, " I said.

"Oh, isn't that cute. Hey Scooter-Wooter, " said Hireen.

"Ahki (Ahki means brother in Arabic) do you want me to finish the story or what?" I asked. "I thought you were asleep anyway! "

"Ok,Ok,Ok! Go ahead and finish. I just had to interrupt when you said your nickname, " Hireen said.

Anyway! It was her mother's intuition. "Please don't go out and do anything crazy son, " she said.

"I'm just hungry mama. I'm not going to do anything, but get me something to eat."

I tried as hard as I could to stay calm. I was ready to get out of that terrible smelling hospital. I didn't know what I was going to do if I didn't. I was sick and tired of hearing everyone saying, "Put it in the Lords Hand's!"

"Come on Pookie, " I said.

I hugged my mom and promised to be right back. When I walked out of the waiting room, I saw the friendly lady out of my peripheral vision, rush towards my mother. I knew she was going to rat me out, so Pookie and I hurried down the stairs instead of waiting for the elevators.

"I know where-Gerald lives," Pookie said when we got in the car. "I know where his grandmother lives and where he hangs out if he isn't at home. He comes to Madison sometimes. You've probably seen him or his car before, " he added.

I didn't have a gun with me, but I had a partner who lived less than ten minutes from the hospital who stayed strapped. I paged him and he called me back by the time I was half way to his house.

"Yeah, who paged Lawrence?" he asked.

"Dis is Styles! What's up nigga?" I asked.

"Styles! " he yelled. "Long time no hear from. Where the hell you been?" he asked.

"I've been chilling, you know? Trying to make that dollar, " I said.

"Where in the hell is your crazy ass brother?" he asked.

"That's why I'm calling you "L". A few guys shot Tim last night. He is in Baptist right now. I need a big favor from you," I said.

"What's up nigga? You want me to go and straighten those bustas?" he asked. "You know Tim is my motherfucking nigga. He's like a brother to me."

"I'm going to handle that, but I don't have any heat with me right now. The guys who blasted Tim live in Pine Hall, and it will be better for me if you let me hold a couple of gats, than me driving all the way back to Greensboro, to strap up. "

"Nigga, you ain't said shit. You got that! Do you want me to get a few niggas and roll with you down there?" he asked again.

"No, I handle it. I'm just going to scout things out right now. But, I don't want to do that without any heat. When the shit gets ready to hit the fan, I'll let you know, " I said.

"'Where are you now? " L asked.

"I'm about a minutes from your crib," I answered.

"I'm sitting here waiting on you," he said.

Lawrence or L, was one of Tim's connects back in the day. He use to box Golden Gloves, and so did Tim. They had boxed each other in a final once and it was a draw. Both of them had respect for each other, inside and out of the ring.

When I pulled up, L walked out in the cool air with shorts, boots and no shirt on, with a blunt in his mouth.

"Stay right here, I'll be right back," I said to Pookie.

L had guns lined up like he was selling them at the coliseum's gun show. He had two 357's, a chrome 380, three 9mm's and a big Desert Eagle sitting on the table. On the floor, beside the table he had a shotgun, a SKS and a Mini 14 that sat on bi-pods.

"Take whatever you want to take. You can take them all if you need them, " he said. "All of them are fully loaded. I have extra mags for each one of them also. You always have to be ready for this type of shit. Are you sure you don't want me to go?" he asked.

Lawrence was talking a mile a minute, while I looked over the weapons.

"No, I'm straight. I just want to find out where this motherfucker lives. I'll let you know when it's on."

One of the 9mm's had an infrared beam attached to it. I picked it up to get a closer look. It felt like it was made especially for my hand as I gripped it and aimed it at nothing.

"Just press that button right there," L touched a small button beside the trigger and a thin red light beamed from the scope. "And put the beam on that nigga's ass and squeeze the fucking trigger. You can't miss. I zeroed this bitch myself, " he said.

I tucked the 9mm away for myself and I grabbed the chrome 380 for Pookie. I looked over at the SKS and the Mini 14 on the floor also. "You don't want to take either one of those unless you're planning to spray the whole block," L said. "And if you're planning to do that, I'm coming along with you."

"After I check things out down there, I'll return your guns," I said to L.

"Take your time. Squirrel jump that nigga. I got a bunch of these babies around here so don't even trip," he said.

I trotted back to the car, holding the Glock 9mm, under the leather belt on my baggy Levi's and the 380 in my jacket pocket. I startled Pookie when I snatched the door open. "For the Good Times," oozed from the Kenwood's. He wiped a tear from his eye as I situated myself in the driver's seat.

"Don't worry about nothing Lil' Bro. Tim is going to be Ok. Let's just ride for him right now like we know he would ride for us, " I said to Pookie.

I couldn't stop thinking about what if that would have been me who got shot? Or 'what if it would have been Pookie? Tim would have murdered everyone in Pine Hall by now. He wouldn't have been messing around! He would have grabbed that shotgun or that SKS and went to work.

Pookie and I didn't speak as we rode to Pine Hall. I could still hear Tim's voice as clear as day, "I love you Lil' Bro, " he said to me .It played over and over in my mind.

For some reason the closer we got to Pine Hall, the calmer I became. I was furious when I left the hospital, but now I felt at peace. Listening to Al Green, reflecting on me and Tim's good times is what caused the calm to cover me. Then again it could have been I knew that it was about to be over for me!

London was a housing community in Pine Hall. Pookie said Gerald stayed with his mother there. "His grandmother lives in London too," he said. "If he isn't at home or at his grandmother's house, he's at Shags. "

Shags was another "hole in the wall, " joint like Peter Rabbits. Only it didn't stay open late at night, and you could buy burnt bologna sandwiches with your cold beer.

When Pookie and I arrived, I read, "Welcome to London, " out loud. It had been years since I'd seen that sign. We lived in London for 2 ½ years when I was in elementary school. After we moved to Madison, I remember returning with my mom to visit only a few times. I hadn't been back since then. Oddly enough, things still looked the same.

"There is his car right there," Pookie said. He pointed at a candy apple red, Escort GT, with shiny chrome wheels and blinds on the back window. When I saw the car I was shocked. "Gerald!" I said under my breath. "That nigga was just in Madison the other day. I know who you're talking about now, " I said to Pookie. In an instant, towering anger razed my calmness.

I was visiting my cousin Shay-Shay, last week when Gerald came over to visit her also. She introduced us to each other. She pulled me to the side and said that he liked her. She even asked me what did I think about him.

"Do you think I should date him?" she asked.

"Does the nigga have any paper?" I asked Shay-Shay.

"Yeah, he hustles in Walnut Cove and Pine Hall, " she said.

"I think you should make him pay if he wants to play. " That was my advice to her.

When I left Shay-Shay's house, I noticed the red Escort GT with the shiny wheels and the blinds on the back window. The same Escort GT, I was looking at now.

"I don't see him though," Pookie said.

The small crowd of people standing outside of Shags watched curiously as we cruised by. A church on the right side of Shags had sharply dressed people in the churchyard conversing. It was obvious that the services were over because a lot of the people made their way to their cars parked along the side of the street.

"There is where his grandmother lives," Pookie pointed to the house on the left side of Shags. An old lady sat on the porch and waved at us like she was in a parade, when we rode by.

"His mom lives down by the school. He may be down there, " Pookie mumbled. I pulled the 380 from my jacket and sat it between me and Pookie. I pulled the 9mm, out of my baggy jeans and loaded one of the hollow tipped bullets. We rode past his mother's house, but we didn't see anyone.

"I just wanted to know where he lived," I said to Pookie. "I don't want to come back and blow up the wrong house," I said seriously.

It was too early for me to get revenge, I thought. Everyone was expecting that. I wanted to be smart when I killed Gerald or his entire family. Doing it in broad daylight was a one way ticket to Central Prison. I wasn't trying to go there.

"Lets get out of here and get back to the hospital," I insisted. "I've seen all I needed to see. Go out the way we came," I said.

I wanted to go out the way we came so I could get a good look at the house we use to live in, which was directly across from Shags.

"Hold up, stop!" I yelled at Pookie. "There is WeeWee."

WeeWee was our homie from Madison, who married a girl who lived in London. If he knew where Gerald was, he'd tell us. He and Tim were close friends too. They graduated from high school together. He would give Gerald up. WeeWee jogged from his small yard to the edge of the street.

"What's up, Styles? What's up Pookie?" he said.

"You know what's up," I abruptly responded.

He leaned over into the car and saw the 9mn sitting in my lap and the 380 sitting beside of me. Everyone in Pine Hall had heard about what had happened to Tim. He was no exception.

"Listen Styles. I know you're mad as hell right now, but now isn't a good time to get Gerald. Everyone is expecting ya'll to do something. Just chill for a minute and creep the nigga later," WeeWee said.

"Yeah, whatever, " I said. "You seen him?"

"No I haven't .Not today, " WeeWee said.

Another old friend I remember from when we lived in London was standing in his yard, across the street from WeeWee's house. I remember Marvin because he was my brother Rodney's age. They played on the same basketball team. Marvin was the only kid in middle school who could dunk a basketball. Since he was from London, I figured his loyalty would be with Gerald. I decided to try him anyway. I told Pookie to let his window down, and I called Marvin over to the car.

"What's happening Marvin? Let me holla at cha, " I said.

"Who is that WeeWee?" he asked, squenching his eyes, trying to focus on who I was.

"It's Dana Styles and his brother Pookie," WeeWee said.

He strolled over to the car and spoke to WeeWee then to me and Pookie.

"What's up Marvin?" I said.

"Nothing much Styles. Long time no see, " he said.

There wasn't any need for me to beat around the bush with Marvin, so I asked him what I called him over to the car for. "Have you seen Gerald today?"

He paused and started to stutter.

"No. ...ah. .ahh.. nah, I haven't seen him. What are you looking for him for?" he asked.

"I just need to see him. I got a message from God for him, " I said.

Marvin stepped back from the car and walked away quickly. He crossed his yard and went into his house. I eyeballed him until he closed his door.

"Let's go Pookie. I'll holla at cha WeeWee," I said.

We pulled off and headed back up the narrow street. Before we reached our old house, I could see in the distance that the church lawn and the street were still packed.

"Slow down when we ride by his grandmother's house. I want to get a good look at her place too," I said.

When we approached his grandmother's house, Pookie yelled out so loud that it made me jump. "Dana! There he is! There that motherfucker is! "

Gerald stood on the small porch with his grandmother. I was right! This was the same guy Shay-Shay introduced me to. Marvin had rushed in his house and called to warn Gerald that we were looking for him. He jumped off the porch and ran up to the small white fence that bordered his grandmother's yard. The fence sat about ten, maybe fifteen feet from the narrow street. But, right now, it felt like he was right in my face. He commenced to smacking his chest like he was a silver back gorilla. "You looking for me motherfucker? You looking for me!" he yelled.

The winos standing outside of Shags and the gossiping church folk, all seemed to stop doing what they were doing .The party and the future gossip was taking place in Miss Louise's front yard, and she watched her grandson almost proudly.

158

"Yeah, I shot your fucking brother!"

That was the last thing I heard Gerald say. My mind went blank. I sprang out of the car, boot legging the 9mm, that felt like it was fashioned just for my grip. In a flash I reached the small fence. Gerald fixed eyes on the 9mm, and whirled. He began to run back towards the porch. All of the gorilla had disappeared from his demeanor. I pressed the round button beside the trigger just like "L" showed me. The scope projected a red beam that tattooed Gerald's white t-shirt.

"You can't miss. I zeroed this bitch myself," I could still hear L's voice. With all the weapons training I had in the Army, I wasn't planning to miss.

BOOM........BOOM...... I squeezed off two stentorian shots. The infrared beams burnt holes in Gerald's shirt. He fell face down.

The drunken winos at Shags and the gossiping church folk, all spread like the plague when they heard the shots. Everyone took some type of cover or concealment. Some took refuge in Shags or under parked cars and the others ran back into the church.

Gerald's grandmother shrieked with terror from seeing her grandson getting blasted. She unassed her rocking chair, desperately trying to make it to her front door. I aimed the pistol and again pressed the small button beside the trigger. The yellow jacket draped over her shoulders enhanced the glow of the red beam.

BOOM.......BOOM......BOOM

The shots hit right where I'd aimed them. Unfortunately, Miss Louise was faster than I thought. Three bullet holes lined the wall, leading to her front door.

After she slammed the door, I turned my pistol back to where Gerald's flimsy body was lying. I couldn't believe what I saw. Nothing! He wasn't there. "You can't miss," I heard again, in my mind. "Bull shit," I screamed.

"He ran around the house, " Pookie yelled. He jumped from the car cradling the 380. "I'm going to cut him off this way, " he said.

He started to run around the right side of the house. I hopped over the fence, just in time to see Gerald slowly turn the back corner of the house. I gave chase, sprinting along the side of the house. When I reached the back corner, Gerald was laying face down in the back yard. Blood gushed from the two holes in his back. He didn't move a single muscle. Pookie stood over him aiming the 380 at his dome.

"Don't shoot...DO NOT SHOOT," I stressed to Pookie. "He's already dead."

Faintly, I could hear the police sirens already responding to the 187, that was in progress. "Lets get the hell outta here, " I said to Pookie.

We both hauled ass back around the house. I leaped over the fence and Pookie was right on my heels. I ran to the driver's side and jumped in. Pookie ran across the hood of the car and snatched the door open. "Man, let's go, " he yelled.

The sirens were getting louder, which means the police were getting closer. My left leg was shaking so much that I couldn't press the clutch to crank the car. "Dana, let's get the fuck outta here, " Pookie screamed again.

With all of my might, I pressed the clutch, starting the car. I crammed the car in gear and like a chicken with his head cut off, I kicked rocks!

I told Shay-Shay less than a week ago, "If Gerald wants to play, make him pay. " I had no earthly idea that I would be the one to make him pay for wanting to play!

CHAPTER 30

Pookie and I didn't take the main roads back to Winston. Instead, we went in the opposite direction. For over an hour, we drove in silence, on back roads, without a destination. We ended up somewhere in the mountains, about eighty miles north of Winston.

"We can't go back to the hospital," I said, finally breaking the silence between me and Pookie. "It'll be crawling with cops looking for us. We might need to break camp if that bitch ass nigga is dead," I said.

"I hope he is dead. The way he shot Tim he deserves to die. I should have peeled his fucking wig back," Pookie said. "What are we going to do now?" he asked.

"We're going to chill out at this girl's house I know in Winston. We're not going to do anything until we find out if Gerald is dead or not. But, I'm sure he is. If that be the case, we're going to be running for the rest of our lives. If not we're still going to be running."

When I got to Rhonda's house, she had no idea of what had happened to Tim. She was blown away when I gave her the run down of the entire situation. She felt bad for Tim and cried when I began to cry. But, she seemed to be more concerned with the fact that I was going to be hiding out at her crib. "At least we'll be able to spend some quality time together," she said.

Two Days Later

I lay back with my hands locked behind my head watching the news. Since I wasn't calling anyone, this was the only way me and Pookie could get information about Tim and Gerald's condition. Tim's condition remained the same. . Poor! The doctors didn't expect him to live from one day to the next, and Gerald was in stable condition. The velocity of the 9mm, rounds were so fast that they passed directly through Gerald's body without hitting anything vital.

"He has the luck of the Irish, " one of the reporters said.

Me and Pookie's pictures flashed on every news channel. Crime stoppers offered a five thousand dollar reward for the information leading to our arrest. We decided to continue laying low.

Four Days Later

I returned the two pistols to L. He joked about me bringing "Hot" pistols back to him. He also threatened to hold me hostage with the hot pistols and call Crime Stoppers. "If the reward was bigger, I'd call the folks on your thugged out ass," he said jokingly.

"You put that beam on that nigga's ass, huh? I told you, you couldn't miss, didn't I?" he asked.

For days my mother had paged me like crazy. I wasn't going to call her back, but I knew she was worried sick about us. When I finally did return her calls, she pleaded with me and Pookie to turn ourselves in to the police. She didn't want anyone else to get hurt. That was out of the question as far as we were concerned. But, I knew it was only a matter of time before Pookie tried to go and visit Tim. That's all he had talked about the past six days. I knew when he did try, the police would be there waiting on him!

It hurt me to my heart that we couldn't visit Tim, but I had to think and plan for long term. I'd rather Tim visit us in some other country, than to visit me in prison. Even though if he did live, he'd probably be in prison with me. . Especially with all the charges he had.

Pookie couldn't take it anymore. He waited until late the following night and he tried to visit Tim. He wasn't in the hospital ten minutes before the police arrested him and took him to the Stokes County Jail. I had briefed Pookie on the inevitable. I told him what to say when he got caught. "Blame it all on me. Tell the police you didn't know that I was going to shoot Gerald."

I figured there wasn't any need for both of us to go to jail for something I'd done. I'd take the beef for my Lil ' Bro anyway.

When Pookie placed the blame on me the Pine Hall detectives made him write a statement against me. The only way the magistrate judge would give him a bond is if I surrendered.

I called my mother after I saw on the news that Pookie got arrested. She told me that Tim still wasn't doing any better. "That boy you shot is fine, " she said.
I listened closely to the tone of my mother's voice. She almost sounded disappointed that Gerald was doing fine. I should have killed him when I had a chance, I thought.

"What are you going to do about your baby brother?" she asked.

"I'm going to turn myself in, but I'm going to wait for a couple of hours. I want to call daddy first to see if he can get with Tommy again, so when I get a bond, everything will be lined up for me to get out."

My daddy talked to Tommy and he said they'd meet me at the Stokes County Jail. I called one of the detectives and informed him I was on my way to turn myself in.

"Make sure you've got my brother's paper work ready so he can leave as soon as I get there," I said.

He gave me his word that it would be done by the time I arrived.

Two Hours Later

When I entered the police station the captain ordered me to get up against the wall. One detective placed his hands on his pistol while another one patted me down. (Like I was going to bring the weapons with me!) I had watched enough t.v, to know that without a weapon the case may be weak.

My daddy and Tommy signed Pookie' s release papers, while I was being questioned. "Where are the weapons you and your brother had?" One of the detectives asked me.

"I bought them from a crack head on 2lst Street in Winston. Then I sold them back to him for half of what I paid him, once I was finished with them," I said.

I knew that would be their first question. I'd briefed Pookie on that question also. The detective's eyebrow rose when I responded. Our answers matched! He couldn't believe it.

"Did your brother know you were going to shoot Gerald?" Another detective asked. "He blamed it all on you," he added.

The cop thought he was saying something slick, by telling me that Pookie blamed it all on me. (Fucking Rookie) Things were happening just like he was trained they'd happen. "Catch one criminal and put the pressure on him and he'll squeal faster than a pig getting slaughtered." That's what he was taught.

I stretched my eyes like a surprised Buckwheat, and shook my head. "What?" I said. I acted like I couldn't believe that Pookie had blamed everything on me. Everything was happening just like I'd planned in reality, not like the cops had planned.

For the next hour I was drilled with questions. It's funny how cops in real life try to act like the cops on t.v. They all ask the same questions and they all use the same scare tactics. I wrote a statement that I did act alone. Pookie didn't have anything to do with me shooting Gerald. After the police read my statement I wrote, they were disappointed. They were hoping that I would tell that Pookie did know about what I was going to do.

After questioning, I was taken in front of the magistrate to see what my bond would be. Because my record was squeaky clean, and I did turn myself in my bond was set at twenty five thousand dollars. Daddy and Tommy signed my release papers and we all headed for the hospital to visit Tim.

My daddy patted me on the back for shooting Gerald. I think that was as proud as he'd ever been of me. The only complaint he had was that I didn't kill the son of a bitch!

The rest of my family, although very few of them said it, appreciated the fact that I dumped 9mm rounds in Gerald. I was the unsung hero, but none of that was important to me. What mattered to me was Tim's condition and that he knew that me and Pookie did ride for him.

Cash was treated and released, but despite all the pain she was in, she refused to go home. She waited in the waiting room with the family and the rest of Tim's girlfriends.

"How is he doing?" I asked the young white nurse, that was changing the bloody dressings on Tim's stomach.

"He is still in very critical condition. Everyday that he makes it is a miracle, " She said.

When she finished, I took Tim's hand, gently holding it in mine. My eyes became swollen with heavy tears. For a while I sat and talked to Tim. What ever came to mind, I said. "I love you! " Came out of my mouth at least a million times. He lied there motionless. A painful look was frozen on his face. "I haven't been here because I've been hiding from the police. Me and Pookie went and found Gerald for you: I shot that motherfucker. I tried to kill his yella ass. He's lying up in here somewhere too," I said. The entire time I talked to Tim I knew he couldn't hear me. He was so, "Out of his mind" it was pitiful. But, due to his extensive damages, the sedation was unavoidable.

After I told him I shot Gerald, his hands tighten around my fingers like a newborn baby's grip. I popped up and the painful look that was chiseled on his face vanished. His weak eyes, barely opened and two colossal tears slid down his face soaking the white cotton sheets.

All I wanted was for Tim to know that me and Pookie did ride for him. For some reason that was important to me. I wanted him to know that something had been done to that busta. Not by the authorities but by my authority!

Just as quick as he responded to what I had said, his infant grip loosened and his watery eyes closed. He knew……....

From that point, I knew my "Better Half," was going to be fine. I felt it in my heart when he squeezed my fingers. Since I had done all that I could do, I decided to put it in the Lords Hand's!

CHAPTER 31

The following morning, Pookie and I went to see an attorney. Dell Olsen, was the "Mattlock" of Pine Hall. He had practiced law for almost thirty years in the small town. He had a reputation of winning big cases. He also had a rep of having high prices. With the seriousness of our charges, I knew that I was about to fork out some unhumorous cash.

Our case was the talk of the surrounding areas. Mr. Olsen loved that. It was free advertisement for him if he won or loss the case. Cases like ours usually caused him to be bombarded with cases afterwards. And I knew it wasn't about me and Pookie, it was about the dough.

Olsen was the first mouthpiece whom I'd met, who didn't start out asking for money. He got all the facts or statements that were suppose to be facts, first. Then he explained a few ways he could combat the case. "A crime of passion," is probably the best way for us to attack it," he suggested.

After we talked about the case it was time to talk about the price. Olsen was also the first attorney I'd met who didn't start out asking for ten thousand dollars. He started out asking for twelve. Twelve thousand smack-a-roos, a piece, to represent me and Pookie. That confirmed half of his rep, that he was high as hell.

When he continued to talk, he revealed why he was so successful. "The sooner I get some of the money, the sooner I can spread it around, " he said.

I had heard that rooster crow before, I thought!

"The object of the game is to payoff quick. We want to put the case off for as long as possible. Get it out of the people's mind. We payoff to put off, " he said. "Then in a few months we'll go to court and win this gotdamn thing! " he screamed. He sounded like my high school football coach, not my attorney. But, I liked him. I had to do some negotiating though.

My step-father, Jimmy taught me never to give a man the first thing he ask for, and to never accept the first thing a man offers to you.

Olsen wasn't expecting me to say that I could pay him all the money at once. That's probably why he said, "The sooner he got some of the money. "

"If I can pay you twenty thousand dollars today, before lunch time, can we forget about the remaining four thousand dollars?" I asked him.

His mouth dropped to the floor. "Ah Yeah! Sure!" he said, his beeddy eyes lit up like Christmas trees.

Twenty grand was a big chunk of the money I'd saved. I knew that I was going to have to do some serious hustling to make that money back. So, for the next three days, half of my time was spent at the hospital with Tim and the other half was spent between my dope spots, school, Madison and Greensboro. I had so much going on, and so much on my mind that it caused me to slip. A fall that would cost me dearly.

Four Days After I Got Arrested

My cousin called me from the Bricks and told me he was out of coke. "It's on like a pot of neck bones, down here too, " he said. "Please bring something down here for me."

I told him that I was tired and that I was going to chill and I'd see him early the next morning. He sounded pissed after I told him that. "Damn Styles, I'm trying to make some money too." "he said before he hung up the phone.

Twenty minutes later he called me again singing the same song. "Are you coming down here? I need some work so I can get paid. I just missed a five hundred dollar sell. I told them that I might be straight in an hour. Nobody has anything around here," he concluded.

I thought for a second and decided that I could drive to the Bricks quickly and return home to get a little rest. I needed the money. "All right. I'll be down there in about thirty minutes. Make sure you're at the top of the Bricks," I said.

I went to my stash spot and pulled out a few half ounces. I grabbed the bags and tucked them inside of my jacket. I hopped into my Mustang and headed for the Bricks.

I took 220 North, from G'boro, and I was in Madison twenty minutes later. I didn't want to ride through town dirty, so I decided to take a few back roads to the Bricks. Since it was so late and there were no cars out on the roads, I began to speed. Trying to save a few minutes. Trying to get to the Bricks! Trying to get that mighty dollar!

When I passed the Madison police car sitting behind the water treatment plant, it was too late for me to slow down. He pulled out behind me, without hesitating and flipped on his blue lights. I jammed the stick into third gear and pressed hard on the gas pedal. I was dirty, out on bond for attempted murder and my licenses were revoked for excessive speeding already! I wasn't about to stop. But, low and behold, when I came over the little hill, another cop had already blocked the road. I hit my breaks, dug into my pockets and pulled out the three bags. I threw two of them out of the window and the third bag fell onto the floorboard. Frantically, I reached, searching for the third bag. I didn't feel it. "Oh shit," I said nervously.

When I did find the bag it was too late to pitch it out of the window. I was blocked in and all eyes were on me!

Moe use to hide his dope under the seat of his Mustang. I remembered that! It was a little spot underneath the seat that you could stuff things. Quickly, I found the spot and stashed the bag.

"Get your hands up buddy!" The police behind me demanded over his intercom. "Stick both of them out of the window."

I placed both hands out the window. The police in front of me had his door ajar and he was ducked down behind the door pointing his weapon at me.

"Now use both hands and open the door. Step out slowly." Came over the intercom. "Now lay flat on the ground and keep your arms and legs spread. "

I followed the cop's instructions and laid on the ground. I had just made bond for shooting Gerald, and now, I was about to go to jail for a stupid drug charge. I'd teased Tim when he got busted back to back, and now it was happening to me. I knew I should have waited until tomorrow, I thought!

The police behind the door jumped and ran over to where I was laying. He cuffed and patted me down. "Why were you going to try to out run my pal?" He asked. "Where is your license?"

"I don't have them with me." I said. "I left them at home on my dresser."
"No license!! Well, that's probable cause for us to search you car. Do you have any guns or drugs in your car?" He asked.

"No sir, I don't. Every black man isn't a drug dealer," I said. I was hoping that the racial statement would discourage him from searching my car, but it didn't work.

I remembered also, how hard it was for me to find the coke Moe hid in his car. Maybe, this pig won't find the bag, I thought. But, I knew I didn't hide it like it was suppose to be hid. I didn't have the time.

The cop helped me up and placed me in the police car behind my car. I sat and watched as the other cop ripped my car apart. He searched the driver's side where the coke was and moved to the passenger's side. While he searched the other cop kept an evil eye on me. I wasn't worried about getting another speeding ticket. I didn't care about going to jail for driving without a license. I had shot a guy! Tickets were small time crimes now. But, I didn't want to go to jail for a drug charge. I knew I'd be facing some serious time.

He moved from the passenger seat to the back seats, then to the trunk. When he popped the trunk, I knew I was home free. I had dodged a silver bullet that was aimed at my head!

Right as the cop was slamming my trunk shut, the K-9 Unit, pulled up. My heart began to pound. I knew I was up shit creek without a paddle if a dog sniffed my car. I watched a big, black and brown German Shepherd leap out of the K-9 van. A police with a Marine crew cut, lead him to the door that I had left open. He wasn't in my car a minute before he was barking like crazy!

The police who searched my car the first time instructed the K-9 police to pull the dog out of my car to allow him to check under the seats again. He got on all fours, like he was a dog, and began to probe under the driver's seat.

"I found it…. ! I found it….!" the skinny police yelled.

He sounded like that broad on the Eureka, vacuum commercials. He jumped up and down with the plastic bag tightly in his hand. "It's crack! I knew he was a drug dealer. Look at the wheels and the radio system in his car. Geez, look at those freak'n necklaces he's got on."

I dropped my head in disbelief. If it weren't for bad luck, I wouldn't have any luck at all. My car was towed and put in the pound as evidence in a drug investigation. I was arrested and placed on another twenty five thousand dollar bond.

They say, "When it rains, it pours! " I don't know who in the hell "They" is but they is right! In less than a week my record went from squeaky clean to dog dirty.

It was indeed pouring. Felonies, that is!

CHAPTER 32

Gerald only spent two weeks in the hospital before he was released. He was arrested and questioned a couple of days later, but he wasn't charged with anything. The detectives didn't want to charge him with attempted murder because if Tim died they wouldn't be able to recharge him with murder. So they released him. My mother was furious because he wasn't detained. I had to break down to her the differences in the two charges.

"Attempted murder won't carry more than ten years, but if we wait, Gerald could get life in prison if Tim dies," I said to mama.

It sounded bad that we were waiting to see if Tim died or not, but we wanted Gerald to get charged with murder if he did die. In the meantime, me and Pookie were facing attempted murder and a rack of other charges.

After Gerald was released from the police station he pulled a "Whoodini" and vanished. A few times I drove through London and all over Pine Hall in an undercover car looking for him. I wanted to finish my job. I never found him, nor did I find out who the other two gunmen were. Neither did the police, but I've never stopped trying to find out.

Tim continued to tight wire life, but deaths gravity pulled from below. In six months he'd had fourteen operations. Most of them were to reconstruct his intestines. He also had bullets lodged in his arms, back and legs. A few of them had been removed in previous operations, but the doctors said he was too weak to have an operation just to extract the remaining rounds. But, he was still holding on to dear life.

Not a day went by without me going to visit Tim. It pained me greatly to see him in the condition he was in. It seemed like it was yesterday that we did everything under the sun together. Now, I didn't know if we were going to ever do anything else together again.

I hired Jack Dunbar to represent me on my drug case. He was another high priced mouthpiece located down town Greensboro. Drug cases were the only cases he'd take. I don't know if it was because of the money he made from them or because he knew exactly how to combat them, since he had a drug charge himself! Nevertheless, he was the "Cock of the Walk" in Greensboro, and eight thousand dollars richer because of my misfortune.

Since I was caught red handed, I didn't have much of a defense. "I'll make sure you won't go to court for this charge until the shooting charge is handled. Then I'll guarantee that I'll have the charges ran concurrent. That way whatever time you have to do for the shooting, you'll be doing the drug time also, " Dunbar exclaimed.

"What if I beat the shooting charges and I don't get any time?" I asked.

"Well, " Dunbar paused. "We'll cross that bridge when we get to it. I have some good friends in high places in Rockingham County. Friends who owe me so don't worry about that."

Each time Mr. Olsen put the shooting charges off, Dunbar would do the same thing with my drug charge. For six months this took place, but now both courts were tired of the delays. Pookie and I were scheduled to be in court for Gerald's shooting in three days. Two days after that, I was scheduled to go to court for the drugs.

Three Days Later

Crowds of people stood in front of the courthouse, dressed in their Sundays best. It only took me a second to realize why they were dressed the way they were.

"Most of those people are probably the ones who were at the church when I shot Gerald, " I yelled to Pookie.

He didn't say anything, he just continued to bob his head to the booming Dr. Dre. His mind was somewhere in California. He looked worried. Everyone turned and watched as we parked. A few people even pointed in our direction, with disgusting looks on their faces, as if to say we had some nerve to be there.

We hopped out of the car and pimped towards the large crowd. Both of us were dressed in slacks with matching serious faces. I searched for a friendly face in the large group of people and I couldn't find a single one. Despite the stares and whispers, we pushed through the crowd and entered the main courtroom.

A few heads turned to see who was walking in when we entered. I saw my mom and my Aunt Puddin sitting in the back row. They both smiled at me and Pookie, and motioned for us to come over.

"Hey Ma, hey Puddin, " Pookie and I said together. We both hugged and kissed our mom and Puddin and exchanged a few words. Then we walked to the first row of the long wooden benches and took our seats.

"There is that lady that use to talk to us and Mama at the hospital, " Pookie said. He waved and smiled at her. "You remember her don't you?" he asked. "The one who's brother got shot also. The "Put it in the Lords Hand's" Lady, " Pookie said.

Lackadaisically, she waved back but she didn't smile. That was odd because she loved to show her teeth to everyone she met. Maybe it was just the courtroom environment, I thought.

She and my mother were very good friends now. I assumed that she attended court to support my mom and us. Then I wondered why she wasn't sitting with my mom and Aunt Puddin? I turned and looked at the crowded bench where my mom and aunt were parked. "That's why! " I said softly to myself. The bench was crowded.

A few minutes after we took our seats, the doors at the back of the courtroom opened and people started to flood the place. I looked at my watch and it was 8:54. Court was about to begin.

The double doors behind the judge's bench opened and a fat, young looking guy, with a black robe emerged. He looked more like a choir director than a judge. "All rise for the honorable Judge Theodore T. Russell," the bailiff cried out. Together, everyone stood facing the judge until he commanded us to be seated. The District Attorney called the docket and court was underway.

The first thirty or forty minutes were all traffic violations. The judge was giving breaks to the traffic violators, which was a good sign, until the charges started getting more serious.

A domestic dispute case was heard following all of the traffic cases. Some young black guy had beat his girlfriend up, but now she didn't want to proceed with the case. The judge informed her if she dropped the charges, that the state had decided to pick them up. "Furthermore, you will be ordered to pay the cost of court and the fine," the judge said. After he said that, the black girl decided to proceed with the case. After both sides of their story was told to the judge, he ordered the young black guy to sit over in the jury box. "It's going to be 180 days before you get a chance to touch her again," the fat judge said. Following that case, everyone who had domestic dispute charges got at least 180 days in the county jail.

I began to think if those guys got 180 days, for hitting someone, I was about to get put under the jail for shooting Gerald's punk ass!

Attorney Olsen came in the courtroom looking like a seasoned vet. He spoke to everyone who thought they were important, including the judge. Then he motioned for me and Pookie to follow him outside.

"There are a lot of people here today to testify against you two .The D.A. has offered you two a plea bargain for three years. He is really happy that you shot Gerald Gibbs, because he has been trying to get him off the streets for a while. I know you two weren't expecting to get any time, but with all these tax paying folks here to testify against you, I'd advise you to take the plea, " he said.

My heart was beating hard as hell! I wasn't trying to go to prison for no amount of time. Neither was Pookie. This was not a part of our deal, I thought. "You said if we put the case off, it was going to become a weak case. If it was weak, we would not get any time," I almost screamed at Olsen. Pookie didn't say one word. He just stood there watching Olsen.

"For crying out loud, you shot the guy in front of a million people," Olsen said as equally as loud. He had flipped the script on us that fast. I had paid him twenty thousand dollars and he was tripping

"Look ah here Mr. Olsen! I paid you twenty thousand dead presidents to represent me and my brother, not to take a plea bargain. When I paid you, you sounded like we were going to win the case hands down. Now, you're sounding like we don't have a damn chance to beat these charges. We are going to trial! We are going to beat this thing. A crime of passion," I said. "A crime of passion!

Olsen shook his wrinkled face from side to side, but he said, "Ok. We'll go in here and give this our best shot and beat this damn thing. Let's just keep our fingers crossed and hope for a miracle."

After our brief conference we all entered the courtroom and Pookie and I returned to our seats. Mr. Olsen took a seat in a red, cushioned chair to the right of the D.A.'s table, along with a few other attorneys.

A few more cases were heard then it was our time to take center stage.

"Your Honor, the next case on the docket is case number 741. The State of North Carolina and Gerald Gibbs, versus Dana and Corey styles. The defendants are being represented by Attorney Olsen," the D.A. said.

Pookie got up first and walked over to the table where Mr. Olsen sat. For some reason, I remained seated for about ten seconds, just watching Pookie. Mr. Olsen looked over at me and motioned for me to get up. I jumped up and quickly walked over and stood beside Pookie.

"You two may be seated, " the judge said.

"Your honor this is a case that I'm sure you're familiar with. We've continued to put it off for six months, but now the State and the defense are ready to proceed, " the D.A. said.

"Is that correct, Mr. Olsen?" asked the judge.

Olsen slid his chair back and stood up. His chunky body stood at the positioned of attention. Olsen gave the D.A., an evil eye and answered the judge. "Yes sir, Your Honor. The defense is ready to proceed at this time."

The judge smiled and nodded at Olsen. He appreciated the respect he had displayed. The D.A. had remained seated while he spoke to the judge. "Then we shall proceed, " the judge said looking at the D.A. furiously.

The D.A. realizing his mistake before stood and began to explain his side of the case. He briefly told the story of Tim getting shot, but he never mentioned Gerald as being the shooter. Then he jumped from that story, to the way Pookie and I infiltrated Gerald's community and shot him in cold blood in front of is grandmother and the church folks, who were all tax payers, he added. Somehow, the D.A. managed to leave out the drunkards at Shags.

"Your Honor, I also have witnesses to testify that Mr. Dana Styles shot Gerald Gibbs in attempt to murder him. His brother Corey Styles, who also possessed a firearm at the time of the shooting aided Dana in trying to kill Mr. Gibbs." The D.A. had blood in his mouth and he was going for the kill. The way he made Pookie and I sound, I was ready to take the plea bargain until I heard Mr. Olsen's opening statements.

Olsen stood up and out of the corner of his mouth he instructed me and Pookie to stand. "Your Honor, I have two brothers here that love their brother Timothy Styles very much. What the D.A. failed to mention in his opening statements is that Gerald Gibbs was one of the guys who shot the defendant's brother, approximately six months ago. Gerald shot Mr. Styles at point blank range, with a 12 gauge shot gun! "

Attorney Olsen continued to speak, illustrating the extent of Tim's damages and trying to establish how much Pookie and I love him. The judge sat attentively listening to Mr. Olsen like he was genuinely concerned. He also mentioned the fact that I was a college student with a 3.2 GPA, and that I'd served in the Army and fought in Operation Just Cause and Desert Storm. That seemed to really get the judges attention. He looked at me in disbelief. Olsen finished his opening statements with eulogistically comments about me and Pookie's character.

The D.A. stood up again and called his first witness. The door to the left of the witness stand opened and a cute little, old lady sashayed out and took a seat. She was sworn in and she testified that she had lived in London for more than thirty years and she hadn't never witnessed anything as tragic as when I shot Gerald. "Especially right beside a church, " she said holding up the Bible that was in front of her. She ended her testimony by saying, "God don't like ugly! And what dem' boys did was sho nuff ugly."

The next three witnesses gave their rendition of the story. Each one made their story sound worse than the one before. Then Gerald's grandmother sauntered from the witness room and testified she saw us the first time we rode past her house. "They rode by slowly as if they were looking for someone. I even waved at them when they rode by," she said. Midway through her testimony, she had the entire courtroom in the palms of her hands, except for my mom and my aunt. Even the lady who befriended us at the hospital, was shaking her head from side to side. I knew Pookie and I were up shit creek without a paddle when she said, ironically in a sweet voice, "That young man right there," she pointed her shaking finger at me." He even tried to shoot me. He shot at me three times, but God wouldn't allow those evil bullets to touch me. I'm a child of God and He protects his own," she said.

A cold chill ran down my spine and I was scared to look up at the judge. Whispers filled the air in the courtroom and the judge had to slam his gavel to bring order back into the court.

Marvin, the guy who ran in his house and called Gerald, was the next witness. He testified that I was looking for Gerald. He made sure he told that I had a 9mm sitting in my lap, when he looked into the car. He ended his testimony reemphasizing that I was hunting Gerald down like he was a wild animal. "Dana told me he was looking for Gerald because he had a message from God for him."

I was sure that the D.A. had finished calling witnesses. He had done more than an adequate job of getting his point across. Which was my actions were premeditated. After Marvin stepped down, the D.A. requested a five minute break. He explained to the judge that he only had two more witnesses and he would be finished. He was granted the break and he walked into the room in which all of his witnesses had emerged. I assumed he was going back to coach his last two witnesses before bringing them to the stand.

Attorney Olsen leaned over and whispered to me and Pookie. "Remember when you take the stand to answer only the questions I ask you. This may sound kind of crazy, but it's ok if you two get emotional on the stand. Sympathy has won a lot of cases for me." he said. Olsen was suggesting to us indirectly that we should cry once on the stand!

He went over a few things until the D.A. returned to the courtroom. "Are you ready to proceed?" The judge, who had sat patiently on his throne, examining files, asked.

"Yes sir, Your Honor,'" the D.A. replied.

"Then call your next witness, " said the judge.

"Your Honor, my next witness is Gerald Gibbs."

I hadn't seen Gerald since the day I ran up on him and pulled a Rambo. Just the sound of his name made my stomach turn flips, and sweat started to form on the tip of my nose. I clenched my fist as tight as I could and took a deep breath. I glanced at Pookie and the look of death covered his face.

Gerald opened the door, walked to the witness stand and took a seat. It was so quiet in the courtroom, you could hear a mouse piss on cotton. I started staring at him as he took his seat, hating the ground he walked on. I hated myself for not killing him. He looked like he had never been harmed. But, Tim on the other hand was in Baptist Hospital, 60 pounds lighter, with Swiss cheese holes in his body and fighting for his life.

He stared directly at the D.A., avoiding me and Pookie's stone faces. The D.A. started asking Gerald questions and he gave his account of the story. When he finished talking he was shaking like a leaf, blowing in March winds. I sat up straight, proud of getting some, "Get Back," for my brother. Seeing him shaking the way he was eased some of my pain.

Gerald stepped down from the witness stand with some help from the bailiff and disappeared into the witness room. The D.A., acting like he was really concerned jumped up and ran to check on him.

I sat on an emotional roller coaster. I was mad as hell a few minutes ago, but now I laughed lightly at the state Gerald was in now. I hoped he'd always be like that. I hoped my name would turn his stomach and make him piss in his pants whenever it was mentioned.

"Your Honor, I'd like to call my last witness to the stand. Mrs. Olivia Butler, " said the D.A.

I wasn't familiar with that name but it was obvious that my mother was. Suddenly, when the D.A. called her name I heard my mom scream "What!" Instead of looking to see who she was, I turned and looked at my mom's shocked face. She had her hand over her mouth shaking her head in disbelief. Her face turned red from anger. When I turned around and looked at the witness stand, I couldn't believe my eyes.

"That sorry bitch!" Pookie said. "Fake ass Christian bitch!"

The put in the Lords Hand's lady, was sitting behind the stand looking at me. "No wonder she half ass waved and didn't smile at us when we came in," he said.

Now I understood why the lady wasn't sitting with my mom. She hadn't showed up for support she showed up to assist the D.A. to burry us alive.

She testified that she heard me planning to go and shoot Gerald. "Air out everything in London, " is what she said I said. "His shooting was very premeditated, " she stressed. "He planned the whole thing. I told him to put it in the Lords Hand's, but I suppose he didn't listen to that." Her testimony put the icing on the cake for the D.A.

Mr. Olsen had declined to cross-examine anyone. His logic was that everyone saw me shoot Gerald in broad daylight. There wasn't anyway he could cross anyone up on the stand and it would be best for us to get them off the stand as soon as the D.A. finished with them. Pookie and I both agreed.

After Mrs. Butler's testimony, we had a short break. When we returned it was Mr. Olsen's time to take the court. He called Pookie to the witness stand first. His main objective with Pookie was to clear him of all charges. He asked Pookie questions about his love for Tim first. Then he began to ask him questions on Tim's condition and Pookie slowly began to break down on the witness stand. I knew they were real tears. Not the tears Olsen had requested. Talking about how bad Tim was doing was a burden on Pookie's heart. I began to hurt because he was hurting. That's how we were raised. If one hurts, then we all hurt. I felt his pain.

Olsen asked Pookie if he had prior knowledge of me planning to shoot Gerald. Just like he was coached, he answered with a convincing, "No!" After fifteen minutes of questioning by Olsen, Pookie was crossed examined by the D.A., who tried to get Pookie to admit to having prior knowledge of me planning to shoot Gerald. The D.A. failed in his attempt. Pookie was too sharp to get crossed up on the stand.

I was called to the witness stand next. Olsen began asking me the same questions as he'd asked Pookie. I answered them with the same intense feelings Pookie had answered with. I noticed the sympathy in the faces of the people when Pookie began to tear up, so I was going to ride that tide all the way to the shore. But, I must admit my tears were real also.

When Olsen began asking me questions about Tim's current condition, I broke down like and old shotgun. The judge even reached over and handed me some tissue. I could tell the feelings in the courtroom were changing and starting to side with us. Gerald"s grandma's "gooey" testimony had been long forgotten. Everyone in the courtroom, even the ones who testified against us had long faces, from hearing my side of the story.

Olsen asked me if Pookie had prior knowledge about the shooting. I told him he did not. "I acted alone. I didn't expect my brother to get caught up in something that I done, " I said.

Olsen continued by asking me, "Why? Why did you shoot Mr. Gibbs?"

"Because I love my brother so much and I didn't want Gerald to get away with shooting him like he was some type of wild animal, " I said with a lot of emotion.

Briefly, I was cross-examined but the D.A. could not cross me up either. I had already admitted to the shooting. I couldn't deny that. He wanted me off the stand so he kept his questions simple and short. He could sense the emotional change in the courtroom's atmosphere too.

The D.A. and Mr. Olsen made closing statements and the judge excused himself and entered his chambers. I knew my testimony had a major impact on him and the rest of the courtroom's occupants, but I also knew that the other testimonies carried significant weight. The more I thought about that plea agreement that was offered to me and Pookie, the more it sounded like something I should have taken into consideration. I was playing chicken, driving a Pinto, going up against a Mack truck! But, there was a chance of Pookie and I walking out of the courtroom "Scott Free".

Everyone stood when the judge walked back into the courtroom. He instructed Pookie and I to remain standing, and allowed everyone else to be seated. Before he started talking, I tried to read his face. I wanted to figure out what was going on inside his head, but I couldn't. His face was expressionless.

"You boys seem to be very good boys. From what Attorney Olsen has said here today, and from some investigation of my own, I find that to be true."

When the judge said that, I knew what was about to happen. Whenever someone starts talking about you and they start out saying things like the judge was saying, they are trying to cushion a forth-coming blow.

It's like when your friend wants to hook you up on a blind date and you ask him, "How does the other girl look?" He always starts by saying how she has a wonderful personality. He starts that way to cushion the blow. Then he says, "But. ...! But she is fat as hell!"

The judge continued to talk. "I know you guys love your brother. I have a couple of brothers myself and if someone shot either one of them, I would probably get a gun and hunt them down myself. But!"

I knew that a "but" was coming. When he said, "but" Pookie looked over to me. I knew he was thinking and feeling the same thing as I was thinking and feeling. Our hearts raced and I braced myself for what he was about to say.

"But, just because that's what I would probably do, and what you have done, doesn't make it right. Attorney Olsen argued that this was a case of " a crime of passion". To be a crime of passion, you'd have had to have been at Peter Rabbits at the time of your brothers shooting. If you had been there and in turn shot Gerald Gibbs, then I might would have agreed with Attorney Olsen. Instead, you found out hours later. We heard the testimony given by Mrs. Butler, that she heard Mr. Dana Styles."

He looked up and pointed at me. The way he talked it sounded like he was directing all of his conversation directly to me. That was good because I wanted Pookie to get acquitted of all charges.

"She said she heard you plan to go and get revenge on Gerald Gibbs, for shooting your brother. By her testimony, I am inclined to believe that this shooting was premeditated. Then you wrote statements and testified that you purchased a weapon from someone in Winston Salem, prior to traveling to Pine Hall. Again, that's grounds for me to believe the shooting was planned."

The courtroom had grown very quiet. My mom and aunt moved from the back row up to the front. They were so close I could hear them whispering something. I began to think about all the things I had planned to do after court. It didn't look like my plans were going to be happening.

The judge paused and flipped through a few papers. He looked up at me and Pookie again and resumed talking.

"You were offered a plea bargain for three years and you declined it." He shook his head in disapproval. "With this type of crime, I'm going to be forced to sentence you two to more than twice that time."

"Oh my God," my mom cried out.

I turned around and my Aunt Puddin hugged my mom tightly. Pookie dropped his head and shook it from side to side. Tears filled his brown eyes. My plan to get him acquitted didn't work.

Attorney Olsen placed his face in the palms of his hands. His face turned beet red. "I can't believe this crap. Damnit Dana, I told you to take the plea bargain, " he said.

"Mr. Olsen, please hold your comments for your clients for later," the judge said. "I hate to give you boys this time but you broke the laws of the state of North Carolina, and I have taken a sworn oath to uphold those laws and that's what I must do today. However, due to the circumstances leading up to your crime, I've decided to take them into consideration."

I stood restively, waiting to hear the sentence the judge was about to impose. All that other bullshit he was talking was frivolous now. He had already said we were about to be broke off with more than twice the time of the three-year plea bargain. He continued to talk as if he had to justify why he was about to give us time. His lips moved, but I didn't hear him saying shit until he said that Pookie and I were sentenced to seven years in the Department of Corrections."

Surprisingly, Mr. Olsen stood up and went to put his arms around my mom who was crying her heart out. She had a right to cry. One of her sons had been shoot a million times, and two of them had just been sentenced to seven years in prison for getting revenge.

The bailiff approached me and Pookie then motioned for us to follow him. Nervously, we started to follow him into the same room all of the witnesses had been in. My mom, Aunt Puddin and Mr. Olsen was tailgating us into the room.

"The judge instructed me to allow you all as much time as you need back here before you two are taken into custody," the bailiff said, his eyes bouncing from me to Pookie to my mom. He turned to walk out of the door and abruptly stopped. "Attorney Olsen, can I have a word with you in private, please?" he asked. He and Mr. Olsen walked to the corner of the room and the bailiff whispered something into Olsen' s ear. Olsen shook his head up and down, signifying he understood. Just as quick as the bailiff marched us in the small room, he turned and walked out into the crowded courtroom and posted up by the side of the huge platform that the judge hid behind.

"We only have about twenty-five minutes before the morning break, " Olsen said. "I know that he said we can take up as much time as we needed, but he is only allowing us to stay until the break. Then you two will have to be taken into custody and dressed out."

My mom hugged Pookie and Puddin had me in the bear hug. "Don't worry, mama we're going to be alright," Pookie said.

"Can we appeal this sentence?" I asked Olsen.

"You can, but it won't do any good. Especially when the Appeals Court review the plea agreement you denied. It will be a waste of your money and of my time if you try to appeal the judge's decision. He could have given you both ten to twenty years! "

Olsen began to explain how if we would have taken a plea bargain that the three years would have been cut to a year and a half. We would have been home in four months. But, now seven years would be cut to three and a half years and with good behavior, we'd be home in eight months to a year and a half. For someone who had never done prison time and didn't expect to get any time, eight months is a long stretch. A year and a half is forever.

We gave our mother a list of things that we needed to be done and departed tearfully. "Make sure both of you call me later, " my mom said.

"Me too, " added my Aunt Puddin.

We were dressed out in orange jumpers and sent to different cellblocks. When I walked in Block "G" there were seven people in the loud block. It sounded like it was twenty-seven! The two card games stopped and they all stared at me. I stared back, just as hard, showing no sign of fear, and carried my bedroll to cell 13. The bottom bunk in the cell was made up and a couple of birthday cards and letters decorated the metal desk.

While I was situating myself, I heard the guys burst into a loud laughter, like they had made a joke about me .One of the guys got up and walked into the cell where I was.

"They told you to move into cell 13?" he asked.

"Yeah, " I said simply.

"They got empty cells and they keep putting motherfuckers in here with me," he said.

When the skinny, tall dude said that I looked over his shoulders and noticed how everyone was watching us .He had been sent to try me!

"If you got a problem with me being in here, you let the police know, and I'll see if I can get moved to another cell," I said. I tossed my bedroll on the top bunk and looked around. I also noticed one of the letters on the metal table had the last name of "Gibbs" on it, written in red ink.

The dude turned and walked out of the cell laughing. "Hey dude, " I said.

He turned. "What?"

"Are you some kin to Gerald Gibbs?" I asked, with my face balled up.

When I asked him that, his eyes opened wide as hell. For a second he did not say shit. Finally, he answered, "No!" That's another set of Gibbs."

I began to stare at him from head to toe. He looked like he could be Gerald's older brother, I thought. I knew they had to be related. He walked past the card table and to the bars and yelled for the police.

The Correctional Officer came to the bars and began to speak with the guy in a low voice. "Ok, wait one second, " the C.O., said and walked away. When he returned, he had two other officers with him. When he opened the cell, the Gibbs guy rushed out. The other two officers entered the block and ordered me to stand over by the other guys at the card table. They went into the cell and packed Mr. Gibbs things.

"What da fuck is going on?" One of the guys at the card table asked.

"That nigga just checked in, " Another one of the guys yelled.

I stood listening, "Green" to what was going on, and what "Checked in" meant.

"What did you say to that nigga?" One of the guys asked.

"I didn't say shit to him, but I did ask him was he Gerald Gibbs' cousin?"

"Oh shit! You're the nigga who shot Gerald, huh?"

I stuck my chest out with pride, "Yeah! Why?" I asked, with an attitude.

"We were just talking about that this morning. That's, that nigga's nephew you shot. He talked all that shit about what he was going to do to you if you came in this block. All of that bullshit and he punked out like a little bitch." They all started laughing and began to introduce themselves.

"You want to play spades?" The guy who said his name was Marc asked.

"Yeah, I'll play, " I said.

"You take that bitch ass niggas place. You're Mr. Miller's partner," he said. They all started to laugh again.

We played cards for hours, until the C.O., said that the lights would be turned off in thirty minutes. I got up and made a million quick phone calls, assuring everyone I was alright. Afterwards, I took a quick shower, made my bunk and laid down. When the lights went out, I gazed into the darkness, still not believing that I was in jail on my way to prison. I thought about Tim. If I had it to do allover again, the only thing I would do differently is give Gerald a head shot, instead of a chest shot! I continued watching the darkness, hating that I wasn't going to be able to see my Better Half for at least eight months. Then a thought hit me hard! Tim may not even live for another eight months. I got out of my bunk and got on my knees and started to pray. Once I got back into my bunk I drifted like a feather from the wings of an eagle, into a deep sleep.

CHAPTER 33

Two Days Later

Surprisingly, I slept like a baby. I didn't realize how jaded my body was. I was so accustomed to "rippin and runnin" the streets, that my body was shocked to receive the proper rest. Actually, I didn't think I was able to sleep unless I was going to the, "Land of Nod" with a cute woman. But, I rested well.

I was dressed out in the same clothes I wore to court two days prior, and transported to Rockingham County Jail. The drug charge had been put off for more than six months also. Now the time had come for me to face the music. My head was still whirling from the seven year blow I'd received, but I wanted to get the drug case behind me too.

I arrived at Rockingham County Jail, and sat in a holding cell from 7:30 a.m. until 9:30 a.m. Then I was escorted by a goofy looking bailiff into the courtroom, bound in shackles and cuff. As soon as I entered the courtroom Attorney Dunbar rushed over to me inquiring about the outcome in Stokes County.

"I was sentenced to seven years, after I declined a three year plea bargain," I explained. He shook his head and smacked his paper-thin, pink lips.

"You should have accepted the plea bargain, " he said.

"No shit," I muttered.

"I've talked to the D.A. and he's going to try to use the shooting charge to make you a two-time felon. But he can't do that because of a new law that was passed a couple of weeks ago. I'm sure I'm going to be able to do what I promised I would do. And if not…" Dunbar paused. He looked like there was something else he needed to say but it wasn't coming out. "If not, I'll refund at least half your money."

I was screwed again, I thought. I didn't like the sound of what he had said.

I scanned the courtroom in search of my mom. I located her perched in the third row, sitting beside her road dog, my Aunt Puddin. Vaguely, I flashed a quick smile and she attempted to smile back. She looked pitiful! I felt bad, because of what I was putting her through.

Dunbar walked over and said something to the D.A. Both of them burst into laughter. He told me before that he had friends in high places in Rockingham County. I hoped and prayed the D.A. was one of them.

After a couple of cases, my name was called. I stood and began to slowly walk, the shackles cutting into my ankles, and I posted behind the chair Dunbar sat in.

"Come on around your attorney son and take a seat, " the judge said.

When I took my seat the D.A. began explaining to the judge the "Said" facts in the case. When he finished, he called the two officers who arrested me to the stand. One by one, both of them gave the same rehearsed testimony. When it was Dunbar's time to take the stage, he started by arguing the weight of the drugs that were found inside my car. He presented the judge with a copy of the lab report, conducted by the S.B.I. (State Bureau of Investigation) The lab report showed that out of 16.7 grams of the drugs I possessed, that only 12.1 grams were actually crack! The other 4.6 grams was cut put on the coke."

"Actually, 4.6 grams is cut and the bag weighs one gram, " Dunbar said to the judge. Both of my eyebrows went north when Dunbar made that statement. That was something only a former drug dealer would know, I thought.

"So that means 11.1 grams were crack, Your Honor, " he said. He continued to argue new laws and I think some of it was made up, but it worked. The judge sentenced me to three years to run concurrent with the seven years I received two days prior. Also, I was ordered to pay a one hundred dollar fine, cost of court, which was sixty dollars, and three hundred dollars storage fee to get my Mustang back. Everything worked out.

Back In Stokes County Jail.

Two weeks had elapsed and I still couldn't believe I was in jail. It was like I was having a long nightmare and couldn't wake up. I even pinched myself a few times to see if I was dreaming.

I missed Tim so much that I felt physical pain in my heart! Needless to say, I missed my daughter and the rest of my family too. Also, I hated Pookie got sentenced to the same amount of time as I did and he didn't do shit.

I'd heard stories of how people flip and turn their backs on you when you're locked up, but I never paid much attention to them. That was my least worry. I was "Dana Styles!" There are only two people in the world like me, and I was both of them! I didn't deal with people who would flip on me. Or at least that's what I thought.

I hadn't heard from Mac, Huntman, Aiesha, Jegbadai or any of the other chickenheads I was sleeping with. I assumed they heard about the seven years along with the three year sentence I received and they all figured I was going to be out of the picture for a while. So they decided to get ghost! When I tried to contact any of those people, no one was ever at home or mysteriously, blocks had been placed on their phones. I tried to get in touch with my partners Tone, Geno and Quayle, but they had vanished also. Zag did show up and hit my mother off with a nice lump sum of cash, and with a message to contact him if I needed anything else. Celeste wrote me daily with promises of never leaving me. And when you're in a situation like I was in, you automatically want to believe that your 'Main Squeeze' will stay down with you for the duration of your bid. And I had faith that she would do just that.

I received mad respect from the other guys that was in my cellblock. Especially, after that punk checked in. Which means he went to the hole. He did that after realizing who I was. After having conversation with the guys a few of them admitted to hearing of me. One guy said he heard I was rolling in Madison and Stoneville. Another one said he heard of the "Styles Boys" a while back. "I heard ya'll will tear some shit up," he said.

Miller was the "Pops" or the oldest guy in the block. He would sit and tell stories as long as we'd sit and listen. He had just got out of Federal Prison two years ago. "After doing an eight year bid, " he said. "Now, I'm back in jail because I got busted with two kilos of cocaine while I was still on probation. He and I became very good friends while I was in Stokes County Jail.

I liked Pops because he was full of advice. "Go and do your little time, get back in college, and leave the drugs alone. That's a dead end street. If you continue to travel down it, you'll end up like me," he said. "Listen Jit," he said. ('Jit is short for jitterbug) "While you're in these white folks prison, life goes on. Your kid will get older and continue to grow. Your woman will leave you and find a new man and you'll find out who your friends really are. Just wait. You'll see. But, that's not the hardest part of doing time. The backbreaking part is when someone in your family, like your mom or dad, dies and you're not allowed to pay your last respects to the ones you love with all your heart. The Feds aren't like the state prisons. The state prison will allow you to be escorted to a funeral, but not the Feds. My dad died while I was in federal prison, three years and seven months ago. I couldn't pay my final respects to my ole man. That was the hardest thing I've had to deal with. It crushed me." Miller started to get tears in his eyes. He needed to talk and he continued to vent. "Now here I am again in prison and my mother is on her death bed. I don't know what I'll do if something happens to her. God willing, she'll recover, but if not, I won't be able to pay my last respects to her either," he said, his eyes becoming more glossy. "And if you get out and go back to the streets, you won't graduate from A&T, but you will graduate from the state system to the federal system. And you don't want to do that."

I sat listening to Mr. Miller, feeling his pain. He made me think about Tim even more. I said a silent prayer for him and Mr. Miller's mother.

.

Two Weeks Later

An entire month had passed and the Department of Corrections hadn't come to get me or Pookie yet. We passed letters to each other daily, and we both were ready to bounce. The county jail was getting old.

What Mr. Miller and I had talked about, and were afraid of happening, happened the night before I was transported to state prison. The C.O. came into the block about

2:00 a.m., and yelled out his name. "Miller…. Donnie Miller…..Miller, " he said loudly. He took a small Mag flashlight and scanned the block. The light bounced from cell to cell waking everyone up.

"Yeah, What?" Miller asked, still half asleep.

The officer shined the light in the direction from which the raspy voice came. Everyone was listening to see what was so important that he had to wake Miller up at 2:00 a.m.

"The federal marshal instructed me to inform you that your mother just died. And since you're not cooperating with them, you won't be going to the funeral." he said in a cold voice. He turned out the bright light and walked out of the block.

I could hear Mr. Miller in his cell, which was two cells down from mine, boohooing. Again, I got out of my bed and said a prayer for him and Tim.

I hoped and prayed that nothing like that would ever happen to me because I knew I couldn't handle it if anyone in my family died and I couldn't pay my last respects. Again, I felt Miller's pain, but deeper than before. So much that I cried for him. Hell, everyone in the block was probably crying.

When the police woke me up later that morning, I packed my things and I called out to Mr. Miller. I walked over to his cell and he was buried under his green, wool blanket. He didn't move a muscle. I walked over to Marc's cell and told him to tell Mr. Miller to keep his head up. I grabbed my things and peeled out, still hurting for him. Still praying that nothing like that would ever happen to me.

CHAPTER 34

Pookie and I were transported to the maximum custody prison in Salisbury. "The High Rise," is what it's commonly referred to in North Click. I had also heard horror stories about the High Rise, but just like the stories of niggas flipping, I didn't pay much attention to them. I never thought I'd end up there!

When the bus backed into the High Rise, it must have been five or six hundred guys standing, sitting or posted up trying to see who was getting off the bus. Some cats were searching for "Fresh Meat." Punks! Others were waiting on family, partners from the same hood or anyone they knew. The remaining spectators just watched because that was the thing to do when a bus of new arrivals surfaced.

I searched the crowd of tan suit wearing niggas for a familiar face. They all seemed to run together and look alike. The bus driver jammed the brakes and stopped the bus! Then armed guards carrying shotguns jumped on the bus. One began to scream.

"Ok. …Ok. . Listen up, " he yelled. The other two stood with their shotguns at portarms. "When you get off the bus, stand against the wall in a single file line. Don't say shit to the faggots on the other side of that fence." He looked over at all the convicts. "Or you'll be in the hole before you can say your damn name. I don't care if you see your daddy, don't say shit to him! You'll be able to talk to those butt pirates later."

The yelling, threats and commands instantly made me have flashbacks of the Army. It was the same exact shit, just a different place.

We filed off the bus amid the screaming convicts, and lined up against the wall. "Hey bitch! I'm going to make you mine," some dude yelled at a punk who stood a few people in front of me. "Whatever you need, come and find Ghetto, " The punk blushed, smiling at Ghetto.

Other cats from across the fence were calling out names also. A few niggas tilted their nappy heads back as if to say, "What's up?" but nobody dared to speak. Then I heard someone calling me and Pookie's name. The voice sounded very familiar. Then about four people started wailing our names.

"Styles..Dana..Pookie! What's happen, Cuz? Welcome to the Big House!" It had been a long time since I'd seen Red. He had been locked up for a while now. I felt good that someone was there that knew me and Pookie. But, Red wasn't the only one there that knew us. His half-brother, Chug, and three more of my cousins were there. Not to mention about five guys who grew up with us. It's bad to say, but this was like a family reunion for me and Pookie.

After we were processed, we were escorted to our assigned units. Pookie was assigned to the unit with Red and I was put in the unit with Chug and a couple of my other cousins and friends.

We talked and Chug gave me the run down on the High Rise. He told me the do's and don'ts, and pointed out who was who in our unit. Then we went to the chow hall where all of us got together and clicked up. Red hated that I was in prison, but he was happy to see me. We embraced each other tightly.

"We all heard how you blasted that bitch Gerald," Red said. There is a certain level of respect one gets when he shoots someone and goes to jail. But, the real respect came because, even though I hadn't seen Red, I continued to drop him money on his account. I hadn't forgotten him like most people had. Including his sorry ass girlfriend, Page. Everyone respected that because it was with my money that Red bought everyone's smokes. Red also told everyone how I was handling my business in the streets. "The shot caller, " Red said. With that being said, I became the shot caller for our little click.

We all got tattoos of pit bulls on our arms or chest. We all use to fight them but that's not why we got them. We got them because that's how our click was representing. Like a pack of pit bulls.

Three Months Later

The "Pit Bull Pack" spent most of the time on the weight pile, preparing for a war we hoped would happen. We didn't mess with outsiders. We all stuck together and did things as a unit.

In the three months at the High Rise, I witnessed some crazy shit. Shit I was use to seeing on t.v. I saw guys getting beat down. I saw guys beat the police down, and of course, I saw the police rough off a few guys. I saw one murder in the chow hall and I saw men having sex with men! That was sickening! It was a wild three months.

Celeste came to visit me weekly. Keeping her promise of never leaving me. She also brought friends of Red's and Chug's. Projects Chicks, that were from the South Side of the Gate City. They were bringing weed in balloons and Red was swallowing them, throwing them back up, and selling the weed. He was making a killing on the yard, so our crew lived large.

I still hadn't heard from Mac, Tone or anyone else I thought was my friend. Mr. Miller was right! I learned quickly that friends were few and far between when you're down and out. I couldn't believe it. All that I had done to help those guys and they failed to keep in touch. I gave Mac a roof over his head when he didn't have one. Tone too. He owed me money for a package I fronted him before I went to court. I expected him to at least take the money he owed me to my mom, so she could send it to me. Daily I thought about them all and I began to hate them with a passion.

Pookie and I were scheduled for a parole hearing in a couple of weeks. Every night when the doors were closed and locked, I prayed that God permitted us to be paroled.

"I hope you get out of jail, " Red said. "Now you see how this prison shit really is."

Red knew that if I were paroled, I would send him twice the amount of money as I'd sent before. Especially, since I seen first hand how hard things are in the Big House when nothing was coming in from the street.

Two Weeks Later

During mail call I received three letters. One from Celeste, one from Lakisha and the other one was from the Parole Commission. I tossed Lakisha's and Celeste's' mail to the side and ripped open the letter from the Parole Commission. It was short and simple. It read in it's entirety:

"Due to the seriousness of your crime, the parole board will not consider seeing you at this time. Depending on your future behavior, the board may or may not see you in four and a half more months."

I dropped the letter in the trash can and.....

"You better not say you started crying, " Hireen said. "You had only done four months and you couldn't do four and a half more?" He asked laughing.

"I can do four and a half months standing on my head in a bucket of cow shit," he said, laughing even louder. "'These seven years have flown by for me."

"Ahki, will you please let me finish telling the story?" I said.

"Ok,Ok, " Hireen said rapidly. "My fault. Go ahead and finish, " he said. He resituated himself and I picked up where I'd left off.

"I dropped the letter in the trash can and climbed onto my bunk. I wanted to cry! That big ass lump came in my throat, but I managed to swallow it. Reading how much Celeste loved me held the tears at bay. Also, I was happy that Lakisha contacted my mother and got my address. She even wrote that she still loved me! That made me feel better also."

Pookie received the same letter from the Parole Commission. He was feeling down too. After we talked to each other, we were both all right. We came to the conclusion that the time we got for the crime I committed was a blessing, considering the judge could have given us up to twenty years.

Compared to everyone else in our crew, we were sitting pretty. We decided not to feel sorry for ourselves. Instead, we sucked it up and continued to drive on.

Red had a beef with a guy who copped some weed from him on credit. The guy kept telling Red his money order was on the way, but he never received it. Red

180

threatened to kill the guy and he checked in. When he checked in, he checked in snitching. He told the whole story about Red and his weed operation. The following day Pookie, Chug, Red, myself and the rest of our crew were locked up in the hole.

"Dag! You stay in the hole don't cha?" Hireen asked.

I paid Hireen's question no attention, and kept talking.

We stayed in the hole for a few days and then we were all sent to different prisons in North Click. Pookie was transferred to Guess Road Prison in Durham. It was a low facility. Red went to Danbury, North Carolina. Both of them were closer to home now, so the snitching was a blessing in disguise for them. The rest of us were spread out over the state like butter on toast. I landed in Brunswick Correctional Institution, in Whiteville. Another maximum joint.

Just like the High Rise, when the bus pulled up, droves of convicts stood around trying to see who they knew on the bus. I was a long way from Madison and Greensboro. I figured since I wasn't in my region, I wouldn't know a soul. And that's exactly how it turned out! I didn't know a single person.

About eleven months had passed since Tim had got shot. He was still in the hospital, but he was doing a lot better. He was well enough to move from I.C.U., into a regular room. He'd had a total of twenty-two operations now, and he still had bullets lodged in his body. His biggest problem was his stomach. The best doctors in North Carolina operated on him, but no one could reconstruct his intestines. They were leaking some type of acid that was poisonous once it entered his blood stream. The micro holes in his intestines is what kept him hospitalized.

Gerald was still in the streets, safe, since Pookie and I were locked up. He'd shot Tim, almost killing him, and he was a free man. Enjoying life. Pookie and I were suffering for something he started, but I wasn't tripping. All dogs have their day was a philosophy of mine.

While I was struggling, carrying my bags to my assigned dorm, a guy ran by me in full stride. Blood poured like water from a faucet, from his horrified face. Another guy chased him with what looked like a sword! A crowd of people ran behind the two screaming, "Get him! Kill em!"

"Where in the hell have they sent me?" I said to myself. Suddenly, I missed Pookie, Red and the rest of the crew.

The first person who said anything to me was a guy named Yahya. As I unpacked my bags, and placed things in my locker, he walked over and spoke.

"What's up brother?" he said.

I turned and eyed him from head to toe. He was a tall and dark skinned brother. His huge head was bald, and he had a large beard.

"What you mean, "What's Up?"" I asked defensively.

"I'm just speaking brother," he said. "I'm Yahya." He extended his large hand and we exchanged a firm shake.

"I'm Styles," I said

"Skyles?" he asked.

"No! Styles. S~T-Y-L-E-S" I spelled out my last name.

"Oh Styles! Like I got style?" Yahya asked.

"Yeah, I said smiling.

"Where you from?" he asked.

"I'm from Madison, but I've been living in Greensboro for a while. Where you from?" I asked.

"I'm from New York, but I caught my case in Raleigh." Yahya responded.

Being the good judge of character I am, I came to the conclusion that Yahya didn't have any motives, so we kicked it for a while. Somehow our conversation got on religion and I found out Yahya was a Muslim.

"I'm a Christian," I said, showing him my black leather Bible. We continued to talk and he invited me to the Islamic services on Friday. I agreed to come, but I wasn't really trying to learn about Islam. I was content with what I was taught and what I believed. That Jesus is the "son" of God and the only way to Heaven.

CHAPTER 35

Two Months Later

Jegbadia got my address from my mom and started to write me. Lakisha was writing on the regular and Celeste was without a doubt still my main squeeze. From Madison to Whiteville was a four hour drive and she drove it religiously every week to see me.

I still couldn't believe how many of my so called friends had jumped ship and turned their backs on me. Once I called Celeste and her brother Orlando gave me the "411" on what was happening around the way. I couldn't believe it when he told me that Tone, Geno, and Quayle all had new GS300 Lexus! They were living high on the hog and hadn't sent me a dime. Since I was their supplier, I thought they would fall off for a while when I got locked up, but the exact opposite happened, they got on.

Zag, my supplier, started missing the loot I use to make for him. Even though he really didn't like Tone, he started to deal with him. He hit them off with twice as much work as I use to give them and they were flipping it like Dominique Dawes. They blew up like a pound of "C-4" when Zag started hitting them off. And after six and a half months of dealing with them, Zag even started to think Tone was "Jive kinda cool," after all.

I attended a few of the Islamic services and became very interested in Islam. I reflected back on the eights months I was in the Middle East, and a lot of things that hadn't made sense to me, made sense to me now. For instance, five times a day I use to hear Arabic blasting through the desert over loud speakers. I use to wonder, "What da hell is that guy saying?" I didn't have a clue as to what he was saying, but the Arabic caused a sense of peace to envelope me. Now that I was attending the Islamic services I learned that the call the guy was making over the fulminating speakers was the Ahdan. The call that invites the Muslims to the five obligatory prayers.

"If Allah wants to bless you, He'll give you the understanding of Islam," Yahya said to me.

I guess Allah was blessing me because the more I attended the services, the more I understood Islam.

I only had two months before the Parole Commission was scheduled to see me, so I planned what I was going to do when I got home. You play like you practice and I had to have a game plan when I hit the streets. My game plan was very simple. To get paid by any means necessary!

Celeste told me she had seen Mac at the mall shopping. He kept the apartment and purchased him some type of small car to get around in.

"He smelled just like weed when I spoke to him, " Celeste said. "Then he told me that was because he sold weed now. "

Even Mac was coming up. He didn't send me a brown penny and he was staying in my apartment and wearing my clothes. If he had enough dough to buy a car, he had enough to send me at least ten or twenty dollars!

My mom brought Sheneka to see me and I couldn't believe how she'd grown in seven months. She missed her daddy, she said and I missed her too. I couldn't wait to get home to spoil her rotten.

Tim was able to write me letters that I looked forward to receiving. In every letter he stressed how he hated being stuck up inside the hospital. For over a year, the hospital had held him hostage. He also mentioned the pain he was in, in each letter. I wished a million times that I could trade places with him, or at least bear his pain. He had suffered enough.

A Month Later

I took my Shahada two weeks prior to my scheduled parole hearing. The Shahada is when one bears witness that there is no god but Allah and that He has no partners or co-equals. Also, you bear witness that Muhammad is the Final Messenger of Allah. This saying is witnessed by other Muslims. By professing this openly, it brings you into the fold of Islam. Allah had blessed me to understand Islam.

I felt like the world had been lifted off of my back after I took my Shahada. My mom and the rest of my family thought I had lost my mind when I told them that I was Muslim.

"So you don't eat pork anymore, huh?" My mom asked sarcastically. "Boy you were born and raised on pork, and now you don't eat it?" she asked.

I tried to explain to her that Islam was much deeper than just not eating pork. But, I was a baby in the deen (Religion) so I couldn't break it down for her.

Back On The Streets

Since January 1993, (almost two years) the Federal government had kept tabs on myself, Tone, Geno and Quayle. Before I got locked up, I was the main one they watched, but since I was locked up, the agents concentrated on watching Tone closely. He was considered, "Most active" between the three.

A week prior to me seeing the board, Tone was stopped by federal agents. He had just met with Zag and he fronted Tone a couple of kilos of coke. Tone also was in possession of a Glock 40, handgun and a digital scale. Tone was scared to death!

The agents took Tone down to their headquarters and interrogated him. They gave him an ultimatum. Either go to prison for the rest of his life or set up his cocaine connection. Tone hadn't ever been to prison and he wasn't trying to go! His ultimatum was a no brainer. He began to sing like Luther.

After a couple of hours went by, Tone gave Zag a call on a bugged phone.

"What's up Zag? I bet you're surprised to hear from me so fast, but I need two more bricks."

"Damn kid, you sold both of them that fast?" Zag asked. "You're balling out of control."

"Yeah, my partners bought both of those. I got some kids waiting on me as we speak, so I need to get with you ASAP. . Meet me at the Pizza Hut on Cone Boulevard in thirty minutes," Tone said.

Zag went back home and relaxed after he met Tone the first time, so he had to put his clothes back on. He wanted to continue to watch the game, but the money was more important. He was glad Tone wanted to meet him at the Pizza Hut, it was only ten minutes from his crib. Tone informed the agents where Zag lived, what route he would probably take to the Pizza Hut, and what type of car he'd be driving.

The agents responded fast and it took them about fifteen minutes to set up to bust Zag. They assumed their positions and anxiously waited for him.

Zag slipped his shoes on. He thought about all the money Tone had made for him since I'd gotten locked up. His opinion of Tone had been wrong. Dead wrong! Tone was a good guy. A real moneymaker. A little flashy, but he was a good guy, Zag thought.

The federal agents sat waiting for a midnight blue, Acura Legend, with chrome and gold wheels. Tone even told them that the personalized plate on the front of the car said " Jerzy".

Just as Tone predicted, Zag cruised down Summit Avenue. He rode in the new "Ack" listening to Monica's " Just One of Those Days," bobbing his head.

He stopped at the light at the intersection of Summit and Cone and put his left turn signal on. Despite Monica's sensuous voice, he could still hear the clicking sound the turn signal made. He reached down and turned the volume up on the Alpine 500, to drown the clicking sound. When he looked back up he was stunned. An undercover cop car zoomed through the intersection and four cops bailed out of the car, stopping traffic. Four more undercover cars, cars that had been riding beside and behind Zag, boxed him in before he had a chance to react. Agents jumped out weapons pointed at Zag's frightened face and told him to place his hands on the roof of the car. He sat puzzled. He had been set up!

Back In Prison, Three Days Before My Parole Hearing

The closer I got to going home, the more enraged I became at the people who had flipped on me. I vowed not to deal with anyone who fronted on me while I was incarcerated. But, I also vowed to do the right thing by those who kept it real with me. That was only a few people. My fam, Zag, Celeste and maybe Lakisha. I couldn't count on Jegbadia, although she began to write me.

Before I left Brunswick, a guy saw her picture in my wall locker. "How you know her?" he asked.

He looked like he admired the picture, but he looked confused, too.

"That's my girl, " I said proudly, rubbing the picture.

He sighed and started to laugh, "Your girlfriend? That's my brother's girlfriend, too! They have been going together since high school," he said.

184

I was floored when those ego wrecking words rolled off his tongue. Jegbadia was trying to be a player. But a player can't run game on a coach. That wasn't going to happen.

I was pissed at everyone, but I was ready to go home. I was ready to see my "Better Half" and the rest of my family. I couldn't wait to see my daughter. Couldn't wait to start going back to A&T, so the girls could see my body! I worked eight and a half months on the weight pile just for that. And I was definitely ready to implement my game plan. To get money!

"Talib, make sure as soon as you get home you go straight to a Masjid and pray," Yahya said to me. (Talib, which means student, was the name given to me by Yahya) "If you do that you'll be starting out on the right path. If not, it's going to be very easy for you to get caught up in the worldly things. The Shatan (devil) makes forbidden things alluring and if you succumb to temptation, you'll end up back in here," he said.

I knew he was telling the truth, but I had already succumbed to the temptation of the streets. I had a plan. It wasn't going to take me long to get on my feet, then I planned to go to a Masjid and become a part of a community. That was my plan, but I didn't tell Yahya that.

"All right, Ahki. That will be the first thing I'll do," I said.

One Day Before My Scheduled Parole Hearing

"Dana Styles, report to the lieutenant's office ASAP, " I heard over the intercom. I was on the weight pile, trying to get a little bigger before I went home. When I heard this, I automatically knew something was wrong. You only go to the lieutenant's office for a few reasons, and they're all bad. Too many people knew that I would probably be paroled after seeing the parole board. I figured someone hating on me, had tried to sabotage that. I hadn't had an infraction in over eight months and the only way the parole board wouldn't see me was if I had a serious write-up.

I put my shirt on, and without saying a word to anyone, I walked slowly towards the lieutenant's office. All types of negative scenarios ran through my mind.

I bet someone put a shank under my locker. I bet somebody put drugs under my mattress. I bet someone…. My mind was running like a wild Mustang over dry Arizona plains. Even though it was cold, I broke out in a profusious sweat, thinking of all the possibilities of why I was being called.

"Are you Dana Styles?" The Lieutenant asked.

"Yes sir, I am, " I said.

"Let me see your I.D. card," He said, extending his hand.

I dug into my pockets and handed him the plastic card with my mug shot on it. He began to study the picture.

"I just received a call from the Parole Board," the lieutenant said. He stopped and looked up at me. His facial expression screamed something was wrong. He shook his head from side to side. My heart fell to the floor. I wasn't going to be paroled.

"They instructed me to release you today. You have to be outta here before 4:00pm. You need to sign these papers."

I was so happy I wanted to cry. "For real?" I asked, smiling like a Chess cat.

"Yep! You need to pack your things and get ready to go. I'll be driving you to the bus station in Lumberton as soon as you're ready," he said.

I ran from the lieutenant's office to my housing unit. I had already promised all of my stuff to Yahya, so I didn't have to pack much. Just my address book and my pictures. I was ready to bounce. My time to go home finally came. Those eight and a half months seemed like eight and a half years, but it was all over now. I was on my way to the crib.

"As Salaamu Alaikum! Yahya! Yahya, wake up, " I said.

Yahya rolled his big body over and looked up at me. "Wa Alaikum As Salaam! What's happening?" he asked.

"I'm going home today. The Parole Commission isn't going to see me, they're just releasing me. Al Hamdulilah! " (All praises due to Allah) I said.

Yahya was wide awake now. "Allahu Akbar," (Allah's the Greatest) he said.

I sat down a bag of personal hygiene items and a bag of snacks. Also, I had two new pair of Chris Webber Nikes that Lakisha had sent me, which I left with Yahya. He was going to need them. He had been incarcerated for eight years and he had twelve more to go. Immediately, he locked everything in his locker, except for a pair of the Nikes. He put them on and walked with me back over to the lieutenant's office.

It took me twenty minutes to walk to the lieutenant's office. I stopped a million times, smacking hands and saying my good-byes. I hugged Yahya and a few more Muslims who jumped on the freedom train to the lieutenant's office, then one of the officers let me inside.

I was given an old pair of Wrangler jeans, a t-shirt that was too small and a fake Members Only jacket to put on. Since I gave my shoes away, I had to wear some state issued "Bobo' s". But I didn't care. I was so happy I would have gone home naked.

"Don't forget what I told you, Talib. Fear Allah! Go to the Masjid first and pray, you'll be on the right track," Yahya yelled.

I walked out the razor wire fence and I didn't look back. I didn't ever want to see that prison or any prison again in my life.

When I arrived at the bus station in Lumberton, I called Celeste and told her to pick me up at the bus station in Fayetteville. She screamed with happiness and promised to be at the bus station as soon as she could get there.

"Don't tell anyone I'm coming home," I said to her. I knew she wouldn't tell a soul because she'd want me all to herself.

"And bring me some clothes and shoes to put on, " I said before I hung up.

The lieutenant made sure I got on the Greyhound. I walked to the back of the bus. It felt like everyone was staring at me trying to figure out why I was escorted on the bus by the police. Or, they could have been staring at the tight ass clothes I had on! But like I said, I didn't care. If they had been through what I'd been through, they wouldn't care either.

I stared out the tinted windows, admiring the scenery. The world had changed in eight months. Well, it seemed that way to me. I prayed that Pookie was on a bus somewhere on his way home also. I couldn't wait to see him either.

CHAPTER 36

Celeste hadn't arrived at the bus station by the time I arrived. From Lumberton to Fayetteville it was about forty minutes. And from Madison to Fayetteville it was about an hour and forty minutes, so I had at least an hour or more before she arrived.

It had been a long time since I had an hour of freedom. I didn't know what to do. I walked out of the bus station delighted at all the Christmas decorations that dressed downtown Fayetteville. Then I strolled across the street to a bench that was spruced up with green, red and silver glittering tinsel. I took a seat and watched the different faces and cars go by. The draft from the cars made me so cold that my teeth began to chatter. After about ten minutes, I got up and walked toward the center of downtown. The fake Members Only wasn't doing anything against the hawk, because I was about to freeze, but it felt great to be free. It was hard to believe that just a few hours ago I was locked up in a maximum security prison, and now I was walking downtown, in my old stomping ground, a free man. That thought made me think of how I use to have it all in Fayetteville. But, now I didn't have nothing but chump change. But, I did have my freedom.

I had $138 in my account when I was discharged from prison. A $138 is all the money I had to my name! My daughter had just had her birthday on December 11th, and Christmas was right around the corner. In spite of the fact that I was Muslim, my daughter wasn't old enough to understand that I didn't celebrate Christmas anymore. She would expect me to have plenty of gifts when she saw me, and I didn't plan to disappoint her.

I had seen enough of downtown and I turned around and started back towards the bus station. I walked past a small antique store and looked at my reflection in the picture frame window. I looked homeless in those tight Wranglers and dirty state shoes.

"I'd rather have this on and look homeless, instead of being locked up," I said out loud to myself. I looked at my reflection once more and continued to walk.

I saw Celeste as soon as she pulled into the parking lot. I walked and stood behind a big pole, beside the bus station's entrance. Celeste opened the door and walked right past me. I eased up behind her and kissed her on the nape of her neck, smelling the weightless perfume. Quickly, she turned around and jumped into my arms, wrapping her thick legs around my waist. We kissed a few minutes like we were on a Close-Up commercial!

"Those are the rags they gave you to come home in? You look like a hobo, but a cute one," she said laughing. "I have some of your clothes in the car."

I grabbed Celeste's hand and we floated to her car. I changed out of the "Hand-me-downs" and donned on my own clothes and shoes. I almost felt like my old self again, except for one thing. My pockets were flat as pancakes and that had to change soon.

I was kissing and feeling all on Celeste as she tried to steer the car. She almost wrecked twice. The first time she ran off the road and the second time she almost ran into the back of a car, so I left her alone! Then we began to talk and she gave me the happs on a few people.

"I heard Zag got busted by the Feds, " she said.

"What! When?" I screamed. I turned her radio down so I could hear all of the details.

"Just a couple of weeks ago. Orlando said that it was on the news. He got caught with a bunch of drugs. That' s all I heard him say. "

I was hurt! My dawg had got knocked by the Feds. I had planned to get Christmas money from him too. Now, what was I going to do?

Celeste hadn't seen Mac anymore, but her girlfriend Tracy, who use to date Mac, told her that he lost the apartment and his car. He was living with a few other guys who were all trying to do something in the rap industry. That news spoiled some more of my plans. I was going to go and kick Mac out of the apartment anyway. Now, I didn't even have a place to stay.

She also visited Tim on the regular. "You're going to be surprised at how well he is doing, " she said.

That was great news. And, after what she'd told me, I needed to hear something good.

From Fayetteville, we made a "B-line" to Baptist Hospital. No……hold up. I take that back, I said to Hireen. We stopped at Sonic in Sanford and I ordered two chicken sandwiches and two chocolate shakes. We ate, kissed and felt on each other some more then we bounced.

"How did that chicken taste?" Hireen asked.

"That chicken sandwich was great. What I wouldn't give to have a boneless chicken breast from Sonic right now, " I said, rubbing my stomach.

"Go ahead and finish the story, " Hireen said. "You're making me hungry."

We left Sonic and went straight to Baptist Hospital. I couldn't wait to see Tim to tell him how much I'd missed him and loved him. Allah had answered my prayers and allowed him to continue to live while I was in prison. I was very grateful for that. I didn't want to end up like Mr. Miller.

I got Tim's room number from the same old lady with the huge glasses and hopped on the elevator. When the elevator stopped on the seventh floor, the shining silver doors parted and I rushed towards room 702. Before I got to Tim's room I could hear my mother laughing. The laughter bounced off the walls and echoed down the hall. The last time I saw her in the hospital, she was crying, so the laughter was music to my ears. I started walking so fast I was leaving Celeste.

"Wait for me, Speedy," she said.

I slowed and finally stopped a few doors from 702. "I got an idea, " I said to Celeste. "You walk in the room and act like you're just visiting Tim. Then ask my mom has she heard from me?"

"Boy, you're going make Brenda have a heart attack," She said smiling, as she proceeded to walk towards the room.

"Hey Brenda! Hey Tim! How are you two today?" Celeste asked.

"Hey Girl! " My mom said.

Tim waved his hand and smiled at Celeste.

"I thought I'd come out and visit my brother-in-law today. Check up on him. I called your house earlier and no one answered. I figured you'd be out here, " Celeste said.

"Yeah, you know this is where I am most of the time. Trying to take care of my baby," my mom said.

I stood outside the door, joyfully listening. I smiled when I heard my mom call Tim her baby. She had five grown sons, and we were still her babies.

"Have you heard from, Dana?" Celeste asked.

"No, I haven't. Not in a few days. I know he is supposed to see the parole board soon." She looked up on a calendar that was beside Tim's bed. "Tomorrow as a matter of fact. I'm praying that him and my Baby get to come home."

When my mom said that I walked into the room. "Oh my God!" she screamed. Her pretty face that never seemed to age, turned red. Her green eyes, that had cried so much in the past due to pain, shed tears of joy. Her Scooter was home.

"I love you, Ma," I said, as I hugged and kissed her. Then I walked over and stood over Tim. I put my arms around his head and gently pulled it to my chest. His eyes filled with tears and it was a contagious thing! My eyes filled with tears and Celeste started to cry, too.

Tim looked a lot better. He gained some of his weight back and despite the tracheotomy, he could speak. His legs, arms and back were still filled with bullets, but by the Grace of Allah, he managed to hang on. His stomach operations resulted in him having a colostomy. That was his biggest problem, but it was a miracle he was alive.

After the ten minutes of emotional "Hellos" I asked mama had she heard anything about Pookie getting paroled. "He was suppose to see the parole people the same day you were," she said.

"Call down to Guess Road and see if they let him go," I said.

She picked up the phone, pressed number nine and got an outside line. She dialed information and information took her calling card number and connected her to Guess Road Prison.

"Guess Road Correctional Institution. This is Officer Johnson," the man said.

"Yes, this is Brenda Vernon, I'm Corey Styles' mother. His prison number is 0249286, and he was supposed to see the parole board today or tomorrow. I want to know if he is going to be paroled or not?" she asked.

"Let me transfer you Mrs. Vernon. You need to speak with someone in the Records Department," the officer said.

"Records Department. This is Officer Razodi. "

"My name is Brenda Vernon. I'm Corey Styles' mother. His prison number is 0249286. "

"Hold on ma'am, " Razodi said.

My mom could hear the keys on the keyboard of the computer being pressed. After a few seconds, Razodi began to speak again. "Ok Mrs. Vernon. What can I do for you?" he asked

"I'm trying to figure out if my son got paroled or not today. Or when does he see the Parole Commission?"

"Hold on," he said again.

I stood in the room talking to Tim and half listening to my mom's conversation. Silently, I prayed that Pookie was on his way home.

"Mrs. Vernon," Razodi called out.

"Yes, I'm still here!"

"According to the records, Mr. Styles was suppose to see the board tomorrow, but from what I'm reading off the screen, they've already denied him. The reason is because he had already had a couple of assault charges in his past criminal history. He is scheduled to see the board in six and a half more months."

Mama just shook her head. A few minutes ago she'd cried tears of joy, now she cried tears of pain. Again.

"Thank you sir, " she said and hung up the phone. "The officer said he was denied because of his past criminal history. He is scheduled to see them in June, " she said calculating the months on her fingers.

"Don't worry about it Mama. He'll be alright. I'm going to see him this weekend, " I said.

I asked mama to give me some time alone with Tim. She looked up and made eye to eye contact with me. She knew that Tim and I were going to discuss Gerald. Her eyes begged me not to get into anymore trouble.

"Don't' worry about it, ma. I'm not going to do anything else," I said. She got up and Celeste followed her out of the room.

"How are you really doing, Big Bro?" I asked.

Although Tim looked a lot better his eyes still looked weak. In a low raspy voice he said, "I'm in constant pain. I've been in pain for so long that I'm almost use to it."

We talked and I gave him a brief summary of my prison stint. He just smiled at some of my wild stories. I showed him my eight dollar tattoo and gave him another hug and kiss.

"Before Mama comes back in here, I want to ask you something. Are you glad I shot Gerald?"

He frowned his face in disbelief. In a low, raspy voice he answered. "I can't believe you ask me that."

Then he said something that I had thought about all along.

"What do you think I would have done to that bastard if he would have shot you like this?" He asked.

That question didn't have to be answered. Anything that's understood doesn't have to be explained! I bent over and kissed Tim. "I love you Bro," I said.

Since Zag had gotten busted, I didn't know what I was going to do about some money for Christmas. I had eight days to work a miracle. I contemplated going to my father's house, where my car was, and taking it to the auction.

"When the funds are low, the jewels must go, " my father use to say, and my funds were extra low. He also used to say, "He that has no choice can not choose. " My back was against the wall. I did have one other choice though. I could go and ask Tone and the rest of those sorry niggas for some cash, I didn't want to do that though. But, I would rather swallow my pride than to sell my Mustang. Especially after I had to pay the large storage fee to get it back.

"You go ahead and go home. I'm going to be down here for a while. I'll see you the first thing tomorrow," I said to Celeste.

She wasn't tripping! She knew how close Tim and I were. Beside, I vowed to keep it real with her. I walked her to her car and gave her another Close-Up, commercial kiss, and she went home.

When I walked back inside I stopped at the pay phones. I pulled out my small address book and dialed Lakisha's number.

"This is an AT&T operator, with a collect call from "Yum Yum" will you accept he call?" the operator asked, laughing at my alias.

I heard Lakisha's soft voice on the other end answering with excitement.

"Yes I certainly will," she said.

"Hey Baby, " I said in my sexiest voice.

"Hey Yum-Yum!"

"I guess you can tell by the way you didn't hear the prison recording that I'm no longer behind bars."

"Dana Styles, you better stop playing with me. Where are you?"

"I'm at the hospital in Winston. I got paroled today. I caught a bus from Lumberton to Winston and my mom picked me up. I'm visiting Tim. "You want to come and see me?"

"Don't ask stupid questions," she said. "I'll be down there in about thirty minutes. What room are you going to be in?"

"I'll be in room 702."

Lakisha was so excited that I was out of prison, that she just hung up the phone without saying bye or anything. She was on her way to get her man!

I held Tim' s hand until he drifted off to sleep. Then mama and I talked about my days in prison and my future plans. She made me promise to stay away from Pine Hall. Even though I was ordered by the courts to stay away!

"I don't want my baby to get into anymore trouble," she pleaded.

I promised her that I'd stay out of trouble, but I didn't know what I'd do or how I'd react if I saw Gerald Gibbs!

I hadn't seen Lakisha the entire time I was locked up. But, that wasn't because she didn't want to see me. I told her since I had a violent charge, and such a short sentence, I wasn't permitted to have visitors. I had to tell her that because I didn't want her and Celeste to bump heads.

When she walked into the room, she spoke to my mom quietly, because she saw that Tim was asleep. Then she hugged and kissed me like my mom wasn't even there.

I looked over her shoulders and my mom rolled her eyes and shook her head. Celeste was her girl. If I had changed, like I told her I had, she couldn't tell.

"I need you to take me to see a few of my partners," I said to Lakisha, as we climbed into her car.

"You drive then. You know where you need to go," she said. I hadn't been behind a steering wheel in eight and a half months. It felt funny when I began to drive down the highway. But driving is just like riding a bike. Once you learn, you never forget.

On my way to Stoneville, I passed a large Masjid in Winston Salem, and I remembered what Yahya had said. I knew I wasn't hurting anyone but myself by not stopping at the Masjid and praying. Temptation had already taken over me!

When I pulled up on the Back Street, it was crammed packed. Just like it was the last time I was down there. Crack heads sat in the cars that lined the street, waiting to be served that butter.

"What in da hell is this place?" Lakisha asked.

I acted like I didn't hear her and patiently waited for the crack heads to move along. I could see the three GS 300' s parked in a row at the other end of the street. A pearl white, black and blue one. Each decked out in chrome and dark tint. These were the cars Orlando told me about. I even noticed a new Jeep Cherokee, parked across from the three Lexus'. The Jeep had a sign that read, "M.O.B." on the front of it. (Money Over Bitches).

I pulled over and told Lakisha I'd be right back. I could see these guys had blown up since I'd been gone. I hated I had to come and ask these guys for anything. All my life I had the ups on these guys. From little league football, to high school fights, and up to the time I went to prison. But, now the coin had flipped. I was on the very bottom looking up to them.

As I walked towards the three of them, I was really dealing with some serious emotions. I wanted to walk up and bitch smack the shit out of each one of them, but that wouldn't get me any Christmas money, so I suppressed those feelings and managed to smile.

When Tone realized who I was, he looked like he wanted to start running. He turned and said something to Geno and Quayle and then the three of them turned, to greet me.

"Wild Styles! What's up Playboy? Welcome home." Tone said.

"When did you get out?" asked Geno.

"Today," I said quickly.

"What's up Styles? I'll be right back." Quayle said. He ran towards a car that had just turned onto the Back Street.

"What's happening?" I asked. "I see y'all niggas are still doing ya thing back here." I looked over at the three new cars and the new Jeep. Tone and Geno's eyes followed mine. Then they looked at each other.

"Yeah, we're trying to do our thing," Tone said.

"Just a lil' sum-something," Geno added.

I tried to be cool, but I blurted out, "Y'all niggas forgot about Styles, huh?"

"Nah man! We didn't forget about you," Tone said and glanced at Geno. "We've just been busy. I was just asking one of your cousins about you the other day. "

I knew I couldn't stand and talk to them much longer without really blowing my top, so I got straight to the point. "Check this out, " I said to Geno and Tone. Right as I was about to get to the point, Quayle ran back to where we were standing. He handed Geno a roll of money and I watched Geno stuff it in his pockets.

"Yo Styles! You alright?" Quayle asked.

I bit my tongue to keep from cursing him out. "Hell nah, I'm not doing alright," I said.

"What's up?" Geno asked.

"Today is the 17th of December, and Christmas is approaching fast. My daughter just had her birthday and I couldn't get anything, but I'm not going to let Christmas be like that," I said.

They stood, staring at me , knowing what was coming next.

"I need something so I can get back on my feet. I'll be straight shortly. You all know that. Whatever y'all do for me, I'll make sure you get it back and then some. That's my word!" I said.

Before Tone and Quayle had a chance to open their mouths, Geno quickly began to speak.

"We have some things going on right now. Actually, all of our money is tied up in something big. It's going to be a few more days before we really get some cash or some more coke."

As Geno spoke he dug deep down into his pockets. He pulled out what appeared to be a ton of cash. Although he was giving me a "Sob Story" he was still about to break me off with some cash, so I didn't care what excuse he made. He stopped talking and started counting. "One, two, three, four hundred, five, six. " Then he stopped counting. He crammed the wad of money back in his pocket and pulled out the money Quayle handed him. He licked his right thumb to grip the dough and counted two twenties and one ten. Fifty bucks!

"Here you go Styles. Just take this for right now. Come back in a few days and I'll see what I can do for you then," Geno said.

If I would have had a gun with me, I would have busted a cap in that punk's ass right then and there. I should have bitch smacked him like I started to, but I was broke. I had to take it. Lakisha had already mentioned that she needed gas money. I was furious. I put the money in my pocket and without saying anything else to them. I turned and walked back to the car.

Lakisha took one look at me and said, "What's wrong with you Baby?"

"Nothing, " I said. "You drive. "

I was too upset to drive. I slammed the door and laid the seat all the way back. I didn't want them chumps to see my face when we rode past them. I directed Lakisha which way to go and she cruised past the three of them. I looked up when I was sure we'd passed them and looked back. They were all laughing and pointing at Lakisha' s car.

"Them niggas tried me." I said.

"How did they try you?" She asked.

"They just did. Believe me, they did, " I said.

For years I had humiliated those three. Now, they had humiliated me in the worse way. I pulled out the fifty dollars. Disgustedly, I counted it as if it was going to me more. I handed it all to Lakisha. "This is for your gas, and for you to get something to eat," I said.

We rode to my daughter's grandparent's house. I figured Kami was at work and Mary, Sheneka's granny, kept her then. She was there, and very happy to see me. I gave her $30 for her birthday and she ran and put it up with the other money she had received for her b-day. When she returned she began telling me everything she wanted for Christmas. Without knowing how I was going to get anything, I promised her that I'd get whatever she wanted.

After sitting and talking for two hours I kissed Sheneka and promised to see her in the next day or so. Lakisha and I got in her car and bounced back to the Gate City.

For more than eight months I had been taking showers and now I was in Lakisha's bathtub, with strawberry smelling bubbles up to my neck. I tried to relax, but I continued to rewind the entire day in my mind. It's funny how one can experience so many different feelings in one day. I'd been the happiest I'd ever been in my life when I got out of jail and went to see my Better Half. I was sad because Pookie didn't get paroled, and mad as hell at Geno and the rest of those punks. All in one day.

Emotionally, I was drained. Physically, I was strong as an ox and horny as a dog in heat. About two hours of constant love making, almost made up for the eight and a half months I was away. Afterwards, Lakisha insisted that I move in with her. I guess she thought that would keep me from sleeping around. She didn't want anyone else to get what she had just received!

I didn't have much of a choice really. Mac had lost the "Best Lil' Ho- House" in Greensboro, and I wasn't going to move back home with my mom. I wanted to move in with Celeste, but she still lived with her mom. Jegbadia had her own place, but she wasn't sure who her boyfriend was! I agreed and decided to move in with Lakisha.

It felt great to sleep in a bed that was big enough for me. In state prison the bunks are so small if you turn over once, you're on the floor. And it was definitely great to be sleeping with a beautiful woman, instead of sleeping alone. I didn't ever want to sleep again, unless I had a beautiful woman under me!

CHAPTER 37

Fake niggas are just like pigeons. You feed them and feed them and when they fly away with full stomachs, they shit all on you!

While I waved my pistol in their faces, that's what I thought about. These niggas had crapped on me after all I had done for them in the past.

"Styles please, dawg...Please don't shoot," Geno begged. His hands were trembling like a wet grimlin.

"We were going to get back with you, and hit you off with some cash before Christmas. I swear to God we were," Tone cried.

"Come on Styles. Just take the loot we have in the back of my car and forget about this whole situation, " Quayle said.

"Now you bitches got something to say, huh? Yesterday, when I asked for some money to get my little girl something for Christmas, y'all didn't have shit to say!" I screamed. I was over acting, but I knew this type of stunt called for extra drama. I made the three of them lay on the ground spread-eagle, while I checked Quayle's trunk. "If one of you moves a muscle, I'm going to shoot all three of you, " I said. "I swear to God I am."

There was at least twenty maybe thirty thousand dollars in the leather bag sitting in Quayle ' s trunk. I zipped the bag and threw it over my shoulders. I ordered Quayle to get up and made him get in the trunk of his car. Then I took Geno and Tone's keys and made them get in the trunk of their own cars.

"Styles, we'll suffocate in her," Tone said.

"I'll send someone to get you all out before that happens," I said, slamming the trunk, hitting Tone's head. "If I don't forget like y'all bitches forgot me," I yelled.

When I woke up it was 10:27 a.m. Lakisha was already woke. She sat in bed naked, watching "Parents who sleep with their children's friends" on Jerry Springer, and eating a bowl of Kellogg's Cornflakes.

"Good morning sleepy head. How did you sleep?" Lakisha asked.

I thought for a second before I answered her question. While in prison I had a million dreams of waking up in the bed with some fine woman and she would ask me the same question in my dreams. I thought I was dreaming again.

Then I remembered the dream I'd just had. I robbed the Stoneville Boys and put them in the trunks of their cars. I smiled as I remembered the dream. I looked at Lakisha and felt her face. She was soft as silk, and she was real!

"How did you sleep?" She asked again.

"I slept like a baby, Baby, " I said.

"Are you hungry?" She asked.

"Yeah, for some more of you, but I'd settle for a bowl of those corn flakes. "

She got out of the bed. The sun burning through the blinds, caused lines to form on her naked body, when she walked past the window. I had forgotten how beautiful she really was. I watched her twist out of the room.

"Damn she looked good! " I said to Hireen.

"Yeah..Yeah, I know. Good enough to eat, right?" He asked.

I closed my eyes trying to recapture that scene. "Go on and finish," Hireen said. "

I took another bath, got dressed and Lakisha drove me to my father's house. He was so happy I was home, but he couldn't understand why Pookie didn't get paroled. We talked about prison, Tim's condition, my parole and probation and what my future plans were. I think my father wanted to hear me say that I was going to finish the job I started with Gerald. Instead, I just left that alone.

He kept insurance on my Mustang and he hadn't driven it but four times in eight months. I told him that I was probably going to sell it to get back on my feet. He understood exactly what I was saying. Getting on my feet meant selling my car, getting the money, buying some coke and flipping the money. It was a cycle. He knew how it went because I told my Ole Man everything.

Lakisha followed me back to Greensboro, but we went our separate ways. She went home and I went to my friend's barbershop.

I grew braids while I was in prison. I was tired of getting my hair done because I was really tender headed. I decided to cut it off, into a nice little fro. I rode to the barbershop thinking about the dream I'd had about the Stoneville Boys. For trying me like I was a crack head, that whole crew had to be checked. I decided that I would ride down to Stoneville, stick up the whole crew and have a Merry Christmas. My back was against the wall and I didn't have a choice.

Leroi had been cutting my hair at Gate City Barber Shop since I got out of the Army. He and I had become very good friends over the past few years. He wrote me a few times when I was in prison, but I didn't expect much from him. He was married with three kids, so I knew his hands stayed full. For this reason, I didn't hate him like I did the others that flipped on me while I was away.

He was glad to see me also. He knew my paper was short so he cut my hair for free. We started talking and I thanked him for the times he did write and for the few dollars he sent. When I told him I never heard from Mac, he couldn't believe it. Mac lied and told him he kept in touch with me all the time. He also told Leroi that he sent me money on the regular.

We talked about Tim too. Leroi visited Tim once every few weeks and cut his hair for free. That meant a lot to me and I expressed my appreciation to him.

When I was getting ready to leave the barber hop, my mouth watered as a black, 600 Benz Coupe, pulled in front of the shop. "Damn that's tight as hell, " I said.

"You know who that is don't you?" Leroi asked.

"Nah, who is it?"

"That's Neon Hall. The one who has the fastest cars at the track."

"Oh yeah, I know who you're talking about, " I said.

Neon's name rang like the Liberty Bell in Greensboro. He had a reputation as being Greensboro's "Number One Ghetto Superstar".   I watched him race a million times at the track, but I had never met him.

He opened the door of the Benz and without his race suit on, and a hat pulled down over his face, he looked a lot different. Younger! He looked like he was my age.

He walked in the shop and spoke to everyone. "What's up? How is everybody doing?" he asked.

A few guys responded with "alright." The others simply answered "fine".

"What's up, Leroi? How many heads you got?" Neon asked.

He cuffed a $50 in his palm and shook hands with Leroi's. Leroi peeped the $50, and smiled.

"Since you had and appointment you're next," he said to Neon.

Neon looked at the time on his platinum watch to make sure he was on time for the appointment he never had. "Whose Mustang is that? Neon asked.

"It's mine," I said.

Leroi took the opportunity to introduce me and Neon. We slapped hands and he continued to say he loved the wheels on my car. "Where did you get them from?" He asked.

"A guy in Stokesdale did it. He can chrome those wheels too," I said pointing at the Benz.

"Can you take me down there? I'll pay you for your time," He said.

"You don't have to pay me shit, playa. What type of time do you think I'm on? I'll take you down there after you finish getting your hair cut," I said.

The leather in the "Six Hundred" hugged me like Lakisha had the night before. But, the leather was even softer than her face! The dashboard looked like the cot pit of a C-130, it had so many lights and buttons on it. I took a deep breath and it smelled like a fruit factory inside the car. There was so much wood grain in the car I was sure that an entire forest was cut down just for the interior of his car. I was amazed! I looked around wishing I was the pilot instead of the co-pilot.

I gave Neon directions and we got on 40 West. "Do you think I should get these wheels chromed out, or do you think I should put some other type of wheels on here?" he asked.

"That white boy got so many types of wheels down there you might want to put something different on here," I said. "He'll even have the exact wheels you have on here now, already chromed."

We turned right on 68 North, still discussing rims, and cars in general. Then Neon asked me a question, I wish he wouldn't have asked. But, then again, it's this question that got him and I connected.

"Are you ready for Christmas?" He asked.

I instantly thought about Geno, Tone and Quayle. How they had played me. I even thought about the dream I had. Just that quick I experienced a 180° mood change.

"Hell nah, I ain't ready. I just got out of prison yesterday," I said.

"For real?" Asked Neon. "You don't mind me asking for what do you?"

"'No, I don't mind. I shot a nigga who shot my brother," I said.

Neon didn't say anything. He just got this look on his face like he was impressed. Then he said, "Hmmmm", like he was trying to figure something out.

196

"IIow long ago was this?"

"About nine months ago. You might know my brother. He was the one who got caught with all those guns a while ago at the track, " I said.

"Oh yeah!" I remember that shit. I did hear he got shot and that his brother shot who shot him. The last I heard the police couldn't find you," Neon said.

"Well, they did, and I did a little bid. My youngest brother who was with me, got the same amount of time just for being with me. He is still locked up."

"That's some real bullshit," said Neon. "This system is ass backwards. I really respect you for hunting that nigga down and blasting his ass. "

"I'm going to get straight for Christmas though. I got some fake ass niggas that I use to look out for prior to getting locked up. They disrespected me and I'm going to put that burna on them real soon. Probably tonight," I said.

Neon looked at the seriousness in my face. "You don't have to do that, playa, " he said.

"I got to do something!" I responded with a slight attitude. Not at him but at the Stoneville Boys.

It didn't take a rocket scientist to figure out that Neon's money was long. I wasn't trying to get him to give me anything, but I was suggesting indirectly that I was desperate for some kind of help.

"Check this out, playa. I don't like to see real niggas get into trouble. I don't fuck around, but I might be able to get someone to help you," Neon said.

"I'd appreciate it, Dawg, but I don't have any loot," I said.

"Don't worry about the paper. My word is good with this nigga. He'll do a favor for me. You can pay him when you get on your feet. "

"Make this left and it's the first right, " I said to Neon.

We pulled into Alumi-Chrome and deaded our conversation. I introduced him to the owner of the rim shop. He showed Neon his super stock of wheels. After looking at a ton of wheels, Neon asked me which rims he should get. "If it was me, I'd put those right there on my "Six." I pointed to some 18" chrome split stars by MoMo.

"Go ahead and put those on there," Neon said, pointing at the MoMo's. "Put some new tires on there too. The best tires you got."

While the wheels and tires were being put on, Neon and I resumed talking about cars. He bragged about his racecar. I listened to him, but I couldn't get my mind off of what he was going to do for me .I had hit a gold mine!

The Benz looked like new money. Neon was so pleased that he tipped the rim man a hundred dollars, and promised to return to do business with him soon.
On our way back to Greensboro, heads turned constantly. Everyone was sweating the Benz. I didn't mind being the co-pilot now. I was content just being on board.

"Do you have a pager?" Neon asked.

"I ain't got shit, but $108 to my name. I can go and buy one though. I knew it takes money to make money, so I didn't mind investing in a pager."

Neon went into his deep pockets and pulled out another $100 bill. He handed it to me and told me to go get a pager when I got back to Greensboro. Then he gave me his pager number and told me to page him and put my number in his pager when I buy one.

"I'll use code 22 when I page you so you'll know it's me, " I said.

I took the crisp Ben Frank along with his pager number and put them both deep into my pocket. I thanked him again. Then our conversation about racecars resumed until he dropped me off at my car.

"I really appreciate you helping me. I'll page you as soon as I get my pager," I said.

"When my partner pages you, he'll use code 44, so you'll know it's him," Neon said. We smacked hands and before I closed his door, I thanked him once more.

I went to the same pager place in the mall as I did when I bought my first pager. They had a sale on cellular phones, so I purchased one of those also. When you're a hustler, you can't be without a cell phone!

I paged Neon and put my pager number in followed by code 22. Just to make sure he received the page I paged him twice. Then I made sure my pager was working. I dialed my own number and entered Neon's number and locked it in my pager.

I had only been home for two days but the way I was making moves, it felt like I never left. More and more, I began to feel like the old Dana Styles!

I called Celeste and she met me on 220. Together, we went to visit Tim again. "He isn't doing good today, " said my mom. "His stomach is acting up again. "

Tim was sedated and he slept like Tyson had knocked him out. I bent over the bed and kissed him. I gave my mom a break from the hospital, so she could go home, shower eat and get some rest.

For hours I waited for Tim to wake up, but he never did. I paced the floor talking to Celeste, telling her horror stories of prison, and constantly checking on Tim. When it got dark I tried to get Celeste to get into the empty bed in Tim's room. "What I'm going to put on you is going to make you scream. I don't want to wake Tim up, " she said.

When my mom returned Celeste and I bounced. I put sixteen dollars in my empty gas tank. With the few bucks I added to the $100, Neon gave me, to get my pager and phone, minus the thirty dollars I gave Sheneka for her birthday, I had $77 left to my name. I explained to Celeste that I didn't have much money and she offered to pay for a hotel room.

"Since tonight is going to be special for you, I want to stay at the Embassy Suites." she said.

I dropped her off at her VW and gave her my new pager and cell number.

"When you get the room call me. I'll be there before you can get naked," I said causing her to laugh. "I got to go to my partners house to grab some of my things. "

I went to Lakisha' s house and picked up a few things. When I picked my car up from my father's house, I packed my clothes in her car. I told her that I had some serious business to take care of. "If you want something for Christmas you won't be tripping," I said, before she had a chance to trip!

I could see the potential of an argument in her face. But, after I mentioned the presents, the wrinkles from her forehead disappeared. I gave her a short kiss and kept it moving.

I couldn't wait to visit Pookie in a few days. Zag's whereabouts were still unknown to me and I only knew one way to find out where he was. I had to locate his friend Robin. She was his plaything from New Jersey. She'd know where he was. I didn't know where she lived, but I did know who her hairdresser was. One of my old flames fixed her hair.

I also had to meet with my probation and parole officers. I knew that I would be given a drug test on the regular, and that I'd be forced to get a real job! The drug test wasn't going to be a problem for me. They could piss test me until the world ran out of piss cups! I didn't care. I hadn't ever used drugs or alcohol, and I wasn't about to start. But, the "J.O.B", that was going to be a problem. I wasn't trying to work for anyone. I needed a real hustle for some real dough! Dope money had spoiled me. And the only way I was going to get real dough was doing what I did best. Hustle!

A&T was going to have to be put on hold. Although, Uncle Sam paid for my college tuition, I wasn't financially set to attend the "Educational Black Mecca". There were things I needed before I enrolled this time. At least two hot whips, a motorcycle, my own apartment and clothes galore.

Celeste called me and gave me the room number. I traveled down Highway 40, in route to the place where I'd stayed a thousand times with a thousand different women. I couldn't wait to make it one thousand one! But, I wasn't going to speed to get there, as much as I wanted to. I still didn't have a valid driver's license. I didn't want to violate my parole and probation before I met my parole officer.

"Buzzzzzzzzz…..Buzzzzzzzz" 555-3103*44, appeared on the screen of my pager. .I dialed the number as fast as I could when I seen the "44" code. I waited for someone to answer the phone. The code 44, let me know that it was Neon's partner. The page I'd been anticipating.

"Yeah!" I heard the deep voice say.
What's happening, playa? This is Styles!"
"Hey playa-playa! What's happening? Neon asked me to call you and set up a time and place to meet with you," he said.
"I'm ready whenever you are," I replied quickly. "You want to meet me now?"
"Nah. Not right now. Meet me tomorrow at the Rock-Ola Cafe' on West Market Street, at 11: 00 pm." he said. "What will you be driving?" he asked.
"I'll be in a maroon Mustang GT. "
"OK, I'll see you tomorrow," he said and hung up the phone.

He didn't give me his name or a description of what he would be driving. I really didn't dig that. Sitting and waiting to meet someone without a face wasn't cool. But my back was against the wall and I didn't have anything to loose and everything to gain.

I pulled into the parking lot of Embassy Suites and I just sat there for a minute. It had been a long time since I stayed there. I had dreams in prison of staying in one of the big suites. That's where I was when the girl in my dream would ask me, "How did you sleep?" Now, here I was. A dream was about to come true and with the one I loved. For real!

I entered the side door and walked to the elevators and pressed number 11, just like the old times. It shouldn't take long before I make it back to the top again, I thought. After a wonderful night of love making, I walked down to the front desk to check out. Celeste had paid a twenty dollar room deposit and I needed that to add to my pitiful funds. I saw Brianna before she saw me this time. The last time I saw her, I gave her some loot to buy her something for herself, after I checked out. "I appreciate a good woman, " was the last thing I said to her before I winked my eye and walked out. She seemed to get more beautiful each time I saw her. She flickered her million dollar smile in another satisfied customer's face, and handed him his change. "Thank you very much, sir. Have a nice day and come back soon," She said, to the man. He was enthralled by her smile. As was I. He looked at her and saw something he knew he could never have.

"Thank you very much. " He said licking his lips.

"Hey Bri- ann-na, " I said stressing every syllable in her name.

Her enormous eyes looked up to see who was speaking to her.

"Oh my God! Hey stranger. Where in the world have you been?" she asked. She leaned over the counter and hugged my neck.

"It's a long story. I'll have to tell you about it when you get some free time. " I said.

"I haven't seen you since you gave me the money to buy myself something. I bought that right there." She pointed her French manicured finger at a brown leather Coach Bag. "It's my favorite bag, " she said flirting with her eyes like she always did.

We started talking and then Celeste walked up and put her arms around me.

"Are you ready to go, Baby?" She asked, looking at Brianna.

"Yeah, I'm ready. I'll talk to you later, Brianna," I said.

Celeste took my hand and almost dragged me out of the door.

Sheneka was in school so I went and ate lunch with her. We both had cheese pizza and a Nutty Buddy ice cream afterwards. I stayed for an hour after lunch and watched as she participated in class. "She is the brains of my class. You should be very proud of her, " Her teacher said to me. "She really doesn't need to be in the first grade. She needs to be in the second maybe the third."

I was proud of Sheneka. She was my pride and joy. She got her looks from her mother, but she got her brains from me .I left the school a very proud father.

I rode to "Spray, Curl and Dye" hair salon when I left the school. The entire time I was incarcerated, I hadn't heard from Cherry. Before I got locked up, she was one of my chicks on the side. She was also Robin's hairdresser. She would know Robin's phone number, so I could find out about Zag. Cherry gave me a million excuses about why she didn't write me. It really didn't matter to me though. She was just another piece of pussy. A good piece I must admit! But all I wanted was Robin's digits. I did get her home number, just in case I wanted some good sex!

I called Robin and she told me Zag was in Hillsboro County Jail. She sounded extremely unhappy. "Tell him Styles is coming to see him this weekend when he calls you," I said.

I left the hair salon and headed for the hospital. From Greensboro to Winston Salem, I thought about meeting Neon's friend. I wondered what he looked like? What kind of car did he drive? I was sure if he was a partner of Neon's he'd have a car that I would love to have. I wondered how much work he was going to give me? Eleven O'clock, couldn't come fast enough for me.

Tim was doing better. He sat up, watching some movie with Bruce Lee kicking everyone's ass. "Mama went home for a while. She said you would be here soon, " Tim said in a low scratchy voice. I embraced and kissed him.

"I love you," I said to him.

"I love you more," He responded.

He was really into his movie, so I pulled up the chair in the corner of the room beside his bed so I could see the t.v. I kicked my shoes off and relaxed.

"Boy, wake up." My mom said. "Tim said you been asleep every since you got here,"

I looked at my watch and it was 10: 13. "Oh, me,me,me. ..." I said, yawning, my mouth wide open.

"Why didn't you wake me up?" I asked Tim

"I went to sleep too," He said.

I picked up the phone and called Lakisha. I told her I'd be home soon. Then I called Celeste, and told her I loved her. I said my good byes to Tim and mama and rushed out to my car. I had less than an hour to get to the Rock-Ola Cafe', to meet "No Face".

It was 10:50pm, when I backed into the parking lot at Rock-Ola. There weren't many cars in the lot. I observed each one of the cars and I didn't see anything that I thought Neon or anyone who dealt with him would drive. I turned the volume up on Tupac and tried to relax. I was ten minutes early anyway.

As soon as the car pulled in, I knew he was the man I was waiting for. A pearl white Corvette with Corvette wheels backed in beside me. It was definelty a car I wished I owned.

A light skinned, fat face, curly head guy tilted his big head back to speak to me. He pressed a button and his window smoothly dropped. I hit my window button also.

"What's up, playa?" he shouted from his ride.

"What's happening?" I said

"Sorry I'm late, but I got caught up doing something." He said.

I looked at my watch and it was 11:02. At least I knew I was about to deal with someone who was punctual, I thought.

"Let's go inside and grab a bite to eat." He said.
We both rolled our windows up and stepped out into the crisp December air. He grabbed a big leather coat and draped it over his colorful Cogi.

"You can tell a lot about a man by the shoes he wears," my Granny used to say. If that colloquialism was true, I'd just learnt a lot about the man, whose name I still didn't know.

He had on pointed toe gator boots. The same color as his coat and the tips of the boots were gold. He was sharp as a tac!

"My name is Rome," he said after taking two steps in my direction.

"I'm Styles," I said.

We shook hands firmly and walked in the restaurant. The place was almost empty. A waiter instructed us to seat ourselves. I followed Rome to a corner table and we took our seats.

He took his coat off, his butterball frame reveling a long platinum Cuban link. I peeled my coat off too and picked up a menu and began to read.

"Neon asked me to meet with you. He said you just got out of the pen and he wants me to give you some work. He also said you were good people. He's a great judge of character. If you're straight with him then you're straight with me." Rome said.

The waiter came and took our orders after a few minutes of conversation. I wasn't hungry, so I just ordered a chocolate shake. Rome on the other hand, ordered like he hadn't eaten in a month. He asked me how long I'd been in prison? What type of gun did I use to shoot Gerald? What were the prices on the work I was getting before I went to prison? And how much was I buying a week?

He asked me questions like I was being interviewed for a job at a Fortune 500 company. After I answered his questions, Rome finally asked me what I'd been waiting to hear. "How much coke do you want me to front you, so you can get back on your fee......"

Before the word "feet" came out of his mouth, I started answering him. "Give me a whole bird," I said.

"Can you handle that much work and you just got out of prison?" he asked. He had a point. It had been a while since I'd sold anything. I didn't know anyone right off hand that would purchase a whole key from me. I thought about the Stoneville Boys, but I was still hot with them. I didn't even know anyone that could buy an ounce! I had lost all my customers while I was incarcerated. But one thing was for certain, if it was good coke it would sell itself!

"Yeah, you're right. Give me a half key," I said.

"If I give you half...." He paused, because he saw the waiter bringing his grub.

"Is there anything else you need, sir?" the waiter asked Rome.

"No, I'm fine, thanks."

"What about you, sir?" he asked me.

"Nah, I'm fine also. Thank you," I said.

The waiter walked away and Rome began talking again. "Instead of fronting you a half a key, I'm going to give you a quarter key. You take that, sell it and have a Merry Christmas. I'm going to give you my numbers to get with me after all the holidays. Then we'll meet again and discuss real business. Take the nine ounces I give you and build some type if clientele. They're going to love this coke, too. It's coming straight from Lima." He said

When Rome said he was going to give me a quarter, I could have kissed his fat ass. Rodney Allen Ripey use to sing about "Santa Claus was a black man!" Until now, I hadn't believed him.

Not only was Sheneka going to have a good Christmas, but it was going to be "on and popping" after the holidays, I thought as Rome swallowed his food.

"Black Santa" finished eating and explained that he wanted to meet me early the next morning at Shoney's. "They have a great breakfast bar. It's all you can eat," he said. "I'll give you the package then. Let's say around 8:30. I have to be at the airport at 9:30. I'm going out of town for the holidays," he said.

We embraced like we had known each other forever. He got in his Vette slowly, moving like a full tick. I watched him pull off and wished I had his Vette again.

I called Cherry on my way to Lakisha's house. For some reason, she had popped into my mind. She was sound asleep, but quickly woke up when she realized it was me. She invited me over and I accepted her invitation gladly. In eight and a half months, she hadn't written me one letter, so I owed her a good grudge fuck! I called Lakisha and told her I was in Madison with my mother. "I'll see you first thing tomorrow, Love." I said to her.

I pulled into Cherry's driveway ready to pay her in full!

8:30 The Next Morning

Rome pulled up this time pushing a black Caddy. He motioned for me to come and get in his car. I got out of my car and jogged around to his passenger's side. We spoke to each other and he handed me a brown paper bag with nine ounces of coke. I quickly pushed the bag inside my coat. Then Rome handed me a piece of paper with three numbers on it. I stuffed the numbers in the front pocket of my jeans. "Don't misplace those numbers. Call me after the New Year," he said.

I promised to call him. A promise that wouldn't be broken with a sledge hammer. He looked at his watch and said he had to hurry up and eat so he could get the airport. We shook hands and Rome tried to say something slick, but it wasn't slick at all.

"I'll see you next year," he said. As if next year was a long time away. I gave him a fake ass laugh and agreed to see him then. I had to go too! I had coke to sell. Christmas was coming fast and I had presents to buy. The White Santa had to get paid now!

CHAPTER 38

I left Rome and headed for down town. My appointment with my parole officer/probation officer was for 9:00am. I parked my car and slid the brown bag underneath my seat.

When I walked in, the secretary asked me my name and instructed me to sign a roster with some more ex-con's names on it. I signed it and took a seat in the waiting room and started reading a Time magazine.

"Mr. Styles, please come this way," the secretary said. She led me down a long hall to a small office with a wonderful view of downtown Greensboro. "Mrs. Braxton will be right with you," she said.

Mrs. Braxton was a short older lady. Probably, in her early fifties. Her hair was jet black with a streak of gray down the center. I could tell by the way she gracefully moved and looked that she was the shit back in her day.

She pranced in the office and sat behind her large wooden desk that consumed the majority of the space. Then she jumped back up like she had forgotten something and pushed the door shut. I looked at her from behind and she still had some junk in her trunk, like most sista's do anyway! Also, I could tell by the muscles in her legs that she still worked out. Fighting a battle against the undefeated, "Time!",

When the door closed, a picture of a younger Mrs. Braxton became visible to me. She was fine! She hated she was getting older, I thought. Without knowing it, I shook my head from side to side, sucking my teeth.

"Good morning, Mr. Styles," she said trying to figure out why I was sucking my teeth. "I'm sure you're happy to be home before Christmas."

"Yes ma'am, I sure am," I said.

"Hmmm...   you'll be doing probation and parole time with me," she said.

"Is that good or bad?" I said.

"It depends on how you make it. Do you smoke, drink or use drugs?" she asked flipping thru a file that was labeled, "D. Styles".

"No, I don't. Nor have I ever done any of the three," I said.

"That's great! You shouldn't have a problem with this drug test today, then." She said. She continued to look thru my file like she was searching for something in particular.

203

"You may not use drugs, but you will sell them, huh?" she asked, looking up from my file.

"That's a mistake I had in the past," I said to Mrs. Braxton.

"Is 16.7 grams a lot?" she asked.

I wanted to say "Not compared to the 250 grams I got in my car right now." But I didn't. "It's not that much," I said.

She closed the file, got up and asked me to follow her. The way she was looking, I didn't have a problem following those legs. After giving her a urine sample, we went back to her office and she asked me more questions that Rome asked me the night before. She seemed impressed by my past, military and college, and advised me to enroll back in school.

"It's going to be mandatory for you to maintain gainful employment," she said.

I was scheduled to see her every other Friday until she said other wise. "Beginning after the holidays," she said.

I also had some community service hours to complete before my probation, parole period was up. I signed a few papers, answered a few more questions and bounced.

I decided to take the nine ounces to the Back Street. After that stunt Geno pulled, he was going to be shocked to see me with some work. Especially, after I was just down there with my palms up, looking for a hand out.

Cars were lined from one end of the Back Street, all the way to the other and it wasn't even 11:30am. I only saw one Lexus parked beside the Old School when I turned in. The license plate read, "G-Wiz" so I knew that it was Geno's car.

I parked beside the Lex and got out. Geno was sitting on the other side of the street with a few of his workers. They stood and turned around him like they were his bodyguards. I walked up grilling all of them and none of them mugged me back.

"What's up, Styles? It's pretty early for you to be out, isn't it?" Geno asked me.

"You told me to get back with you in a few days, didn't you?" I asked Geno.

Geno started to stutter, "Ah...ah...yeah," he stammered.

"Well, I don't need shit from you now. Instead, I came to see if you wanted to make a deal with me."

Geno looked relieved when I said I didn't want anything. But he also looked confused. "What kind of deal you talking about?" he asked.

"Come on over to my car and I'll show you."

He followed me to my car and I retrieved the brown bag from underneath my seat and handed it to him. He acted like he was afraid to look inside the bag, but he opened it and peeked inside. I looked back across the street and his soft ass homeboys were hawking me like I was going to kidnap him or something.

"That's nine ounces of uncut funk," I said.

Geno couldn't understand how three days ago I didn't have a pot to piss in, but now I was back offering him a deal. "I'll sale it all to you for fifty five hundred and after the New Year, I'm really going to be connected to the big fish," I said.

"Let me get someone to test it," Geno said.

"Be my guest," I said knowing somehow that it was good coke.

"Come here, Tank!" Geno yelled.

Tank rushed across the street to see what his boss wanted. He was the official tester on the Back Street.

"Test that powder to see if it's any good," Geno said to Tank.

Tank's eyes gleamed and his mouth watered. Geno untied one of the bags and Tank baptized his pinky finger, which had a nail that looked like it was a mile long, into the bag. He shoveled some of the coke and without dropping any, stuck his lengthy nail inside his nose. He sniffed hard, like a small kid trying to keep snot from running out his nose. When he yanked the long nail away from his nose, all the coke had disappeared.

"Oh shit," Tank said.

"What? What is it?" asked Geno.

"That's the Strawberry Coke. That's the best shit on the market," Tank yelled, rubbing his nose. "When you cook that Strawberry Coke, it makes grade A crack. Motherfuckers go crazy over it!" he said. "Everytime you bring your ass up here, you bring the bomb," He said to me.

Geno dug his hands in his pockets and pulled out a roll of money. He counted out fifty five hundred and handed it to me. "Here is my pager number. After the holidays, I'll really be straight. Better than I've ever been. I got the best hook up around now." I said. "Call me. Tell Tone and Quayle I said what's up? Tell them Tony Montana said, Feliz Naveda" I said trying to sound Cuban.

I left the Back Street and went to pick up Sheneka. I took her to the mall and let her get everything she wanted and then some. I bought a few more gifts also. For my mom, Celeste, Lakisha and a pair of new Air Jordans for Pookie. I called my aunt and got Red's address and hit him off with some loot. After taking care of everything. I still had money to burn.

I visited Tim and spent a few hours with him. It still hurt me to my heart that he was in the condition he was in, but I was just glad Allah blessed him to continue to live.

Whenever I left the hospital, I'd cry almost all the way back to G'boro. This particular night, I realized that I would never be the "Old Dana Styles" if Tim didn't get better. How could I be, if he was my Better Half?

I stopped in Hillsboro to see Zag before I went to Durham to visit Pookie. He had been locked up almost a month. He looked like he'd been locked up a year. He was at least twenty pounds lighter than when I last saw him. He hadn't shaved and his hair was matted to his head. He didn't look nothing like the smooth playa I was accustomed to seeing. Stress was breaking him down.

"When you come home, I get locked up." Zag said speaking thru the small hole in the glass.

"How are you doing?" I asked.

"Not so good, dawg. These Feds ain't playing. They are trying to give me an elbow."

I had learned in state prison that an "elbow" of "L" meant a life sentence.

"What happened?" I asked,

"I think your homeboy, Tone set me up. I had fronted him two kilos then he called me for two more. When I was taking them to him, the Feds ran down on me like white on rice."

"I thought you didn't deal with Tone like that? I thought you said you didn't like him. That it was something strange about him that you didn't like."

"I shouldn't have started dealing with him. I missed that money you use to make for me. I ran into him at a gas station and we talked. I got greedy, I should have just left well enough alone." He said.

"Do you know for sure that Tone set you up, or are you just speculating?" I asked.

"No, because the agents said they have watched me for a couple of years. They do have pictures and shit of me dealing with Tone. But, you couldn't tell who was in any of the flicks. It's possible that I just got knocked, but I think he had something to do with it."

I knew Tone, Geno and Quayle could be shady when it came to business, but I didn't think that either one of them would tell on anyone! Zag caught me off guard when he made that accusation about Tone being a snitch. I knew him well enough to know that wasn't true. So I defended Tone's honor.

We continued to talk and he warned me about the Feds. "They can arrest you on a conspiracy charge if they can't catch you with anything. It's a few guys in here that didn't get caught with shit." He began to name a list of things they didn't get caught with. "No coke! No large sums of money! No weapons! No pictures of them or nothing! No phone taps or any type of recordings. No nothing! But they've been sentenced to twenty and thirty years. Those motherfuckers are playing dirty. Them crackers are taking niggas lives over that crack. It's as simple as that! You need to stop messing around now and go back to school. Leave them bitch ass niggas alone. They're going to get you fucked up one way or another. Especially Tone! He said.

For years Tone had been one of my best friends. I knew him and I were too close for him to tell anything on me. We grew up together. Ate from the same plate. That wasn't even a thought I was going to entertain. I felt Zag's pain, but he was wrong this time. Dead wrong! He just got greedy. He shouldn't have dealt with Tone anyway!

I promised Zag anything he needed done I would do for him or brake my back trying. I gave him Lakisha's number and left a couple hundred dollars on his books. He kept it real with me while I was locked up and I planned to keep it real with him. But I wasn't going to stop dealing with Tone or anyone of the Stoneville Boys. Not because of his misfortune. I appreciated the advice he gave me even though I didn't believe that bullshit about the conspiracy. How could anyone get twenty or thirty years and they don't get caught with anything? I figured Zag was just trying to scare me out of the game. I appreciated that too, but it hadn't worked. I was going to ball until I fall!

Pookie was very happy that I was out of prison. He still couldn't believe that I got paroled before he did. Especially, after I testified he didn't have anything to do with me assaulting Grerald.

He wanted to know how Tim was doing and I made Tim sound better than he actually was. I knew Pookie was worried about him. I gave him his Air Jordans and talked to him about a few things I had going on. Before I left, I broke bread with him too. I left a few hundred on his books and promised to visit him every weekend. I hugged and kissed him and drove back to Greensboro with a bunch of mess on my mind. I listened to the O'Jays "Stairway to Heaven" and reflected on the great times Tim and I had had together. I thought about Mr. Miller also. I prayed that both of them were going to be ok.

CHAPTER 39

Every New Year's Eve after Celeste and I hooked up, was spent with me serenading her at some hotel. Every year I would make the same New Year's resolution. "To be a better boyfriend!" This year was no exception besides the fact that we spent New Year's Night together also. I was really trying to be a better boyfriend.

For two days I'd been missing in action. I knew Lakisha was going to be tripping when I got home. I put my clothes on without taking a shower and bounced.

Sixteen days had passed and Lakisha and I had lived together in perfect harmony. But when I walked into her house she began to curse me out without even asking for an explanation. When she finished I flipped the script on her. After I told her that I spent my New Years' Night at the hospital with Tim while she was out partying her hot ass off, she apologized to me. So we were still living in perfect harmony!

A lot happened over the holidays. While Lakisha bathed me in my favorite sun ripened raspberry bubble bath I thought about how my plan was coming together. Dealing with Rome, promised to make me some serious money.

On Christmas Day, Mac had the nerve to show his face down my mom's house. He had heard it thru the grapevine that I was home. He had more excuses than Cherry did as to why he didn't keep in touch with me.

After cursing him out, him and I were cool again. I just had to vent. Our friendship was bigger that eight and a half months of ignorance on his behalf! It was about getting our music together and trying to make it big time. So, I told him he was forgiven.

Also, I decided to forgive my homies back on the Back Street. I was getting ready to start taxing them anyway. They carried me real greasy while I was in prison and when I came home. But, as soon as their money started filling my pockets, I would have the last laugh.

I visited Zag and Pookie twice over the holidays. Zag was still advising me that I needed to slow down and to watch out for Tone. "Slow down," wasn't in my vocab. I hadn't even got started yet. And as far as Tone goes, he'd probably be one of my best customers, I thought. But, I played it off and pretended to take his advice to heart.

Pookie was parlaying in Durham now that I was home. Doing his time with ease. He was still pissed that he didn't get paroled, but happy that I did. He knew I was going to look out for him and look out I did. Each time I visited him I took him money, weed and when I left I tossed the bottle of Easy Jesus (E&J) over the fence.

The doctors discussed Tim coming home. He would still be confined to the house but it would be better than being crammed in that small hospital room he'd been in for so long. He learned to basically take care of himself. He could start his own I.V.'s, change all of his bandages and change his colostomy. The doctor's were very impressed with him. I was convinced he would be home soon.

No one knew that Tone had got knocked and set Zag up. All Geno and Quayle knew was that Zag got popped and since then, they'd had trouble finding a steady connect. As much as they hated to, once again they were getting ready to start copping from me and I planned to make them pay dearly.

Tone made a deal with the Feds that gave him full immunity. As long as he worked and got people busted, he was safe. In order to do so, the Feds gave him the green light to continue to hustle so that things would appear normal with him. And he did just that. He continued to ball!

I broadcasted the word over the holidays that immediately after all the shiny tinsel was gone, I would have more coke to sell than Nino Brown. It was January 2nd (96) and my pager was beeping like horns in a New York City traffic jam. I wanted to wait a few more days before I paged Rome, but my big mouth had written a check my ass had to cash, so I paged him from Lakisha's cordless phone.

Lakisha was drying me off when Rome called me back. To my surprise, he said he had been waiting for me to call. I was pleased to hear that. After a few minutes of hearing him brag about his Carribean vacation and a few Christmas tales from both of us, I explained that I had a few people paging me already.

"Just tell me what you need and I'll tell you where to meet me." He said.

"Today?" I asked.

"Yeah! Anytime today. Fun time is over. It's time to get down to the nitty gritty, now. He said.

"Let me return all those pages first. Then I'll call you back to let you know what I need."

I got dressed and called back the cats that had been paging me. I took orders using coded talk with each call. "You need one whole pizza," I asked one customer. That set the tone. Every other caller from that point on ordered pizzas instead of coke and I took orders like I was the Dominos Pizza Man. Then I set up appointments like a secretary. Nine people called me and everybody wanted a half key or more. That was great because the fifty-five hundred I made from the nine ounces was almost gone.

Rome couldn't believe it when I told him all the work that I needed. "I need three whole pizzas and six half pizzas for my big homecoming party." I said.

"Oh yeah! The party is jumping like that and it just got started?" he asked quickly decoding my order. "Meet me in thirty minutes at Elizabeth's Pizza on Summit Avenue," he said.

I tied up my Timberlands and explained to Lakisha I had some business to handle. "I might be gone most of the day," I said. I pulled out five twenties and handed them to her. Killing any conceivable tension and walked out the door.

When I got ready to back out the small driveway, Lakisha ran to the door and motioned for me to come back. I let the window down to see what she wanted. "You have a phone call. It's from your brother."

I turned the key back, killing the growling engine. I ran back into the house and answered the phone. "What's up, Bro? I asked,

"Asalaamu Alaikum," a soft voice responded.

"Wa alaikum asalaam…..Yahya!," I yelled.

"You didn't tell me you had another brother named Yahya," Lakisha mumbled.

"What's up Ahki?" I asked "How are you and the other brothers?"

"We're fine, alhamdulilah. We want to know how you are doing? We haven't heard from you and we thought we would have by now."

"Yeah, I've been busy trying to get things back in order. I haven't forgot about you brothers though."

Yahya continued talking asking me questions. "Have you been making your salat? Did you go to a masjid as soon as you got out? You're not messing around are you?"

I knew he was talking about selling drugs and I answered "no". I felt bad about telling a lie. I hadn't done anything he asked. I looked at my watch and realized I only had a few minutes before I was supposed to meet Rome. Yahya was still talking, preaching a bunch of stuff I wasn't trying to hear. It was easy for him to preach like that because anyone can say anything when they're locked up, I thought. I did! I knew I wasn't doing what I was supposed to be doing. But I had to live!

"Check this out, Yahya," I interrupted. "I got to bounce. I'm supposed to be at the hospital with my brother and I'm late. Call me back later," I said.

Elizabeth's Pizza was owned and operated by people from the Boot. A big screen t.v. was tuned in on a soccer game when I walked in and half of the employees sat and cheered as Italy kicked America's ass. I walked to the counter and ordered a slice of cheese pizza, a large lemonade and a bag of Wise sour cream and onion potato chips. I sat down with the employees and watched the soccer game until my order was ready.

Rome walked in and went straight to the counter. He ordered a bunch of stuff, as always and came and sat beside me. "When you finish eating, look in the back seat of that old green car parked next to yours. There is a grocery bag and it's got nine boxes of laundry soap in the bag. The Cheer boxes have the half joints in them and the Tide boxes have the whole birds. Do you remember the prices?" her asked.

"Yeah, I remember them"

"Just call me as soon as you finish dropping them off and I'll tell you where to meet me again," he said.

I ate my slice of pizza quickly, scooped my chips and lemonade and rolled out. An old LTD the ugliest green I'd ever seen in my life was parked beside my car. I opened the heavy door and grabbed the grocery bag. I slammed the stiff door and opened my door. I put the bag in my backseat and jumped in and pulled off.

When I got back to Lakisha's she was gone. That one hundred dollars was burning a hole in her pocket. I locked the door and pulled one of the Tide boxes out of the Food Lion bag. I examined the box closely. The boxes hadn't been opened. Rome said the coke was in the boxes! "What kind of stupid games is this nigga playin?" I said out loud. I pulled at the tab on the side of the box spilling specks of Tide on the wooden living room floor. I lifted the top back and I didn't see anything but washing powder. I dug my hand deep in the soap and I felt it! As hard as a brick. I pulled the block, wrapped in brown paper and yellow tape off the box. Soap was all over the floor now. "This nigga is slick! I can't believe this shit," I said giggling. I got the broom and swept up the mess I'd made. I poured the Tide from the dustpan, back into the box and sat it in the pantry.

I called everyone who was waiting for the pizzas to make sure it was still on. They were all waiting for me to come through.

I loaded the car with the boxes and made all the drop offs. Everyone questioned me when I handed them a box of laundry soap in exchange for their money.

"It's in there," I'd say. "Trust me. When you open it up, page me and tell me what you think about my idea." I said to each customer, taking Rome's brilliant idea as my own. And each one called me back satisfied. I had given a new meaning to the term "washing powder'!

CHAPTER 40

Mrs. Braxton informed me that I had two weeks to find a job. "You've got to have some way to pay your probation and parole fee, " She said.

I didn't need a job. I had just made nine thousand dollars the day before. I wanted to pullout a fat bankroll and slap her with it for insulting me. But, I complied, promising to have a job before two weeks was up. I didn't have any idea where I would work though. It had been years since I'd had a job. The last two jobs I had, when I got out of the Army, didn't work out. I didn't see the next one working out either.

Huntman didn't even know I was out of prison. I ran into him and Tammy at a gas station on West Market Street. He said he had moved back to Pittsburgh for about six months after I got locked up. "That's why you hadn't heard from me, " He said. He went on to explain that he and Tammy had fallen out. "That's why I left." Then he said that she was about to have his child. The real reason he left, I thought.

I told Huntman about the connect I had and invited him to get down with me. He declined and for good reason. He invested all his money he had saved up in a natural springs water company, and he was doing very well. "You can come and work with me. There isn't any future in the dope game. I learned that years ago when we almost got trapped off, " He said. "It's easy work and you can be your own boss. All you do is drive around to different companies and change out their five gallon water jugs. I never thought that people would pay for water the way they do. I'm selling water like coke! I'm making a killing, " Huntman said.

My old partner sounded content with his business. He went from balling out of control to a regular John Doe. He definitely wouldn't be getting back into the game. I decided then and there to just leave him alone and let him live a regular John Doe life.

"Neon told me to tell you not to shoot anyone," Rome said to me. I laughed and told Rome to tell him I'm keeping a low profile, and I promise I won't dump on anyone, unless they mess with me first.

From time to time, Tone would get ghost. He claimed to have a honey in V.A. "I got a fine ass red bone in Petersburg. She went to A&T also. She's an A.K.A." He said to me. "I met her in the mall in Greensboro."

That was possible, but it wasn't true. The truth was Tone was putting in work for the Feds in Virginia. He was getting guys set up left and right, in V.A., and North Click.

I finally saw Jegbadia while I was "Ho-Hopping" on A&T's campus .She flagged me down and jumped out of her car and ran over to mine.

"Dana Styles!" She exclaimed in her Liberian accent, with her hands on her thick hips. "When did you come home? You better not tell me that you been home." She bent over and hugged my neck. Then she puckered up her sizable lips to kiss mine, but I turned my head. Jegbadia was looking so good that it was hard for me to refrain from sticking my tongue down her throat.

"What's wrong with you?" She asked.

"Do you know Norman, from Durham?" I asked coldly. My question caught her off guard, because her head went up and down and her lips moved but nothing came out.

"I was locked up with him and he told me about you and his brother. He said you two have been together since you been in this country. You didn't have to lie to me and say you didn't have a man."

As many lies as I told her and every other female I dealt with, I shouldn't have been tripping, but it was an ego thing. She tried to play the coach!

"I really appreciate you keeping in touch with me while I was locked up, but I'm not playing the role of your fool," I said.

She tried to explain how they had been together, on and off, for a while. "But, when you and I met, we wasn't together," she said.

A line of cars on both sides of the street had formed and impatient students and ho-hoppers alike, started to lay down on their horns.

"I'll see you around," I said. Slowly, she walked back to her car and I pulled off quickly.

I was getting tired of staying with Lakisha, so I stayed at hotels more often. Of course with different broads! I was in the process of getting my own place, but I wanted to find the perfect spot. Something that would be impressive to the ladies.
Most of the time I hid out at the Embassy Suites. Brianna even gave me a discount when I stayed there. She and I became very good friends. Everyday that she worked, she'd call me on her breaks and we would discuss different things. From her marriage to all the women she'd seen me with over the years, and even the possibility of us getting together was discussed. But, I wasn't really taking Brianna seriously. I figured she was just bored with her marriage and talking on the phone to another man was all the cheating she was going to do. After all, her husband was already kicking her ass, and he'd probably kill her if he found out she was talking to another man. He'd definitely kill her if she gave up the gold mine between her legs .

When I told her I had to have a job in a few days, she suggested that I come and work at the Embassy Suites. "You stay here enough, you might as well get a job here. I can't picture you flipping burgers at some fast food restaurant, " She said laughing at me. "Maybe we can go out for lunch then," she added.

That wasn't a bad idea. I did have to have a job, and with all the rooms at the Embassy Suites, I was sure that I could persuade Brianna to slip off so I could have her for lunch.

"Yeah, lunch is a good idea, " I said. "I'll be out there tomorrow to fill out an application."

I hung up the phone and tried to picture myself checking someone into a room, or pushing that little cart from room to room cleaning up. I couldn't picture either one of them. But, I could picture flipping Brianna and not burgers in one of those rooms.

Usually, when someone fills out an application, they're broke as hell and in need of a job. In my case, I filled out the application with a pocket full of cash. I hated I had to work. My probation, parole period was for a year. That meant I was going to have a real job for twelve months! Fifty-two weeks of working! Three hundred and sixty five days of hell!

"Do you know anything about maintenance?" A skinny, dark brown haired man, with a Hitler mustache asked me .He was dressed in an all gray uniform with a tool belt that had to weigh a ton.

"No sir, I don't But, I do learn fast. "

The guy just looked at me with a serious look on his face and shook his head up and down. Finally, the mug was broken with a slight smile. "Most people would have told a lie and said they know a little bit, knowing good 'n and damn well they don't know shit, just to get a job. I appreciate your honesty. I could use someone who learns fast. My name is Kenny Paper, " He said extending his hand. I shook it firmly. "Everyone calls me Ken. "

When I was letting go of his hand, he tried to end our shake with the "Soul Shake". I almost started to laugh in his face, but I let him have his black moment and finished filling out the application.

Little did Ken know I was about a half a second away from saying that I knew a little bit, about maintenance. I signed my name on the application and handed it to him. "When do I start?" I asked.

"Can you come up here tomorrow for an interview. I'll definitely hire you but there is some paper work that has to be done. "

"What time?" I asked.

"Tomorrow at 1: 00 p.m. will be good."

Brianna stood behind the counter smiling like she had won the lotto. As soon as Ken stepped off, she said, "I can't believe he talked to you like that. He is usually an ass hole to everyone. You must be something special."

"I am something special. You haven't figured that out by now?" I asked.

The following day Ken hired me. He gave me the option to work full time or part time. Since I didn't want to work at all, I choose to work part time. I explained to Ken that I would be enrolling back into college soon also. He said that I could work any four hours out of the day, just as long as I worked five days a week and one weekend out of every month. That was sweet! I couldn't ask for anything better than that.

Mrs. Braxton was satisfied with the job I had. I was ordered to pay sixty-nine dollars a month for my probation/parole fees. I told Mrs..Braxton that I think I could handle paying that much, sounding unsure. I wanted her to think the fee was going to be hard for me to pay. And I still wanted to smack her with a roll of my dough!

Mac and I started working on our music again. While I was incarcerated, I wrote a gang of songs and I was ready to drop them on wax.

"Drop them on wax. What cha mean by that?" Hireen asked.

"That means I was ready to record them. I forgot, just because you're Muslim, doesn't mean you're hip to the hip talk," I said.

"OK! Whatever! Go ahead and finish the story, " Hireen said.

Mac had written a lot of songs while I was away also. We began to work on our second record. Whenever I had time, we'd buy studio time and go record a few songs.

The doctor told Tim if he continued to do well he'd be home in less than two weeks. That was a blessing to us all. Tim had came a long way and we all encouraged him to be strong so he could hurry up and come home.

My daddy, whom I'd grown even closer to since Tim got shot, prepared a place at his house for Tim's hospital bed. He stayed sick a lot himself and he joked that he and Tim could be at home sick together. "At least I'll be able to see him," My father said. He hadn't been able to get back and forth to the hospital at all. Now, I would be able to kill two birds with one stone. I could visit Tim and spend time with my Ole Man.

One Week Later

Ken asked me to check the sinks in all the empty rooms for leaks. "If you find a sink that leaks, put the room out of order in the computer, and I'll have Reggie or Gilley to come up to fix them," he said.

All morning, I went from room to room, inspecting sinks and showers heads for leaks. I wasn't use to all the walking around and after two hours my feet got tired. I stopped in room 539, closed the door and locked it. I picked up the phone and pressed zero for the front desk.

"Front desk! This is Brianna. How can I help you?"

"You can help me if you take a break and come up to room 539," I said.

Brianna started laughing lightly. "Dana, what are you doing?" She whispered.

"I'm up here in this big ass room, all alone waiting for you. That's what I'm doing. When is your next break?"

"I can take one now if I need it because we're not busy, but I don't need one."

Since I had started talking to Brianna on the regular, I found out she was unhappily married. Her husband was a jealous jerk, who didn't want her to do shit but go to work and cone home.

"He never massages my back, and if I ask him to rub my tired feet, he looks at me like I'm crazy, " she had said to me in a previous conversation.

He also roughed her up from time to time, so being at work was a break for her. A break from him.

"Sure you need a break. You need your back massaged. You need your tired feet rubbed and your toes sucked. And I know you need a man to make love to you like I know you deserve, " I said.

"My breaks are only fifteen minutes. I don't think you can do all of that in that short period. "

Obviously, Brianna didn't know who she was talking to. In fifteen minutes I was capable of making her feel like a brand new woman, or the only women on God's green earth!

"Of course I can. While I'm eating you, I'll massage your chest and stomach. Then I'll rub and suck your toes while I'm making sweet love to you. And your back! When I turn you over, I'll massage it then," I said.

Brianna's breathing became heavy. "Damn! What room are you in?"

"I'm in 539. Type in the computer that the room is occupied. Don't put it's out of order in the computer, because Ken is going to send Reggie or Gilley to all of the out of order rooms."

Brianna didn't say anything she just hung up the phone. I reached over the huge bed and turned the clock radio on, and kicked off my boots. The thought of Brianna being on her way up to the room made my nature rise!

For a long time me and Brianna had been attracted to each other. For years we had flirted with each other, over the counter! We talked about getting together, but since she was married it was hard for her to shake her covetous hubby.

As I waited for her, I wondered if she suggested that I work at the Embassy Suites because she really wanted what was about to happen to happen?

She'd seen me with a bunch of different women, so I knew she was curious about what I had down south. I wondered if she had planned this? It didn't matter though. I was about to show her why I was someone special!

Room 539 was right by the fire escape. Brianna walked from the front desk, past the break room in the back of the hotel, and up the fire escape. The rooms had the type of doors that could be opened only with coded cards. She made one to open 539 before she left the front desk, and I heard the door open and close. I eased up and met her in the doorway of the bedroom. There wasn't time to procrastinate, so without saying a word I latched my arms around her curvy waist and commenced to kissing her. Her arms wrapped around my neck and she pulled, standing on her tiptoes and she kissed me almost violently. My hands slithered from her waist to her round behind. I lifted her skirt with my left hand, pulled at her white, cotton panties with my right. They were soaked!

She unfastened my pants and pulled them down. As she stepped out of her panties, I kicked my pants and boxers off. While she fumbled with the tiny buttons on her shirt I guided her to the large bed and pushed her back. The clock radio seemed like it was playing louder for some reason. Then I realized it wasn't playing louder, it was just the song that was playing that caught my attention. Barbara Weathers of Atlantic Star sang, "Secret Lovers…...that's what we are! " How appropriate I thought.

I opened her big brown thighs and she bent both of her knees, and rested her heels on the edge of the bed. I dropped down to my knees and began to eat her out, sucking and blowing on her long clit. Just like I promised, I massaged her breast softly, lightly squeezing her nipples. Delightfully, she moaned and begged me not to stop. I had no intentions of stopping until she came in my mouth. That happened faster than I expected. After about three minutes, Brianna started convulsing and moaning she was about to come.

While she was still trembling, I slowly entered her. I pushed her legs up in the air and pulled her three inch heels off her tiny feet. Slowly, I thrusted her while licking every inch of her feet.

"Yes, Dana...Oh God, this is what I need. This is what I need," Brianna kept saying. Then all of a sudden she started to curse out her husband. "That motherfucker ain't shit. I ought to leave his ass. Make me leave his sorry ass Dana. I hate him! "

I pulled out of Brianna and instructed her to turn over. So far, I had kept all of my promises except for rubbing her back. I began to hit her doggie style and firmly massaging her back at the same time. Then, I smacked her ass and pulled her silky hair at her request. She looked over her shoulder, biting her sappy lips and begged me again.

"Please don't stop Dana. Please don't stop!"

"I'm about to come, " I said.

"Come inside of me! " She demanded. "Don't take it out Dana. Please!" She pleaded.

Brianna was a married woman that wasn't on the pill. I knew this from past conversation also. She wasn't on the pill because her husband was sterile. I wasn't about to get her pregnant!

"Will you suck me baby?" I asked, already pulling out of her.

"Yes, I will. Hell yeah! " She cried. "Let me suck your dick!"

I was about to explode. She turned around and took Frankie in both of her hands and sucked like a porn vet. I came in her mouth and she was still sucking. I laid back on the bed, moaning myself, now. "Brianna. ...Please," I said.

I sounded like she had a few minutes ago, and I felt like cursing the next broad out! Whatever she was doing with her tongue, I couldn't take it. I pushed her away and pointed at the clock radio. A Baby Face song played, and exactly fifteen minutes had elapsed.

"I don't believe this shit," Brianna whispered, like someone else was in the room.

"What?" I asked. "That you cheated on your husband?"

"Hell nah! " She responded quickly and almost adamantly. "I can't believe how good that shit was. I won't miss a damn day of work while you're working here, " She said with a big childish smile.

"Now I see why you run in and out of here with different women." Brianna's curiosity had been totally satisfied. Finally.

"You better hurry up and get your fine ass back to work. They're going to miss you up front. "

"I can't move a muscle right now. They are going to have to miss me for a few more minutes until I can get myself together. "

I picked up my pants and Tommy Boxers, and proudly walked to the bathroom. I took a bird bath and started to get dressed.

"You did to me in fifteen minutes, what no man, including my sorry ass husband, has ever done. You made me have multiple orgasms. I even had an orgasm when I was performing oral sex on you. And that has definitely never happened before."

"Now it's called oral sex! Just a few minutes ago it was called, "Let me suck your dick, " I thought.

"You're something special alright, " She yelled from the bedroom. She finally got up, staggered to the bathroom and washed up. I kissed her, on her cheek, and told her that I'd be down to the front desk to see her later.

When Ken hired me, Brianna sounded like she had hit the lotto. From the way she was smiling now, it looked like I was her winning ticket!

A Week Later

Rome was happy as hell at the way I sold kilos, like the Waffle House sold waffles. So happy that he gave me his customers. He only wanted to deal with me, he said.

"I'm going to give you my customers to deal with. These are guys that buy a kilo or two a week from me. You've been selling so much coke, I'll let you handle them and you can make a cut from them also."

That was just fine with me. I was trying to get a new car and buy a condo, anyway. The more the merrier. I needed all the customers I could get.

After almost a year and a half in the hospital, Tim, got to come home. He was doing about the same, but he was home. I was so pleased when he got to my father's house that I cried tears of joy.

I visited Pookie with the good news and he cried too. He feared that Tim might pass while he was locked up. Now that he was home he felt like Tim was out of the danger zone. And so did I.

Since I was in the maintenance department, I had keys to every lock in Embassy Suites. I used this to my advantage and stored boxes of washing powder in the landscaping storage. But, only after I changed the locks so that I would be the only one with a key. I had my own personal safe house.

I began to conduct all of my business at the hotel. Needless to say, everyone was dumbfounded when they showed up and I greeted them in an Embassy Suites uniform. I actually had a job, and I was getting laid while I worked. I loved my job. It didn't get any better than that.

Two Weeks Later

Neon sent a message to me by Rome for me to call him. When I did, he asked me to meet him at the Apple Bees on Battleground Avenue. I agreed to meet him the following night.

Lakisha started really tripping. I spent less and less tire with her. Our perfect harmony was no more. I couldn't understand why she got so upset with me though. I paid her rent, made sure her hair and nails stayed done, and she was never without spending money. She didn't want for anything but my time. I was moving too fast to give her anymore than she was already receiving.

Celeste was still hanging in there with me, but I knew she wasn't going anywhere. She had been tested. Even though I was a dog she continued to think that one day she would be able to change me into the man she knew I could be.

I paid my probation and parole fees and started my community service at Country Park on Lawndale Drive. Mrs.Braxton stopped giving me the drug test everytime I reported in, and changed our appointments to once a month. Things were looking good for me. I had come a long way since I'd gotten out of prison. I even forgave everyone who flipped on me while I was locked up. I got back with Aiesha and made up with my African Queen, Jegbadai. I had fat pockets again and a stash to boot. There wasn't any need for me to continue to have an attitude. Especially over some niggas and broads

The Following Night

Neon recognized my Mustang when I pulled into the parking lot. I parked and looked for the black 600 Benz, sitting on new MoMo's, but I didn't see it. "Beeeep Beeeeep" I heard a horn and I looked to see where the sound was coming from. I saw Neon sitting in a gold Toyota Land Cruiser, decked with huge chrome wheels and some big Mickey Thompson tires that gleamed like patton leather. It was nice as shit! He motioned for me to come over. I closed and locked my door, and being extra cool, dapped over to the passenger side of the Land Cruiser. I heard his electric locks, and I pulled the door open. Neon burst into laughter as soon as I climbed into the truck. He sat in the parking lot watching a small tv screen that was mounted on his dash. Chris Tucker screamed at Ice Cube that Worm was going to kill them for smoking his weed. I looked around and there were tv screens mounted in the back of each head rest also. This nigga was doing the damn thing, I thought.

"I just want to see this part right here, and then I'll be ready," Neon said. He watched another minute of "Friday" and turned it off. "That's my favorite movie. Chris Tucker is a funny nigga," Neon said.

We got out and went inside of Apple Bees and ordered. Neon and I kicked it for a few minutes then he explained how Rome continued to tell him how much coke I was selling for him.

"Since he has been dealing with you, he has made ten times as much money as he use to, " He said.

When Neon said that I knew what was coming next. He wanted to thank me for doing right by Rome. He had went out on a limb to get me hooked up and I delivered! But, that's not what came next.

"I know I told you that Rome was my man, and that he would do me a favor if I asked him to, but the truth is Rome looked out for you because I told him to. He works for me."

I tried to look surprised and confused, but I had already put two and two together. He continued to explain. The way he was sounding I owed him the money for the nine eggs Rome gave me. "So what exactly are you saying? That I owe you for the coke that Rome gave me when I first met him?" I asked Neon.

Neon started laughing like he was still watching "Friday. " "Hell nah, Playa! I don't care about no eighteen ounces. I don't care about eighteen keys," He said.

"Did you say eighteen?" I asked.

"Yeah! Isn't that what Rome gave you?"

"No! He only gave me nine," I said quick on the trigger.

"That petty nigga. He was suppose to give you a half brick. I'll fix his ass. I'm cutting that nigga off from this point on. I'm going to start hitting you off instead of him. And if you like Rome's prices, you're going to love mine. "

Right then and there I realized that if Neon undercut Rome that easy, he would do the same to me. Especially if someone came along and sold coke like McDonald' s fries. But, right then that didn't matter. What mattered is that I wanted my own place and a new car. The Mustang was still my baby, but "Big Fish" didn't ride around in 5.0's. They pushed big expensive whips. Beemers, Lexus' and Benzs'!

"Do you still have my pager number?" He asked.

"Yeah, it's locked in my pager." I pulled my pager off and double checked to make sure it was still there. "Yeah I still have it."

"From now on I'm going to hit you off. I only need nine for a half and eighteen for the whole ones. I don't sell anything under that. What I'll do is give you so many per week and if you need more, hit me on my hip and I'll get you straight. That way you won't have to page me a hundred times a day. The less we meet and deal, the better off we are. "

I understood that, so I shook my head up and down, but I didn't say a word.

"What code are you going to use when you page me?" He asked.

"I'll use code 22," I said.

"If you ever have an emergency, use code 22, with 911 behind it and I'll hit you right back. But, never use 911 unless it's an emergency," He stressed.

Rome had taxed me two thousand on the halfs and twenty five hundred on the whole birds. That meant I was going to make that much more on each sell. I was with that.

I called my homies on the Back Street and informed them that in the future I'd be giving them and only them better deals. They couldn't understand how I got on so fast, and why I was looking out for them the way I was. But, they didn't question it. In fact they loved it. Loved the money they were making. All the bad feelings from the past had subsided. Money! Lots of it, tends to make everything better!

CHAPTER 41

A Week Later

Rome was highly pissed that he had to get his coke from me now. He didn't say anything, but I could see it in his face and hear it in his voice. I still gave him the coke for the same price Neon charged him, before his demotion, but he was still heated like ovens. I had infiltrated his good thing and took over. For a couple of months he was my boss, now the tables had turned. Due to my promotion I gave him his customers back and a few of mine.

I moved to Woodbridge Condos and laced my pad. Neon had a hook up with furniture and big screens tv's, therefore, I put pink and green leather furniture in the living room, with big screens in each room. (I color coordinated my crib with black college sororities) After I moved in I stacked my paper because I intended to pay for my car with cash. I decided that I wanted a new 740 BMW. According to my calculations I would own one in about a week or two.

All of my pictures from the Army, pictures of me and my brothers, books, tapes, CD's and my clothes got thrown away by Lakisha. Priceless possessions were gone forever. All because she didn't want me to move. I wanted to beat her ass for that, but I knew it would hurt her more if I just left her alone. Thus, that's what I did.

Pure Passion's was a strip club that opened while I was in prison. Every swinging dick in Greensboro, High Point, Winston Salem and the surrounding cities flocked to Greensboro's number one attraction. The word on the streets was that every broad that worked there was a dime. If you wanted any play from the dancers, your money had to be long. Until now, I considered my money to be short. But, I was plugged in now. My money was growing daily like the hair on the back of a "Chia Pet." I wanted to go to Pure Passion's as soon as I got out of prison, but I made up in my mind that I wouldn't show my face in the place until my loot was long. And it was long now!

I bought a brand spanking new, 740il BMW from a car dealership that one of Neon's partners owned. I paid cash for it, but put it in my Ole Man's name. Neon's friend fixed it so it would look like my daddy put five grand down and had a monthly payment of five twenty. I took it straight to the rim man in Stokesdale and decked it out with the new Lorenzos and tinted the windows. The next day I took it to Car Toys and let them fill my trunk with some serious bang!

Now, I sat in the big parking lot of Pure Passion's, flossing, talking to Neon, who sat parked beside me in his new 850 Beemer.

I had long money and it was time for me to let my presence be known. And what better place to do it in than a strip club, where everyone thinks they are someone!

When we walked in Neon and I littered the stage with money as Rio, jiggled her moneymaker. From that night on, niggas and dames knew that my money had to be long if I tossed it like I didn't care about it. And it was coming so easy, I didn't care!

Neon and I started hanging daily. We went to the clubs, drag strips, shopping sprees and ho-hopping together. We hung out so much that people, even those that already knew him, thought we were brothers.

I agreed to meet Tone at Gate City Barber Shop. He had a friend he wanted to introduce to me. "This guy buys two and three bricks at a time." Tone said. "He wants to cop one today to make sure it's good product. Just give me a few hundred dollars when I bring him to meet you."

If the guy bought two and three bricks at a time, and I was making twenty five hundred, more than I was before on each one, I didn't care about giving up a few hundred dollars. So I agreed to pay Tone.

Tone pulled up in his Lexus and I walked out to greet him and his friend. He introduced me to "Country" and told me he was from Eden. "He got Eden on lock, " Tone said referring to Country. Country blushed when Tone gave him his accolades. We all discussed a few girls from Eden, then we got down to business. After minor wrinkles were ironed out I told Tone and Country to follow me.

I went to Dee's apartment and served Country. He was skeptical about paying twenty~four G's for a box of Tide .He opened the box and was surprised as I was the first time I opened a box.

Dee was a honey I met at the phone company one day while paying my bill. We both were leaving and I saw her getting into a taxi. I offered her a ride and she said she had a few places she needed to go. I offered to take her whereever she needed to go, and paid the cab driver for waiting on her. We rode to Duke Power, Belk's and Rhodes Furniture and Dee paid her bills. As we rode we got acquainted and we were really feeling each other.

"Feeling each other! You just met her and you were feeling on each other. ?" Hireen asked.

I just looked at him and shook my head. "Ahki, you're tripping, " I said.

"What? You said y'all were feeling each other, didn't you?"

"That means we hit it off, Hireen. Not that we were physically touching each other," I explained.

"Oh. I didn't know. You been feeling on everybody else and their mama, throughout the story, I just wanted to make sure.

Dee was twenty four years old, with two daughters. She worked at New Image Hair salon, but she hadn't finished cosmetology school yet. "I have four more weeks at Carolina Beauty School and I'll graduate. Then I want to open up my own shop, " She said to me.

We rode to Carolina Beauty School so she could pay her last installment of her tuition. While she was inside some girls began to gossip about who she was riding with. "Guuuurl, you're with the biggest "HO!" in Greensboro," One girl said. "Yeah, but I heard he was an animal in bed, " Another girl said. "One of my girl's use to mess with him and she said he doesn't have a problem dishing out those green backs. " "I heard he could eat some cat," An old lady said, who was sitting under a hair dryer. Everyone paused and looked at her in disbelief.

Dee paid her bill and returned to the car. "You're a very popular person, Styles!" She said. "Just about every girl in there has heard about you. Some said I was crazy for riding with you and some said they'd love to be in here with you."

I put the Beemer in gear and hurried out the parking lot. From then on Dee and I became an item. She knew I was a Ho, and a thug, but she was still feeling me. She allowed me to use her apartment as one of my stash spots she felt me so much.

Country was more than happy with my price. It was two thousand dollars cheaper than what he'd been paying. I called Tone in the kitchen before they left and paid him five hundred dollars. He said he had to use the bathroom after I paid him his money. That gave me the opportunity to speak to Country alone.

I walked back into the living room and told Country if he wanted a better deal that he should come to the barbershop the next day. "Don't bring Tone," I whispered.
I thought about it and Tone hadn't sent me a dime while I was in prison. The five hundred smacks I paid him wasn't nothing to me, but I wasn't about to let him eat from my plate again. I had forgiven those niggas, but I refused to forget the past. Besides, I'd learned this was a nasty game. A game of crossing out people. A cut throat game!

Tim was doing a lot better. The move home had lifted his spirits amazingly. He was able to get out of his bed and he was sitting around the house now. And soon afterwards, he became strong enough to ride around with me .The only thing was, he had to bring half of the machines in his room with him, but he could ride around and that's exactly what we did.

I honestly loved working at the Embassy Suites, and everyone there loved me.
I brought breakfast and paid for lunch everyday that I worked, for the people at the front desk and my co-workers in maintenance department. I loaned money to the people in my department and didn't care if they paid it back or not. Twenty dollars here and thirty there wasn't going to hurt me at all. I started to pay Ken for punching my time card for me .I did that because being on a time card, I'd always have an alibi while I did my dirt. I gave him whatever I made on my checks. After I started showing him love like that, he gave me a raise and according to my time card I worked at least eight hours a day.

Neon had graduated from South Carolina State with a bachelors degree in Business Management. He wasn't the average Ghetto Superstar. He learned from college and from his Uncle Roy (whom I called my uncle too) about investing his money. Uncle Roy schooled him on cleaning his dirty money also. Roy was a big time heroine dealer in the Gate City back in the late 50's early 60's up until the mid 70' s. He invested his money in some retirement homes in Greensboro, which made him a very rich man. And even though he spent seventeen years in prison, mostly for drugs, he didn't have to raise a finger now. Neon learned from and capitalized on Uncle Roy's mistakes. He dealt with an eclectic team and cleaned his money as soon as he got it. For the most part he tried to keep a very low profile, but that was impossible for him to do.

Neon was only thirty years old and he already owned seven Subway Restaurants, a rack of houses and he co-owned three Bo Jangles' in Atlanta. He was easily a multi millionaire, but he couldn't break his ties with the tempting streets, so he continued to hustle. His latest project was a club he had bought. I was knocked off my feet when I found out what club it was that he bought.

"Side Effects" had been closed for a while because so many people were getting shot there. Eventually it became just as bad if not worse than Moore's. (The club across the street). The City Board voted to close both of the clubs down. Neon spread a few bucks around and got a permit to open it back up again.

"If you invest twenty thousand, I'll let you be co-owner of the club, " he said after revealing his plans to me. I declined the offer because I knew no matter how much money was spent to renovate the club, it was still going to be viewed the same by the public. It was always going to be Side Effects, and people stopped going to that club before the city elected to close the doors.

Neon was full of advice. He got that from Uncle Roy too. He stressed that I should do something with the money I was making. "You got to invest your loot, playa. Clean it up or those folks are going to be watching your ass. You don't need that and neither do I."

I thought about how I wanted to invest my money. I contemplated saving it and investing into the Subway franchise like Neon, but that would require too much work from me. I even reconsidered investing in the club, but something told me the club wasn't going to be a success. Finally, I came to the conclusion to open a barbershop in Madison. There was only one small shop down there and I planned to open a much larger one. When I shared my plans with Neon he liked them and offered to help me anyway he could.

Also, I learned that Neon had a lot of celebrity friends. Once I popped up over his crib and DL Hugely was there. They were on the phone with Chris Tucker, and I realized why Neon like "Friday" so much. A huge box of clothes were delivered to his house one day, compliments of Karl Kani. He and I went to a Mary J show in the Queen City and she had her bodyguards to meet us on the back side of the coliseum, to escort us inside. Neon stood and talked to Mary J before she performed and afterwards she invited us to travel on the tour bus with her to Tennessee. Whenever OutKast would come to North Carolina, they'd page Neon. We'd take strippers to where ever they were staying, complements of G'Boro's Number One Ghetto Superstar!

After I realized the people he knew in the music business, I knew that me and Mac were going to be stars. With the people he knew, we couldn't miss. It was just a matter of time.

One Month Later

Dee cursed me out for flirting with the tall, slim chick, that lived a few apartments down from her. Sandy was her name and she was eye filling. A few guys that I dealt with in the Grove told me that everyone was gunning at her. That made me want her even more. "She is the Prize Possession in the Grove, right now," one of my partners said. I had to have her just to prove the point that I was "Da Man"

I purchased a spot in the new shopping center in Madison for my barbershop. All the work to set the shop up was conducted by the same guys who worked on Neon's club. Compliments of Neon. It was mid-April, and I planned to open up the first week in May. Country became one of my best customers. He truly had Eden and a few other spots on lock. He bought between ten and twelve bricks a week from me. And he had a partner that purchased about four bricks a week in addition to his twelve. That was great!

My homies from Stoneville were doing their thing also. We got close again, and every now and then we'd get together and blow a couple thousand dollars at Pure Passion's. They never questioned why I looked out for them, but they were very curious about who my connection was. They saw me and Neon together a million times at the track and elsewhere, and they tried to put two and two together. Tone even asked me once, "Is Neon your connect?" If I didn't know how cut throat Neon was and if I didn't think Tone's good coke selling ass would infiltrate my good thing, like I did Rome, I probably would have answered him truthfully. Except, I lied. I'm glad I did because I found out later that Tone was wired up that day.

"Nah, we're just good friends. He doesn't deal drugs anyway. Everyone thinks just because he caked up, he has to be selling drugs. The guy has a college degree in Business and he owns a lot of shit fool, " I said and walked away.

Tim could get around using a walker now. He was back talking shit again and everything! When we rode around he didn't have to bring half of the equipment as he did before. My mom paged me one day and when I called her back I could not believe what she was telling me.

"Guess who I just passed on the highway driving?" She asked excitedly.

I thought she had passed the president or Michael Jackson, the way she asked the question. "I don't know, who?"

"Your brother Tim! He was driving his jeep by himself!"

In the four months that I had been home Tim had made a miraculous recovery. If he wasn't out of the danger zone before, he certainly was now.

Robin called me crying like a baby. Zag had been to court and he was sentenced to seventeen years in Federal Prison. My heart hit the floor when I got the news. I felt sorry for him and her.

"He told me to tell you he was right about your boy Tone. He did set him up, " Robin said.

I only knew one way to solve the problem I was having. I'd heard Zag's side of the story, and now it was time to hear Tone's side. I needed to get him alone and talk to him. I called Tone and asked him to meet me at the Four Season's Mall.

When he arrived, he could sense something was wrong. "What's up Styles?"

"Why do you think something is up?" I said.

"Because of the expression on your face. It's all frowned up," he said.

I didn't say anything else. I motioned for Tone to follow me. I went inside the bathroom and he followed me. I checked in all the stalls to make sure there wasn't anyone else in the bathroom. I faced Tone and put my finger over my lips. "Shhhhh." I said. I didn't want him to make a sound. I pulled my pistol out and pointed it at his chest. I waved the pistol and tilted my head to the right, signifying I wanted him to go in the last stall to my right. Without saying shit, quickly he moved into the last stall. I closed the door and patted him down with one hand while I kept the pistol on him with the other.

"What da fuck are you doing?" Tone asked through clenched teeth.

I didn't say anything until I was convinced he wasn't wired up. "I heard it was you that got my nigga Zag popped. I got the word today that he said he knows it was you for a fact. " I still had the pistol pointed at his chest.

"What! You're crazy as hell nigga! Why in the hell would I do that? He looked out for me when you got locked up. "

I could tell by Tone's eyes that he was scared to death. He knew I was crazy. And he knew I would bust a cap in his pretty boy ass!

He started to name reasons why he'd never do anything as insane as having the hand that feeds him cut off and he sounded convincing. You must think I'm trying to have you set up. Did Zag tell you that too? If that was the case, your ass would be locked up now. I've dealt with you a thousand times since that nigga got arrested."

Tone was right. We'd had numerous dealings since Zag got knocked. I think the money was making me. "Noid" just like it had made Zag.

"He just got busted coming back to meet me. That's not my fault. I heard the Feds had been watching him for a while anyway. That's what they said on the news the night he got arrested. I sat and watch him getting arrested. He saw me and I thought he was going to point me out. I was scared as hell too."

Zag did tell me that the Feds had been watching him for a couple of years.

"It was just bad luck that he got popped when he did, " Tone concluded.

That made sense to me. So I believed Tone. I put my pistol away and apologized to him. He fixed his clothes that I had tugged on, and we both came out of the stall. Neither one of us had heard anyone enter the bathroom but an older white man stood at the sink washing his hands when we walked out. He looked at us in the mirror and without drying his hands he hurried out the door.

I felt bad for questioning Tone the way I did. For more than half our lives we had been friends and now I was tripping. Zag was a good dude, but his word didn't weigh more than Tone's word. To compensate for my erratic behavior and questioning his integrity, I bought Tone some new Air Jordans and the new sweat suit to go with it. He accepted the gifts and my apology.

Not only was I knocking off Brianna at work, but I started to sleep with a few of the housekeepers too. And all of them were married, so I didn't have to worry about anyone of them saying anything to the other.

Ken gave me another raise and he asked me if I knew anyone else "Like myself" who wanted a job. He was trying to get paid too.

Tim and I stayed on the road. He couldn't travel too far, but he rode with me all around G'boro while I did my thing. All he talked about was seeing Pookie. He couldn't wait until he came home. He wasn't able to visit Pookie because there was too much stuff he'd have to take inside the prison. Certain things, such as the oxygen tank wasn't permitted inside.

Tim also told me that he wasn't going to testify against Gerald. He wanted to settle the score himself. "Even if it takes me years, I'm going to make him suffer, like I'm suffering."

"God made us men, but what men do makes them heroes." That's a quote Tim use to say to me. He was a real soldier. He was without a doubt my hero.

A Month Later

Tim had been doing too much too fast. His stomach started giving him serious problems and he was admitted back into the hospital. His intestines started leaking those fluids that were poisonous once they entered into his blood stream. Everything started going wrong!

He regressed to how he was when he first got shot. When I visited him the day after he was admitted he wasn't even conscious. The glow that overcast his brown face a few days prior, was no more. He looked like he was more in the danger zone than ever before.

I opened the barbershop and named it after Pookie. We use to call him "PK", short for Pookie, so I named it PK's Barber Shop. When I told him the name of the shop you couldn't tell him shit! I took pictures of the sign that hung over the shop and the painting on the window (That said PK' s). I took them to him and he showed them to everyone while we were on visit. Bragging that he had his own barbershop. One that he opened while he was locked up. "Big Boy Shit, " He bragged.

I gave Pookie the good news about the shop, but I explained I had some bad news too. "Tim is in the danger zone again, " I said, not making him better than he actually was this time. He needed to know the truth. That news rained on his whole parade.

Not only was Tim sick, but daddy got seriously ill at the same time. He was in Annie Penn Hospital in Reidsville and he was in the danger zone too. One day I'd drive to Baptist and stay with Tim and the next day, I'd roll down to Annie Penn and sit with my daddy. I did this and still hustled like there was no tomorrow. Not to mention that I still worked and finished my community service. In a sense things couldn't have been better for me. I owned my own business, had long money, the best connect in NC and women galore. But, on da flip side things couldn't have been worse. My youngest brother was still locked up, my mom was worrying herself to death and my two favorite people in the world were in the hospital fighting for their lives.
 I couldn't win for losing!

CHAPTER 42

I sat in 539, like I'd paid for the room. I picked up the remote control and flicked through a few channels. Brianna finished washing up and rushed to get dressed. She was ten minutes late from returning from her break already. In the heat of passion my tool belt and radio had been tossed on the floor and somehow kicked underneath the bed. I heard Ken's voice amid the static calling for me. I got on all fours and pulled my radio from under the bed.

"Go ahead Ken. This is Styles. "

"Can you go to channel three, Styles?"

I don't know why he always did that. Everyone who had a radio was going to go to channel three to see what he had to say to me. "10-4, " I said. When I got to channel three Ken asked me to call him in the maintenance shop. I just laughed and agreed to call. He could have asked me to do that on channel one.

"Your mom just called and she sounded upset. She said that you need to get to the hospital. She said that your brother isn't doing good at all, and that you should be there," he said.

Brianna stood by the window and peeked out. "The coast is clear. I'm gone," She said. She slipped out and I got dressed quickly.

Pookie had been approved to be paroled on June 17th. The day after his birthday. That was only ten days a way. In route to the hospital I prayed that Tim wouldn't pass while Pookie was still locked up. All Tim talked about was seeing Pookie and all Pookie talked about was coming home to see Tim.

My hazard lights flashed as I drove like a maniac down Highway 40. I dipped in and out of traffic with nothing but Tim on my mind. I began to cry as I passed cars that wouldn't respect my hazard lights. I steered the Beemer to the far left and right shoulders of the highway, in attempt to gain some time. I felt in my heart and soul that every second counted. I hated every person, in every car, in front of me. I could actually feel my Better Half leaving me. That feeling made me press the accelerator harder. It seemed like the faster I drove the less ground I covered. Winston Salem, never seemed so far away.

When I got to the hospital, I jumped out of my car, neglecting to lock the doors. I ran through the entrance and straight to the elevators. Tim was in I. C .U .The same place he was in when this nightmare kicked off. I pressed the up arrow and waited for the mirror like doors to open.

When I reached the 12th floor, it was like deja vu. Rodney and Ronnie struggled to hold my mom up. She was crying so much she didn't even see me. Jimmy, my step-dad, pulled up a chair for my mom so she could take a seat.

I dashed off the elevator and ran to my mother's side. I knelt and embraced her. Kissing her red face. "Tim is going to be alright ma. You know he's strong," I said, trying to reassure her. But, I had the feeling that wasn't going to be the case.

Tim was a fighter. But, at some point, even the best fighters get worn out. And he was tired! During one of our rides around G' boro, he told me himself. "I'm tired of living like this Lil'Brah," He said simply, and out of the blue. I knew exactly what he was talking about, so I didn't ask him any questions or make a comment. I just left it alone.

"What did the doctors say the problem is? Is it still his stomach?" I asked my mom.

"It's his stomach, but the big problem is his heart," she said peering at me through teary eyes. Her soft voice started cracking, but she continued to talk. "It stopped earlier today and they can't get it beating again. He's on life support."

I got up and rushed to 12 D. I hit the electric door opener, and I listened to the sound the opening doors made. "Shhhhhhhhhh.." I walked over to Tim's bed, that was surrounded by doctors. All of them moved like they were in a life or death situation. Each one doing something that seemed to help the other, but nothing was helping Tim. He lay on the bed with no expression on his face. Tubes ran from his nose, arms and even his legs, but he didn't show any sign of being in pain.

"You're going to be alright Tim," I said loud enough for the doctors to hear me. One doctor turned and looked at me. He shook his head agreeing that Tim was going to be alright. For a moment I stood watching the doctors move around like working ants. Then I pressed the door openers again.

"Shhhhhhhhh" I backed out of the I.C.U. , watching Tim's face until the doors closed, and walked back to the waiting room.

Peachie, my mom's first cousin had arrived, while I was in the I.C.U. She sat beside my mom, clutching her hands. Throughout this entire ordeal she had consoled and supported my mother. She whispered something in my mother's ear that made her smile subtly, as I entered the waiting room. She was my mom's other sidekick.

Two Hours Later

The same doctor who had been working like mad and who turned and shook his head when I told Tim he was going to be alright, walked into the waiting room which was filled with family and friends now. He still had on his latex gloves and the white covering

225

over his nose and mouth. He walked over to my mother and Peachie and removed the covering from his face. "I'm sorry Mrs. Vernon, we did all that we could do."

When those words flowed from the doctor's lips, it was like he was blowing tear gas over the entire waiting room. There wasn't a dry eye in the house! Mama buried her face in her hands and Peachie embraced her. Jimmy ran over and placed his big arms around Mama and Peachie stepped back out of his way. He tried to comfort her, but there aren't any words that can comfort a mother when she loses a child.

Those words that the doctor spoke hurt me deeply. I felt like Tim took a part of me with him. My Better Half was gone forever! I'd never be my old self anymore.

Slow-footed, my mom, myself along with Jimmy and my brothers, walked back to the I.C.U. where Tim's lifeless body rested. As I stood over my brother, tears dropped on his face and a million flashbacks ran through my mind. I bent over and kissed Tim on his lips. I thought about how mama used to make us kiss each other on the lips when we were younger if she'd catch us fighting. It had been humiliating back then. I thought about that as I kissed him, and I wished I could turn back the unforgiving hands of time, to one of our fights. One that mama broke up.

After I kissed Tim, all the love and pain I felt transformed into rage. I turned and began to run out of the I.C.U. When I reached the electric doors I didn't push the square plates on the wall. I couldn't stand to hear the "Final breath" of the doors at that moment. Instead, I snatched the doors open and kept running.

I made it to the fire exit, next to the elevators, before Rodney and Ronnie caught me. I tried fervently to get away but they wrestled me down and held me on the floor.

Tim told me he wanted to settle the score with Gerald himself. "Even if it takes me years, " He'd said to me. Those years would never come for Tim. He'd never get to settle the score with Gerald, so I was on my way to settle the score for him. Everyone knew that!

A warrant was issued for Gerald's arrest as soon as Tim was pronounced dead. An hour later, he was picked up and booked on first degree murder charges. He was more safe in jail than he was on the street. That's how I felt and he probably felt the same way.

I thanked God that I wasn't locked up. I didn't know how in the world Pookie was going to handle Tim's death. I hurt for him. What I feared most missed me, but hit him head on.

Instead of calling to inform him that Tim passed, we thought it would be best if we all went to Durham and told him face to face. My Aunt Puddin called, informed the administration of what was going on, and we all were on our way to Guess Road Prison.

When we all showed up with long faces and puffy eyes, Pookie knew what time it was. He was crushed! Before anyone opened their mouth, he spread his arms and buried his face deep into my chest .He cried and kept asking "Why?" No one had an answer for him. Mom tried to answer him saying that now we know he isn't suffering anymore. That may have been true, but it still didn't explain "Why", and now we were all suffering.

The next couple of days I spent under my mom. I wanted to stay close to her to make sure she was alright. I was numb. The only reason I was standing strong, but somebody had to be. But, that was just on the outside. On the inside I was torn into a kazillion pieces! I couldn't believe that Tim was really gone. Forever gone. I couldn't believe that I wouldn't ever ride down the street and pass him again. I'd never talk to him on the phone again. Couldn't believe that I'd never see him acting a fool at the club, or see him in the mall again. I couldn't picture a family reunion without Tim. The life of all our get-togethers. I couldn't believe that God took him away from me.

Two Days Later

The warden at Guess Road, granted Pookie a three day furlough. He sat beside my mother in a daze. I sat beside him and looked at the side of Tim's made up face. I felt like I was watching a sad movie, starring me.

The funeral home was jammed packed. There were people from as far away as Cali that came to pay their respects to Tim. As people filed by the "body box", to view Tim, conversations of death, that Tim and I use to have, played in my mind.

"I couldn't imagine looking at you in a body box, " Tim said to me once.

"Don't bury" me in a suit that I never owned and don't bury me with a tie on. Bury me in my own clothes, " He said.

I could hear his voice so clear that it was scary. I promised him that I would die before him. "I couldn't stand to see you in a body box either," I had said to him. I sat, upset at him for making me go through so much pain.

I did keep my promise to Tim. He had on some of his own clothes. A pair of his favorite jeans and his favorite sweater.
Through a constant stream of tears, I looked at him and wished that I'd left this world first.

The Following Day

Instead of riding in the big Caddy that the funeral home provided for the family, I drove my own car. Pookie and my two half sisters (my old man's seed's) rode with me. The line of cars with beaming headlights, stretched for at least a mile or more. As we rode, nobody said anything. All of us sat hypnotized by Minnie Ripperton's, Back Down Memory Lane, " reminiscing of better days.

It's crazy the things you hope, wish and even pray for when someone dies. I sat in the front row of the church, this time beside my oldest brother Ronnie. I wished, hoped and prayed that Tim would just wake up. Get up and walk out of the church and leave with me. I couldn't accept the fact that he was gone. I planted my head deep in Ronnie's chest and watched a million feet walk past the coffin to view Tim's body, one at a time. I had tried to be strong, but the funeral broke me down like kryptonite broke Super Man down. I was too weak to lift my head and look at the sad faces that extended their condolences to our family. I cried and cried, until Ronnie's shirt was soaked.

Instead of listening to someone who didn't know Tim well make eulogistical comments, I mustered up enough energy with Pookie's help and addressed the people in the church. I spoke about the conversations of death that Tim and I use to have. I shared with everyone that I loved Tim more than I loved myself. Some of our deepest conversations were revealed that day.

"If I could trade places with him I would. I swear to God I would. Not a day will go by without me missing you, " I said, looking down at my brother. "I'll mourn you until I join you Tim!"

After a couple of minutes of talking I got so choked up that I couldn't speak anymore. Pookie put his arm around my waist and we leaned on each other, softly crying. We both stood there until one of the ushers escorted us back to our seats.

The preacher spoke his peace for a few minutes then the youth choir performed an original song. When they neared the end of the song, the mortician watched as the preacher nodded his head, which was his cue to close the casket.

As the top to the gold and black box slowly dropped, I hated the mortician. He was forever severing Tim's ties to this world.

Friends of Tim's, then joined the mortician in his conspiracy and carried the casket out to an extra clean hearse that sparkled in the sun light. The preacher then gave the ushers a cue, and row by row, we were filed out of the church. Everyone loaded their cars and followed the slow hearse to the gravesite.

Once there, I sadly watched my brother being lowered into the ground. Fed to the hungry earth. It was there that I realized that life wasn't fair. Life often gives dust to a crying man dying of thirst. "Hope," Tim's final companion, forsaked him and left him in 12 D to face death alone. After tussling with death for almost two years, death, The Inevitable. The Invincible, defeated Tim Dawg. Twenty-eight years young. So few were his days. I miss him today more than ever.................

CHAPTER 43

A Month Later

An entire month had elapsed since Tim had passed. I hadn't lifted a finger to do anything. I hadn't hustled or went back to work. Nor, had I reported to Mrs. Braxton. I was thinking that if I violated my parole and probation that maybe somehow I'd end up in the same prison as Gerald. I hadn't even had sex! I was literally sick from missing Tim.

Neon came by the crib daily to check on me. He'd done so religiously since 'Tim had passed. He made sure I had everything I needed and anything I wanted. Neon had been more than a friend to me during this trying time. He had become like a brother to me. Tim's demise created an unbreakable bond between the two of us.

Business was kind of slow at first at PK's Barber Shop, but it picked up after a month or so. Pookie didn't have a barber's license, but he cut most of the heads and ran his house! Working at the shop something was good for him. It took his mind off of Tim, for at least a few hours a day.

There were six chairs in the shop and I rented each chair for a "Cee Note" a week (except for Pookie's chair). The rent on the building, and the other bills combined totaled $470 a month. The first week of chair rental paid the bills for the month. The other three weeks were a nice profit.

I registered for summer school, but I enrolled in different classes than I was taking before I went to prison. Since I had a felony, I couldn't be a school teacher. So, I decided to major in Electronics and Computer Technology. I needed something challenging to occupy my mind other than revenging Tim's death. Advanced Calculus and Statistics was the temporary solution.

Renovations had been underway for a year in Neon's club. Finally, it was completed and opened. His friend who owned the car dealership, Tino, took him up on his offer and invested twenty thousand dollars into the club. Like Neon, Tino was very business minded. He handled all the promotions and advertisements for Club Sensations and all his planning paid off.

The first night "Club Sensations" opened, it was lines, ten times as long as the lines had ever been at Side Effects. I should have known that if Neon, Greensboro's Number One Ghetto Superstar, had anything to do with a club, that it was going to be a success. I don't know what I was thinking about. His hands were like King Midas. Everything he touched turned to gold.

Everyone welcomed me back to work with open arms and full smiles. Brianna and my other married friends were especially happy that I was back. But, no one was as happy as Ken. He hadn't been getting paid since I was absent. "You don't know how I'm glad that you're back. We've missed your smile around here," he said, trying to sound sincere. It wasn't me that he missed. He missed those checks, but they were about to start again.

Extreme smiles and wider arms welcomed me back to the street game. For good reason too. There was a drought all over the country. Only a few people around the Gate City had coke, and Neon was one of the few. Whatever caused the nation wide drought hadn't affected his connection at all.

"He who has the gold makes the rules, that's the golden rule, " Neon said. "We're going to jack the prices up on this yeayo. It's the law of supply and demand. The demand is high, but the supply is low. But, not my supply."

Neon used his college education to enhance his dope game. "Supply and Demand" I'd never heard of such. "So, we're going to charge these fools what we want to and nobody will buck the system."

One And A Half Months Later

Because of the drought I was getting rich! The few people in Greensboro who did have coke, had been reduced to even fewer. But, my supplier was pumping me work like OPEC pumps oil. Without Neon telling me to, I jacked the already high prices even higher when I realized that I didn't have much competition. Just like Neon had said, nobody tried to buck the system.

Well almost nobody. My homies from the Back Street complained, so I taxed them more than I taxed anyone. All because they didn't throw me something to get on my feet when I got out of prison. (I thought I was over those bad feelings, but I guess not!) They were going to have to pay for a long time, or until I decided they had paid enough. From the way things were happening that didn't look like it was going to be anytime soon either, because Geno and Company were still trying to cross me.

Tommy Creadell was the best motorcycle mechanic around. He souped up my new GSXR-1100 and brought it to the track for me to race. I'd set up a race with a guy from High Point, named Peanut, for five thousand dollars. When I got to the track Peanut said he wasn't going to ride his motorcycle in the race. "I'm kinda of sick. I'm going to let my homeboy B-Scott ride for me," He said.

I peeped the game. Peanut wasn't sick, but B-Scott was about twenty-five pounds lighter than both of us. Also B-Scott was one of the better riders at the track. Twenty-five lighter pounds, and a hell of a rider, will may a big difference when it came to racing, so I decided to do the same thing.

"New York" was one of Neon's cousins. (He was really from Mississippi, but he went to New York once for the summer when he was small and he faked like he was from New York every since then). He was half my size and known for his motorcycle riding skills. He was also known to tell amazing fibs! Just so happened, I saw him at John's Curb Market prior to coming to the racetrack. He didn't have a way to the track, but he wanted to come and watch the races. "I heard you were going to race Peanut, " he said. "I'd love to come see you kick that non-riding nigga' s ass." I let New York ride with me and I was glad I did. Now, he was about to do a lot more than watch the race, he was about to ride my bike in the race.

When the bikes lined up, New York gave B-Scott the middle finger. B-Scott shot him two birds back. New York looked over at me and gave me two thumbs up. Both riders revved the bikes up and waited for the green light. When the light turned green, B-Scott got the jump on New York. B-Scott was riding a ZX-ll Ninja, and I thought it was going to be impossible for New York to catch him. He trailed the ZX-ll half way down the track on one wheel. When he sat the front wheel down, he reeled B-Scott in like fishing twine, and won by a half a bike. The crowd went crazy and I sighed with relief.

Afterwards, New York parked the bike and walked around with his tiny chest stuck out, I paid him five hundred dollars for his services and he was elated. The five hundred dollars was burning through his pockets though. He walked in the center of a large crowd of ballers and began placing small bets on the up and coming races.

Geno was the first person who made a bet with him "I bet you fifty dollars that Quayle kicks Hough's ass," Geno said.

"That's a bet," New York said.

New York took Geno's fifty and put it in his shirt pocket. He continued to bet until his bets equaled five hundred dollars. When he was walking away getting ready to go and watch the races he betted on, Geno called him. "Hey New York. Let me holla at cha son. "

New York bebopped over to where Geno was standing, hoping that he wasn't going to renig on his bet. "Yeah, what's up?" Asked New York.

"Check this out. " Geno looked over his shoulders to make sure no one was listening. "I see you're rolling with Styles today. What's up with you and that nigga? Does he hit you off with work or what?"

"Hell nah son. You got me fucked up. I hit that kid off with mad bricks." New York lied so much it came natural to him. But, this time he thought about the lie he'd just told and couldn't believed he had fixed his lips to tell it. But, he'd got started now. Lying was like an addiction to him, once he started he had to continue.

"That's why you don't hardly ever see me down here. I want to keep a low profile. I don't want niggas to see my new cars and bikes. "

New York sounded really convincing to Geno. Just that easy Geno fell for the "Okie-doke". He figured he had lied enough, so he turned to walk a way, from Geno, before he dug a hole that he couldn't get out of. "Hold up! " Geno called out, screaming over the loud roars of motorcycles and race car engines.

"I'm trying to cop a bird from you, if you're the man. I don't need to continue seeing Styles. "

New York had done it. And he knew it! He'd dug himself a hole he couldn't get out of. Even though they didn't act like it Geno and the rest of the gang hated that they had to buy dope from me. They knew that I was taxing them, but they also knew why. And dope was scarce. That they couldn't do anything about. Geno saw New York as an opportunity to cross me and he took full advantage of it.

"I'm trying to get one bird tonight. What's your pager number?" Geno asked. New York patted both sides of his jeans, feeling for a pager that he knew wasn't there. He didn't own a pager. He couldn't afford one. He didn't have a pot to piss in or a window to throw it out of. But, he did have game and a gang of lies. "I don't even have my pager on me. Low profile!" New York said. "Give me your pager and I'll call you around ten tonight."

Geno stopped a cute girl walking by, and borrowed a pen from her and wrote his pager number down on a one dollar bill. He handed the dollar to New York and told him not to forget to page him. Then he turned around and gave the shorty her pen back.

"Write your number down for me baby girl," he said. Without hesitation, she began to scribble her number down for the baller!

A couple hours later I found New York and told him I was ready to leave the track. He was also ready to bounce. He had won most of his bets and he was ready to spend his money. "I'm going to get me some Dro tonight and get high as a kite. Thanks for giving me a ride down here and letting me race your bike. I needed some loot. B-Scott didn't have a snowballs chance in hell from the start. I knew he couldn't out ride me, that country nigga."

From the track all the way back to where New York was staying, we kicked it about the big race. I made him the official rider of my bike when the other rider was lighter than I was.

"Let me bounce," I said, as we sat in front of some girl's house, where we'd been chopping it up for the past ten minutes. New York acted like he didn't want to get out. He acted like something was bothering him.

"Styles, I need to tell you something."

"What?"

"That nigga Geno, I know you deal with him, but that punk ain't shit. He was asking me all the questions about dope and I fronted like I was the man. "

I laughed at New York. I couldn't figure out how anyone would fall for the lie he told. You could look at him and tell he wasn't the man. His Timberlands had to be at least two years old!

"He asked me if I worked for you and I told him you worked for me." He looked over expecting me to respond, but I didn't, so he continued.

"Then he said he wanted to buy a bird from me tonight. He gave me his pager number." He pulled out the dollar bill from his back pocket. He pointed at the scribbling on the bill. "That nigga hates to deal with you. I can see it in his eyes and hear it in his voice," New York said.

I was pissed that Geno was still trying to cross me. Now I was going to make them all pay for him trying to cut my throat.

"What time did you say you'd page him?" I asked.

"Around ten. "

I checked my watch and it was 8:17 pm. "I'll be back over here around 9:30. I'm going to let you make a few G's if you want to," I said to him.

"Hell yeah, I want to. I need some money. "

I rode over to the Grove and found "Killer. " He was a homeless man that I looked out for whenever I saw him. I fed him and gave him a few bucks that he purchased wine with. All of my old shoes and clothes went to him also. He even stayed at my crib a couple of times.

"Hey Styles," Killer yelled. Whenever he saw anyone of my cars he'd come running.

"What's up Old Timer? You alright?" I asked.

"Hell nah! I'm broke and I'm hungry as hell, " he said.

I pulled out a ten and a five dollar bill and gave it to him. "I need you to do me a favor tonight Killer. I need you to be over in Creek Bend around twelve tonight. Just stand at the entrance and wait for me. I'm going to come through and ask you have you seen New York? You say you seen him with a bunch of bags in his car like he was in a hurry. And he left about an hour ago. I'm going to pull off and cone back in about thirty minutes and give you a hundred dollars, " I said.

Killers eyes opened wide. "Ok….Ok…I'll do that. Shit yeah, I'll wait. I'll be there the whole gotdamn night for a hundred dollars!" He was so excited he showered me with speckles of spit when he answered.

"Get there a little early and I'll see you thcn, " I said, wiping the spitballs from my face.

I rode to the Food Lion on East Market Street and bought a box of Uncle's Ben's Rice. The box was about the same size as a kilo of coke, but it was a lot lighter. I took it home and stuffed the box with flour, until it weighed 2.4 pounds, just a little more than a kilo. I wrapped the box in brown paper with yellow tape so it would look like the kilos I had been serving. Then I took a half ounce of coke in a small zip lock bag and placed it in one corner of the wrapped box. Once the coke was properly placed, I taped over it, but I made the corner where the coke was very loose. That way when Geno attempted to open the package, he would go to the spot that was raveled. I looked at my watch and an hour had gone by. I jumped in the car and made my way back to New York's place.

Before I arrived at New York's, I paged Geno and he called me directly back. "What's up, Styles?"

"What's up, Homie?" I said. "I'm calling you because I saw you talking to New York today at the track. When we left he told me he was going to get with you tonight on some business. I'm calling to let you know that he is fronting his ass off. He ain't got shit!"

Geno burst into laughter. "Stop hating on that man Styles! Let him make his money. I found out today that he is Neon's cousin. He is the one whose been hitting you off. He just has a real low profile. You're just hating because I'm getting ready to eliminate the middle man."

We talked for a few more minutes, but I couldn't convince Geno not to deal with New York. Which was my plan! I hung up on him and I started to laugh.

I pulled up at New York's place and he sat on the porch, blowing smoke rings from the bag of Dro he'd purchased. He jumped from the porch and hopped into the car and I drove him to a pay phone to page Geno. Geno called him right back also. New York set it up so that Geno could meet him at 11: 00 p.m., at the Super K-Mart on Battleground Avenue. He was selling Geno his first bird for twenty four thousand. That was four thousand dollars cheaper than my "Drought Prices. "

I knew if I showed up driving New York, Geno and the rest of them would think that I really did work for him. So that's what I did.

I pulled up and before New York got out to do his business with my homies, I told him to wait a minute and let me have a few words with them. I got out and walked over to Tone's van .The door opened and each one of them sat staring at me. Nobody said shit.

"I know y'all think I'm trying to stop this cat from getting money, but I'm not. I'm just letting you all know that this dude has a rep other than racing bikes. He got one as being a habitual liar," I said.

For a second there was silence. Then Tone, the one I thought that was my real friend spoke up. "We got to hurry up, Styles. We've got some people waiting on us."

I turned and walked back to the Beemer with my head down. I opened the door and winked at New York. That was his cue to proceed. He popped out of the car and barreled to the van. He jumped inside and the door closed.

"What's up fellas?" He asked once seated in the van.

Everyone responded in syncopation. "'What's up?"

"What's up with that nigga Styles?" Geno asked. "Why he hating on you?"

New York knew this was going to be the last time he'd ever "BS" Geno, so he iced the cake. "I don't know what's up with that bitch ass nigga. I'm getting ready to cut him off though. Hopefully, I can put you niggas on and have him buying dope from ya'll. You feel me son, " New York said.

Almost everyone in the van smiled from ear to ear after New York spoke his piece. The thought of me buying coke from them was thrilling. Tank set in the back of the van. He couldn't wait to taste the coke. He didn't smile. New York pulled the package from underneath his shirt and handed it to Geno.

"Do you mind if we test it?" Geno asked.

"No! Go ahead," New York said half laughing, insinuating that wasn't necessary. He was nervous as hell, but nobody could tell.

Geno pulled out a small black and silver hawk bill knife. He probed the block, in search of a place to cut it open. His hands stopped on the frayed tape. He made an incision with the razor sharp knife, until he saw the flakes of coke. He gave the brick to Tank and he dug his long nail into the cut. He scooped out a nail full of coke and sniffed with aggression.

"Yep.....Hell yeah! That's the same shit. That strawberry coke. That's the same shit that lying ass Styles had," Tank said.

Geno passed New York a bag filled with cash. "We got to hurry up, " Tone said.

"What's your pager number?" Geno asked New York. New York gave him a bogus number and told him to call him any time.

The van door opened and New York slid out. Tone pulled the van beside my car and him and Quayle laughed and waved at me. Geno opened the door and waved too. They all continued to laugh and they pulled off.

New York got in the car and handed me the brown paper bag. There were twenty four rolls, a thousand dollars each, in the bag. I counted out four rolls and gave them to New York. He cuffed them and thanked me with a bright smile.

35 Minutes Later

Geno paged me ten times in a row. When he got back to Stoneville, he opened the brick and found a half ounce of coke, some flour and Uncle Ben's black face smiling at him.

"Yeah, what's up?" I asked Geno coolly.

"Styles........Where ya man at?" he asked.

"Who?..........Neon!"

"Nah nigga. That little, ugly bitch New York, " Geno said angrily.

"I don't know where he is. I dropped him off at this girl's apartment. "Why?" I asked.

"He got us…………"

There was a brief pause.

"What cha mean he got ya'll?"

"He sold us some bullshit! "

"The shit ain't no good?" I asked.

"Hell nah, it ain't no good. It's a box of fucking rice!"

"What!" I yelled. "A box of rice. I told y'all niggas not to fuck with that kid. You thought I was hating. I was just trying to help your greedy ass out! Hurry up and get back up here and I'll take y'all to where I dropped him off. Meet me at Falonda' s house, " I said to Geno.

Falonda was Tone's sister. I had been knocking her off for a long time, but Tone didn't know about it. I wanted to meet at her house because I knew Tone wouldn't allow any shit to jump off there. I played them like suckas, but I knew they weren't punks. They had a history of being involved in a lot of gun play.

30 Minutes Later

I kept a 10mm Glock at Falonda' s house. I strapped up and loaded one in the chamber. I tucked it in the front of my pants and hurried to the van. The door opened and just like before, in the parking lot of Super K, nobody said shit. I pulled my pistol out and jumped in the van.

"Do you know where Creek Bend is?" I asked Tone, observing the van. Quayle sat beside me with his 45 Beretta in his lap. Geno and Tone had two Glock 40's sitting between them on the armrest.

"Yeah, I know where it is, " He said harshly.

"That's where I dropped him off. He fucks with some broad over there."

I glanced at my watch and it was 12: 10. I hoped that Killer was where I told him to be.

As soon as we turned into Creek Bend, I saw Killer standing against a light pole. We rode past him and I directed Tone which way to go. "Turn left, right here, " I said pointing.

We turned into the "B" section of the apartments and I pointed to an area where New York ' s car was suppose to have been. "There is where his car was parked. I don't know which one of these apartments he stays in."

"Let's just go and knock on every door in the section, until we find out," Geno suggested.

234

We banged on about fourteen doors, and no one knew who "New York" was. "Never heard of em! " One old man screamed and slammed the door in my face. We consolidated at the van and Quayle said something that made a lot of sense.

"He probably got dropped off here and drove to where he was actually staying. It's probably not even down here in Creek Bend."

"You're right. There is no use for us to keep banging on people's doors. These crazy niggas will start shooting after a while. Take me back to my car," I said.

With disappointed faces, they loaded the van. I climbed in, clutching my pistol. Silence filled the van until I broke it. "Pullover to where that old man is standing, " I said.

"Excuse me, Old Timer, " I yelled.

Killer looked over at the van. "Who you talking to? Me! " He asked, pointing at himself.

"Yeah! Come here for a second."

He walked slowly to the van and suspiciously, peered inside.

"What's up Old Timer?" I asked.

"Ain't nothing up. What cha want wit me?" Killer asked, with a disturbed frown on his face. He was playing his role to a tee!

"Do you know New York" I asked.

"Yeah, I know him."

"Have you seen him?" Quayle asked quickly.

"I seen him with a bunch of shit in his car when he was leaving. He was driving like a crazy man. Almost hit me."

"Fuck!" Geno screamed.

"Thank you, sir, " I said.

Killer stepped back as the van pulled off.

"He's probably on his way back to New York by now. I told y'all niggas not to fuck with him. Take me back to my car. "

I acted like I was frustrated and they all acted like the cat had their tongues. Nobody said anything until we reached my car. I clutched my pistol and my eyes danced from Quayle to Tone to Geno. When the van stopped, Tone began to speak. "Styles, I'm going to tell you right now that we think you had something to do with all this bullshit."

When Tone said that, I pointed my pistol at Quayle's head. Then I took his pistol out of his lap and stuffed it in my Pelle Pelle's. Geno froze behind the wheel and Tone's mouth hit the floor.

"Nigga if you think I got something to do with this bullshit, we're going to handle it right now!" I screamed. Doing a damn good job of acting myself.

"Styles, please get that gun out of my face. I don't think you had anything to do with this shit," Quayle cried.

"Me either, " Geno said.

I leaned over to pick up Geno's and Tone's pistols. As I did, the barrel of my pistol touched Quayle s face. "Please Styles,........Please get that pistol out of my face before it goes off," He begged.

I tucked one of the Glock 40's away with the 45 and the other one I pointed at Geno's head.

"I don't think you set it up Styles. I just think you could have told us more about New York." Tone said. He tried to explain the statement he'd made, but I could barely hear him because Quayle and Geno were pleading for me to move the pistols out of their faces.

"Open the damn door for me," I ordered Tone. "When I get out, you pull off or I'll fill this bitch with lead," I said to Geno. "If I see the break lights, I'm going to start dumping and I won't stop until these motherfuckers are empty. " I waved the two pistol around like a mad man. Tone opened my door and I eased out of the van. Before my feet hit the ground, they were out of sight.

That night I learned two things. First, it doesn't pay to think you got all the sense. Secondly, I learned a scared motherfucker follows great orders!

I got into my car and pulled out a hundred dollars from the stack of money that was packed in the brown paper bag. I drove back to Creek Bend and picked up Killer. I gave him a hundred dollars and a bonus fifty for acting so damn good.

"Do you need me to stand and wait for you somewhere else?" Killer asked. "For a hundred and fifty dollars I'll be your own personal actor anytime you need me to be! " 442

"I'll let you know if I need you again, Killer. You did a damn good job though. You could have been like Mel Gibson or somebody, " I said.

Killer wanted to go to John's Curb Market, so I dropped him off there and went home. Twenty thousand dollars richer!

CHAPTER 44

A Few Weeks Later

I pulled into the crowded parking lot of Club Sensations and whipped my new SC 400 Lexus Coupe, (Complements of the Stoneville Boys) into a parking space Neon reserved for me. The twenty inch chrome Anterras, gleamed in the night lights, causing heads to do a double take.

In eight months I had purchased two cars. Two dream cars for some! Both with cash money. My reputation around G'boro was growing also. To some, I was known as Greensboro's up and coming Ghetto Superstar, second to my main man, Neon.

The club was hopping and had been since the opening night. Weekly, the lines to get into the club grew longer. And every weekend Neon and I ended up tricking with some of the finest women in Greensboro. All of whom "Just wanted to be down, " with some real ballers.

Neon and Tino were making a killing. Business was off the hook. Every night when the club closed, I helped count the money that was made. And every night I helped count the money, I wanted to kick my own ass for not investing in the club.

PK's became the hangout for all the young cats and some older ones too, who thought they were young. I added another barber's chair, a few video games and a couple vending machines to the shop. I increased my advertisement in the local newspaper and on the radio. This was Tino's advice and it caused PK's business to triple.

The advanced calculus and statistics was more mind boggling than I anticipated. I hired a tutor to assist me in both of the classes. Vernon Simmons was a math wiz, who majored in Chemistry. He had the ability to explain difficult problems, and make them seem simple. I was doing good, thanks to him and I was proud of that.

Why would I set someone up? Especially if it's someone that's been buying coke from me. You don't bite the hand that feeds you! Everyone knows that.

The word on the streets was that I had my own homies set up to be robbed. Not too many people, if any at all believed it. That wasn't my M.O.S. I was a player, and hustler and definitely a thug, but not a stick up kid.

I called Tone and told him to keep my name out of his mouth. "Tell Geno and Quayle the same thing," I said to him. "That bull shit that y'alll are spreading can mess up my rep. And that's going to cause some problems!"

"That shit is squashed, " Tone said. "We should have listened to you when you told us not to fuck with New York. That fake ass nigga!"

I pulled the phone a way from my face and snickered like Muttley. (From the cartoon The Wacky Racers) "Chi-chi-chi-chi-chi"

We talked and smoothed things out. That was to their benefit though. They needed me now. Although, I will admit to missing the money I made off of them, but I was still getting paid. They were in a slump.

"Shit has been fucked up for us, " Tone explained.

That was music to my ears. He shouldn't have told me that, I thought. Now, I planned to really jack my prices up even higher for them.

"We've only had coke once since the incident," He said.

Even higher now, I thought. The drought had niggas messed up.

"I'm still holding strong. Do y'all need to see me?" I knew it was hard for him to swallow his pride, but he did. Money does that.

"We need to see you today. As soon as you get time for us," He said.
Tone was still working for the Feds. He had the green light to deal with anyone and everyone. He became so use to helping the police that he actually felt like he was a real agent. They even gave him cash to fund certain deals. He put a lot of their money in his own pocket too. He was one of them because he was on their pay roll

A few times in the past Tone tried to make conversation with Neon. He questioned Neon about the prices of different things. "How much did the motor in your blue car cost? How much did it cost you to get your red car running under five seconds?"

That automatically turned Neon off. He tried to be low key and he became leery when anyone who he didn't deal with, start talking about money and inquiring about the prices of his possessions.

"I don't see how you deal with that nosey ass nigga," Neon said, referring to Tone. "He's a snake. Tell that nigga to stay out of my business."

When Neon called Tone a snake, I came to Tone's defense. "He's just a friendly person. He doesn't mean any harm. He just doesn't meet any strangers."

Later on what Neon said made me think. I recalled what Zag said about Tone. Now, Neon was saying basically the same thing. What did they see in a guy that they've known for a short period of time, and I've known all of my life? I asked myself.
I decided that Neon was like Zag. Paranoid! When your money is long, being paranoid came with it. It had to be that!

Two Months Later

The Stoneville Boys got the notion to clean their money. PK's was doing so good they offered me a large sum for it. I discussed selling it to them.

"If your, money is right, you can get it. Just let me think it over for a while," I said to Geno.

Country and I became good friends. He was making tons of cash in Eden and in Log Town, Virginia. In turn, he was making me tons of cash. He made me so much money that I started giving him the coke for almost what I got it for. I charged him five hundred dollars in addition to what Neon expected in return, but everyone else got taxed almost five thousand dollars extra.

I enjoyed my job at Embassy Suites, so much, that I decided to keep working after my parole and probation period. It was a perfect front for my real job. Hustling! Not to mention that I had daily sexual rendezvous. Sometimes two and three times a day. I truly had the world's greatest job.

With Vernon as my math tutor I was doing considerably well in school.

When it came to the honeys, I was doing better than considerably well. I had a long list of prospects who wanted to ride in the Lex and the Beemer or on the back of my GSXR 1100, Zuke. And I had a philosophy. "Ass, gas or grass, nobody rides for free." I didn't smoke weed and I sure as hell didn't need any gas money. So you know what they rode for! The process of elimination is a bitch!

A Few Months Later

The drought was slowly coming to and end. More and more people around G'boro began to have dope. I lowered my prices for everyone including my homies in Stoneville. I had made so much money during the drought that I came up with a slogan.

"Do you want to hear it?" I asked Hireen.

"Yeah! What was it?" Hireen asked.

I took a deep breath and sat up. "I was happy as shit, when the drought hit, so I kept bricks and got rich in 96, " I said.

Hireen giggled. "That was corny, " He said.

I locked my hands behind my head and laid back. I began to reminisce about some wild events that happened in "96. " A unfathomed smile configurated on my face.

"What are you smiling about?" Hireen asked.

"I wasn't smiling, " I said.

"Yes you were. I'm looking at cha, " He said

"Well, it's nothing." I shook my head like I was getting things back in order upstairs. I batted my eyes quickly, and came back to reality.

"It had to be something the way you was cheesing. Your mind was out in the streets. "

"You're exactly right! Way out in the streets, but what I was thinking about doesn't have anything to do with this story, " I said.

"If it's about you it does. You might as well tell me, you've told me everything else."

"I was thinking about something that happened with me and these three fine ass chicks."

"Three! " He said loudly.

238

"Yeah, three! One, two, three," I said holding three fingers up in his face.

"What happened?"

"Do you remember the girl I told you about, Dee? The girl I met at the phone company and then I took her to pay her other bills?" I asked.

"Yeah, the girl who was feeeeeeeeling you?" He said sarcastically.

"That's the one. She had a cousin who knew I was a "Ho" somehow. She tried to get Dee to leave me alone. When I found out she was trying to put salt in the game, I cursed her ass out. Then about two weeks later, I saw her at a gas station. She had two more girls with her that was fine as hell!

"How did Dee's cousin look?" Hireen asked.

"On a scale from one to ten, she was a hundred. She looked better than both of the girls that were with her. All of them were dimes though, " I said.
I was putting gas in the BMW to go to this club in Raleigh called Plumb Crazy's .I acted like I didn't see her, but she spoke to me and apologized for getting into my business. I accepted her apology and was about to leave when she asked me where was I going?

When I told her Plumb Crazy's, her two friends screamed that they wanted to go with me. And as fine as they were, I wanted them all to go. Then she asked. "Can we ride with you down there?" At first I said, "No! " I thought that she just wanted some more bullshit to tell Dee. But, they kept asking to go with me and I finally gave in, and told them they could go. To make a long story short, they smoked weed and drank some White Zinfindale on the way to the club. They were high as the North Star in no time. All they were talking about was sucking dicks and eating pussy. Then they all started talking about how Dee boasted about me eating her out. This conversation went on all the way to Raleigh.

When we reached Plumb Crazy's, it was so packed that no one else was allowed to enter. So, we sat in the car and just bugged out. Then one of the girls said to me, "Styles, if you can eat pussy that good eat this one." She pulled up her mini skirt, pulled off her panties, and threw them at me.

She was so fine I didn't have to think twice about it. I positioned myself and bent over and ate her. Dee's cousin and the other girl was laughing and screaming, asking, "Can he eat some pussy girl!?"

Then Dee's cousin pulled her panties off and said, "If you don't eat this pussy, I'm telling Dee! " We all started laughing, except for the girl I had just finished eating. She was still shaking from her orgasm. I ended up eating all three of them in the parking lot.

"What!?" Hireen yelled. "Dude, you're a freak'n maniac! Then what happened next?" He asked.

"We left the club and went to a hotel room. I let one sit on my face. One rode me like the stud I am and I fingered the other one. We went on all night long, like the Mary Jane Girls! "

"Nothing like that ever happens to me! " Hireen said.

"That's the type of shit that happens to ballers and playa's, not bank robbers, " I said to Hireen.

"What happened after that night?" He asked, laughing at my bank robber comment.

"They told me not to tell anyone, because all of them had boyfriends. "If you tell anyone, all three of us will deny it, but if you don't tell, whenever we want to do it again we'll call you," they all said to me."

"Did you ever tell anyone?"

"Kinda, " I said. "I told Mac and Neon, but I didn't tell them the girls names. Both of them were dying to know. "

"Did they ever call you again?"

"They called me so much that I gave them a key to my condo. This occurred until I got knocked by the Feds."

"What happened......... ?"

I cut Hireen off. If I didn't, I would have spent the rest of the night telling him about my three fine freaks.

"Let me finish telling you the other story first. If I have time, I'll tell you the rest of the story, about the girls." I said.

"Ok......... But, now I see why you were cheesing. It was the bricks from 96, and it was the chicks from 96!"

After almost a year, Mrs. Braxton terminated my parole and probation. Since I paid my fines and fees on time, had steady employment and never tested positive on a urine test, she said I deserved a break. So, she gave me one. Her timing was perfect too.

A few days afterwards, Neon and I flew to Las Vegas, to the Mike Tyson fight. Just when I thought I had an idea of the caliber of person Neon was, he'd do something to amaze me.

On the morning of the fight, Neon was invited by Mike to eat breakfast with him and his camp. "I met Mike at a club in New York once while I was with some of the guys from the group Black Street," He said to me, when I asked him, "How do you know Mike Tyson?"

When we returned from Sin City, we hung out daily. I continued to sell so much coke for him, even he couldn't keep enough of it for me to distribute. Neon had helped me pay for Tim's funeral. When he did that that really made me have respect for him. But, something else happened that proved his brotherly love for me.

It was close to the end of the year, around November of 96. I went home one evening and some young guys that were cousins of one of my neighbors, were out in front of his condo rolling dice. I walked up and asked if I could join the game. They let me join and I, being the cheater that I was would set the dice before I rolled them. My first nine rolls were either seven's or eleven's. In less than thirty minutes, I had three G's of the youngster's cash in my pocket. That wasn't nothing to me, but to those young guys, it was more than half of what they had.

After I won that much. I told them, "Kenny Rogers said, you got to know when to fold em! So, I'm folding. " They got mad when I quit and we began to argue. I walked a way talking shit to them. I pulled their money out of my pocket and waved the wrinkled up bills in their long faces.

After I went inside and took a bath, I got dressed. I came back outside and I was getting into my car and I heard my neighbor call me.

"Hey, what's up Styles?"

"What's happening?" I said.

"Did you get into it with my cousins today, while rolling dice?" He asked.

"I sure did! You need to teach that young punk some respe…….."

Before I could get the whole word "respect" out of my mouth, the youngest boy, whom I'd took about two thousand dollars from, started busting shots at me. My neighbor and the rest of their crew pulled out gats and followed suit. They began to squeeze off rounds and I hit the ground and crawled behind one of my other (better) neighbor's car's.

Obviously they didn't expect me to be strapped. I pulled out my pistol and started returning fire. After I clapped the first three shots, they all scattered, like kids running to get out of the rain. When they bolted, I got up and made a break towards my crib. As I unlocked the door, they started shooting at me inside my condo. I picked up my phone and called Neon. He answered his cell and I told him what was going down. Within ten minutes, he pulled up on the backside of my pad, and eased inside.

The shooters had disappeared by the time he arrived, and one police car was on the scene. The reason there was only one cop there was because there is a Woodbridge Condo's and a Woodbridge Projects, in Greensboro. When the calls were placed to the G'boro Police Department, the dispatcher sent the cops to the projects instead of the condos. Shit like that happened all the time in Woodbridge Projects!

Neon came inside and I briefed him on the situation again, but in full detail. We agreed to wait for a few minutes and go out on the backside from which he came. When we did, we walked right into an ambush.

The youngsters regrouped and expected us to exit from the backside. When we walked out of the rear door, they opened fire on us. Neon and I shot it out with about eight guys, right in front of the one police. Neon's gun jammed after firing about ten shots and he turned and ran back inside the condo. I was trapped outside once again.

The cop radioed for back up, which arrived fast this time. The shooting finally stopped and I high tailed it back inside the condo myself. Neon and I were blessed not to get hit. The other guys weren't so fortunate. One guy got shot in the gut and another one in the arm. The two that got shot, along with two more, got caught by the cops. The other four got a way.

Neon took his pistols and mine and beat feet. He walked out of the front side because all the police were on the backside asking questions. I gave him a few minutes and tried to follow him, but my escape wasn't successful.

I heard another one of my neighbors yell, "There he is! He was shooting. They shot up my new Benz, " He cried.

The police stopped me and asked had I been shooting? I denied the allegations and agreed to let them search my house, when asked. Nothing was found. "I don't know who was shooting, " I said.

Another witness surfaced and said she saw me shooting too. The police arrested me for questioning, and took me down town. They put that shit on my arms to see if I'd fired a weapon and my whole body glowed like a lighting bug in June.

Before I was booked, Neon called Joe Lee, Greensboro's biggest attorney and Neon's close friend. Joe came down town and got me out of jail. He talked to a few people and I was released. I don't know what he said, or what Neon gave him, but I never heard anything else about that charge! Joe had power!

When Neon went to war with me like that, I felt his brotherly love, so I felt loyal to him. There was nothing he couldn't ask me to do for him. That situation really made us like brothers. What he did is what Tim would have done. We'd become like two peas in the same pod, that's how close we'd become.

CHAPTER 45

A Couple Of Months Later

I bumped into the two girls that said they were pregnant by Tim. Together! Before, they were best friends, until they fell out over Tim. Now that he had passed, they resolved their differences and became best friends, again. Even closer now that their children were brother and sister.

I took one look at the kids. I didn't have to study either one of them to determine if Tim was their father or not. They fathered themselves. Strong genes caused that to happen. Tim could have spit them out, they looked so much like him.

I opened another barbershop in Greensboro, and sold the one in Madison to Geno and Crew. But, I still wasn't finished making them pay for what he had done......or should I say, what he didn't do when I came home.

I opened the second shop and told all the barbers to come and work for me in G'boro. "For the first three months you can work there without paying chair rental. " I enticed them all with an offer they couldn't refuse. All of them quit PK's and followed me to PK's II.

When I put out a rumor, that if any barber goes and works for the Stoneville Boys, they were going to have some major problems. After that rumor circulated for a month or so, I sold the shop to them for four times as much as I put into it, and four times the amount I'd made from it since it had been opened.

Two Months Later

For two months, Geno searched for a barber so they could open the shop. They couldn't understand why the shop was booming when I owned it, and now it was like a ghost town.

After eight years of being in love, I got rid of my baby. We had been through a lot together, but it was time for a change. A white guy had eyes for her, so I sold her to him. He offered me a price for my Mustang even I couldn't refuse. I hardly drove it anymore anyway! I hardly drove the Beemer either, now that I had the Lex. So, I sold it also. I had bought the 850 Beemer from Neon. He never drove it! And of course everything was paid for with cash. "If you can't pay cash for it, you can't afford it," Neon use to say. I agreed and adopted another philosophy.

All of my free time was spent in the recording studio with Mac. We became local celebrities in G'boro. Well, I was already one, but his rep was boosted due to his rapping skills. He and I became like brothers too. Mac wanted to get down and make money with me, but I knew he wasn't a hustler. I made sure he was straight though. I kept cash in his pockets and he had spare keys to my cars and condo. If I wasn't driving it, then he could.

Local celebrity status wasn't good enough for me. I wanted to be a national star. International even! I wanted to put the dope down and make dope money rapping. It was just a matter of time before that happened. With Neon's connections in the industry, we were going to blow up big time. He promised. And what ever he promised, you could bank on it.

My daddy and I were already close, but since Tim had passed, we'd become closer. He was deeply affected by Tim's death. Even though I was named after him, Tim was more like him.

During Tim's funeral, daddy was so sick that he just sat in his car on the side of the road mourning from a distance. While Tim stayed at his house they'd developed an unbreakable bond also.

"Sometimes I hear that water machine bubble like Tim is back there getting some water. And one time, I was sitting on the bed and I felt the bed sink down. It felt like someone sat down beside of me. It was probably Tim," Daddy said. He missed Tim a lot. Tim had taken half of him too. So together, him and I made a whole.

Neon and I started to spend a lot of time in Hot Lanta. He had a partner named Paris who co-owned the BoJangles in Atlanta with him and a conglomerate of other businesses. Paris was extra large in the ATL. Every club owner recognized him as a major baller in the city. I learned back in my Fayetteville days, that another way to determine how much loot a nigga got is based on how the club owners handle him. If a nigga got short paper, his ass will be standing in line with the regular Joes. But, if his cheese is long, he'll be escorted to the VIP section on sight. No matter what! And this is how the club owners carried Paris.

It didn't take me long to put it all together either. The way most niggas brown nose around Neon in the Gate City, is how Neon did around Paris. I knew Paris had to be the real Ghetto Superstar!

Six Months Later

I was doing my thing in school. Either I was going to be a rap star, or I was going to have a good "legal " job in the electronics field. Either way I was getting closer to putting down the coke.

Paris got OutKast to agree to do a single with me and Mac. We signed to his record label, "Ice Cold Records" and we were on our way to stardom.

Despite my hectic schedule I still managed to eat lunch with my beautiful daughter a few times a month. I even received the "Most Involved Parent" award from her school. Probably because I was the only involved parent without a real job! But, nevertheless, I didn't miss a field trip or anything she was involved in at her school.

"You keep talking about your daughter but when I asked you before you started telling this long ass story, you said you had a son and a daughter, " Hireen interjected.

"I haven't got to that part. He wasn't born yet. Pump your breaks, I'm about to get to that part now," I said.

When no one would work for the Stoneville Boys, at the barbershop, I offered to buy the shop back from them. The shop had been open for a long time and only one guy cut hair there.

"You'll never guess who?" I said to Hireen.

"Who?" He asked.

"Tank! The coke tester, " I said.

"Dag, they were desperate, huh?"

243

"Actually, he was a barber turned crack head, so he could cut, he just needed a job."

When I made my proposition Geno accused me of sabotaging his business, and he cursed me out. I started out offering him half of what he gave me, but I went all the way up to three fourths of what he paid me. I asked him to meet me at the barbershop so we could talk face to face.

"I'll be down there in an hour," He said.

I messed around Madison for an hour and went down to the shop. Geno hadn't arrived, so I walked up to the Family Dollar Store to get some Charlie's Soap to wash my cars with. As I neared the cash register, I heard the bell dingling on the entrance door. Curiously, I turned to see who it was and it was a girl named Micki.

Micki was from Stoneville also. I knew her, but I hadn't seen her in years. She dated a white boy, who wanted to be black, and moved with him to Charlotte. She'd been gone for more than six years. Everybody use to talk about her because she was so fine, yet she had the nerve to have jungle fever.

When she walked through the door, I thought heaven's bells were ringing. She was breath taking. Her skin was golden brown, like a graham cracker, that had been baked perfectly. There wasn't a hair on her beautiful head out of place. The hills, valleys and every curve on her body was sacred ground. Ground that I'd love to worship. Micki was finer than Janet! A little slimmer than Mary, but she was thicker than Jada! God had to break the mold after he made her.

She smiled at me and obliterated what I thought was a perfect smile. Brianna's smile was no more. Micki's smile replaced hers in the "Perfect Smile" category, in my mind.

"Hey, Dana Styles, " She said sounding less country than most people in Stoneville.

"Hey, What's up? How are you?" I asked.

"I'm fine, " She said. "What about yourself?"

"Now that I've been blessed to see you, I'm doing a lot better," I said.

I eyed Micki from head to toe, back to her breast. She had on a black shirt that was cut into a deep "V" neck. Her breast, real, looked like perfect implants. The shirt was cut above her belly button also, revealing impeccable abs. Her jeans, by D&G, were so tight that I could see her coochie print! And her toes, they were the cutest. She blushed and walked closer to me.

"What are you doing in Madison? I thought you were still living in the Queen City. As a matter of fact, I thought the city was named after you, because you are a queen!

Micki smiled and said, "I moved back home a week ago. I rode down here with Geno to meet you actually. He is down at the shop now, " She said.

"You're dating Geno now?" I asked in disbelief.

Micki was so fine I couldn't picture her with Geno. She was too fine for that clown.

"We've been out twice since I've been home, but there is no commitment," she said.

That was the go ahead for me to ask her out, but to me that would have been tacky. Almost like "Playa Hating " So, I didn't ask her. To be honest, I really didn't get a chance. The bell started dingling on the door again, and when we both turned around, Geno was walking in our direction.

"What's up Styles?" He said, looking at Micki awkwardly. She turned and walked a way. Disappearing down one of the aisles.

"Nothing much, " I said as I paid the cashier for the Charlie's Soap. She took the money and watched the silent drama with pleasure. "Thank you," She said.

"Where Tone and Quayle?" I asked Geno.

"They're down at the shop waiting on you."

We walked out of the dingling door and I looked back just in time to catch one last smile from Micki.

I didn't pay them seventy five percent of what they gave me for the shop. I only paid them a little over half and I gave them a few ounces of coke to make them think they broke even, or at least close to it.

Three days later, I had the barbershop open and fully operational like it never closed.

"What's any of this got to do with your son?" Hireen asked.

"Brother please! Let me finish, " I said.

"I just can't make the connection," He added looking sleepy as ever.

The connection is, I saw Micki about two weeks later, after an OutKast concert. She was with her cousin Wendy and they were on their way back to Stoneville. I was on my way to pick up some strippers that were going back to the Park Lane Hotel with me.

Whenever OutKast came to North Click, they would get in touch with me or Neon and we'd set it out for them, like playa's do for each other. They were at the Park Lane waiting for me to return with the dancers.

"Beep. beep. ...beep. ." "Dana, " I heard a horn blowing and someone screaming my name. I turned Biggie down, and looked over two lanes. That same beautiful smile that floored me in Family Dollar, was taking my breath again. "Pullover Dana!" Micki yelled from her car .

We pulled over at the McDonald's on Lee Street and got out of our cars. Micki was eye candy! She looked even better now than she did a couple of weeks ago.

"I need to get a hug tonight," I said. "I couldn't get one a couple of weeks ago."

When I hugged Micki, she smelled as good as she looked. I inhaled deeply and squeezed her firm body. I looked over her shoulder, down to her ass. Perfect, I thought.

"Where are you going?" She asked.

I explained to her that I was in the process of going to pick up some strippers to take them back to meet OutKast. "You're probably going to get them for yourself," She said jokingly. She and Wendy starting laughing.

"Would you two like to come and meet them also?" I asked.

"Sure, why not," Micki said.

"Hell yeah, I want to meet them. I might be able to hook up with one of them and get paid," Wendy said. And she was dead serious!

They followed me to pick up the dancers and then to the Park Lane Hotel. Once inside the Park Lane the dancers immediately went to work. Dollar bills went flying all over the place. "What's up girl?" Big Boi said to Micki in a country drawl.

"Nothing much, " She said.

"Come on outta dem threads fo a nigga"' he said, blowing smoke like a broken stove.

"Oh no. I don't do that!" Micki responded embarrassed.

"You da finest thing in here and don't want to get naked." Big Boi pulled out a big wad of cash and fanned it in her face.

Wendy was smoking weed with some nigga from Atlanta, who was just down with OutKast. She stood in the corner with him, shaking her ass like she was one of the strippers.

I got up because I had some more things to take care of. I announced that I was leaving and slapped a thousand high fives. I promised Dre and Big Boi that I'd see them when I came to Atlanta or when they came back to Raleigh in a couple of weeks.

Micki got up and walked over to the door with me. "You're not leaving me in here. I'm leaving with you. I don't know these guys and I'm not staying in here with them. I don't care who they are," She said.

"Get Wendy's hot ass and come on," I said laughing at her. "I thought you wanted to get with these cats. You know they're caked up?"

"I don't care how much money they got. I don't know them and I don't want their money."

Micki and Wendy hung out in Greensboro with me and we went and ate breakfast at I-HOP, on Wendover Avenue. After that we went to my house and sat up all night long and talked about the past.

"So, you're use to staying up all night long and running your mouth, huh?" Hireen asked. I paid him no attention and kept talking.

Finally, we all fell asleep in the living room, in front of the big screen tv. Before Micki left the following morning, we exchanged numbers and made plans to go out on a date.

I started promoting a comedy show on Wednesday night at Sensations. So much money was being made at the club, I had to get my piece of the pie. I averaged close to three thousand dollars a week off of the comedy show. Believe it or not, I gave up my job at the Embassy Suits! I had to. I had too much going on in my life.

I didn't give up Brianna though. I continued to see her for two reasons. First, I had some feelings for her. Secondly, I had to continue getting my employee rate whenever I traveled outside of Greensboro.

Ken almost cried when I told him I had to quit. He had gotten use to getting an extra five or six hundreds every other week. (Or whatever he paid me).

Micki and I began to see each other daily. We couldn't get enough of each other. I had her open and she had me turned out, but we both were too afraid to admit it. Geno found out that I was seeing her and his ego was crushed. That was a slap in his face. Once again, I got the up's on him. I had snatched his girl or who he wanted to be his girl.

Four Months Later

Celeste was still down with me. Her family, friends and anyone else who knew us, told her that she was too fine and much too smart to put up with my bullshit. But, love is blind. She couldn't see the forest for the trees. She was certain about one thing though, that if I was faced with an ultimatum, to be with her or Janet Jackson, Janet would be shit out of luck, because I really did love her. But, I loved how I was living too.

Over the years more than a few situations had popped up with chicks giving me ultimatums between themselves or Celeste. And every time, Celeste walked a way with me! Celeste had confronted me in front of a few girls that I was sleeping with too, girls that I claimed to have loved.

"It's either me or her," Celeste said each time. And each time, I professed my love for her right in front of the other girl. I loved her like no other. I was just a "Bow-WOW"!

I thought that whenever situations like that occurred and I declared my love for Celeste, that made her love me even more.

"That was a pretty beef headed thought, " Hireen said. "This girl been through thick and thin with you and you thought dragging her in front of some hoochie you're boning is going to make her love you more, just because you said you loved her? Stupid. stupid. stupid!" He said.

"Well, I was young and dumb, and you know the rest, " I said.

"The Feds surrounded the Back Street and arrested Geno, Quayle, Tank and about seven other do-boys, " Tone said to me calmly.

I was shaken upon receiving this news. Zag had told me horrifying stories about the Feds, and the long sentences they gave out. Stories I didn't pay much attention to before, but now this Fed shit was hitting closer to home.

But, why did the Feds want the guys from the Back Street? Why did they want Tank? He was nothing but a crack head. The theory about the Feds was that you had to be considered "Big Time" in order for them to come at you. Four or five kilos, here and there, wasn't considered big time. If the Feds arrested those guys, then I knew they could get me, because I was a bigger fish! I sold cocaine to them. All types of thoughts raced through my head, that suddenly started to hurt.

"Where are they now? What do we need to do to get them out?" I asked Tone.

"They're all in Greensboro Jail. They don't have a bond right now. We can't do shit but wait and hope for the best."

"What did they get caught with?" I asked.

"All of them had guns first of all, and most of them are already convicted felons. Geno had about twenty five thousand dollars in his car, and Quayle had about a whole brick of hard in his car. The do-boys, had grams, quarters and stuff like that on them. " Tone continued to talk and inform me about the situation. "Geno and Quayle are facing at least thirty years in prison. The other guys will probably get at least ten years a piece. "

"When did you talk to them?" I asked.

"I haven't," Tone said.

"You haven't!"

Tone knew an awful lot without having talked to anyone. I didn't bother asking him how he got his info, but my mind raced even more.

"Where were you when then got busted?" I asked.

"I left the Back Street to go and get us all something to eat. When I got back from 220 Restaurant, I saw the whole Back Street blocked off. The Feds were everywhere. I kept driving passed the Back Street and came straight to Greensboro.

Two Days Later

I didn't do anything but go to school and back home for the first two days after the bust in Stoneville. On the second day Geno called me. Since the Micki situation, our dealings had become strictly business. Very limited! But, this was a very serious situation and that petty crap had to be tossed aside.

"I might need some help paying an attorney," Geno said. Before I had a chance to answer he was talking again. "They tried to get me to say I dealt with you. I told them we were just homies."

Quayle was in the same cellblock as Geno. I talked to him to make sure he was ok also. Before he hung up he said the same thing as Geno. "I might need some help paying for an attorney too. "

Six months ago Zag warned me about the Feds. He told me to stop dealing with the Stoneville Boys. He told me to stop dealing period! But, I had to make the money. "There are people in here that didn't get caught with shit. They got arrested because other people told on them," He'd said to me.

Now, more and more I thought about that. Zag's advice was haunting me. I couldn't hardly sleep for thinking about all he'd said. I hoped and prayed that what he said wasn't true.

Geno had a 1995, Pearl white, 300 ZX, Twin turbo, that he needed to sell. He had more than $8, 000, in the engine and suspension, and bout the same amount in the stereo system.

"Just give me ten thousand for it and I'll be straight. I'm going to put that with the money I have for an attorney. "

I took the money to Geno's sister the following day and picked up the car. I even told him when he came home he could have his car back, in hopes he kept my name out of his mouth.

Manny was on the Back Street when the big bust went down. He had come from Eden to cop a half a key from Geno and got caught up. He was the only one out of the crew that got a bond.

"They didn't know anything about me. Geno and them had been under investigation for a few years," He said. "But, not me. Geno told me that you could get me straight. He called me yesterday and gave me your number."

I listened to Manny and something didn't sound right. He was talking too fast or something. I hadn't ever talked to him, now he was telling me that Geno told him to call me about some work. I knew that was a lie. Geno knew how I was about the phone.

Suddenly, Manny said, "I need two keys of crack!"

I had learned years ago that you don't talk business over the phone. And if someone did it was because they were trying to have you set up.

"Nigga, I don't sell no fucking drugs!" I yelled and slammed the phone down.

The Next Day

I informed Neon that I was going to lay low for a while. After I explained why, he co-signed my suggestion. "Just chill and concentrate on school. Let the smoke clear. You've stacked enough paper to chill for a while," He said.

Four Months Later

The smoke had long cleared and I was moving and shaking again. If the Feds didn't come for me by now, then I knew they weren't going to come.

My homies had kept my name out of their mouths and Manny's rootless attempt to set me up had failed. I figured the Feds were leaving me a lone. I was too clever to get caught anyway! That proved my point. You had to get caught red handed before the Feds rolled on you.

Micki was three months pregnant and tripping. When Celeste found out Micki was pregnant, she tripped out like never before. She had reason to trip though. For years we had been together and I put her through "pure-d-hell". While I was in Dessert Storm, she waited for me faithfully. She wrote me everyday for eight months. When I got out of the Army all the promises I made from Saudi Arabia were broken. Shattered! I ran buck wild after everything that had on a skirt! Then for years I thought I was showing her how much I loved her, but I wasn't showing her love, I was humiliating her and I was too stupid to realize it. When I was locked up she visited me weekly, because she loved me like no other. And how did I pay her back for staying down with me when I came home? I couldn't control my dick and got another woman pregnant! She couldn't take it anymore.

"I love you Dana, but you've hurt me for the last time, " She cried.

CHAPTER 46

While I was in Club Nikki's one of Atlanta's hottest strip clubs, throwing away money and trying to trick with the gorgeous dancers, Micki was being rushed to the hospital. She was only six months pregnant, but she had went into labor.

My mother paged me and told me that I needed to get to the hospital as soon as possible. And as soon as possible was going to be at least the next day.

The Following Day

When I arrived at the hospital, Micki had given birth to my son. He was only two pounds and eleven ounces. He was definitely in the danger zone. His small, red body looked like it could fit in the palm of my hand. Tubes, IV's, and other machines were hooked up to his little body. It hurt me to my heart when I saw him like that. It made me automatically think of Tim.

The name Chandan was written on a piece of paper and stuck to the incubator, in which he lied. I looked around at the other new born babies and read the first and last name on each incubator. Micki noticed me observing the other names and she spoke. Almost like she was reading my mind. "If your ass wouldn't have showed up today, I was going to give him my last name instead of yours." She rolled her eyes, too exhausted to fuss with me. She had just given birth, yet she was still breath taking, I thought.

"If he was my son you would have named him after me," I said to Micki. I was starting some shit because I knew Micki was too weak to argue.

"Where in the hell were you last night?" She asked. Her scratchy voice grating against my ear like sand paper. "Probably out fucking some skank ho, while I'm in here giving birth to your son." She wasn't that exhausted.

"You was only six months pregnant, Micki. How in the hell was I suppose to know you were going to go into labor? Most women carry their loads for nine months, " I said holding up nine fingers.

A Month Later

I hit my breaks after Chandan was born. I didn't have a choice. He was fighting hard for his life. Most of my time was spent between A&T and the hospital. I'd go to school during the day, then I would leave school with my laptop and all my work and head straight to the hospital.

On and off, I had completed three years of college. I could see the graduation light at the end of the tunnel. The fun and games were over for me as far as school was concerned. I wanted to graduate! I didn't see anything else but the light.

Well, that's kind of a lie. Occasionally, I still got with a "phat" Aggiette. But, I knew with a degree in Electronics and Computer Technology, I could lay the dope down forever. That's what I really wanted to do. With two kids, that's what I had to do! And with everyone around me going to prison that's what I planned to do.

A Couple Months Later

Celeste became very distant. I wasn't really tripping though, because she wasn't seeing anyone else. That's all that mattered to me. She knew that I still loved her with all of my heart. Plus, she confronted me in front of Micki and as always I told her that I loved her more than anything in the world. She was just bent out of shape because Chandan was born. Her family and friends really encouraged her to move on after that. I tried to keep her close, but I was smart enough to give her some breathing room.

Geno was sentenced to twenty-two years. Quayle got knocked in the head with twenty seven. Tank and the other do-boys, got nothing less than ten years. My heart ceased upon receiving the terrible news. I hated that with a passion, but I was glad it wasn't me!

After I got wind of their long sentences, I solemnly promised myself that after I peddled the coke I had in my possession, I was going to get out of the game for good. That was my word to my damn self! I wasn't going to wait until I graduated. I had a clearance sale on the coke I had stashed. I wasn't concerned about making much profit, I just wanted to get rid of it. I called Country and told him what I was doing and he wanted a few of them, he said. He came from Eden to pick up three kilos. When he got there we discussed the drug bust that occurred in Stoneville. We both agreed that something was fishy about Tone. Country then told me something he should have disclosed to me a long time ago. "I heard Tone got a few people set up in Log Town, VA. Rumor is, he's been working for dem folks for a while. I wanted to tell you, but I knew that was your nigga," He said.

While Country and I were talking about Tone, he paged Country. "Damn, that nigga must hear you talking about him," I said.

"I talked to him earlier today and he said he knew some guys from Charlotte that was looking for some work. He even said they're still paying drought prices. "

I saw the dollar signs in Country's eyes. All that shit he'd just talked about Tone being the police and he was still going to deal with him. Just to get those few extra dollars. Greedy, dumb ass nigga, I thought.

I started not to sell the three bricks to Country because I knew he was going to sell them to Tone. In a way I was setting my ownself up for the downfall. But, I wanted to get rid of the coke. Greedy, dumb ass nigga, I thought about myself.

"He said he paged you, but you didn't call him back, " Country said.

"I didn't get his page, " I responded. I lied! Tone paged me five consecutive times, but I didn't nor was I ever going to call him back.

I sold the rest of the coke and called Neon. I told him I needed to sit down and talk with him. We went to eat at the House of Prayer, a huge church on East Market Street, that had an enormous cafeteria in it. Neon's favorite spot to eat in Greensboro.

We both ordered the mouth watering, macaroni and cheese, but different side dishes, and began to talk. "I sold my last gram of coke today, " I said. "Niggas are getting busted and they're dropping like flies. The Fibbies are giving out so much time that it isn't funny. I'm going to finish school and continue promoting the comedy show. Between the comedy show, and the barber shops and your deep pockets, " I smiled, "I'll be straight. "

Neon understood where I was coming from. He even admitted to feeling some heat. Joe Lee, his powerful attorney friend, had told him the day before that all eyes were on him also. "They're watching your ass with a million eyes," Joe said to Neon, referring to the Feds. So, Neon was feeling where I was coming from.

As we ate and talked some more we watched the local news on the tv, that hung over our table. The weather was going to be wonderful the entire weekend. The extended forecast was the same all the way through the next weekend, which was Bike Rally Weekend, in Myrtle Beach. An event that Neon and I loved equally. There was a bad accident on Holden Road, and the Greensboro Bats had won their last eight games, the newsman reported.

"I'm thinking about getting Bruce-Bruce to come to the comedy show and perform. You know that's my partner too, don't you?" Asked Neon.

I shook my head up and down, not surprised that Neon knew Bruce-Bruce, but I continued to watch the news. Nothing in the world could have prepared me for what was about to be shown on the screen.

I saw a brown leather bag on a round table with guns, three kilos of coke and a stack of money. Three black guys covered their faces with their t-shirts as the police walked high and mighty, around the table pointing at the contents, then pointing at the guys .

I dropped my fork covered with macaroni, in my lap. "Oh shit!" I said loudly.

"Man, we're in a church, " Neon said looking around at the old faces that stared at us in disgrace. I didn't care though. I couldn't see the t-shirt, covered faces, but the brown leather bag belonged to me. It was a bag I brought while I was in high school. I used it in college now. It was my favorite bag. Country had needed something to put his coke in and I let him use my bag because he promised to bring it back the next day.

Two Days Later

Chandan was doing much better. In four months, he gained seventeen pounds. He was eating like it was going out of style too. Micki and I were getting along, but we were not the love birds we'd been ten months ago. We still had each other open, but still wouldn't admit it.

It was taking me longer than I thought to smooth things out with Celeste. Having another kid with someone else, after she'd stuck by me was too much for her to forgive. It was the straw that broke the camels back!

I changed my cell phone and pager numbers. I didn't want Tone to have anyway to contact me. Then I got up the nerve to call Country's mom. I gave her my new numbers and asked her to call me on three-way when Country called her. I wanted to help him anyway I could. I wasn't worried about him telling anything on me. We were too close for that. I wanted to help him because that's what real friends are for.

Two Days Later

Country called me finally. He told me what happened when he got busted.

"I was on my way to meet Tone. He had the police waiting for me at Winn Dixie. I was stupid for fucking with him. We'd just talked about that hot ass nigga too, " Country said. He added that he didn't need anything. His sister had hired and paid an attorney already. "I'll let you know if I need anything, but I should be ok. "

Country sounded too cool on the phone. That befuddled me. Country was the quiet, scary type. Something of this magnitude should have scared the shit out of him. Especially after seeing what happened to Geno and Quayle. But, he was cool. I'm his partner. "Why shouldn't he be cool," I thought. I was getting very paranoid for nothing.

Bike Rally Weekend

Mac and I finished our masterpiece. An eighteen song CD entitled, "Somebody's Gotta Die." Of course we were talking about Gerald's bitch ass, and we dedicated the CD to Tim Dawg.

Dakim, a friend of mine from college, and I loaded the Lexus with CD's and Mac and three strippers, whom I recruited to help sell the CD's, loaded the 850 in route to Myrtle Beach, South Carolina.

Once we got there I really couldn't enjoy myself. I continued to think about Country, Geno, Quayle and the other ones who had gotten locked up. Zag's advice about Tone haunted me too. I waited for someone to come up and tap me on the shoulder. "Excuse me, are you Dana Edward Styles III?" They'd ask.

"Yes I am, " I'd answer. "You bought my CD and you want my autograph, right?"

"No! I'm agent so and so, and you're under arrest.

I was just paranoid! Finally, I told Dakim that I'd seen enough of the Bike Rally. "I'm ready to bounce back to Greensboro, " I said to him. I knew he was having the time of his life, but he acted like he was ready to go too. I hated to be the one who spoiled the party for him, but my mind wasn't at the Bike Rally, so there was no need for my body to be there.

I went to Pookie ' s room to let him know that I was leaving. That's when my cousin Tina showed up and introduced me to Nina. They were ready to leave the Bike Rally also. We coupled up and rode back to Greensboro together.

Two Months Later

I finished summer school and only had twenty-two more hours before I graduated. I sold both barber shops, the 850 Beem, and the 300ZX. I liquidated my possessions

252

because Nina and I planned to open a group home for kids with behavioral problems. She loved kids like myself and wanted to do something to help them.

The house that I was going to buy cost $144,000, and of course I was going to pay for it in cash. Neon, the "Hook up King" had a friend who owned a real estate company. He agreed to do the deal under the table for me because I was a friend of Neon's.

The house could accommodate five kids. Each kid would be worth, the minimum of $4,500, a month. It wasn't coke money, but it was legal money and enough for me to live comfortably.

It had been some time since Geno and Company got knocked, and two months since Country's empire fell. I made it my business to keep in touch with them. That way I was sure they weren't going to rat me out. Hell, I really didn't care now. I was living drug "dealing" free. Since I wasn't hustling anymore I was out of the danger zone. I knew I couldn't be locked up if I wasn't doing anything.

Also, I was ready to settle down and be a real man. Things were coming together in my life and…..

"Wait a second, wait a second! What did you just say? You settle down! Mr. Don Juan himself, " Hireen said. "You'd die if you settled down. "

"Are you going to let me finish? I'm almost through," I said.

I wanted to settle down. Lucky for me, Celeste and I were getting close again. I done a lot of ass kissing, but we were on the verge of working things out.

Micki had my son. It would be nice to raise him like he needed to be raised. With his mother and father in the same house. Married not just shacking up.

Nina and I clicked like clock work from day one. For two months we had seen each other almost daily. I was still infatuated by her intoxicating green eyes.

Aeisha wasn't out of the picture either. Neither was Jegbadia. But, then there was Clovia. She was very….

"Hold up again, " Hireen said quickly, holding up a finger. "Who in the world is Clovia. I've heard of everyone except her."

I had met Clovia three weeks before I got arrested. Our paths crossed at Sensations one Wednesday night. She came to the comedy show and a mutual friend introduced us.

"What did she look like?" Hireen asked.

"Ah man. She was gorgeous! She put you in the mind of that broad Mike Tyson married. The one who took his cheese."

"Oh,oh. ..Robin, what's her name?"

"Givens, " I said. "Yeah, Robin Givens, but she looked better than Robin."

The day after I met her, I stayed with her every night, up until the day I got busted. She had just graduated from A&T, and she was getting ready to move to Atlanta, to start her career in engineering.

"So she's down here now?" Hireen asked.

"Yeah, she came to see me a few times."

"Why were you thinking about settling down with someone you just met?"

"It was something about her! During those three short weeks we bonded faster than I bonded with any woman. Including Celeste! We just seemed to be right for each other, " I said. "There were some others who were in the running to become Mrs. Styles, but I haven't mentioned them, so I won't mention them now. But, I was ready to settle down."

"Yeah right! You just named fifty women you were sleeping with, and oh yeah, in love with, but you were ready to settle down." He shook his head. He couldn't believe that I said I was ready to settle down.

"So you stayed with Clovia the night before you got arrested, and then you went over to. ..." Hireen paused and closed his eyes. He was trying to remember a name from my long list of lovers. "Let me see…. Sandy! Right?" He said, snapping his fingers.

"Yeah, " I said. "I stayed with Clovia and got up early because I had an 8:00 a.m. class. I went home showered and dressed and headed for campus. On my way to class guess who I saw for the first time in a long time?"

"Who?" Hireen asked.

"I saw Tone. I hadn't seen him in a while. Now, all of a sudden he was riding behind me in his new Benz. It spooked me too. I wanted him to pull over because I had some questions for him. Although, I already knew the answers to them. I knew he was the police. I knew he'd had everyone from Zag to Country set up. I wanted to know why he saved me? I wanted to bitch slap him!

I stuck my arm out the sunroof and pointed to the Krispy Kreme's parking lot we were quickly approaching. He stuck his arm out his sunroof and pointed to the parking lot too. I slowed down and turned in, and Tone slowed down like he was turning into the lot also. But, he didn't! Instead of turning in, he mashed out!

When he did that, I knew without a doubt in my mind that he wasn't right. Here is this guy, that I've known all my life. Since we were knee high to a duck's ass, and he wouldn't stop and talk to me.

I went to class and stayed on campus until 11: 00 a.m. When I got out of class at 11: 00, I was dog tired and hungry as a hostage, from sexing Clovia all night. I drove over to the House of Prayer to get something to eat. I had another class at 11: 50, so I had to hurry up and eat and get back to campus.

When I walked into the House of Prayer there wasn't anyone inside, except one old man. He sat all the way at the back of the cafeteria watching one of the tv's hanging from the wall. He turned around when I walked in and we smiled and waved at each other.

"What time do they open young fella?" He yelled.

I walked towards him so I didn't have to yell back. "I don't know sir. I thought they were opened already," I said. I looked behind the serving line and through the windows on the swinging doors, and I didn't see a soul, "You'd think someone would be in here. Someone could come in here and take those pretty tv's and anything else they wanted right now, " I said. I walked back to the table where the old man was sitting and copped a seat across from him.

"You're not going to find to many people stealing from a church though," he responded.

The old man was dark skinned. Almost blue he was so black. He had a long silver beard that connected perfectly with his mustache and goatee. His benign old face was veiled with netted wrinkles. He looked like a black Father Time! Yet his eyes were youthful. Snow white, with sable pupils that examined me as I sat down.

He smiled again, revealing a mouth full of white choppers. I couldn't tell if they were real or false teeth. He closed his mouth too fast.

"You're right sir. I don't think too many people will steal from a church. I hope they hurry up and open," I said in the same breath.

I checked my watch and it was 11:12 a.m. If they opened at 11:30 I would have twenty minutes to order, eat and get back to campus. If they open later than that, I was going to be hungry! The problem was, we didn't see anyone to ask what time they opened.

"Do you usually come up here this early?" The old head asked.

"No sir. I usually come up here in the evenings. I was in class, " I turned and pointed towards A&T, because the college is directly across the street from the church. "And I got hungry, so I decided to come over here and grab a bite to eat. "

"Oh, you go to A&T?"

"Yes sir. "

"What's your major?"

"Electronics and Computer Technology ."

"What's your classification?" He asked.

"I'm a senior. I only have twenty-two more hours before I graduate, " I said proudly.

"Do you believe in God?" The old man asked me unexpectedly, his black eyes looking deep into mine. The question caught me off guard. I instantly thought about Yahya. I hadn't talked to him in a while. I needed to be getting myself together! Yahya asked that question once. Then I thought about the times I'd been to a mosque since I had been home from prison. I could count them on one hand.

"Yes sir, I believe in God. The One God. The Creator of All Things. I believe in Allah!" I said. (Based on how I'd been living, you couldn't tell.)

He shook his head. He was familiar with Islam. I could tell because he didn't look confused by my response. "Do you believe God has a perfect plan for you?" He asked.

"Yes sir, I do."

"Do you know what your calling is?" He asked.

"Yes sir. I think I know. "

The old man was asking a lot of questions, but it didn't bother me. I loved to sit and talk with old heads. I picked up all the jewels they dropped.

"Can I see your hand?" He asked.

When Father Time asked me that, I thought "This is about to get real funny! "

"I'm going to tell you what your calling is," He said.

I stretched out my arms, palms up. His crinkled hands covered mine. His four knuckles looked like small, dusty pitchers mounds, blanketed with scratched skin from decades of fighting. His palms were rough too. Evidence of seasons of hard work.

He gripped my hands tightly and closed his eyes as if he was reading my mind. He jerked like a bolt of electricity had jolted him. My calling was dealing with troubled youths. That's what I felt it was.

Nina and I were closing the deal on the house the following day for the group home. I couldn't wait to start helping the kids. I couldn't wait to educate them about the perils of the street. I wanted to have a "Say No To Drugs" class. Especially since I wasn't dealing anymore. I'd come a long way. A lot of my friends waited too late to get out of the game. I was blessed! I beat the odds. I got out before I got locked up or killed and now I planned to prevent it from happening to the youth.

He released my hands and opened his eyes. Then he slid his chair closer to mine and showed his teeth again. False! Too straight to be real, I thought.

"Your calling has something to do with today's troubled youth, " He almost whispered.

I was stunned when he said those words. "You're right!" I said all fired up. "I'm closing on a house tomorrow that's going to be a group home for troubled kids."

The old man shook his head from side to side. "No...No That's not what I'm talking about. It's a lot deeper than a group home. A lot bigger. Something that's going to reach the masses. Something big is about to happen to you. It's going to change your entire life. Then you're really going to be able to help the kids, " He said.

A small framed lady walked out of the swinging doors, behind the serving line and smiled and spoke to us.

"What time do you all open. " I asked.

"We open at twelve, " She said.

I looked at my watch and it was 11:28. I had to get back to campus for my 11:50 class. "It was a pleasure talking to you sir. I'll probably see you up here again soon. "

The old timer smiled and nodded his head. I turned and walked towards the door. When I pushed the door open the old man yelled, "That's why I came up here this morning. I realize it now. God wanted me to tell you something was bout to happen to you. Something real big. I usually don't come up here in the morning, but God told me to come this morning. You better get ready!" he said.

I didn't know what to say so I didn't say anything. I just nodded my head like he'd done and I let the door close. I wanted to laugh at the old man but something inside of me wouldn't allow me to laugh. Honestly, I was kind of spooked. I walked to my car thinking how strange the past seventeen minutes had been. I'd been spooked twice in one day, I thought.

I left the House of Prayer, still hungry and went to class. Unable to concentrate, I sat in the front of the large classroom looking down the instructor's throat. I was trying to figure out what was going to happen to me that was going to be so big? Father Time had me sitting in class tripping!

Maybe my CD was going to take off and I was going to become famous. My lyrics were conscious lyrics....well some were. Maybe the group home was going to be a major success. Nah. He said it was deeper than the group home. I thought of a lot of stuff that I wished would happen. Then I reflected on our entire conversation. I realized, Father Time never said that the "Something" was going to be good!

Needless to say my mind became swamped with bad thoughts. But, what happened never crossed my mind.

"When I got out of class I told you I went to Sandy's apartment." I said to Hireen.

"You never said how you got with Sandy though, " Hireen said.

"She lived down the sidewalk from Dee. Eventually, Dee and I feel out because I kept flirting with Sandy every time I saw her. So I left Dee alone and starting messing with her."

"So Sandy thought it was Dee paging you but it was Nina?" Asked Hireen.

256

"Yep! It was Nina. She was trying to tell me the Feds were looking for me. If I would have just answered my pager! "

CHAPTER 47

I was taken to some old building down town. Black and blue unmarked cars dressed the parking lot in unflawed formation. Slowly, I looked around. I'd passed by the building a million times and hadn't ever noticed the cars.

"Maintain your cool, Rock., " continued to play in my mind. A part of me was still scared as hell, but the other half of me was calm as a mill pond. For good reason too.

When the Feds ambushed and kidnapped me, they didn't find anything. They ripped Money apart and searched Sandy's apartment. Still, they found nothing. To top that off, the Head Nigga In Charge had the nerve to ask me for permission to go and search my place.

"You can snatch me off the streets for nothing, but you have to ask to go and search my house? Hell nah, you can't go and search my fucking house," I said.

For about fifteen minutes the agents drilled me with simple questions. "Do you know Tone and Geno?" Do you Quayle and Barry? Oh, you probably call Barry, Country," One of the agents said.

"Yeah, I know them. I grew up with them all except for Country. I know him from Piedmont Drag Strip."

"Did you forget something? Like you use to supply them with kilos and kilos of crack?" Another agent asked.

"Nah, the hell I didn't. I haven't sold drugs since 94. And I went to prison for that petty bullshit!"

I didn't care if the agents knew I sold drugs back in 1994. That was four years ago. I'd done my time for that crime already. I wasn't an attorney but I knew enough about the law that those charges in 1994, couldn't be used against me again.

"Do you know how much time Geno and Quayle received? Do you know your friend Country is facing more time than they got!?" An agent yelled at me, trying that same t.v. bullshit to get me to talk.

I knew exactly how much time Geno and Quayle received, and I knew how much time Country faced. I was helping them all in one way or the other. I denied knowing anything about anyone of them though. But, I also knew that they all had one thing in common. Including Zag. The all got popped in possession of drugs. I didn't.

"We're going to take everything you own, and anything else that you may have your dirty hands in," The H.N.I.C. said. "Like Club Sensations. We're checking as we speak to see if your name is on any of their papers." The H.N.I.C. paused. Then he confirmed the rumor, and reason I was there.

"Unless you do like your homeboy Tone is doing and work for us!" He might as well had cuffed me behind my back and let Mike Tyson hit me right in the kissers. I was out cold!

Zag and Neon had been right. Tone was a snake in the grass. I never saw it in him and I'd known him for years.

"Man, fuck you house nigga! " I said. I was more mad now than scared. No wonder Tone wouldn't stop this morning, I thought. He had flipped on me too.

That "Fuck you house nigga," rolled right off the H.N.I.C. He paid no attention to me and continued to talk. "If you can call Neon right now and get him to meet you with a package you won't do a day in jail, opposed to doing life. Look at Tone. He hasn't done a damn day. He got popped months and months ago and he is still in the streets. Even if you can get Neon to mention anything about drugs on the phone, we'll take care of you when you go to court." The Head Nigga In Charge talked long and fast. I couldn't believe how much shit he'd just said in one breath. He was high-strung about the possibility of me cooperating with his team.

"You didn't hear me the first time Billy D? Fuck You! " 'I screamed.

The other agents found it funny that I called their boss, Billy D. They made small jokes about the statement, until, Billy D, grilled them.

"Neon doesn't sell drugs fool. I don't know him like that. We're not that close. " I said.

"'Nah! I know you two are like brothers," he said without even thinking. "We know he owns a lot of shit too. We're just not sure of how much shit. We may be able to work something out so you can get some of his shit if you only cooperate. You're the closest we've ever been to him. Set him up and we'll put you on the pay roll. Just like Tone!"

My stomach turned. I felt something thick beginning to climb my esophagus, but I managed to keep it down. What I was hearing was making me sick.

"I want to call my attorney, " I said.

The agents laughed in unison, like I had told a joke, when I mentioned "attorney". One of them got up and left. He returned with an old black rotary phone. He slammed it down in front of me so hard I heard the ringer inside.

"Dinnnnnnnggggg."

"Who is you attorney?" The H.N.I.C. asked.

"Joe Lee," I responded with a bit of pride. "Can I see a phone book?" Nobody laughed when I said that Joe was my attorney.

"555-3881" said Billy D.

I didn't realize he was talking to me. I stared at my lap, waiting for one of the agents to return with the phone book.

The H.N.I.C. reached over the table and handed me the receiver. "That's Joe's number. 555-3881, " He said.

Puzzled, I began to dial the number on the ancient phone. The H.N.I.C. rattled Joe's number off the top of his dome like he talked to Joe daily. I didn't know if that was good or bad.

Joe remembered me from the shooting in Woodbrigde. "Your partner already called me." he said, being extra careful not to say Neon's name. "Have you told them anything?" Joe asked.

"No sir, I haven't," I answered.

"Good. Don't say anything to them. About nothing! I'll see you sometime tomorrow. Let me talk to whoever's in charge, " he said.

258

I handed the phone to the H.N.I.C. He laughed and talked to Joe, like they were old war buddies or something. Finally, he hung up the phone and I was taken to Greensboro Jail.

The Following Day

Joe met with Neon prior to visiting me. I thought prices, fees, etc… were going to be discussed, but they were not!

"It won't be a good idea for me to represent Styles," said Joe to Neon.

"Why not? I want the best for him," Neon said.

"That's why? If I represent him now and he decides to flip on you later I can't represent you. It'll be a conflict of interest;" he said. "I suggest you get someone else to represent him. Unfortunately, they can't be from my firm. I think it'll be best if you hire Rhyan Pardelo. He's cheap, and he'll do whatever I tell him to do. He'll tell us if Styles starts to talk."

From the inception of my incarceration my "Ace-Boon-Coon" Neon, Greensboro Number One Ghetto Superstar, crossed me out. He allowed Joe Lee to spook him. He had so little faith in me that he wouldn't allow Joe to represent me. That was just a fraction of the betrayal to come.

Joe was accompanied by Rhyan Pardelo. He explained to me that he was too busy to handle my case. "But, I will be assisting Mr. Pardelo." he said to me.

He suggested Neon hire Pardelo, who wasn't a part of his firm. I didn't understand that. I knew that Joe had at least ten more attorneys in his firm. But, what was most important is that I didn't have a pubic defender, but a paid lawyer. You get what you pay for. And if you are represented by an attorney you haven't paid a dime, he isn't going to be worth one cent! At least I had someone with my best interest at heart.

Two Weeks Later

Tone, Geno, Quayle and the whole Back Street gang wrote statements on me. I was hurt because I was trying to do what I could, to help Geno and Quayle. Because despite all our differences, I thought we were closer than we were. I guess they all had plenty of time to think about all the shit I'd done in the past. Shit that cost them tons of cash, and probably more pride. This was their way of getting back at me.

Even that punk Manny wrote statements on me. I never dealt with that nigga a day in my life. The only time I ever spoke to him was when he called me with that bullshit, "He needed some crack! ".

"If he walked in this cell right now, I wouldn't know him from Adam," I said to Hireen.

Country made statements on me also. I was shocked that he squealed on me! That nigga told the Fed's everything. He told them shit that didn't have to be told. Shit like how many women I had! And how many big screens I had in my crib! I knew he was too calm when I last spoke with him. I can see that nigga now. Telling on every swinging dick he ever dealt with. And that's just what he did. I didn't feel so shocked when I found out he told on his own father! I should have known because he was a scary type nigga.

Zag was right again when he said the Feds didn't have to catch you with shit. Not even a speck of coke .Not even one dollar! They can come and lock you up for life based on what another motherfucker says. That's how the government kidnapped me.

259

Everyone who wrote statements against me, agreed to come to court and testify against me at my trial. In exchange for their testimony, they all were promised a reduction in their sentences, or a "Time Cut" up to 65% and no less than 50%.

I had always had the upper hand on the guys from Stoneville, and since I'd met Country, I had the ups on him too. And I always got the last laugh in any of our clashes. From little league football to adult hood, I had the last laugh. Now, they had the upper hand on me. And if it was going to be some laughing going on, they'd be the ones laughing, not me. All the way to the courthouse.

Most of my entire life I had known the Stoneville Boys. Yet, in all of their statements they said that they met me in 95 or later. They inflated the drug amounts and instead of saying I sold them cocaine, they all wrote, I sold them crack! Crack gets you more time than cocaine does. And since I wasn't cooperating, the H.N.I.C. promised me a shit load of time. The ratio is 100 to 1. You'd have to sell 100 kilos of cocaine to equal 1 kilo of crack. According to the statements, I was responsible for the distribution of thousands of kilos of crack, which guaranteed me an elbow!

But, that's **DA FLIP SIDE** of this nasty game. For every action there is a consequence. But, I didn't consider the consequences when I was making more money than I could spend. And those charges in 94…the ones I had already done time for…the same ones I didn't think they could use against me…well, I was wrong. The prosecutor was using those charges, the shooting charge, even driving charges to make me a career offender. That was another life sentence. Like I'm a fucking cat or something! For two years I prayed that God allowed me to be living and healthy, when Gerald got out of prison. And guess what? I was. Those prayers were answered, but I was in Forsyth County Jail when he went home.

When I called home and found out that Gerald had been released from prison, I went to my cell and cried like a baby. I wanted to be home so I could settle Tim's score.

Not until that day had I thought about "Father Time" and the miraculous shit he predicted. "Something big is going to happen to you that's going to change your entire life. Something big," He had said.

Something big had happened. And then I thought it was something bad. It wasn't until then that I realized that it wasn't God's will that I do anything else to Gerald when he came home from prison. Something had definitely happened to me to change my life forever. And it was much bigger than I ever imagined!

Ten Months Later

Micki found out so much trash on me she changed her phone number and wouldn't bring Chandan to see me. Celeste didn't change her number, but she never answered her phone. Probably sat looking at her caller ID when I called! She stopped writing so much also. She had rode with me through one war and one prison bid. I guess she wasn't going to fall into the same hole twice.

If someone would have told me that all the women who where fussing, crying and fighting over me, were going to drop me like a hot potato, if I got locked up, I would have called them a liar.

When you're making money, everything is lovely. But, when you're out of sight, you're out of mind. Especially, when it comes to women! Definitely, when your money runs out. They're quick to jump on the bandwagon of another Ghetto Superstar! Believe that.

And even though I feel like all those women I had betrayed, betrayed me in return, I got to keep it real. I was a D.O.G. while I was in the streets. I'm well aware that you reap what you sow too. Just like I've had a chance to sit and think about all the things I could have, and should have done, I'm sure all of those women have too. Now, I'm reaping what I sowed........Nothing!

I guess Jeffery Osborne said it best when he sang for L.T.D. "It takes separation, to bring about appreciation. " (Concentrate On You), because I would appreciate anyone of those women now.

When you start hustling, your goal is to reach that first key. Everyone that has sold drugs, and reached that level of kilos, has a story to tell about, "When they got their first brick. " "When they copped their first bird" Or whatever they elected to call it. Their first one thousand grams. It's something you never forget. Sort of like a man getting his first piece of pussy. He never forgets it and he loves to talk about it!

But, nobody likes to talk about the shit that people need to hear. Like the first time they found themselves in solitary confinement. Where the dirty walls are so close together, you can lay on your hard ass bunk and touch all four.

I hustled to have a nice place to live. To have a big bed to sleep in, with a beautiful woman. It was a rude awakening for me the first time I was thrown in the hole. There, I faced the ugly reality of the consequences of hustling. And I hated them! Hated that my freedom had been reduced from the entire world to an eight by ten, cold cell.

What's worse than that is when they stick two more grown ass men in the cell with you. The system is over crowded so the government stacks inmates in cells like supplies on a shelf. One guy goes on the upper bunk, and one goes beside you on the floor. Did I mention that you only get to shower three days out of the week. And the toilet! Imagine being arms length away from a grown ass man, who hasn't showered in a couple of days, and he is taking a shit? Imaging that.

"You never hear those stories on the streets or on these rap CD's, do you?" I asked Hireen.

He didn't answer me. He just looked at me like he was in a trance.

"You only hear the ones about the kilos, right?" Hireen shook his head up and down.

You never hear the stories about this bullshit that these folks serve for you to eat. I hustled so I could eat the best foods at the best restaurants. So I could go and buy whatever I wanted to eat, when I wanted to eat. Cook when I wanted to cook, or have someone's daughter cooking for me. But, now I'm forced to eat this bullshit that they serve, when they serve it, if they serve it, or starve to death. What I wouldn't give to eat a meal that has been prepared by a woman!

"Think about that," I said to Hireen. "Every meal that you have eaten in the past seven years was prepared by hard heads! I yearn for a woman's touch, even if it's just in my food!" There isn't a man in this world that can add a woman's touch to anything.

You won't hear that story in the streets or on these tv's shows. But, you will hear that some knucklehead bragging about his first kilo, bragging about the first time he paid a couple hundred dollars for one plate of food at the Chop House, Lucky 32's or anywhere else it cost an arm and leg to eat. Because, that adds to his reputation when he is eating at spots like that. Baller Spots!

I hustled so I could spoil my children rotten. I wanted Sheneka and Chandan to have everything I wanted as a child and more, but I didn't get. Couldn't get. I've heard a thousand tales from guys "Get'n money" about how they always wanted a go-cart or a mini-bike when they were young. But, Ma Dukes couldn't afford it and Pops was a dead beat dad, or in prison for drugs. Now, that they're getting paid, by way of the drug trade, they can afford the go-cart and the mini-bike for their shorty's. And don't forget to deck shorty out in the Nikes and the freshest gear, you wanted as a youth, but couldn't afford. Just listen to the guy who tells you about his first kilo. He'll have a story that's similar.

But, you'll never hear someone telling about the years that went by without seeing those same children they intended to spoil rotten. Why? Because it hurts too much to tell that story. Never will you hear the story of how a man's daughter was a skinny runt with pony tails the last time he saw her, and after years upon years in prison, his skinny runt has a skinny runt with pony tails of her own. That's how long he's been gone. Never will you hear that story!

That's "Da Flip Side" of the drug game. When you start your prison bid as a "Jit" and end it as a "Pops", or in a body bag. That's "Da Flip Side" of having the reputation as "Da Man!"

When I was getting ready for trial, I sat in a small holding cell waiting to go into the courtroom. I almost cried as Tone, Geno, Quayle, Country and the rest of the Back Street crew, fourteen in all, filed into the courtroom. All armed with vicious testimonies!

"There is no way in hell you can win this trial Styles, " Pardelo said. "These guys will give you a natural life sentence if you let them take the stand. The D.A. has offered you a plea bargain for seventeen years. You have less than ten minutes to decide what you want to do." He said.

For ten months, I had thought about going to trial. Dreamt about beating the case, marching out of the courtroom and going home. The Feds didn't catch me with shit, so I wanted to make them prove I was guilty of selling all the coke they accused me of selling. Then Pardelo told me something that sunk my battle ship.

"If the jury finds you guilty of selling one and a half kilograms of crack, you're going to get a life sentence."

"Just one and a half?" I asked.

Ten months of courage building, was destroyed with a moment of rational thinking.
"I'll take the plea bargain," I said sadly

Pardelo informed the D.A. that I was going to accept the plea agreement. All the guys, my so called homies, were marched out of the courtroom. I watched each one of them as they quickly walked by. Not one of them could look at me in the eyes. And all of them looked relieved that they didn't have to take the stand. They would still receive their "Time Cuts". They had the upper hand on me now, "Fo-Sho!"

I sat in the courtroom listening to Pardelo serenade the judge with accounts from my past. He harped on the fact I'd been in the "UNITED STATES!" Army for four years. He read a list of schools that I completed while in the Army, and that I'd fought in "Not one, but two wars! " He said to the judge. "Panama and Desert Storm. Receiving metals and awards from both wars!"

When Pardelo mentioned those wars, hot oil rushed through my veins. I was so young when I joined the Army and fought in those wars. Wars that didn't have shit to do with me. I didn't care back then though. I loved this country. I even called myself a patriot.

"Do you believe that?" I asked Hireen, not expecting an answer.

I was nineteen years old when I parachuted into Panama. Twenty one when I went to Desert Storm. Now, I'm fighting this country for my life. For my children's lives. Because this system is designed for my son to follow in my footsteps, and for my daughter to be on welfare. Needless to say how I feel about this country now. As a matter of fact I will say how I feel. "I hate this crooked, society deceiving, murderous country now!"

When the government can snatch you from the street because of "Hear say" and give you a life sentence, something has to be done. I can't change this country with my hands. At least not alone. That's just being real, but I can speak out against it and hate it in my heart.

Since my conspiracy charge ran from January 1993 to December 1997, Pardelo argued that the 1994 charges, couldn't be used to enhance my sentence.

"Those charges happened during the time of the conspiracy, Your Honor," Pardelo said to the judge, who agreed.

That helped me. I went from seventeen years to fourteen years   When I realized I was receiving a fourteen year sentence, I was very pleased. I'd dodged a life sentence and got my plea bargain reduced by three years.

Whenever someone is pleased to receive a fourteen year sentence, and he didn't kill anyone, you know this system is wicked. Gerald only received a seven year sentence for killing Tim and that was cut to three and a half years.

The Head Nigga In Charge wasn't playing the radio! The Feds took the Lex and a couple other cars I had in my father's name. One agent testified that I said I put most of everything I own in my father's name, which was a lie, but the judge believed him.

Speaking of my father, he had been in and out of the hospital since I was in Forsyth County Jail worried sick about me. He was the only one that I called daily, when he wasn't in the hospital. He was the only one who could make me forget the situation I was in and make me laugh. That's what best friends do. He was the "Only" one I called when I needed to cry too. That's what best friends are truly for.

Ten months had elapsed and I hadn't seen him once. I missed him like crazy. "I'm too sick to come to Winston, " He said sadly on the phone.

But I knew he wasn't too sick. He just couldn't stand the sight of me being behind bars. He cried most of the time I called him. Even the times he made me laugh, he cried.

Once he told me he felt like he would never see me again. My response was that he was talking crazy, but I knew damn well that was a serious possibility.

"I'm too sick Dame." He said. Dame is what he used to call me. "They gave you all that damn time like you killed somebody. " That day, we both sat on the phone and cried. Missing each other.

I filed a Direct Appeal, but Pardelo said I should drop it because I'd be wasting my time and money. He just didn't want to do it. Ten months on one case was more than

263

enough for him. He said I should file a motion called, "2255". "You'll have to find some one else to do it though, " He said.

That someone else was Nina. She was still down with me, which was a big blessing. Actually, in the ten months, she and I fell madly in love with each other. So she took over as my attorney.

I left Forsyth County and was sent to Leavenworth, Kansas, the roughest joint in the Federal System. I thought I'd seen some wild stuff in state prison, but Leavenworth was a hundred times worse than the High Rise or Whiteville.

When I got to Leavenworth the few letters that I received from Celeste stopped completely. The only time I heard from Micki was when I called home to talk to Chandan. She was still upset at all the mess she found out about me. Most of which wasn't true! But, Nina was still in my corner.

"And guess who else was still hanging in there with me?" I asked Hireen.

"Who? The African Chick," He said, shrugging his shoulders.

"Nah, not her. Clovia," I said.

"The girl you just met before you got knocked?" Hireen asked.

"Yep! Now you see why I was thinking about settling down with her?"

I stayed in Leavenworth for a little over a year. Then I was transferred to Estill, South Carolina. On December 19, 1999, my greatest fear of being locked up, walked me down. On a cold winters midnight, I was told by the captain that my father had passed. My "Other Half!" When Tim passed, he took part of me with him. When my Ole Man passed, he took the rest! Or that's how I felt.

Four years prior, when Miller's mom died while we were in Stokes County Jail, I cried because I felt his pain. Miller told me that the hardest part of a bid is when your mother or father passes and you can't pay your final respects to them.

I had prayed years ago and begged God not to ever allow that to happen to me. "I couldn't take it," I said to God. "I couldn't take not being able to pay my last respects to someone I loved so much!"

I didn't think I could bear the burden. But, for some reason, And Allah Knows Best, the same thing happened to me. My father had said he felt like he'd never see me again and he was right.

I wasn't able to pay my respects to my beloved father. The man who helped bring me into this world. The man I was named after. This was definitely the hardest part of my bid. And that will hurt me forever!

"You'll never hear any of those stories, will you Hireen?" I asked, still not expecting, or even wanting an answer.

These are the stories that we never hear. I think in order to keep our youth from following into our footsteps, "Da Flip Side" of the dope game must be told. Maybe that's what Father Time meant. Maybe that's my calling. To educate the masses of youth, or anyone who'll listen about the other side of the dope game. But how? I asked myself. I paused for a second to think.

Nothing is cool about sitting in prison watching your kids grow up without you. Nothing is hip about not being able to pay your last respects to family and friends when they pass. Yep, living large was fun while it last. The things I've seen and done, movie stars don't do. But, those things are costing me fourteen years of my life.

There isn't a stripper, house or car on God's Green Earth, that's worth fourteen years of my life.

In February 2000, I got locked up because those Hill Billies in Estill, wouldn't allow the Muslims to pray in congregation. That was eight months ago. I've been here, in the hole ever since. Waiting to go back to that hell hole, Leavenworth.

Hireen just shook his head at my story. I know it made him really think about some things. That's what he was doing now. He didn't even look sleepy anymore.

"I just want to get home and get in a bath tub," He said. If someone would have told me that I was going to have to use the same showers as a hundred men or more, use daily, I would have thought twice before running up in that bank. Seven years of taking showers. I'm ready for a long hot bath." He said. "I hate to stand in the showers and smell piss and look at all the crap on the walls. That's what I hate," He added.

I heard some keys and then the police kicked the door.

Bang…Bang…Bang…

"Styles! Get your things together. You're leaving in a few minutes."

I can't say I was happy because I was going back to Leavenworth, but I was happy to be getting out of the hole. Eight months of eight by ten feet of freedom. Eight months without any sunlight. Yeah, I was happy to be leaving. I didn't care where I was going, just as long as I was getting out of the hole.

"You talked all night long," Hireen said. He watched as I moved around like a wild animal, about to be let out of his cage. I packed my things with aggression.

"How you know? You were asleep half the time," I said.

"Nah, I wasn't. I listened to the whole story."

I looked at him and smiled. I knew he had slept through a chunk of the story and he knew I knew.

"You should write a book." Hireen said. "Let the world know that there is a flip side to the drug game. A side that's glorified, and a side that's never told. That's how you can reach the children in masses," He said.

The officer came back and unlocked the door. I picked up my things and embraced Hireen.

"As salaamu alaikum, Ahki.. Stay on the Straight Path," I said.

"Wa alaikum asalaam. You do the same thing Brother," He said.

"I will insha Allah, and I think I'm going to write a book. I'm going to call it what you just said. Da Flip Side! The side that's glorified and the side that's never told. Yeah, I'm going to do that. Insha Allah."

"Styles let's go. You're holding me up!" The officer yelled.

I hugged Hireen again and rushed out of the door.

265

EPILOGUE

Maybe we love a thing that's bad for us and we hate a thing that's good for us! This is how Allah addresses all of mankind in the Noble Quran. To make us ponder and reflect on our daily lives. So, before you continue reading, read the first sentence over, and reflect! Let the sentence marinate!

All things that occur in each of our lives happen because Allah decrees them to happen. Whether we think they are good things or bad things, we must still give all praise to Allah alone, and ponder on the situations we find ourselves in.

At times, especially the times we call bad, in order to find good in a situation, you must have patience. Sometimes, years and years of patience. But, Allah tells us repeatedly in the Noble Quran, that He loves the patient ones.

Our minds can't conceive the plan that Allah has for us. We are quick to say that "God's plan is perfect," until we're touched with affliction. Then we are even quicker to forget that we said, "God's plan is perfect."

Allah also tells us in the Noble Quran that, "We'll be tried certainly, with something of fear, hunger, loss of wealth, lives and fruits, but give glad tidings to the patient."

Those before us were tried, and we will be tried with afflictions also!

This time in prison has been hard on me. Sometimes harder than other times. But, it has made me realize that life is about preparing for death. Preparing to return to the Creator of All Things. The hereafter is where we will find true success. If indeed the Most Gracious, the Most Merciful is pleased with us.

Not in the things that man covets and cherishes, like women, silver, gold, will he ever find success….No, I take that back. There is temporary success in this world. But most purchase that success at the price of the hereafter!

If I wouldn't have been arrested, I don't think I would have ever prepared anything for death. I was too deep in the streets! So, as crazy as this may sound, and as hard as it is for me to say this, I must keep it all the way real. I got rescued from the streets! I was a man on the verge of gaining the whole world and lost everything, but I gained my soul. It was a blessing that I got locked up.

Allah had mercy on me. He has allowed me to see life's conceptual picture. I've been blessed to have the chance to get back on the Straight Path! And insha Allah, I'll stay on the Straight Path, until I return to the All Knowing!

A WINTER'S MIDNIGHT
(For My Daddy)

There are shimmering altitudes of "Heartache Mountain"
That only a handful may know

On a Winter's Midnight
I found it's crown
Scorching cold,

Upon receiving the detestable tidings
Of your demise
I cried,
Sotto voce

My spirit became feeble,
Struggling to reflect a light
That was once brilliant

I sat me down
In Silent Rage
Telling my soul to stop weeping
So the world may not know We died……..
 Tonight,

I tried to recollect
The last time I fixed brown eyes on you
The last time I broke silence with you
But, I can't

It's been years
Yet, tears cascade
Still,

Like it was last night
When I escalated
To the depths of sorrow,

Which feeds off of pain
Tomorrow
Only promises to bring
The same thing
When I think of you

Another
Winter's Midnight

                                        James E. Lowe, III

I don't generally enjoy this genre, but I loved this book! Lowe's fast paced, visceral narrative, will keep you turning pages, leading you on a chaotic journey along with his characters who get a glimpse behind the veil. Your illusions may be shattered along with theirs when they learn that the "American Dream" is like all dreams-made of paper which burns so quickly, so easily.

V. Turner Whitely

can someone please pass this book on to…**OPRAH**

ISBN 141200769-0